GREAT TALES
OF
TERROR

Edited and with
an Introduction by

S. T. Joshi

DOVER PUBLICATIONS, INC.
Mineola, New York

DOVER HORROR CLASSICS
GENERAL EDITOR: S. T. JOSHI

Bibliographical Note

Great Tales of Terror, first published by Dover Publications, Inc., in 2002, is a new selection of twenty-three stories reprinted from standard editions.

Library of Congress Cataloging-in-Publication Data

Great tales of terror / edited by S. T. Joshi.
      p. cm. — (Dover horror classics)
    ISBN 0-486-41938-X (pbk.)
    1. Horror tales. I. Joshi, S. T., 1958–   .

PN6120.95.H727 G74 2001
808.83'8738—dc21

2001047461

Manufactured in the United States of America
Dover Publications, Inc., 31 East 2nd Street, Mineola, N.Y. 11501

Contents

IV. The Terror of the Superhuman

V. The Terror of Fantasy

VI. The Terror of the Cosmic

Introduction

Why do people read tales of terror? Since 1764, when Horace Walpole published *The Castle of Otranto*, stories of horror, terror, the supernatural, and psychological suspense have represented a distinctive contribution to European letters, the roots of which can be traced as far back as the anecdotal ghost stories found in Greek, Latin, and other ancient literatures. And yet, the sensation of fear cannot be said to be a pleasant one; no one, in real life, would wish to be subject to it, whether it be the sublime terror of a haunted castle or the more mundane but no less clutching fear of bodily harm at the hands of a criminal or a madman. Why, then, are certain people drawn inexorably to the experiencing of such emotions by way of literature?

As early as 1773, Anna Laetitia Barbauld discussed the matter in a brief essay, "On the Pleasure Derived from Objects of Terror." Already in her time, she states, "The greediness with which the tales of ghosts and goblins, of murders, earthquakes, fires, shipwrecks, and all the most terrible disasters attending human life, are devoured by every ear, must have been generally remarked." Barbauld first conjectures that it is merely curiosity that leads us to reach the end of a work once we have begun it, even though it is full of horrors that may actually cause us pain as we read. But this solution dissatisfies her, because it cannot account for our fondness for rereading tales of terror whose outcomes we already know. It is at this point that Barbauld states a principle of great importance:

> A strange and unexpected event awakens the mind, and keeps it on the stretch; and where the agency of invisible beings is introduced, of "forms unseen, and mightier far than we," our imagination, darting forth, explores with rapture the new world which is laid open to its view, and

rejoices in the expansion of its powers. Passion and fancy
cooperating, elevate the soul to its highest pitch; and the
pain of terror is lost in amazement.

In other words, it is *imaginative liberation* that readers are
seeking. Realistic accounts of mundane events, gripping as they
can be in their penetrating portrayals of character and society,
nonetheless fail to satisfy what appears to be an inbred human
desire to surpass the bounds of the ordinary and to approach (in
Poe's imperishable formulation)

> a wild weird clime that lieth, sublime,
> Out of Space—out of Time.

That this kind of imaginative liberation has also been sought
by a wide variety of writers—many of whom are or were chiefly
known for their realistic writing—is evident in the tales in this
volume. It is, of course, unwise to assert that all writers of weird
tales are motivated by any single or simple purpose; but that
many of them have relished the freedom from mundane realism
afforded by the tale of terror is evident in a great majority of the
contributions in this book.

It is misleading, however, to speak of the tale of terror as a
definite genre, analogous to the detective story, the tale of science fiction, or the love story. Rather, terror is frequently only
one component—perhaps not even the dominant one—in many
of the tales included here, and it becomes quickly evident that a
variety of elements utilized by writers of weird fiction are
manipulated as a means of symbolically conveying messages that
could not be conveyed in any other fashion. It is, indeed, in
exactly this way that the tale of terror gains literary substance.
The mere exercise of literary imagination, however distinctive,
is not sufficient; that imagination must be harnessed in order to
shed light on the human condition. As H. P. Lovecraft pointed
out:

> A serious adult story must be true to something in life.
> Since marvel tales cannot be true to the *events* of life, they
> must shift their emphasis toward something to which they

can be true; namely, certain wistful or restless *moods* of
the human spirit, wherein it seeks to weave gossamer
ladders of escape from the galling tyranny of time, space,
and natural law.

Lovecraft's formulation is exemplified in many tales of terror.
The ghost or revenant, perhaps the most ancient element of the
weird tale, frequently serves as a kind of imaginative shorthand
for the human conscience. The spirit of a murder victim who
comes back from the dead to gain revenge on its murderer is
perhaps nothing more than a vivid depiction of the guilt, fear, or
trepidation that plagues even the most hardened criminal; but
this motif is still capable of surprisingly powerful effects, as
exemplified in various ways by Sir Arthur Quiller-Couch's "The
Haunted Dragoon," William Sharp's "The Graven Image," and
Lafcadio Hearn's "Of a Promise Broken." Related to the notion
of the ghost is the idea of the persistence, and possible transmi-
gration, of the soul; and this conception, however implausible it
may now seem to be, gains surprising power in Robert Hichens's
lengthy tale, "The Return of the Soul."

The haunted house, castle, or region is similarly a trope of
great antiquity. The human mind is inexorably led to fear those
locales where a great many people have died, perhaps under
mysterious circumstances. Is it then strange that, in "The
Ghosts of Austerlitz," William Waldorf Astor, adroitly combining
the tale of terror with historical fiction, finds terror on the
bloody fields of one of the most significant battles of Europe?
The haunted locale becomes ambulatory in Violet Hunt's "The
Coach," but resumes more orthodox forms in James Hopper's
tale of a haunted school.

Many weird writers found the ghost, and such of its analogues
as the vampire and the werewolf, rather too conventional for
effective use in the tale of terror. The advance of science had
shown that all these conceptions were merely the fallacious
products of the primitive mind, so that their vestigial emotive
resonance had, by the middle of the nineteenth century, worn
quite thin. New creatures of wonder and terror had to be
sought. Théophile Gautier answered the call by hypothesizing
not an entire ghost, but only a portion of one, in "The Mummy's

Foot." The sardonic Ambrose Bierce tartly envisions a demon being terrified by the appearance of a ghoul, the loathsome creature that eats the dead. Finally, W. F. Harvey, in "The Tortoise," is one of many authors who sought terror in imagining the possibility of animals endowed with human emotions—particularly the baleful emotion of vengeance.

Lovecraft's notion of escaping from the "galling tyranny of time, space, and natural law" is nowhere better exemplified than in those many tales of superhuman figures that dominate the literature of the weird. Whether he is called Faust, Melmoth, or Dr. Frankenstein, the human being who surpasses his fellows—by extraordinary knowledge, anomalous physical endowments, or the conquest of such inevitable concomitants of the human condition as age and death—has been a figure of compelling fascination. In many ways, such tales are cautionary accounts of the dangers of knowledge—specifically scientific knowledge—unharnessed by moral restraints. The protagonist of E. Nesbit's "The Three Drugs" learns, to his doom, that even in fleeing the law it is not wise to give one's trust too readily to a stranger. Barry Pain's "The Diary of a God" etches poignantly the sensations of a man whose development of superhuman power is only imaginary, and as a result this story crosses over into the realm of psychological suspense. That realm—exemplified in our day by such well-known works as Robert Bloch's *Psycho* and Thomas Harris's *The Silence of the Lambs*—is only on the borderline of the weird, but when it presents a vivid depiction of aberrant psychology—as in H. L. Mencken's "The Window of Horrors"—it becomes an authentic branch of the tale of terror.

At the opposite extreme from the nonsupernatural tale of psychological suspense is the tale of fantasy. Here all, or many, of the earmarks of the real world are boldly abandoned, and the author's imagination is allowed the widest play. Some critics have maintained, indeed, that this branch of the tale of terror represents art at its most quintessential. Clark Ashton Smith once wrote: "imaginative art is surely the highest and purest art"; and elsewhere, "I am far happier when I can create *everything* in a story, including the milieu." The danger of such tales is that they will have so little connection to "reality" that they will fail to elicit a response in the reader, or that they will be merely ventures into empty escapism. How this danger can be avoided is shown by three skillful and haunting tales: Erckmann-Chatrian's "The Queen of the Bees" (a "benign" fantasy that exhibits the anomalous mental union between a blind girl and a horde of bees), Gertrude Atherton's "The Caves of Death" (a fantasy where a dreamer crosses over to the "House of Death" and encounters the souls of the dead suffering the varied fates brought upon them by their actions in life), and Arthur Machen's "The Soldiers' Rest" (where the souls of dead soldiers in World War I find an unexpected haven).

The tale of terror can be said to reach its most awe-inspiring scope in those accounts of cosmic wonder and awe. We learn early on in life that the human race—and, indeed, the entire history of all life on this earth—is a thing of vanishingly small importance in the well-nigh infinite reaches of space and time; but, encumbered by mundane concerns, we quickly put this awesome and depressing knowledge out of our minds. On occasion it is salutary to be reminded of it; and it is perhaps exactly this that the protagonist of Algernon Blackwood's "The Man Who Found Out" learns to his horror. All humanity is a "negligible experiment" in J. D. Beresford's cosmic vignette, while R. H. Barlow's "The Root-Gatherers" speaks casually of the destruction of entire civilizations. In science fiction, the endless gulfs of space and time are scenes of thrilling exploration and adventure; but in the tale of terror, the incalculable light-years of the galaxy and the oppressive burden of ages past and to come can only be the sources of awe tinged with horror and melancholy.

The tale of terror, in all its multitudinous forms, offers virtually unlimited scope for imaginative development. Is it any accident that authors generally known for a very different kind of writing have so frequently tried their hands at it? Novelists of social realism such as Charles Dickens, Henry James, and F. Marion Crawford; writers of sentimental love stories such as Robert W. Chambers and Daphne du Maurier; even essayists and critics such as H. L. Mencken and Sir Arthur Quiller-Couch have all produced ventures into the weird, and with notable success. It is exactly the possibility of imaginative liberation that has led so many writers to explore this corner of literature; and in this sense, few will contest H. P. Lovecraft's rousing declaration:

> The imaginative writer devotes himself to art in its most essential sense. . . . He is a painter of moods and mind-pictures—a capturer and amplifier of elusive dreams and fancies—a voyager into those unheard-of lands which are glimpsed through the veil of actuality but rarely, and only by the most sensitive. . . . He is the poet of twilight visions and childhood memories, but sings only for the sensitive.

Let us hope that there will continue to be a sufficient modicum of "sensitive" readers to appreciate this most elusive and tenuous of literary productions.

—S. T. JOSHI

Great Tales of Terror

I. The Terror of Revenants

The Haunted Dragoon

Sir Arthur Quiller-Couch

Beside the Plymouth road, as it plunges down hill past Ruan Lanihale church towards Ruan Cove, and ten paces beyond the lych-gate—where the graves lie level with the coping, and the horseman can decipher their inscriptions in passing, at the risk of a twisted neck—the base of the churchyard wall is pierced with a low archway, festooned with toad-flax and fringed with the hart's-tongue fern. Within the archway bubbles a well, the water of which was once used for all baptisms in the parish, for no child sprinkled with it could ever be hanged with hemp. But this belief is discredited now, and the well neglected: and the events which led to this are still a winter's tale in the neighbourhood. I set them down as they were told me, across the blue glow of a wreck-wood fire, by Sam Tregear, the parish bedman. Sam himself had borne an inconspicuous share in them; and because of them Sam's father had carried a white face to his grave.

My father and mother (said Sam) married late in life, for his trade was what mine is, and 'twasn't till her fortieth year that my mother could bring herself to kiss a gravedigger. That accounts, maybe, for my being born rickety and with other drawbacks that only made father the fonder. Weather permitting, he'd carry me off to churchyard, set me upon a flat stone, with his coat folded under, and talk to me while he delved. I can mind, now, the way he'd settle lower and lower, till his head played hidey-peep with me over the grave's edge, and at last he'd be clean swallowed up, but still discoursing or calling up how he'd come upon wonderful towns and kingdoms down underground, and how all the

3

kings and queens there, in dyed garments, was offering him
meat for his dinner every day of the week if he'd only stop and
hobbynob with them—and all such gammut. He prettily doted
on me—the poor old ancient!

But there came a day—a dry afternoon in the late wheat
harvest—when we were up in the churchyard together, and
though father had his tools beside him, not a tint did he work,
but kept travishing back and forth, one time shading his eyes
and gazing out to sea, and then looking far along the Plymouth
road for minutes at a time. Out by Bradden Point there stood a
little dandy-rigged craft, tacking lazily to and fro, with her mains'le
all shiny-yellow in the sunset. Though I didn't know it then, she
was the Preventive boat, and her business was to watch the
Hauen: for there had been a brush between her and the *Unity*
lugger, a fortnight back, and a Preventive man shot through the
breast-bone and my mother's brother Philip was hiding down in
the town. I minded, later, how that the men across the vale, in
Farmer Tresidder's wheat-field, paused every now and then, as
they pitched the sheaves, to give a look up towards the churchyard, and the gleaners moved about in small knots, causeying
and glancing over their shoulders at the cutter out in the bay;
and how, when all the field was carried, they waited round the
last load, no man offering to cry the *Neck,* as the fashion was,
but lingering till sun was near down behind the slope and the
long shadows stretching across the stubble.

"Sha'nt thee go underground today, father?" says I, at last.

He turned slowly round, and says he, "No, sonny. 'Reckon us
'll climb skywards for a change."

And with that, he took my hand, and pushing abroad the bel-
fry door began to climb the stairway. Up and up, round and
round we vent, in a sort of blind-man's-holiday full of little glints
of light and whiffs of wind where the open windows came; and
at last stepped out upon the leads of the tower and drew breath.

"There's two-an'-twenty parishes to be witnessed from where
we're standin', sonny—if ye've got eyes," says my father.

Well, first I looked down towards the harvesters and laughed
to see them so small: and then I fell to counting the church-
towers dotted across the high-lands, and seeing if I could make

out two-and-twenty. 'Twas the prettiest sight—all the country round looking as if 'twas dusted with gold, and the Plymouth road winding away over the hills like a long white tape. I had counted thirteen churches, when my father pointed his hand out along this road and called to me—

"Look'ee out yonder, honey, an' say what ye see!"

"I see dust," says I.

"Nothin' else? Sonny boy, use your eyes, for mine be dim."

"I see dust," says I again, "an' suthin' twinklin' in it, like a tin can——"

"Dragooners!" shouts my father; and then, running to the side or the tower facing the harvest-field, he put both hands to his mouth and called:

"*What have 'ee? What have 'ee?*"

—very loud and long.

"*A neck—a neck!*" came back from the field, like as if all shouted at once—dear, the sweet sound! And then a gun was fired, and craning forward over the coping I saw a dozen men running across the stubble and out into the road towards the Hauen; and they called as they ran, "*A neck—a neck!*"

"Iss," says my father, "'tis a neck, sure 'nuff. Pray God they save en! Come, sonny——"

But we dallied up there till the horsemen were plain to see, and their scarlet coats and armour blazing in the dust as they came. And when they drew near within a mile, and our limbs ached with crouching—for fear they should spy us against the sky—father took me by the hand and pulled hot foot down the stairs. Before they rode by he had picked up his shovel and was shovelling out a grave for his life.

Forty valiant horsemen they were, riding two-and-two (by reason of the narrowness of the road) and a captain beside them—men broad and long, with hairy top-lips, and all clad in scarlet jackets and white breeches that showed bravely against their black war-horses and jet-black holsters, thick as they were wi' dust. Each man had a golden helmet, and a scabbard flapping by his side, and a piece of metal like a half-moon jingling from his horse's cheek-strap. 12 D was the numbering on every saddle, meaning the Twelfth Dragoons.

Tramp! tramp! they rode by, talking and joking, and taking no more heed of me—that sat upon the wall with my heels dangling above them—than if I'd been a sprig of stonecrop. But the captain, who carried a drawn sword and mopped his face with a handkerchief so that the dust ran across it in streaks, drew rein, and looked over my shoulder to where father was digging.

"Sergeant!" he calls back, turning with a hand upon his crupper; "didn't we see a figger like this a-top o' the tower, some way back?"

The sergeant pricked his horse forward and saluted. He was the tallest, straightest man in the troop, and the muscles on his arm filled out his sleeve with the three stripes upon it—a handsome red-faced fellow, with curly black hair.

Says he, "That we did, sir—a man with sloping shoulders and a boy with a goose neck." Saying this, he looked up at me with a grin.

"I'll bear it in mind," answered the officer, and the troop rode on in a cloud of dust, the sergeant looking back and smiling, as if 'twas a joke that he shared with us. Well, to be short, they rode down into the town as night fell. But 'twas too late, Uncle Philip having had fair warning and plenty of time to flee up towards the little secret hold under Mabel Down, where none but two families knew how to find him. All the town, though, knew he was safe, and lashins of women and children turned out to see the comely soldiers hunt in vain till ten o'clock at night.

The next thing was to billet the warriors. The captain of the troop, by this, was pesky cross-tempered, and flounced off to the "Jolly Pilchards" in a huff. "Sergeant," says he, "here's an inn, though a damned bad 'un, an' here I means to stop. Somewheres about there's a farm called Constantine, where I'm told the men can be accommodated. Find out the place, if you can, an' do your best: an' don't let me see yer face till to-morra," says he.

So Sergeant Basket—that was his name—gave the salute, and rode his troop up the street, where—for his manners were mighty winning, notwithstanding the dirty nature of his errand—he soon found plenty to direct him to Farmer Noy's, of

Constantine; and up the coombe they rode into the darkness, a dozen or more going along with them to show the way, being won by their martial bearing as well as the sergeant's very friendly way of speech.

Farmer Noy was in bed—a pock-marked, lantern-jawed old gaffer of sixty-five; and the most remarkable point about him was the wife he had married two years before—a young slip of a girl but just husband-high. Money did it, I reckon; but if so, 'twas a bad bargain for her. He was noted for stinginess to such a degree that they said his wife wore a brass wedding-ring, weekdays, to save the genuine article from wearing out. She was a Ruan woman, too, and therefore ought to have known all about him. But woman's ways be past finding out.

Hearing the hoofs in his yard and the sergeant's *stram-a-ram* upon the door, down comes the old curmudgeon with a candle held high above his head.

"What the devil's here?" he calls out.

Sergeant Basket looks over the old man's shoulder; and there, halfway up the stairs, stood Madam Noy in her night rail—a high-coloured ripe girl, languishing for love, her red lips parted and neck all lily-white against a loosened pile of dark brown hair.

"Be cussed if I turn back!" said the sergeant to himself; and added out loud—

"Forty souldjers, in the King's name!"

"Forty devils!" says the old Noy.

"They're devils to eat," answered the sergeant, in the most friendly manner; "an', begad, ye must feed an' bed 'em this night—or else I'll search your cellars. Ye are a loyal man—eh, farmer? An' your cellars are big, I'm told."

"Sarah," calls out the old man, following the sergeant's bold glance, "go back an' dress yersel' dacently this instant! These here honest souldjers—forty damned honest gormandisin' souldjers—be come in his Majesty's name, forty strong, to protect honest folks' rights in the intervals of eatin' 'em out o' house an' home. Sergeant, ye be very welcome i' the King's name. Cheese an' cider ye shall have, an' I pray the mixture may turn your forty stomachs."

In a dozen minutes he had fetched out his stable-boys and farm-hands, and, lantern in hand, was helping the sergeant to picket the horses and stow the men about on clean straw in the outhouses. They were turning back to the house, and the old man was turning over in his mind that the sergeant hadn't yet said a word about where he was to sleep, when by the door they found Madam Noy waiting, in her wedding gown, and with her hair freshly braided.

Now, the farmer was mortally afraid of the sergeant, knowing he had thirty ankers and more of contraband liquor in his cellars, and minding the sergeant's threat. None the less his jealousy got the upper hand.

"Woman," he cried out, "to thy bed!"

"I was waiting," said she, "to say the Cap'n's bed——"

"Sergeant's," says the dragoon, correcting her.

"—Was laid i' the spare room."

"Madam," replies Sergeant Basket, looking into her eyes and bowing, "a soldier with my responsibility sleeps but little. In the first place, I must see that my men sup."

"The maids be now cuttin' the bread an' cheese and drawin' the cider."

"Then, Madam, leave me but possession of the parlour, and let me have a chair to sleep in."

By this they were in the passage together, and her gaze devouring his regimentals. The old man stood a pace off, looking sourly. The sergeant fed his eyes upon her, and Satan got hold of him.

"Now if only," said he, "one of you could play cards!"

"But I must go to bed," she answered; "though I can play cribbage, if only you stay another night."

For she saw the glint in the farmer's eye; and so Sergeant Basket slept bolt upright that night in an armchair by the parlour fender. Next day the dragoons searched the town again, and were billeted all about among the cottages. But the sergeant returned to Constantine, and before going to bed—this time in the spare room—played a game of cribbage with Madam Noy, the farmer smoking sulkily in his armchair.

"Two for his heels!" said the rosy woman suddenly, halfway through the game. "Sergeant, you're cheatin' yoursel' an' forgettin' to mark. Gi'e me the board; I'll mark for both."

She put out her hand upon the board, and Sergeant Basket's closed upon it. 'Tis true he had forgot to mark; and feeling the hot pulse in her wrist, and beholding the hunger in her eyes, 'tis to be supposed he'd have forgot his own soul.

He rode away next day with his troop: but my uncle Philip not being caught yet, and the Government set on making an example of him, we hadn't seen the last of these dragoons. 'Twas a time of fear down in the town. At dead of night or at noonday they came on us—six times in all: and for two months the crew of the *Unity* couldn't call their souls their own, but lived from day to day in secret closets and wandered the country by night, hiding in hedges and straw-houses. All that time the revenue men watched the Hauen, night and day, like dogs before a rat-hole.

But one November morning 'twas whispered abroad that Uncle Philip had made his way to Falmouth, and slipped across to Guernsey. Time passed on, and the dragooners were seen no more, nor the handsome devil-may-care face of Sergeant Basket. Up at Constantine, where he had always contrived to billet himself, 'tis to be thought pretty Madam Noy pined to see him again, kicking his spurs in the porch and smiling out of his gay brown eyes; for her face fell away from its plump condition, and the hunger in her eyes grew and grew. But a more remarkable fact was that her old husband—who wouldn't have yearned after the dragoon, ye'd have thought—began to dwindle and fall away too. By the New Year he was a dying man, and carried his doom on his face. And on New Year's Day he straddled his mare for the last time, and rode over to Looe, to Doctor Gale's.

"Goody-losh!" cried the doctor, taken aback by his appearance—"What's come to ye, Noy?"

"Death!" says Noy. "Doctor, I bain't come for advice, for before this day week I'll be a clay-cold corpse. I come to ax a favour. When they summon ye, before lookin' at my body—that'll be past help—go you to the little left-top corner drawer o' my wife's bureau, an' there ye'll find a packet. You're my executor," says he, "and I leaves ye to deal wi' that packet as ye thinks fit."

With that, the farmer rode away home-along, and the very day week he went dead.

The doctor, when called over, minded what the old chap had said, and sending Madam Noy on some pretence to the kitchen, went over and unlocked the little drawer with a duplicate key, that the farmer had unhitched from his watch-chain and given him. There was no parcel of letters, as he looked to find, but only a small packet crumpled away in the corner. He pulled it out and gave a look, and a sniff, and another look: then shut the drawer, locked it, strode straight down-stairs to his horse and galloped away.

In three hours' time, pretty Madam Noy was in the con- stables' hands upon the charge of murdering her husband by poison.

They tried her, next Spring Assize, at Bodmin, before the Lord Chief Justice. There wasn't evidence enough to put Sergeant Basket in the dock alongside of her—though 'twas freely guessed he knew more than anyone (saving the prisoner herself) about the arsenic that was found in the little drawer and inside the old man's body. He was subpœna'd from Plymouth, and cross-examined by a great hulking King's Counsel for three- quarters of an hour. But they got nothing out of him. All through the examination the prisoner looked at him and nodded her white face, every now and then, at his answers, as much as to say, "That's right—that's right: they shan't harm thee, my dear." And the love-light shone in her eyes for all the court to see. But the sergeant never let his look meet it. When he stepped down at last she gave a sob of joy, and fainted bang-off.

They roused her up, after this, to hear the verdict of *Guilty* and her doom spoken by the judge. "Pris'ner at the bar," said the Clerk of Arraigns, "have ye anything to say why this court should not pass sentence o' death?"

She held tight of the rail before her, and spoke out loud and clear—

"My Lord and gentlemen all, I be a guilty woman; an' I be

ready to die at once for my sin. But if ye kill me now, ye kill the child in my body—an' he is innocent."

Well, 'twas found she spoke truth; and the hanging was put off till after the time of her delivery. She was led back to prison, and there, about the end of June, her child was born, and died before he was six hours old. But the mother recovered, and quietly abode the time of her hanging.

I can mind her execution very well; for father and mother had determined it would be an excellent thing for my rickets to take me into Bodmin that day, and get a touch of the dead woman's hand, which in those times was considered an unfailing remedy. So we borrowed the parson's manure-cart, and cleaned it thoroughly, and drove in together.

The place of the hangings, then, was a little door in the prison-wall, looking over the bank where the railway now goes, and a dismal piece of water called Jail-pool, where the townsfolk drowned most of the dogs and cats they'd no further use for. All the bank under the gallows was that thick with people you could almost walk upon their heads; and my ribs were squeezed by the crowd so that I couldn't breathe freely for a month after. Back across the pool, the fields along the side of the valley were lined with booths and sweet-stalls and standings—a perfect Whitsun-fair; and a din going up that cracked your ears.

But there was the stillness of death when the woman came forth, with the sheriff and the chaplain reading in his book, and the unnamed man behind—all from the little door. She wore a strait black gown, and a white kerchief about her neck—a lovely woman, young and white and tearless.

She ran her eye over the crowd and stepped forward a pace, as if to speak; but lifted a finger and beckoned instead: and out of the people a man fought his way to the foot of the scaffold. 'Twas the dashing sergeant, that was here upon sick-leave. Sick he was, I believe. His face above his shining regimentals was gray as a slate; for he had committed perjury to save his skin, and on the face of the perjured no sun will ever shine.

"Have you got it?" the doomed woman said, many hearing the words.

He tried to reach, but the scaffold was too high, so he tossed up what was in his hand, and the woman caught it—a little screw of tissue-paper.

"I must see that, please!" said the sheriff, laying a hand upon her arm.

"'Tis but a weddin'-ring, sir"—and she slipped it over her finger. Then she kissed it once, under the beam, and, lookin' into the dragoon's eyes, spoke very slow—

"Husband, our child shall go wi' you; an' when I want you he shall fetch you."

—and with that turned to the sheriff, saying: "I be ready, sir."

The sheriff wouldn't give father and mother leave for me to touch the dead woman's hand; so they drove back that evening grumbling a good bit. 'Tis a sixteen-mile drive, and the ostler in at Bodmin had swindled the poor old horse out of his feed, I believe; for he crawled like a slug. But they were so taken up with discussing the day's doings, and what a mort of people had been present, and how the sheriff might have used milder language in refusing my father, that they forgot to use the whip. The moon was up before we got halfway home, and a star to be seen here and there; and still we never mended our pace.

"'Twas in the middle of the lane leading down to Hendra Bottom, where for more than a mile two carts can't pass each other, that my father pricks up his ears and looks back.

"Hullo!" says he; "there's somebody gallopin' behind us."

Far back in the night we heard the noise of a horse's hoofs, pounding furiously on the road and drawing nearer and nearer.

"Save us!" cries father; "whoever 'tis, he's comin' down th' lane!" And in a minute's time the clatter was close on us and someone shouting behind.

"Hurry that crawlin' worm o' yourn—or draw aside in God's name, an' let me by!" the rider yelled.

"What's up?" asked my father, quartering as well as he could. "Why! Hullo! Farmer Hugo, be that you?"

"There's a mad devil o' a man behind, ridin' down all he comes across. A 's blazin' drunk, I reckon—but 'tisn' *that*—'tis the horrible voice that goes wi' en—Hark! Lord protect us, he's turn'd into the lane!"

Sure enough, the clatter of a second horse was coming down upon us, out of the night—and with it the most ghastly sounds that ever creamed a man's flesh. Farmer Hugo pushed past us and sent a shower of mud in our faces as his horse leapt off again, and 'way-to-go down the hill. My father stood up and lashed our old gray with the reins, and down we went too, bumpity-bump for our lives, the poor beast being taken suddenly like one possessed. For the screaming behind was like nothing on earth but the wailing and sobbing of a little child— only tenfold louder. 'Twas just as you'd fancy a baby might wail if his little limbs was being twisted to death.

At the hill's foot, as you know, a stream crosses the lane—that widens out there a bit, and narrows again as it goes up t'other side of the valley. Knowing we must be overtaken further on— for the screams and clatter seemed at our very backs by this— father jumped out here into the stream and backed the cart well to one side; and not a second too soon.

The next moment, like a wind, this thing went by us in the moonlight—a man upon a black horse that splashed the stream all over us as he dashed through it and up the hill. 'Twas the scarlet dragoon with his ashen face; and behind him, holding to his cross-belt, rode a little shape that tugged and wailed and raved. As I stand here, sir, 'twas the shape of a naked babe!

Well, I won't go on to tell how my father dropped upon his knees in the water, or how my mother fainted off. The thing was gone, and from that moment for eight years nothing was seen or heard of Sergeant Basket. The fright killed my mother. Before next spring she fell into a decline, and early next fall the old man—for he was an old man now—had to delve her grave. After this he went feebly about his work, but held on, being wishful for me to step into his shoon, which I began to do as soon as I was fourteen, having outgrown the rickets by that time.

But one cool evening in September month, father was up digging in the yard alone: for 'twas a small child's grave, and in

the loosest soil, and I was off on a day's work, thatching Farmer
Tresidder's stacks. He was digging away slowly when he heard
a rattle at the lych-gate, and looking over the edge of the
grave, saw in the dusk a man hitching his horse there by the
bridle.

'Twas a coal-black horse, and the man wore a scarlet coat all
powdered with pilm; and as he opened the gate and came over
the graves, father saw that 'twas the dashing dragoon. His face
was still a slaty-gray, and clammy with sweat; and when he
spoke, his voice was all of a whisper, with a shiver therein.

"Bedman," says he, "go to the hedge and look down the road,
and tell me what you see."

My father went, with his knees shaking, and came back again.

"I see a woman," says he, "not fifty yards down the road. She
is dressed in black, an' has a veil over her face; an' she's comin'
this way."

"Bedman," answers the dragoon, "go to the gate an' look back
along the Plymouth road, an' tell me what you see."

"I see," says my father, coming back with his teeth chattering,
"I see, twenty yards back, a naked child comin'. He looks to be
callin', but he makes no sound."

"Because his voice is wearied out," says the dragoon. And
with that he faced about, and walked to the gate slowly.

"Bedman, come wi' me an' see the rest," he says, over his
shoulder.

He opened the gate, unhitched the bridle and swung himself
heavily up in the saddle.

Now from the gate the bank goes down pretty steep into the
road, and at the foot of the bank my father saw two figures waiting. 'Twas the woman and the child, hand in hand; and their
eyes burned up like coals: and the woman's veil was lifted, and
her throat bare.

As the horse went down the bank towards these two, they
reached out and took each a stirrup and climbed upon his back,
the child before the dragoon and the woman behind. The man's
face was set like a stone. Not a word did either speak, and in this
fashion they rode down the hill towards Ruan sands. All that my
father could mind, beyond, was that the woman's hands were

passed round the man's neck, where the rope had passed round her own.

No more could he tell, being a stricken man from that hour. But Aunt Polgrain, the housekeeper up to Constantine, saw them, an hour later, go along the road below the town-place; and Jacobs, the smith, saw them pass his forge towards Bodmin about midnight. So the tale's true enough. But since that night no man has set eyes on horse or riders.

The Graven Image
Being the Narrative of James Trenairy

William Sharp

There is an old house in Kensington which is to me, dweller in the remotest part of Cornwall though I am, the most solitary place I know. It is not far from the eastern boundary of Holland Park, yet, I am sure, few even of the residents on Campden Hill, or other Kensingtonians, are aware of its existence.

The house is a small square building, set far back in a walled garden. The approach is by an unattractive byway, which has all the appearance of a *cul-de-sac,* though there is really a narrow outlet which leads ultimately to High Street.

"The Mulberries," as it is called, was, some years ago, occupied by my father's old friend, John Tregarthen: as it was, in years back, by at least three successive John Tregarthens before him. The Tregarthens have always been a solitary and even somewhat eccentric race, but where the last representative of the family differed from his kin was in his dislike to his native Cornwall. He was the most confirmed Londoner I have ever known, though by this I mean only that he never left the metropolis, and seldom roamed beyond Kensington. So far as social intercourse was concerned, however, he might as well have lived in the lighthouse of Tre Pol, or at his own desolate ancestral home, Garvel Manor.

In the autumn of last year, on my way to spend the winter in Italy, I stayed for a few days in London. One afternoon I was in the Campden Hill neighbourhood, vainly in search of the studio of an artist friend, who seemed to me to have done his utmost to make his abode indiscoverable. It was while on this quest that I meandered through small streets and byways, and found myself at last at an unkempt gateway, whereon I could just decipher the words, "The Mulberries."

I confess that I had forgotten the very existence of Mr. John Tregarthen. Several years had passed since my father's death, and I had never had occasion to communicate with the owner of "The Mulberries." Now, however, that I was there, I was prompted by various feelings, but particularly by that clannish sentiment which distinguishes the true Cornishman, to seek Mr. Tregarthen himself.

To avoid needless details, I may say at once, and succinctly, that I found Mr. Tregarthen within; that he gave me a cordial welcome,—cordial, that is, for a man of so austere a life and so sombre a cast of mind; and that I was persuaded to remove my impedimenta from my Bloomsbury hotel, and to spend my two remaining spare nights at "The Mulberries."

When, a few hours later, I drove up to the house and rang the gate-bell, I feared that my host had forgotten our appointment and gone off on some errand or walk. Time after time I rang, but without any result; and as a dull November rain was dripdripping from the few discoloured leaves still clinging to the chestnuts and elms, my position was not an agreeable one.

At last, however, Mr. Tregarthen came slowly along the garden path and opened the door to me. In the misty gloom, unrelieved by even a flickering gas-jet, I could not discern his features; but I fancied that he spoke constrainedly, and, indeed, as if he had already repented of his pressing invitation.

True, when once we were housed from the rain and chill, and the outer world was, as it were, locked away for the night, he became more genial, and even expressed heartily his pleasure at seeing me there as his guest. None the less, so gloomy was the lonely, silent house, so cheerless the aspect of the room where we sat, notwithstanding the bright flame of a wood fire and the yellow glow of a large reading-lamp, that I could not but regret the cheerful, if commonplace comforts of my hotel, the opulence of light and sound, the pleasant intimacy of familiar things enjoyed in common.

Still, I enjoyed my evening. We had a very simple dinner, for Mr. Tregarthen's one servant, an elderly Cornishwoman, was no vagrant from the culinary straight path to which she had been accustomed in her youth; but the wine was exceptionally good. My host talked well and intelligently, and, recluse though he was, I could see that he took at least a casual interest in the various matters of international policy which were at that time occupying so much attention in the press.

After dinner we adjourned to a small room, which he told me was his sanctum. There we had coffee, and sat for a long time in silence, watching the play of the firelight along the dark bookcases which lined the room, and listening to the dreary intermittent cry of the autumnal wind. Mr. Tregarthen had either forgotten, or had intentionally omitted, the lighting of his lamp. Though in ordinary circumstances, nothing delights me more than to sit and dream by the fireside in a dark room, I admit that on this occasion I should have preferred the serene company of a lamp, or even the unwavering effrontery of a gas jet. Again, I am a smoker, though indifferent to the pipe, and I could not but yearn for that postprandial luxury to which I had grown so accustomed. No cigar was offered, however, and I was quick to discover proofs that tobacco in any form was not to be found at "The Mulberries."

After a long silence, following some casual chit-chat about the places in Italy where I hoped to sojourn, my host suddenly made a remark that surprised me, wholly inconsequent as it seemed.

"You never knew him, did you?"

Again I noticed that strange constraint of voice, as if the mouth spoke while the mind was otherwise preoccupied.

"Him . . . whom?"

"My brother Richard."

"No, never. I heard—"

"What have you heard?" broke in Mr. Tregarthen, at once so imperiously and so sharply, and with so keen an accompanying glance the while he stooped in order to scrutinize me more fully in the upswing of the flame, that I realised his constraint was due to no mere dreamy indolence of mind.

"Oh, merely that he was always a wanderer, and that he came here at last broken in health, and died of some long-standing but mysterious trouble."

"Ah!" ejaculated my companion, and said no more. I did not care to broach the subject again, for I knew that it was one which could not be welcome. Indeed, I had heard more than I was willing to admit to Mr. Tregarthen, though I knew not how much was mere rumour. I remembered, however, that my father, a man as exact in the spirit of his statements as precise in the expression of them, had told me of some tragic misunderstanding having long separated John and Richard Tregarthen, and that there was something very strange in the return of the younger to his brother's house, whence he had departed years before with a curse upon him heavy as woe and unforgettable as death. Moreover, I recollected some vague particulars concerning a beautiful girl, one Catherine Tregaskis, belonging to an old family neighbouring our own, whom, as I understood, both men had loved, and who, in the manner of women, was a cause of infinite disturbance to both.

I was about to rise at last, for a fret of impatience was on me. The dull sound of the wind had grown to a moaning sough, that, in my then mood, could be hearkened with equanimity only in affluence of light and comfort. I thought that if I went to the bookcase near the fire my host would suggest the lighting of the lamp; but before I stirred, he broke the silence once more.

"We have scarce spoken of our own parts yet. I wish to know something about our neighbours of old. Tell me, who lives now at Malfont? Is James Tregaskis still alive and well?"

"Yes," I replied, "Mr. Tregaskis is still alive, though he lives in as recluse a fashion as you do. His wife died three years ago. Childless and wifeless, the old man is very lonely. He has never been himself since—since—"

Here I stopped, embarrassed; but Mr. Tregarthen quietly finished my sentence,—

"Since the death of his daughter Catherine, you were going to say?"

I bowed slightly in affirmation.

"Will you tell me the actual wording of the inscription on the memorial tablet which he has raised in the family burial-ground behind the little private chapel on Malfont Heath?"

"Well—to say the truth, I don't know—that is to say, I have forgotten," I muttered, confusedly, reluctant as I was to communicate anything on a subject fraught with so much that would be painful.

"Does it run thus?" went on Mr. Tregarthen, quietly, though with a suggestion of irony in his voice. "Does it run thus, for I am sure you can at least correct me if I am wrong? First, the date of the year; and then—

"'TO THE MEMORY
of
EDWARD TREGASKIS, aged 29: Slain in war.
OLIVIA TREGASKIS, aged 26: Drowned at sea.
CATHERINE TREGASKIS, aged 25: Not yet avenged.'

Tell me, am I right?"

I admitted that he was, and even ventured to add that in our neighbourhood people thought trouble had perverted James Tregaskis' judgment.

"And, of course," I went on, "when he lost his youngest and best-loved child, the third terrible bereavement in a single year, it is no wonder that he imagined vain things, and turned away from those who would have won him to a more generous, if not a more resigned, view."

Mr. Tregarthen looked at me curiously, and I fancied that for a moment a sarcastic smile hovered across his face.

He said no more, however. After a brief interval he rose abruptly, lighted the lamp, and drew my attention to some rare books on Etrurian remains which he thought would interest me, as I was on my way to Volterra and other dead cities and towns of the Etruscan region.

I am not accustomed to late hours, and I suppose that I showed the weariness I felt. At any rate, when my host asked me if I was inclined to go to my room, I assented gladly.

Yet, when I was alone, my sense of sleep was no longer a

pleasant languour. The room was a long oak-panelled chamber, both in height and appearance quite unlike what one would expect from an outside view of "The Mulberries." The bed, an old-fashioned four poster with heavy hangings, stood with its back to the same wall in which was the door; beyond it, on the right, was a fireplace, in which one or two logs sullenly smouldered. For the rest, there was nothing but a few stiff chairs set along the dark panelled walls, and a great gaunt badly-carved escritoire and bookcase of bog-oak.

I do not like gloomy rooms, and so it was natural that I should again think with regret of my comfortable lodging at the hotel, where, for old associations' sake, I always put up when I go to London. But I had the good sense to undress and go to bed, hopeful of sleep.

Whether it was the singular silence within, or the moaning voice of the wind without, with a swift slash of rain ever and again upon the panes, or the coffee I had drunk, or I know not what, but sleep I could not. The longer I lay the more restless I became, and at last I thought I would rise and see if there were any readable volumes in the oak bookcase.

There were not, and I turned discontentedly to the fire, which I had replenished before I went to bed. I leaned on the mantelpiece for some time, looking into the flickering tongues and jets of red and yellow flame beneath, when I chanced at last to stand back and look up.

For the first time I noticed that what seemed a large bronze bas-relief was deeply set in the wall. I know not why I had not noticed it before; doubtless because the fire was low and the shadow deep, while I had not moved the candle away from the small book-table near the door where I had placed it on entrance.

I was glad of anything to distract me. So I lit my candle, and held it so that I could scrutinize the ornament, as it appeared to be. I saw at once that it was something out of the common. It seemed to be a sheet of bronze or copper, along the sides and at the base and summit of which were strange and perplexing arabesques and other designs, most notably what I presumed to be flaming swords, somewhat as represented by Leonardo da Vinci.

But in the centre was a head, life-size, which so far as I could tell was moulded in wax, hardened and tinted.

I did not apprehend these and other details till later, for my first feeling was one of startled curiosity, my second of something akin to fear.

The face was that of a woman; no doubt, of a beautiful woman, though the expression was so evil, or, rather, I should say, so forbidding, that I was blind to the native loveliness of the features.

What amazed me was the extraordinary lifelikeness. The face before me seemed almost as though it were alive. The clustering black hair, drawn back from the high pale brows, appeared to droop with its own weight; the compressed mouth, the distended nostrils, the intent staring gaze, simulated a painful and distressing actuality.

For some time I was fascinated by this strange portrait or imaginative study. I regarded it with something of the same blended curiosity and repugnance with which most of us look at some rare and terrible reptile. No, I felt sure, that woman *lived* once; through those sombre eyes came fire of passionate love or passionate hate; from those delicately-curved lips issued words fanged with scorn or sweet with perilous seduction.

At last I scrutinized the base. There, wrought in deep, strong lines, I read:

"THE GRAVEN IMAGE:"

with below it the words,

"Lo, I made unto myself a graven image, that unto the end of my days the eyes of the body should likewise know no peace."

The inscription was mysterious,—nay, I admit that to me it had a terrifying suggestiveness.

I could look no more. Had I not been ashamed of my weakness, I should have dressed and gone down to the sitting-room. Determined, however, not to yield to my nervous disquiet, I went back to my bed. It was with a sense of relief that I felt my weariness growing upon me, and the stealthy tide of sleep draw nearer and nearer.

When I awoke, I know not how much later, it was with that abrupt sickening sensation which is indescribable, but is familiar to any one who has been aroused by the unheard but subtly apprehended entrance of another person into the room.

I lay for a few moments in a cold perspiration, trembling the while as though in terror. Then I opened my eyes.

I did not need to raise myself. The fire was burning dimly, but I could clearly see a woman standing beside it, looking fixedly into its embers. So much of her face as was turned towards me was in deep shadow. She was tall, and of a fine grace of figure, and though simply dressed in a long gown of a soft gray material, I imagined her to be of good birth and breeding.

I know not how it was that for that brief while fear left me, and that I could lie and speculate thus quietly. I perceived, of course, that my visitor was not Mr. Tregarthen's old servant, but it occurred to me that she might be an inmate of the house. For all I knew to the contrary, Mr. Tregarthen might be married; and, if so, this might be his wife or daughter come to my room unknowing me to be there, or, mayhap, as a victim to somnambulism.

But when suddenly a flame spurted upward from the heart of the fire, almost simultaneously with the sound of an approaching step along the passage, and the woman turned her face towards the door, so that I saw it plainly, my heart seemed as though it would burst.

For with a sense of unutterable fear I recognised in a flash the beautiful but terrifying face of the "Graven Image."

Startling as was the discovery, I had no time for thought, even if I had not lain as though paralysed.

The vindictive fury and scorn that shone in her eyes affrighted me. If it was Mr. Tregarthen who had come along the passage and was now knocking slowly at the door, his reception promised to be a dramatic one.

Whether the door opened or not, I cannot say. All I know is that I saw the woman draw back, as a tall dark man, whose features were quite unknown to me, slowly advanced.

Neither seemed to be aware of my presence; certainly they took no note of it.

I wondered he did not quail under that fierce, that inexpressibly malignant scorn.

As it was, he stopped abruptly. What tragedy of love turned to hate was this! In the dark scowl of the man I interpreted an insatiable fury. Yet I shuddered less at this speechless anger than at the lacerating contempt of her unwavering stare.

I looked to see the man spring at her, to do her some violence. But, leaning against the fireplace, he stood watching her intently. On her face was such a shadow of tempest as made me sick with a new and poignant terror.

I saw his lips move; the scowl on his face deepened. He drew himself erect, and as he did so I thought I heard him utter a name mockingly.

She did not answer, did not move. Outside I heard the wind rise and fall, monotonously crying in a thin shrewd wail. The patter of the rain had ceased, but so intense was the stillness that the drip, drip, from the soaked leaves upon the sodden ground was painfully audible.

Then so swiftly that I scarce saw her move, she sprang forward. There was a flash, a hoarse cry, and the man staggered back, with the blood from a knife-thrust spurting from his left shoulder.

She stood motionless. He, staring at her, panted hard as he slowly stanched the blood.

Suddenly she began to scream. I thought my blood would freeze with horror at the awful sound; scream after scream of deadly terror, and yet neither she nor the man moved.

But, looking at him, I saw that murder flamed in his eyes. Before I could spring from the bed to interfere, he leaped upon her like a beast of prey. In a moment both were on the floor, and I could see that he was strangling her to the death.

With a savage exclamation I dashed to the spot, but tripped, and the next moment lay unconscious, for my forehead fell against a corner of the oaken bookcase.

When I woke, or came out of my stupor, I was still on the

floor where I had fallen, though the sunlight streamed in at the window. There was no sign of the horrible tragedy that had been enacted before me. With a shudder I looked at the "Graven Image," and recognised with a new and horrible distinctness, the appalling verisimilitude of the waxen face.

It was impossible to remain in the room. I dressed hurriedly, and made my way downstairs. The front door was open, and I passed into the garden. The fresh air, damp as it was, was cool and soothing to my throbbing nerves, and, before long, I had almost persuaded myself that I had been victim to nightmare.

Suddenly I caught sight of Mr. Tregarthen. He was sitting in his sanctum, and beckoned to me. From the appearance of the room, and, indeed, of himself, I guessed that he had been there all night.

"Well?" he said, quietly: his sole greeting.

I thought it best to be frank.

"I have had a bad night," I began.

"I know it. I heard you cry out."

I looked at him amazedly and in some fear. Abruptly, I demanded, in an imperative tone:

"Who was the original of the 'Graven Image'?"

"Catherine Tregaskis, my betrothed wife."

I was silent, intensely surprised as I was.

Mr. Tregarthen leaned forward and handed to me a vignette portrait.

It was that of a handsome, dark-haired, dark-eyed, black-bearded man. I recognised the face at once, with a thrill of horrified remembrance.

"Who—who—is this man, Mr. Tregarthen?"

"My dead brother, Richard."

•   •   •

I write this a year after my visit to "The Mulberries," which I left that morning. Mr. Tregarthen is dead. "The Mulberries," under another name, is still untenanted; but I should be poor and forlorn indeed before I accepted again the shelter of that roof.

The Return of the Soul

Robert Hichens

"I have been here before,
But when, or how, I cannot tell!"
ROSSETTI.

I.

TUESDAY NIGHT, *November 3rd.*

Theories! What is the good of theories? They are the scourges that lash our minds in modern days, lash them into confusion, perplexity, despair. I have never been troubled by them before. Why should I be troubled by them now? And the absurdity of Professor Black's is surely obvious. A child would laugh at it. Yes, a child! I have never been a diary writer. I have never been able to understand the amusement of sitting down late at night and scrawling minutely in some hidden book every paltry incident of one's paltry days. People say it is so interesting to read the entries years afterwards. To read, as a man, the *menu* that I ate through as a boy, the love-story that I was actor in, the tragedy that I brought about, the debt that I have never paid—how could it profit me? To keep a diary has always seemed to me merely an addition to the ills of life. Yet now I have a hidden book, like the rest of the world, and I am scrawling in it today. Yes, but for a reason.

I want to make things clear to myself, and I find, as others, that my mind works more easily with the assistance of the pen. The actual tracing of words on paper dispels the clouds that cluster round my thoughts. I shall recall events to set my mind at ease, to prove to myself how absurd a man who could believe in Professor Black would be. "Little Dry-as-dust" I used to call

26

him. Dry? He is full of wild romance, rubbish that a school-girl would be ashamed to believe in. Yet he is abnormally clever; his record proves that. Still, clever men are the first to be led astray, they say. It is the searcher who follows the wandering light. What he says can't be true. When I have filled these pages, and read what I have written dispassionately, as one of the outside public might read, I shall have done, once for all, with the ridiculous fancies that are beginning to make my life a burden. To put my thoughts in order will make a music. The evil spirit within me will sleep, will die. I shall be cured. It must be so—it shall be so.

To go back to the beginning. Ah! what a long time ago that seems! As a child I was cruel. Most boys are cruel, I think. My school companions were a merciless set—merciless to one another, to their masters when they had a chance, to animals, to birds. The desire to torture was in nearly all of them. They loved to bully, and if they bullied only mildly, it was from fear, not from love. They did not wish their boomerang to return and slay them. If a boy were deformed, they twitted him. If a master were kind, or gentle, or shy, they made his life as intolerable as they could. If an animal or a bird came into their power, they had no pity. I was like the rest; indeed, I think that I was worse. Cruelty is horrible. I have enough imagination to do more than know that—to feel it.

Some say that it is lack of imagination which makes men and women brutes. May it not be power of imagination? The interest of torturing is lessened, is almost lost, if we can not be the tortured as well as the torturer.

As a child I was cruel by nature, by instinct. I was a handsome, well-bred, gentlemanlike, gentle-looking little brute. My parents adored me, and I was good to them. They were so kind to me that I was almost fond of them. Why not? It seemed to me as politic to be fond of them as of anyone else. I did what I pleased, but I did not always let them know it; so I pleased them. The wise child will take care to foster the ignorance of its parents. My people were pretty well off, and I was their only child; but my chief chances of future pleasure in life were centered in my grandmother, my mother's mother. She was immensely rich, and she lived here. This room in which I am writing now was her favourite sitting-room. On that hearth, before a log fire, such as is burning at this moment, used to sit that wonderful cat of hers—that horrible cat! Why did I ever play my childish cards to win this house, this place? Sometimes, lately—very lately only—I have wondered, like a fool perhaps. Yet would Professor Black say so? I remember, as a boy of sixteen, paying my last visit here to my grandmother. It bored me very much to come. But she was said to be near death, and death leaves great houses vacant for others to fill. So when my mother said that I had better come, and my father added that he thought my grandmother was fonder of me than of my other relations, I gave up all my boyish plans for the holidays with apparent willingness. Though almost a child, I was not short-sighted. I knew every boy had a future as well as a present. I gave up my plans, and came here with a smile; but in my heart I hated my grandmother for having power, and so bending me to relinquish pleasure for boredom. I hated her, and I came to her and kissed her, and saw her beautiful white Persian cat sitting before the fire in this room, and thought of the fellow who was my bosom friend, and with whom I longed to be, shooting, or fishing, or riding. And I looked at the cat again. I remember it began to purr when I went near to it. It sat quite still, with its blue eyes fixed upon the fire, but when I approached it I heard it purr complacently. I longed to kick it. The limitations of its ridiculous life satisfied it completely. It seemed to reproduce in an absurd, diminished way my grandmother in her white lace cap, with her white face and hands. She sat in her chair all day and looked at the fire. The cat sat on the hearthrug and did the same. The cat seemed to me the animal personification of the human being who kept me chained from all the sports and pleasures I had promised myself for the holidays. When I went near to the cat, and heard it calmly purring at me, I longed to do it an injury. It seemed to me as if it understood what my grandmother did not, and was complacently triumphing at my voluntary imprisonment with age, and laughing to itself at the pains men—and boys—will undergo for the sake of money. Brute! I did not love my grandmother, and she had money. I hated the cat utterly. It hadn't a *sou!*

This beautiful house is not old. My grandfather built it himself. He had no love for the life of towns, I believe, but was passionately in touch with nature, and, when a young man, he set out on a strange tour through England. His object was to find a perfect view, and in front of that view he intended to build himself a habitation. For nearly a year, so I have been told, he wandered through Scotland and England, and at last he came to this place in Cumberland, to this village, to this very spot. Here his wanderings ceased. Standing on the terrace—then uncultivated forest—that runs in front of these windows, he found at last what he desired. He bought the forest. He bought the windings of the river, the fields upon its banks, and on the extreme edge of the steep gorge through which it runs he built the lovely dwelling that today is mine.

This place is no ordinary place. It is characteristic in the highest degree. The house is wonderfully situated, with the ground falling abruptly in front of it, the river forming almost a horseshoe round it. The woods are lovely. The garden, curiously, almost wildly, laid out, is like no other garden I ever saw. And the house, though not old, is full of little surprises, curiously shaped rooms, remarkable staircases, quaint recesses. The place is a place to remember. The house is a house to fix itself in the memory. Nothing that had once lived here could ever come back and forget that it had been here. Not even an animal—not even an animal.

I wish I had never gone to that dinner-party and met the Professor. There was a horror coming upon me then. He has hastened its steps. He has put my fears into shape, my vague wondering into words. Why cannot men leave life alone? Why will they catch it by the throat and wring its secrets from it? To respect reserve is one of the first instincts of the gentleman; and life is full of reserve.

It is getting very late. I thought I heard a step in the house just now. I wonder—I wonder if *she* is asleep. I wish I knew.

Day after day passed by. My grandmother seemed to be failing, but almost imperceptibly. She evidently loved to have me near to her. Like most old dying people, in her mind she frantically clutched at life, that could give to her nothing more; and I believe she grew to regard me as the personification of all that was leaving her. My vitality warmed her. She extended her hands to my flaming hearthfire. She seemed trying to live in my life, and at length became afraid to let me out of her sight. One day she said to me, in her quavering, ugly voice—old voices are so ugly, like hideous echoes:

"Ronald, I could never die while you were in the room. So long as you are with me, where I can touch you, I shall live."

And she put out her white, corrugated hand, and fondled my warm boy's hand.

How I longed to push her hand away, and get out into the sunlight and the air, and hear young voices, the voices of the morning, not of the twilight, and be away from wrinkled Death, that seemed sitting on the doorstep of that house huddled up like a beggar, waiting for the door to be opened!

I was bored till I grew malignant. I confess it. And, feeling malignant, I began to long more and more passionately to vent myself on someone or something. I looked at the cat, which, as usual, was sitting before the fire.

Animals have intuitions as keen as those of a woman, keener than those of a man. They inherit an instinct of fear of those who hate them from a long line of ancestors who have suffered at the hands of cruel men. They can tell by a look, by a motion, by the tone of a voice, whether to expect from anyone kindness or malignity. The cat had purred complacently on the first day of my arrival, and had hunched up her white, furry back towards my hand, and had smiled with her calm, light-blue eyes. Now, when I approached her, she seemed to gather herself together and to make herself small. She shrank from me. There was—as I fancied—a dawning comprehension, a dawning terror in her blue eyes. She always sat very close to my grandmother now, as if she sought protection, and she watched me as if she were watching for an intention which she apprehended to grow in my mind.

And the intention came.

For, as the days went on, and my grandmother still lived, I began to grow desperate. My holiday time was over now, but my parents wrote telling me to stay where I was, and not to think of returning to school. My grandmother had caused a letter to be sent to them in which she said that she could not part from me, and added that my parents would never have cause to regret interrupting my education for a time. "He will be paid in full for every moment he loses," she wrote, referring to me.

It seemed a strange taste in her to care so much for a boy, but she had never loved women, and I was handsome, and she liked handsome faces. The brutality in my nature was not written upon my features. I had smiling, frank brown eyes, a lithe young figure, a gay boy's voice. My movements were quick, and I have always been told that my gestures were never awkward, my demeanour was never unfinished, as is the case so often with lads at school. Outwardly I was attractive; and the old woman, who had married two husbands merely for their looks, delighted in feeling that she had the power to retain me by her side at an age when most boys avoid old people as if they were the pestilence.

And then I pretended to love her, and obeyed all her insufferably tiresome behests. But I longed to wreak vengeance upon her all the same. My dearest friend, the fellow with whom I was to have spent my holidays, was leaving at the end of this term which I was missing. He wrote to me furious letters, urging me to come back, and reproaching me for my selfishness and lack of affection.

Each time I received one I looked at the cat, and the cat shrank nearer to my grandmother's chair.

It never purred now, and nothing would induce it to leave the room where she sat. One day the servant said to me:

"I believe the poor dumb thing knows my mistress can't last very much longer, sir. The way that cat looks up at her goes to my heart. Ah! them beasts understand things as well as we do, I believe."

I think the cat understood quite well. It did watch my grandmother in a very strange way, gazing up into her face, as if to mark the changing contours, the increasing lines, the downdroop of the features, that bespoke the gradual soft approach of death. It listened to the sound of her voice; and as, each day, the voice grew more vague, more weak and toneless, an anxiety that made me exult dawned and deepened in its blue eyes. Or so I thought.

I had a great deal of morbid imagination at that age, and loved to weave a web of fancies, mostly horrible, around almost everything that entered into my life. It pleased me to believe that the cat understood each new intention that came into my mind, read me silently from its place near the fire, tracked my thoughts, and was terror-stricken as they concentrated themselves round a definite resolve, which hardened and toughened day by day.

It pleased me to believe, do I say? I did really believe, and do believe now, that the cat understood all, and grew haggard with fear as my grandmother failed visibly. For it knew what the end would mean for it.

That first day of my arrival, when I saw my grandmother in her white cap, with her white face and hands, and the big white cat sitting near to her, I had thought there was a similarity between them. That similarity struck me more forcibly, grew upon me, as my time in the house grew longer, until the latter seemed almost a reproduction of the former, and after each letter from my friend my hate for the two increased. But my hate for my grandmother was impotent, and would always be so. I could never repay her for the *ennui,* the furious, forced inactivity which made my life a burden, and spurred my bad passions while they lulled me in a terrible, enforced repose. I could repay her favourite, the thing she had always cherished, her feline confidant, who lived in safety under the shadow of her protection. I could wreak my fury on that when the protection was withdrawn, as it must be at last. It seemed to my brutal, imaginative, unfinished boy's mind that the murder of her pet must hurt and wound my grandmother even after she was dead. I would make her suffer then, when she was impotent to wreak a vengeance upon me. I would kill the cat.

The creature knew my resolve the day I made it, and had even, I should say, anticipated it.

As I sat day after day beside my grandmother's armchair in the dim room, with the blinds drawn to shut out the summer sunlight, and talked to her in a subdued and reverent voice, agreeing with all the old banalities she uttered, all the preposterous opinions she propounded, all the commands she laid upon me, I gazed beyond her at the cat, and the creature was haggard with apprehension.

It knew, as I knew, that its day was coming. Sometimes I bent down and took it up on my lap to please my grandmother, and praised its beauty and its gentleness to her. And all the time I felt its warm, furry body trembling with horror between my hands. This pleased me, and I pretended that I was never happy unless it was on my knees. I kept it there for hours, stroking it so tenderly, smoothing its thick white coat, which was always in the most perfect order, talking to it, caressing it.

And sometimes I took its head between my two hands, turned its face to mine, and stared into its large blue eyes. Then I could read all its agony, all its torture of apprehension: and in spite of my friend's letters, and the dulness of my days, I was almost happy.

The summer was deepening, the glow of the roses flushed the garden ways, the skies were clear above Scawfell, when the end at last drew near. My grandmother's face was now scarcely recognizable. The eyes were sunk deep in her head. All expression seemed to fade gradually away. Her cheeks were no longer fine ivory white; a dull, sickening, yellow pallor overspread them. She seldom looked at me now, but rested entombed in her great armchair, her shrunken limbs seeming to tend downwards, as if she were inclined to slide to the floor and die there. Her lips were thin and dry, and moved perpetually in a silent chattering, as if her mind were talking and her voice were already dead. The tide of life was retreating from her body. I could almost see it visibly ebb away. The failing waves made no sound upon the shore. Death is uncanny, like all silent things.

Her maid wished her to stay entirely in bed, but she would get up, muttering that she was well; and the doctor said it was useless to hinder her. She had no specific disease. Only the years were taking their last toll of her. So she was placed in her chair each day by the fire, and sat there till evening, muttering with those dry lips. The stiff folds of her silken skirts formed an angle, and there the cat crouched hour after hour, a silent, white, waiting thing.

And the waves ebbed and ebbed away, and I waited too.

One afternoon, as I sat by my grandmother, the servant

entered with a letter for me just arrived by the post. I took it up. It was from Willoughby, my school-friend. He said the term was over, that he had left school, and his father had decided to send him out to America to start in business in New York, instead of entering him at Oxford as he had hoped. He bade me good-bye, and said he supposed we should not meet again for years; "but," he added, "no doubt you won't care a straw, so long as you get the confounded money you're after. You've taught me one of the lessons of life, young Ronald—never to believe in friendship."

As I read the letter I set my teeth. All that was good in my nature centred round Willoughby. He was a really fine fellow. I honestly and truly loved him. His news gave me a bitter shock, and turned my heart to iron and to fire. Perhaps I should never see him again; even if I did, time would have changed him, seared him—my friend, in his wonderful youth, with the morning in his eyes, would be no more. I hated myself in that moment for having stayed; I hated still more her who had kept me. For the moment I was carried out of myself. I crushed the letter up in my burning hand. I turned fiercely round upon that yellow, enigmatic, dying figure in the great chair. All the fury, locked within my heart for so long, rose to the surface, and drove self-interest away. I turned upon my grandmother with blazing eyes and trembling limbs. I opened my mouth to utter a torrent of reproachful words, when—what was it?—what slight change had stolen into the wrinkled, yellow face? I bent over her. The eyes gazed at me, but so horribly! She sat so low in her chair; she looked so fearful, so very strange. I put my fingers on her eyelids; I drew them down over the eyeballs: they did not open again. I felt her withered hands: they were ice. Then I knew, and I felt myself smiling. I leaned over the dead woman. There, on the far side of her, crouched the cat. Its white fur was all bristling; its blue eyes were dilated; on its jaws there were flecks of foam.

I leaned over the dead woman and took it in my arms.

·　·　·

That was nearly twenty years ago, and yet tonight the memory of that moment, and what followed it, bring a fear to my heart which I must combat. I have read of men who lived for long spaces of time haunted by demons created by their imagination, and I have laughed at them and pitied them. Surely I am not going to join in their folly, in their madness, led to the gates of terror by my own fancies, half-confirmed, apparently, by the chance utterances of a conceited Professor—a man of fads, although a man of science.

That was twenty years ago. After tonight let me forget it. After tonight, do I say? Hark! the birds are twittering in the dew outside. The pale, early sun-shafts strike over the moors. And I am tired. To-morrow night I will finish this wrestle with my own folly; I will give the *coup de grâce* to my imagination. But no more now. My brain is not calm, and I will not write in excitement.

II.

WEDNESDAY NIGHT, *November 4th.*

Margot has gone to bed at last, and I am alone. This has been a horrible day—horrible; but I will not dwell upon it.

After the death of my grandmother, I went back to school again. But Willoughby was gone, and he could not forgive me. He wrote to me once or twice from New York, and then I ceased to hear from him. He died out of my life. His affection for me had evidently declined from the day when he took it into his head that I was only a money-grubber, like the rest of the world, and that the Jew instinct had developed in me at an abnormally early age. I let him go. What did it matter? But I was always glad that I had been cruel on the day my grandmother died. I never repented of what I did—never. If I had, I might be happier now.

I went back to school. I studied, played, got into mischief and out of it again, like other boys; but in my life there seemed to be an eternal coldness, that I alone, perhaps, was conscious of. My deed of cruelty, of brutal revenge on the thing that had never done me injury, had seared my soul. I was not sorry, but I could not forget; and sometimes I thought—how ridiculous it looks written down!—that there was a power hidden somewhere which could not forget either, and that a penalty might have to be paid. Because a creature is dumb, must its soul die when it dies? Is not the soul, perhaps—as *he* said—a wanderer through many bodies?

But if I did not kill a soul, as I killed a body, the day my grandmother died, where is that soul now? That is what I want to arrive at, that is what I must arrive at, if I am to be happy.

I went back to school, and I passed to Oxford. I tasted the strange, unique life of a university, narrow, yet pulsating, where the youth, that is so green and springing, tries to arm itself for the battle with the weapons forged by the dead and sharpened by the more elderly among the living. I did well there, and I passed on into the world. And then at last I began to understand the value of my inheritance; for all that had been my grandmother's was now mine. My people wished me to marry, but I had no desire to fetter myself. So I took the sponge in my strong young hands, and tried to squeeze it dry. And I did not know that I was sad—I did not know it until, at the age of thirty-three, just seventeen years after my grandmother died, I understood the sort of thing happiness is. Of course, it was love that brought to me understanding. I need not explain that. I had often played on love; now love began to play on me. I trembled at the harmonies his hands evoked.

I met a young girl, very young, just on the verge of life and of womanhood. She was seventeen when I first saw her, and she was valsing at a big ball in London—her first ball. She passed me in the crowd of dancers, and I noticed her. As she was a *débutante* her dress was naturally snow-white. There was no touch of colour about it—not a flower, not a jewel. Her hair was the palest yellow I had almost ever seen—the colour of an early primrose. Naturally fluffy, it nearly concealed the white riband that ran through it, and clustered in tendrils and tiny natural curls upon her neck. Her skin was whiter than ivory—a clear, luminous white. Her eyes were very large and china-blue in colour.

This young girl dancing passed and repassed me, and my glance rested on her idly, even cynically. For she seemed so happy, and at that time happiness won my languid wonder, if ingenuously exhibited. To be happy seemed almost to be mindless. But by degrees I found myself watching this girl, and more

closely. Another dance began. She joined it with another part-
ner. But she seemed just as pleased with him as with her former
one. She would not let him pause to rest; she kept him dancing
all the time, her youth and freshness spoken in that gentle compelling. I grew interested in her, even acutely so. She seemed to
me like the spirit of youth dancing over the body of Time. I
resolved to know her. I felt weary; I thought she might revive
me. The dance drew to an end, and I approached my hostess,
pointed the girl out, and asked for an introduction. Her name
was Margot Magendie, I found, and she was an heiress as well
as a beauty.

I did not care. It was her humanity that drew me, nothing else.

But, strange to say, when the moment for the introduction
arrived, and I stood face to face with Miss Magendie, I felt an
extraordinary shrinking from her. I have never been able to
understand it, but my blood ran cold, and my pulses almost
ceased to beat. I would have avoided her; an instinct within me
seemed suddenly to cry out against her. But it was too late: the
introduction was effected; her hand rested on my arm.

I was actually trembling. She did not appear to notice it. The
band played a valse, and the inexplicable horror that had seized
me lost itself in the gay music. It never returned until lately.

I seldom enjoyed a valse more. Our steps suited so perfectly,
and her obvious childish pleasure communicated itself to me.
The spirit of youth in her knocked on my rather jaded heart, and
I opened to it. That was beautiful and strange. I talked with her,
and I felt myself younger, ingenuous rather than cynical,
inclined even to a radiant, though foolish, optimism. She was
very natural, very imperfect in worldly education, full of fragmentary but decisive views on life, quite unabashed in giving
them forth, quite inconsiderate in summoning my adherence to
them.

And then, presently, as we sat in a dim corridor under a rosy
hanging lamp, in saying something she looked, with her great
blue eyes, right into my face. Some very faint recollection awoke
and stirred in my mind.

"Surely," I said hesitatingly—"surely I have seen you before?
It seems to me that I remember your eyes."

As I spoke I was thinking hard, chasing the vagrant recollection that eluded me.

She smiled.

"You don't remember my face?"

"No, not at all."

"Nor I yours. If we had seen each other, surely we should recollect it."

Then she blushed, suddenly realizing that her words implied, perhaps, more than she had meant. I did not pay the obvious compliment. Those blue eyes and something in their expression moved me strangely; but I could not tell why. When I said good-bye to her that night, I asked to be allowed to call.

She assented.

That was the beginning of a very beautiful courtship, which gave a colour to life, a music to existence, a meaning to every slightest sensation.

And was it love that laid to sleep recollection, that sang a lullaby to awakening horror, and strewed poppies over it till it sighed itself into slumber? Was it love that drowned my mind in deep and charmed waters, binding the strange powers that every mind possesses in flowery garlands stronger than any fetters of iron? Was it love that, calling up dreams, alienated my thoughts from their search after reality?

I hardly know. I only know that I grew to love Margot, and only looked for love in her blue eyes, not for any deed of the past that might be mirrored there.

And I made her love me.

She gave her child's heart to my keeping with a perfect confidence that only a perfect affection could engender. She did love me then. No circumstances of today can break that fact under their hammers. She did love me, and it is the knowledge that she did which gives so much of fear to me now.

For great changes in the human mind are terrible. As we realize them we realize the limitless possibilities of sinister deeds that lie hidden in every human being. A little child that loves a doll can become an old, crafty, secret murderer. How horrible!

And perhaps it is still more horrible to think that, while the human envelope remains totally unchanged, every word of the

letter within may become altered, and a message of peace fade
into a sentence of death.

Margot's face is the same face now as it was when I married
her—scarcely older, certainly not less beautiful. Only the
expression of the eyes has changed.

For we were married. After a year of love-making, which
never tired either of us, we elected to bind ourselves, to fuse the
two into one.

We went abroad for the honeymoon, and, instead of shorten-
ing it to the fashionable fortnight, we travelled for nearly six
months, and were happy all the time.

Boredom never set in. Margot had a beautiful mind as well as
a beautiful face. She softened me through my affection. The
current of my life began to set in a different direction. I turned
the pages of a book of pity and of death more beautiful than that
of Pierre Loti. I could hear at last the great cry for sympathy,
which is the music of this strange suffering world, and, listening
to it, in my heart there rang an echo. The cruelty in my nature
seemed to shrivel up. I was more gentle than I had been, more
gentle than I had thought I could ever be.

At last, in the late spring, we started for home. We stayed for
a week in London, and then we travelled north. Margot had
never seen her future home, had never even been in
Cumberland before. She was full of excitement and happiness, a
veritable child in the ready and ardent expression of her feelings.
The station is several miles from the house, and is on the edge of
the sea. When the train pulled up at the wayside platform the day
drew towards sunset, and the flat levels of the beach shone with
a rich, liquid, amber light. In the distance the sea was tossing and
tumbling, whipped into foam by a fresh wind. The Isle of Man
lay far away, dark, mysterious, under a stack of bellying white
clouds, just beginning to be tinged with the faintest rose.

Margot found the scene beautiful, the wind life-giving, the
flat sand-banks, the shining levels, even the dry, spiky grass that
fluttered in the breeze, fascinating and refreshing.

"I feel near the heart of Nature in a place like this," she said,
looking up at a seagull that hovered over the little platform, crying to the wind on which it hung.

The train stole off along the edge of the sands, till we could see only the white streamer of its smoke trailing towards the sun. We turned away from the sea, got into the carriage that was waiting for us, and set our faces inland. The ocean was blotted out by the low grass and heather-covered banks that divided the fields. Presently we plunged into woods. The road descended sharply. A village, an abruptly winding river sprang into sight.

We were on my land. We passed the inn, the Rainwood Arms, named after my grandfather's family. The people whom we met stared curiously and saluted in rustic fashion.

Margot was full of excitement and pleasure, and talked incessantly, holding my hand tightly in hers and asking a thousand questions. Passing through the village, we mounted a hill towards a thick grove of trees.

"The house stands among them," I said, pointing.

She sprang up eagerly in the carriage to find it, but it was hidden.

We dashed through the gate into the momentary darkness of the drive, emerged between great green lawns, and drew up before the big doorway of the hall. I looked into her eyes, and said "Welcome!"

She only smiled in answer.

I would not let her enter the house immediately, but made her come with me to the terrace above the river, to see the view over the Cumbrian mountains and the moors of Eskdale.

The sky was very clear and pale, but over Styhead the clouds were boiling up. The Screes that guard ebon Wastwater looked grim and sad.

Margot stood beside me on the terrace, but her chatter had been succeeded by silence. And I, too, was silent for the moment, absorbed in contemplation. But presently I turned to her, wishing to see how she was impressed by her new domain.

She was not looking towards the river and the hills, but at the terrace walk itself, the band of emerald turf that bordered it, the stone pots full of flowers, the winding way that led into the shrubbery.

She was looking at these intently, and with a strange puzzled, almost startled expression.

"Hush! Don't speak to me for a moment," she said, as I opened my lips. "Don't; I want to—— How odd this is!"

And she gazed up at the windows of the house, at the creepers that climbed its walls, at the sloping roof and the irregular chimney-stacks.

Her lips were slightly parted, and her eyes were full of an inward expression that told me she was struggling with forgetfulness and desired recollection.

I was silent, wondering.

At last she said: "Ronald, I have never been in the North of England before, never set foot in Cumberland; yet I seem to know this terrace walk, those very flower-pots, the garden, the look of that roof, those chimneys, even the slanting way in which that great creeper climbs. Is it not—is it not very strange?"

She gazed up at me, and in her blue eyes there was an expression almost of fear.

I smiled down on her. "It must be your fancy," I said.

"It does not seem so," she replied. "I feel as if I had been here before, and often, or for a long time." She paused; then she said: "Do let me go into the house. There ought to be a room there—a room—I seem almost to see it. Come! Let us go in."

She took my hand and drew me towards the hall door. The servants were carrying in the luggage, and there was a certain amount of confusion and noise, but she did not seem to notice it. She was intent on something; I could not tell what.

"Do show me the house, Ronald—the drawing-room, and—and—there is another room I wish to see."

"You shall see them all, dear," I said. "You are excited. It is natural enough. This is the drawing-room."

She glanced round it hastily.

"And now the others!" she exclaimed.

I took her to the dining-room, the library, and the various apartments on the ground-floor.

She scarcely looked at them. When we had finished exploring, "Are these all?" she asked, with a wavering accent of disappointment.

"All," I answered.

"Then—show me the rooms upstairs."

We ascended the shallow oak steps, and passed first into the apartment in which my grandmother had died.

It had been done up since then, refurnished, and almost completely altered. Only the wide fireplace, with its brass dogs and its heavy oaken mantelpiece, had been left untouched.

Margot glanced hastily round. Then she walked up to the fireplace, and drew a long breath.

"There ought to be a fire here," she said.

"But it is summer," I answered, wondering.

"And a chair there," she went on, in a curious low voice, indicating—I think now, or is it my imagination?—the very spot where my grandmother was wont to sit. "Yes—I seem to remember, and yet not to remember."

She looked at me, and her white brows were knit.

Suddenly she said: "Ronald, I don't think I like this room. There is something—I don't know—I don't think I could sit here; and I seem to remember—something about it, as I did about the terrace. What can it mean?"

"It means that you are tired and overexcited, darling. Your nerves are too highly strung, and nerves play us strange tricks. Come to your own room and take off your things, and when you have had some tea, you will be all right again."

Yes, I was fool enough to believe that tea was the panacea for an undreamed-of, a then unimaginable, evil.

I thought Margot was simply an overtired and imaginative child that evening. If I could believe so now!

We went up into her boudoir and had tea, and she grew more like herself; but several times that night I observed her looking puzzled and thoughtful, and a certain expression of anxiety shone in her blue eyes that was new to them then.

But I thought nothing of it, and I was happy. Two or three days passed, and Margot did not again refer to her curious sensation of pre-knowledge of the house and garden. I fancied there was a slight alteration in her manner; that was all. She seemed a little restless. Her vivacity flagged now and then. She was more willing to be alone than she had been. But we were old married folk now, and could not be always in each other's sight. I had a great many people connected with the estate to see, and had to gather up the tangled threads of many affairs.

The honeymoon was over. Of course we could not always be together.

Still, I should have wished Margot to desire it, and I could not hide from myself that now and then she scarcely concealed a slight impatience to be left in solitude. This troubled me, but only a little, for she was generally as fond as ever. That evening, however, an incident occurred which rendered me decidedly uneasy, and made me wonder if my wife were not inclined to that curse of highly-strung women—hysteria!

I had been riding over the moors to visit a tenant-farmer who lived at some distance, and did not return until twilight. Dismounting, I let myself into the house, traversed the hall, and ascended the stairs. As I wore spurs, and the steps were of polished oak and uncarpeted, I walked noisily enough to warn anyone of my approach. I was passing the door of the room that had been my grandmother's sitting-room, when I noticed that it stood open. The house was rather dark, and the interior was dim enough, but I could see a figure in a white dress moving about inside. I recognised Margot, and wondered what she was doing, but her movements were so singular that, instead of speaking to her, I stood in the doorway and watched her.

She was walking, with a very peculiar, stealthy step, around the room, not as if she were looking for anything, but merely as if she were restless or ill at ease. But what struck me forcibly was this, that there was something curiously animal in her movements, seen thus in a dim half-light that only partially revealed her to me. I had never seen a woman walk in that strangely wild yet soft way before. There was something uncanny about it, that rendered me extremely discomforted; yet I was quite fascinated, and rooted to the ground.

I cannot tell how long I stood there. I was so completely absorbed in the passion of the gazer that the passage of time did not concern me in the least. I was as one assisting at a strange spectacle. This white thing moving in the dark did not suggest my wife to me, although it was she. I might have been watching an animal, vague, yet purposeful of mind, tracing out some hidden thing, following out some instinct quite foreign to humanity. I remember that presently I involuntarily clasped my hands together, and felt that they were very cold. Perspiration

broke out on my face. I was painfully, unnaturally moved, and a
violent desire to be away from this white moving thing came
over me. Walking as softly as I could, I went to my dressing-
room, shut the door, and sat down on a chair. I never remember
to have felt thoroughly unnerved before, but now I found myself
actually shaken, palsied. I could understand how deadly a thing
fear is. I lit a candle hastily, and as I did so a knock came to
the door.

Margot's voice said, "May I come in?"

I felt unable to reply, so I got up and admitted her.

She entered, smiling, and looking such a child, so innocent, so
tender, that I almost laughed aloud. That I, a man, should have
been frightened by a child in a white dress, just because the twilight cast a phantom atmosphere around her! I held her in my
arms, and I gazed into her blue eyes.

She looked down, but still smiled.

"Where have you been, and what have you been doing?" I
asked gaily.

She answered that she had been in the drawing-room since
tea-time.

"You came here straight from the drawing-room?" I said.

She replied, "Yes."

Then, with an indifferent air which hid real anxiety, I said:

"By the way, Margot, have you been into that room again—
the room you fancied you recollected?"

"No, never," she answered, withdrawing herself from my
arms. "I don't wish to go there. Make haste, Ronald, and dress.
It is nearly dinner-time, and I am ready." And she turned and
left me.

She had told me a lie. All my feelings of uneasiness and discomfort returned tenfold.

That evening was the most wretched one, the only wretched
one, I had ever spent with her.

•   •   •

I am tired of writing. I will continue my task to-morrow. It
takes me longer than I anticipated. Yet even to tell everything to

myself brings me some comfort. Man must express himself; and despair must find a voice

III.

THURSDAY NIGHT, *December 5th.*

That lie awoke in me suspicion of the child I had married. I began to doubt her, yet never ceased to love her. She had all my heart, and must have it till the end. But the calm of love was to be succeeded by love's tumult and agony. A strangeness was creeping over Margot. It was as if she took a thin veil in her hands, and drew it over and all around her, till the outlines I had known were slightly blurred. Her disposition, which had been so clear cut, so sharply, beautifully defined, standing out in its innocent glory for all men to see, seemed to withdraw itself, as if a dawning necessity for secrecy had arisen. A thin crust of reserve began to subtly overspread her every act and expression. She thought now before she spoke; she thought before she looked. It seemed to me that she was becoming a slightly different person.

The change I mean to imply is very difficult to describe. It was not abrupt enough to startle, but I could feel it, slight though it was. Have you seen the first flat film of waveless water, sent by the incoming tides of the sea, crawling silently up over the wrinkled brown sand, and filling the tiny ruts, till diminutive hills and valleys are all one smooth surface? So it was with Margot. A tide flowed over her character, a waveless tide of reserve. The hills and valleys which I loved disappeared from my ken. Behind the old sweet smile, the old frank expression, my wife was shrinking down to hide herself, as one escaping from pursuit hides behind a barrier. When one human being knows another very intimately, and all the barricades that divide soul from soul have been broken down, it is difficult to set them up again without noise and dust, and the sound of thrusting bolts, and the tap of the hammer that drives in the nails. It is difficult, but not impossible. Barricades can be raised noiselessly, soundless bolts—that keep out the soul—be pushed home. The black gauze veil that blots out the scene drops, and when it is raised—if ever—the scene is changed.

The real Margot was receding from me. I felt it with an impotence of despair that was benumbing. Yet I could not speak of it, for at first I could hardly tell if she knew of what was taking place. Indeed, at this moment, in thinking it over, I do not believe that for some time she had any definite cognisance of the fact that she was growing to love me less passionately than of old. In acts she was not changed. That was the strange part of the matter. Her kisses were warm, but I believed them premeditated. She clasped my hand in hers, but now there was more mechanism than magic in that act of tenderness. Impulse failed within her; and she had been all impulse? Did she know it? At that time I wondered. Believing that she did not know she was changing, I was at the greatest pains to guard my conduct, lest I should implant the suspicion that might hasten what I feared. I remained, desperately, the same as ever, and so, of course, was not the same, for a deed done defiantly bears little resemblance to a deed done naturally. I was always considering what I should say, how I should act, even how I should look. To live now was sedulous instead of easy. Effort took the place of simplicity. My wife and I were gazing furtively at each other through the eye-holes of masks. I knew it. Did she?

At that time I never ceased to wonder. Of one thing I was certain, however—that Margot began to devise excuses for being left alone. When we first came home she could hardly endure me out of her sight. Now she grew to appreciate solitude. This was a terrible danger signal, and I could not fail to so regard it.

Yet something within me held me back from speaking out. I made no comment on the change that deepened day by day, but I watched my wife furtively, with a concentration of attention that sometimes left me physically exhausted. I felt, too, at length, that I was growing morbid, that suspicion coloured my mind and caused me, perhaps, to put a wrong interpretation on many of her actions, to exaggerate and misconstrue the most simple things she did. I began to believe her every look premeditated. Even if she kissed me, I thought she did it with a purpose; if she smiled up at me as of old, I fancied the smile to be only a concealment of its opposite. By degrees we became shy of each other. We were like uncongenial intimates, forced to occupy the same house, forced into a fearful knowledge of each other's personal habits, while we knew nothing of the thoughts that make up the true lives of individuals.

And then another incident occurred, a pendant to the incident of Margot's strange denied visit to the room she affected to fear. It was one night, one deep dark night of the autumn—a season to affect even a cheerful mind and incline it towards melancholy. Margot and I were now often silent when we were together. That evening, towards nine, a dull steady rain set in. I remember I heard it on the window-panes as we sat in the drawing-room after dinner, and remarked on it, saying to her that if it continued for two or three days she might chance to see the floods out, and that fishermen would descend upon us by the score.

I did not obtain much response from her. The dreariness of the weather seemed to affect her spirits. She took up a book presently, and appeared to read; but, once in glancing up suddenly from my newspaper, I thought I caught her gaze fixed fearfully upon me. It seemed to me that she was looking furtively at me with an absolute terror. I was so much affected that I made some excuse for leaving the room, went down to my den, lit a cigar, and walked uneasily up and down, listening to the rain on the window. At ten Margot came in to tell me she was going to bed. I wished her good-night tenderly, but as I held her slim body a moment in my arms I felt that she began to tremble. I let her go, and she slipped from the room with the soft, cushioned step that was habitual with her. And, strangely enough, my thoughts recurred to the day, long ago, when I first held the great white cat on my knees, and felt its body shrink from my touch with a nameless horror. The uneasy movement of the woman recalled to me so strongly and so strangely the uneasy movement of the animal.

I lit a second cigar. It was near midnight when it was smoked out, and I turned down the lamp and went softly up to bed. I undressed in the room adjoining my wife's, and then stole into hers. She was sleeping in the wide white bed rather uneasily, and as I leaned over her, shading the candle flame with my outspread hand, she muttered some broken words that I could not catch. I had never heard her talk in her dreams before. I lay down gently at her side and extinguished the candle.

But sleep did not come to me. The dull, dead silence weighed upon instead of soothing me. My mind was terribly alive, in a ferment; and the contrast between my own excitement and the hushed peace of my environment was painful, was almost unbearable. I wished that a wind from the mountains were beating against the window-panes, and the rain lashing the house in fury. The black calm around was horrible, unnatural. The drizzling rain was now so small that I could not even hear its patter when I strained my ears. Margot had ceased to mutter, and lay perfectly still. How I longed to be able to read the soul hidden in her sleeping body, to unravel the mystery of the mind which I had once understood so perfectly! It is so horrible that we can never open the human envelope, take out the letter, and seize with our eyes upon its every word. Margot slept with all her secrets safeguarded, although she was unconscious, no longer watchful, on the alert. She was so silent, even her quiet breathing not reaching my ear, that I felt impelled to stretch out my hand beneath the coverlet and touch hers ever so softly. I did so.

Her hand was instantly and silently withdrawn. She was awake, then.

"Margot," I said, "did I disturb you?"

There was no answer.

The movement, followed by the silence, affected me very disagreeably.

I lit the candle and looked at her. She was lying on the extreme edge of the bed, with her blue eyes closed. Her lips were slightly parted. I could hear her steady breathing. Yet was she really sleeping?

I bent lower over her, and as I did so a slight, involuntary movement, akin to what we call a shudder, ran through her body. I recoiled from the bed. An impotent anger seized me. Could it be that my presence was becoming so hateful to my wife that even in sleep her body trembled when I drew near it? Or was this slumber feigned? I could not tell, but I felt it impossible at that moment to remain in the room. I returned to my own, dressed, and descended the stairs to the door opening on to the terrace. I felt a longing to be out in the air. The atmosphere of the house was stifling.

Was it coming to this, then? Did I, a man, shrink with a fantastic cowardice from a woman I loved? The latent cruelty began to stir within me, the tyrant spirit which a strong love sometimes evokes. I had been Margot's slave almost. My affection had brought me to her feet, had kept me there. So long as she loved me I was content to be her captive, knowing she was mine. But a change in her attitude toward me might rouse the master. In my nature there was a certain brutality, a savagery, which I had never wholly slain, although Margot had softened me wonderfully by her softness, had brought me to gentleness by her tenderness. The boy of years ago had developed toward better things, but he was not dead in me. I felt that as I walked up and down the terrace through the night in a wild meditation. If my love could not hold Margot, my strength should.

I drew in a long breath of the wet night air, and I opened my shoulders as if shaking off an oppression. My passion for Margot had not yet drawn me down to weakness; it had raised me up to strength. The faint fear of her, which I had felt almost without knowing it more than once, died within me. The desire of the conqueror elevated me. There was something for me to win. My paralysis passed away, and I turned toward the house.

And now a strange thing happened. I walked into the dark hall, closed the outer door, shutting out the dull murmur of the night, and felt in my pocket for my matchbox. It was not there. I must inadvertently have laid it down in my dressing-room and left it. I searched about in the darkness on the hall table, but could find no light. There was nothing for it, then, but to feel my way upstairs as best I could.

I started, keeping my hand against the wall to guide me. I gained the top of the stairs, and began to traverse the landing, still with my hand upon the wall. To reach my dressing-room I had to pass the apartment which had been my grandmother's sitting-room.

When I reached it, instead of sliding along a closed door, as I had anticipated, my hand dropped into vacancy.

The door was wide open. It had been shut, like all the other doors in the house, when I had descended the stairs—shut and locked, as it always was at night-time. Why was it open now?

I paused in the darkness. And then an impulse seized me to walk forward into the room. I advanced a step; but, as I did so, a horrible low cry broke upon my ears out of the darkness. It came from immediately in front of me, and sounded like an expression of the most abject fear.

My feet rooted themselves to the ground.

"Who's there?" I asked.

There came no answer.

I listened for a moment, but did not hear the minutest sound. The desire for light was overpowering. I generally did my writing in this room, and knew the exact whereabouts of everything in it. I knew that on the writing-table there was a silver box containing wax matches. It lay on the left of my desk. I moved another step forward.

There was the sound of a slight rustle, as if someone shrank back as I advanced.

I laid my hand quickly on the box, opened it, and struck a light. The room was vaguely illuminated. I saw something white at the far end, against the wall. I put the match to a candle.

The white thing was Margot. She was in her dressing-gown, and was crouched up in an angle of the wall as far away from where I stood as possible. Her blue eyes were wide open, and fixed upon me with an expression of such intense and hideous fear in them that I almost cried out.

"Margot, what is the matter?" I said. "Are you ill?"

She made no reply. Her face terrified me.

"What is it, Margot?" I cried in a loud, almost harsh voice, determined to rouse her from this horrible, unnatural silence. "What are you doing here?"

I moved towards her. I stretched out my hands and seized her. As I did so, a sort of sob burst from her. Her hands were cold and trembling.

"What is it? What has frightened you?" I reiterated.

At last she spoke in a low voice.

"You—you looked so strange, so—so cruel as you came in," she said.

"Strange! Cruel! But you could not see me. It was dark," I answered.

"Dark!" she said.

"Yes, until I lit the candle. And you cried out when I was only in the doorway. You could not see me there."

"Why not? What has that got to do with it?" she murmured, still trembling violently.

"You can see me in the dark?"

"Of course," she said. "I don't understand what you mean. Of course I can see you when you are there before my eyes."

"But——" I began; and then her obvious and complete surprise at my questions stopped them. I still held her hands in mine, and their extreme coldness roused me to the remembrance that she was unclothed.

"You will be ill if you stay here," I said. "Come back to your room."

She said nothing, and I led her back, waited while she got into bed, and then, placing the candle on the dressing-table, sat down in a chair by her side.

The strong determination to take prompt action, to come to an explanation, to end these dreary mysteries of mind and conduct, was still upon me.

I did not think of the strange hour; I did not care that the night was gliding on towards dawn. I was self-absorbed. I was beyond ordinary considerations.

Yet I did not speak immediately. I was trying to be quite calm, trying to think of the best line for me to take. So much might depend upon our mere words now. At length I said, laying my hand upon hers, which was outside the coverlet:

"Margot, what were you doing in that room at such a strange hour? Why were you there?"

She hesitated obviously. Then she answered, not looking at me:

"I missed you. I thought you might be there—writing."

"But you were in the dark."

"I thought you would have a light."

I knew by her manner that she was not telling me the truth, but I went on quietly:

"If you expected me, why did you cry out when I came to the door?"

She tried to draw her hand away, but I held it fast, closing my fingers upon it with even brutal strength.

"Why did you cry out?"

"You—you looked so strange, so cruel."

"So cruel!"

"Yes. You frightened me—you frightened me horribly."

She began suddenly to sob, like one completely overstrained. I lifted her up in the bed, put my arms round her, and made her lean against me. I was strangely moved.

"I frighten you! How can that be?" I said, trying to control a passion of mingled love and anger that filled my breast. "You know that I love you. You must know that. In all our short married life have I ever been even momentarily unkind to you? Let us be frank with one another. Our lives have changed lately. One of us has altered. You cannot say that it is I."

She only continued to sob bitterly in my arms. I held her closer.

"Let us be frank with one another," I went on. "For God's sake let us have no barriers between us. Margot, look into my eyes and tell me—are you growing tired of me?"

She turned her head away, but I spoke more sternly:

"You shall be truthful. I will have no more subterfuge. Look me in the face. You did love me once?"

"Yes, yes," she whispered in a choked voice.

"What have I done, then, to alienate you? Have I ever hurt you, ever shown a lack of sympathy, ever neglected you?"

"Never—never."

"Yet you have changed to me since—since——" I paused a moment, trying to recall when I had first noticed her altered demeanour.

She interrupted me.

"It has all come upon me in this house," she sobbed. "Oh! what is it? What does it all mean? If I could understand a little—only a little—it would not be so bad. But this nightmare, this thing that seems such a madness of the intellect——"

Her voice broke and ceased. Her tears burst forth afresh.

Such mingled fear, passion, and a sort of strange latent irritation, I had never seen before.

"It is a madness indeed," I said, and a sense almost of outrage made my voice hard and cold. "I have not deserved such treatment at your hands."

"I will not yield to it," she said, with a sort of desperation, suddenly throwing her arms around me. "I will not—I will not!"

I was strangely puzzled. I was torn with conflicting feelings. Love and anger grappled at my heart. But I only held her, and did not speak until she grew obviously calmer. The paroxysm seemed passing away. Then I said:

"I cannot understand."

"Nor I," she answered, with a directness that had been foreign to her of late, but that was part and parcel of her real, beautiful nature. "I cannot understand. I only know there is a change in me, or in you to me, and that I cannot help it, or that I have not been able to help it. Sometimes I feel—do not be angry, I will try to tell you—a physical fear of you, of your touch, of your clasp, a fear such as an animal might feel towards the master who had beaten it. I tremble at your approach. When you are near me I feel cold, oh! so cold and—and anxious; perhaps I ought to say apprehensive. Oh, I am hurting you!"

I suppose I must have winced at her words, and she is quick to observe.

"Go on," I said; "do not spare me. Tell me everything. It is madness indeed; but we may kill it, when we both know it."

"Oh, if we could!" she cried, with a poignancy which was heart-breaking to hear. "If we could!"

"Do you doubt our ability?" I said, trying to be patient and calm. "You are unreasoning, like all women. Be sensible for a moment. You do me a wrong in cherishing these feelings. I have the capacity for cruelty in me. I may have been—I have been— cruel in the past, but never to you. You have no right to treat me as you have done lately. If you examine your feelings, and compare them with facts, you will see their absurdity."

"But," she interposed, with a woman's fatal quickness, "that will not do away with their reality."

"It must. Look into their faces until they fade like ghosts, seen only between light and darkness. They are founded upon nothing; they are bred without father or mother; they are hysterical; they are wicked. Think a little of me. You are not going to be conquered by a chimera, to allow a phantom created by your imagination to ruin the happiness that has been so beautiful. You will not do that! You dare not!"

She only answered:

"If I can help it."

A passionate anger seized me, a fury at my impotence against this child. I pushed her almost roughly from my arms.

"And I have married this woman!" I cried bitterly. I got up.

Margot had ceased crying now, and her face was very white and calm; it looked rigid in the faint candle-light that shone across the bed.

"Do not be angry," she said. "We are controlled by something inside of us; there are powers in us that we cannot fight against."

"There is nothing we cannot fight against," I said passionately. "The doctrine of predestination is the devil's own doctrine. It is the doctrine set up by the sinner to excuse his sin; it is the coward's doctrine. Understand me, Margot, I love you, but I am not a weak fool. There must be an end of this folly. Perhaps you are playing with me, acting like a girl, testing me. Let us have no more of it."

She said:

"I only do what I must."

Her tone turned me cold. Her set face frightened me, and angered me, for there was a curious obstinacy in it. I left the room abruptly, and did not return. That night I had no sleep.

I am not a coward, but I find that I am inclined to fear that which fears me. I dread an animal that always avoids me silently more than an animal that actually attacks me. The thing that runs from me makes me shiver, the thing that creeps away when I come near wakes my uneasiness. At this time there rose up in me a strange feeling towards Margot. The white, fair child I had married was at moments—only at moments—horrible to me. I felt disposed to shun her. Something within cried out against her. Long ago, at the instant of our introduction, an unreasoning sensation that could only be called dread had laid hold upon me.

That dread returned from the night of our explanation, returned deepened and added to. It prompted me to a suggestion which I had no sooner made than I regretted it. On the morning following I told Margot that in future we had better occupy separate rooms. She assented quietly, but I thought a furtive expression of relief stole for a moment into her face.

I was deeply angered with her and with myself; yet, now that I knew beyond question my wife's physical terror of me, I was half afraid of her. I felt as if I could not bring myself to lie long hours by her side in the darkness, by the side of a woman who was shrinking from me, who was watching me when I could not see her. The idea made my very flesh creep.

Yet I hated myself for this shrinking of the body, and sometimes hated her for rousing it. A hideous struggle was going on within me—a struggle between love and impotent anger and despair, between the lover and the master. For I am one of the old-fashioned men who think that a husband ought to be master of his wife as well as of his house.

How could I be master of a woman I secretly feared? My knowledge of myself spurred me through acute irritation almost to the verge of madness.

All calm was gone. I was alternately gentle to my wife and almost ferocious towards her, ready to fall at her feet and worship her or to seize her and treat her with physical violence. I only restrained myself by an effort.

My variations of manner did not seem to affect her. Indeed, it sometimes struck me that she feared me more when I was kind to her than when I was harsh.

And I knew, by a thousand furtive indications, that her horror of me was deepening day by day. I believe she could hardly bring herself to be in a room alone with me, especially after nightfall.

One evening, when we were dining, the butler, after placing dessert upon the table, moved to leave us. She turned white, and, as he reached the door, half rose, and called him back in a sharp voice.

"Symonds!" she said.

"Yes, ma'am?"

"You are going?"

The fellow looked surprised.

"Can I get you anything, ma'am?"

She glanced at me with an indescribable uneasiness. Then she leaned back in her chair with an effort, and pressed her lips together.

"No," she said.

As the man went out and shut the door, she looked at me again from under her eyelids; and finally her eyes travelled from me to a small, thin-bladed knife, used for cutting oranges, that lay near her plate, and fixed themselves on it. She put out her hand stealthily, drew it towards her, and kept her hand over it on the table. I took an orange from a dish in front of me.

"Margot," I said, "will you pass me that fruit-knife?"

She obviously hesitated.

"Give me that knife," I repeated roughly, stretching out my hand.

She lifted her hand, left the knife upon the table, and at the same time, springing up, glided softly out of the room and closed the door behind her.

That evening I spent alone in the smoking-room, and, for the first time, she did not come to bid me good-night.

I sat smoking my cigar in a tumult of furious despair and love. The situation was becoming intolerable. It could not be endured. I longed for a crisis, even for a violent one. I could have cried aloud that night for a veritable tragedy. There were moments when I would almost have killed the child who mysteriously eluded and defied me. I could have wreaked a cruel vengeance upon the body for the sin of the mind. I was terribly, mortally distressed.

After a long and painful self-communion, I resolved to make another wild effort to set things right before it was too late; and when the clock chimed the half-hour after ten I went upstairs softly to her bedroom and turned the handle of the door, meaning to enter, to catch Margot in my arms, tell her how deep my love for her was, how she injured me by her base fears, and how she was driving me back from the gentleness she had given me to the cruelty, to the brutality, of my first nature.

The door resisted me: it was locked.

I paused a moment, and then tapped gently. I heard a sudden rustle within, as if someone hurried across the floor away from the door, and then Margot's voice cried sharply:

"Who's that? Who is there?"

"Margot, it is I. I wish to speak to you—to say good-night."

"Good-night," she said.

"But let me in for a moment."

There was a silence—it seemed to me a long one; then she answered:

"Not now, dear; I—I am so tired."

"Open the door for a moment."

"I am very tired. Good-night."

The cold, level tone of her voice—for the anxiety had left it after that first sudden cry—roused me to a sudden fury of action. I seized the handle of the door and pressed with all my strength. Physically I am a very powerful man—my anger and despair gave me a giant's might. I burst the lock, and sprang into the room. My impulse was to seize Margot in my arms and crush her to death, it might be, in an embrace she could not struggle against. The blood coursed like molten fire through my veins. The lust of love, the lust of murder even, perhaps, was upon me. I sprang impetuously into the room.

No candles were alight in it. The blinds were up, and the chill moonbeams filtered through the small lattice panes. By the farthest window, in the yellowish radiance, was huddled a white thing.

A sudden cold took hold upon me. All the warmth in me froze up.

I stopped where I was and held my breath.

That white thing, seen thus uncertainly, had no semblance to humanity. It was animal wholly. I could have believed for the moment that a white cat crouched from me there by the curtain, waiting to spring.

What a strange illusion that was! I tried to laugh at it afterwards, but at the moment horror stole through me—horror, and almost awe.

All desire of violence left me. Heat was dead; I felt cold as stone. I could not even speak a word.

Suddenly the white thing moved. The curtain was drawn sharply; the moonlight was blotted out; the room was plunged in darkness—a darkness in which that thing could see!

I turned and stole out of the room. I could have fled, driven by the nameless fear that was upon me.

Only when the morning dawned did the man in me awake, and I cursed myself for my cowardice.

• • • • • •

The following evening we were asked to dine out with some neighbours, who lived a few miles off in a wonderful old Norman castle near the sea. During the day neither of us had made the slightest allusion to the incidents of the previous night. We both felt it a relief to go into society, I think. The friends to whom we went—Lord and Lady Melchester—had a large party staying with them, and we were, I believe, the only outsiders who lived in the neighbourhood. One of their guests was Professor Black, whose name I have already mentioned— a little, dry, thin, acrid man, with thick black hair, innocent of the comb, and pursed, straight lips. I had met him two or three times in London, and as he had only just arrived at the castle, and scarcely knew his fellow-visitors there, he brought his wine over to me when the ladies left the dining-room, and entered into conversation. At the moment I was glad, but before we followed the women I would have given a year—I might say years—of my life not to have spoken to him, not to have heard him speak that night.

How did we drift into that fatal conversation? I hardly remember. We talked first of the neighbourhood, then swayed away to books, then to people. Yes, that was how it came about. The Professor was speaking of a man whom we both knew in town, a curiously effeminate man, whose every thought and feeling seemed that of a woman. I said I disliked him, and condemned him for his woman's demeanour, his woman's mind; but the Professor thereupon joined issue with me.

"Pity the fellow, if you like," he uttered, in his rather strident voice; "but as to condemning him, I would as soon condemn a tadpole for not being a full-grown frog. His soul is beyond his power to manage, or even to coerce, you may depend upon it."

Having sipped his port, he drew a little nearer to me, and slightly dropped his voice.

"There would be less censure of individuals in this world," he said, "if people were only a little more thoughtful. These souls are like letters, and sometimes they are sealed up in the wrong envelope. For instance, a man's soul may be put into a woman's body, or *vice versâ*. It has been so in D——'s case. A mistake has been made."

"By Providence?" I interrupted, with, perhaps, just a *soupçon* of sarcasm in my voice.

The Professor smiled.

"Suppose we imitate Thomas Hardy, and say by the President of the Immortals, who makes sport with more humans than Tess," he answered. "Mistakes may be deliberate, just as their reverse may be accidental. Even a mighty power may condescend sometimes to a very practical joke. To a thinker the world is full of apple-pie beds, and cold wet sponges fall on us from at least half the doors we push open. The soul-juggleries of the before-mentioned President are very curious, but people will not realize that soul transference from body to body is as much a plain fact as the daily rising of the sun on one half of the world and its nightly setting on the other."

"Do you mean that souls pass on into the world again on the death of the particular body in which they have been for the moment confined?" I asked.

"Precisely: I have no doubt of it. Sometimes a woman's soul goes into a man's body; then the man acts woman, and people cry against him for effeminacy. The soul colours the body with actions, the body does not colour the soul, or not in the same degree."

"But we are not irresponsible. We can command ourselves."

The Professor smiled dryly.

"You think so?" he said. "I sometimes doubt it."

"And I doubt your theory of soul transference."

"That shows me—pardon the apparent impertinence—that you have never really examined the soul question with any close attention. Do you suppose that D—— really likes being so noticeably different from other men? Depend upon it, he has noticed in himself what we have noticed in him. Depend upon it, he has tried to be ordinary, and found it impossible. His soul manages him as a strong nature manages a weak one, and his soul is a female, not a male. For souls have sexes, otherwise what would be the sense of talking about wedded souls? I have no doubt whatever of the truth of reincarnation on earth. Souls go on and on following out their object of development."

"You believe that every soul is reincarnated?"

"A certain number of times."

"That even in the animal world the soul of one animal passes into the body of another?"

"Wait a minute. Now we are coming to something that tends to prove my theory true. Animals have souls, as you imply. Who can know them intimately and doubt it for an instant? Souls as immortal—or as mortal—as ours. And their souls, too, pass on."

"Into other animals?"

"Possibly. And eventually, in the process of development, into human beings."

I laughed, perhaps a little rudely. "My dear Professor, I thought that old notion was quite exploded in these modern scientific days."

"I found my beliefs upon my own minute observations," he said rather frigidly. "I notice certain animals masquerading—to some extent—as human beings, and I draw my own conclusions. If they happen to fit in at all with the conclusions of Pythagoras—or anyone else, for that matter—well and good. If not, I am not much concerned. Surely you notice the animal— and not merely the animal, but definite animals—reproduced in man. There are men whose whole demeanour suggests the monkey. I have met women who in manner, appearance, and even character, were intensely like cats."

I uttered a slight exclamation, which did not interrupted him.

"Now, I have made a minute study of cats. Of all animals they interest me the most. They have less apparent intensity, less uttered passion, than dogs, but in my opinion more character. Their subtlety is extraordinary, their sensitiveness wonderful.

Will you understand me when I say that all dogs are men, all cats women? That remark expresses the difference between them."

He paused a moment.

"Go on—go on," I said, leaning forward, with my eyes fixed upon his keen, puckered face.

He seemed pleased with my suddenly-aroused interest.

"Cats are as subtle and as difficult to understand as the most complex woman, and almost as full of intuitions. If they have been well treated, there is often a certain gracious, condescending suavity in their demeanour at first, even towards a total stranger; but if that stranger is ill disposed toward them, they seem instinctively to read his soul, and they are in arms directly. Yet they dissemble their fears in a cold indifference and reserve. They do not take action: they merely abstain from action. They withdraw the soul that has peeped out, as they can withdraw their claws into the pads upon their feet. They do not show fight as a dog might, they do not become aggressive, nor do they whine and put their tails between their legs. They are simply on guard, watchful, mistrustful. Is not all this woman?"

"Possibly," I answered, with a painful effort to assume indifference.

"A woman intuitively knows who is her friend and who is her enemy—so long, at least, as her heart is not engaged; then she runs wild, I allow. A woman—— But I need not pursue the parallel. Besides, perhaps it is scarcely to the point, for my object is not to bolster up an absurd contention that all women have the souls of cats. No; but I have met women so strangely like cats that their souls have, as I said before souls do, coloured their bodies in actions. They have had the very look of cats in their faces. They have moved like them. Their demeanour has been patently and strongly feline. Now, I see nothing ridiculous in the assumption that such women's bodies may contain souls—in process of development, of course—that formerly were merely cat souls, but that are now gaining humanity gradually, are working their way upwards in the scale. After all, we are not so much above the animals, and in our lapses we often become merely animals. The soul retrogrades for the moment."

He paused again and looked at me. I was biting my lips, and

my glass of wine was untouched. He took my agitation as a compliment, I suppose, for he smiled and said:

"Are you in process of conversion?"

I half shook my head. Then I said, with an effort: "It is a curious and interesting idea, of course. But there is much to explain.
Now, I should like to ask you this: Do you—do you believe that
a soul, if it passes on as you think, carries its memory with it, its
memory of former loves and—and hates? Say that a cat's soul
goes to a woman's body, and that the cat has been—has been—
well, tortured—possibly killed, by someone—say some man,
long ago, would the woman, meeting that man, remember and
shrink from him?"

"That is a very interesting and curious problem, and one
which I do not pretend to have solved. I can, therefore, only
suggest what might be, what seems to me reasonable. I do not
believe that the woman would remember positively, but I think
she might have an intuition about the man. Our intuitions are,
perhaps, sometimes only the fragmentary recollections of our
souls, of what formerly happened to them when in other bodies.
Why, otherwise, should we sometimes conceive an ardent dislike of some stranger—charming to all appearance—of whom
we know no evil, whom we have never heard of nor met before?
Intuitions, so called, are often only tattered memories. And
these intuitions might, I should fancy, be strengthened, given
body, robustness, by associations—of place, for example. Cats
become intensely attached to localities, to certain spots, a particular house or garden, a particular fireside, apart from the people who may be there. Possibly, if the man and the woman of
whom you speak could be brought together in the very place
where the torture and death occurred, the dislike of the woman
might deepen into positive hatred. It would, however, be always
unreasoning hatred, I think, and even quite unaccountable to
herself. Still——"

But here Lord Melchester rose from the table. The conversations broke into fragments. I felt that I was pale to the lips.

We passed into the drawing-room. The ladies were grouped
together at one end, near the piano. Margot was among them.
She was, as usual, dressed in white, and round the bottom of her

gown there was an edging of snow-white fur. As we came in, she moved away from the piano to a sofa at some distance, and sank down upon it. Professor Black, who had entered the room at my side, seized my arm gently.

"Now, that lady," he whispered in my ear—"I don't know who she may be, but she is intensely cat-like. I observed it before dinner. Did you notice the way she moved just then—the soft, yielding, easy manner in which she sat down, falling at once, quite naturally, into a charming pose? And her china-blue eyes are——"

"She is my wife, Professor," I interrupted harshly.

He looked decidedly taken aback.

"I beg your pardon; I had no idea. I did not enter the drawing-room tonight till after you arrived. I believed that lady was one of my fellow-guests in the house. Let me congratulate you. She is very beautiful."

And then he mingled rather hastily in the group near the piano.

The man is mad, I know—mad as a hatter on one point, like so many clever men. He sees the animal in every person he meets just because his preposterous theory inclines him to do so. Having given in his adherence to it, he sees facts not as they are, but as he wishes them to be; but he shall not carry me with him. The theory is his, not mine. It does not hold water for a moment. I can laugh at it now, but that night I confess it did seize me for the time being. I could scarcely talk; I found myself watching Margot with a terrible intentness, and I found myself agreeing with the Professor to an extent that made me marvel at my own previous blindness.

There was something strangely feline about the girl I had married—the soft, white girl who was becoming terrible to me, dear though she still was and must always be. Her movements had the subtle, instinctive and certain grace of a cat's. Her cushioned step, which had often struck me before, was like the step of a cat. And those china-blue eyes! A sudden cold seemed to pass over me as I understood why I had recognised them when I first met Margot. They were the eyes of the animal I had tortured, the animal I had killed. Yes, but that proved nothing, absolutely nothing. Many people had the eyes of animals—the soft eyes of dogs, the furtive, cruel eyes of tigers. I had known such people. I had even once had an affair with a girl who was always called the shot partridge, because her eyes were supposed to be like those of a dying bird. I tried to laugh to myself as I remembered this. But I felt cold, and my senses seemed benumbed as by a great horror. I sat like a stone, with my eyes fixed upon Margot, trying painfully to read into her all that the words of Professor Black had suggested to me—trying, but with the wish not to succeed.

I was roused by Lady Melchester, who came toward me asking me to do something, I forget now what. I forced myself to be cheerful, to join in the conversation, to seem at my ease; but I felt like one oppressed with nightmare, and I could scarcely withdraw my eyes from the sofa where my wife was sitting. She was talking now to Professor Black, who had just been introduced to her; and I felt a sudden fury in my heart as I thought that he was perhaps dryly, coldly, studying her, little knowing what issues—far-reaching, it might be, in their consequences—hung upon the truth or falsehood of his strange theory. They were talking earnestly, and presently it occurred to me that he might be imbuing Margot with his pernicious doctrines, that he might be giving her a knowledge of her own soul which now she lacked. The idea was insupportable. I broke off abruptly the conversation in which I was taking part, and hurried over to them with an impulse which must have astonished anyone who took note of me. I sat down on a chair, drew it forward almost violently, and thrust myself in between them.

"What are you two talking about?" I said, roughly, with a suspicious glance at Margot.

The Professor looked at me in surprise.

"I was instructing your wife in some of the mysteries of salmon-fishing," he said. "She tells me you have a salmon-river running through your grounds."

I laughed uneasily.

"So you are a fisherman as well as a romantic theorist!" I said, rather rudely. "How I wish I were as versatile! Come, Margot, we must be going now. The carriage ought to be here."

She rose quietly and bade the Professor good-night; but as she glanced up at me, in rising, I fancied I caught a new expression in her eyes. A ray of determination, of set purpose, mingled with the gloomy fire of their despair.

As soon as we were in the carriage I spoke, with a strained effort at ease and the haphazard tone which should mask furtive cross-examination.

"Professor Black is an interesting man," I said.

"Do you think so?" she answered from her dark corner.

"Surely. His intellect is really alive. Yet, with all his scientific knowledge and his power of eliciting facts and elucidating them, he is but a featherheaded man." I paused, but she made no answer. "Do you not think so?"

"How can I tell?" she replied. "We only talked about fishing. He managed to make that topic a pleasant one."

Her tone was frank. I felt relieved.

"He is exceedingly clever," I said, heartily, and we relapsed into silence.

When we reached home, and Margot had removed her cloak, she came up to me and laid her hand on my arm.

So unaccustomed was her touch now that I was startled. She was looking at me with a curious, steady smile—an unwavering smile that chilled instead of warming me.

"Ronald," she said, "there has been a breach between us. I have been the cause of it. I should like to—to heal it. Do you still love me as you did?"

I did not answer immediately; I could not. Her voice, schooled as it was, seemed somehow at issue with the words she uttered. There was a desperate, hard note in it that accorded with that enigmatic smile of the mouth.

It roused a cold suspicion within me that I was close to a masked battery. I shrank physically from the touch of her hand.

She waited with her eyes upon me. Our faces were lit tremblingly by the flames of the two candles we held.

At last I found a voice.

"Can you doubt it?" I asked.

She drew a step nearer.

"Then let us resume our old relations," she said.

"Our old relations?"

"Yes."

I shuddered as if a phantom stole by me. I was seized with horror.

"tonight? It is not possible!"

"Why?" she said, still with that steady smile of the mouth.

"Because—because I don't know—I——To-morrow it shall be as old, Margot—to-morrow. I promise you."

"Very well. Kiss me, dear."

I forced myself to touch her lips with mine.

Which mouth was the colder?

Then, with that soft, stealthy step of hers, she vanished towards her room. I heard the door close gently.

I listened. The key was not turned in the lock.

This sudden abandonment by Margot of the fantastic precautions I had almost become accustomed to filled me with a nameless dread.

That night I fastened my door for the first time.

IV.

FRIDAY NIGHT, *November 6th.*

I fastened my door, and when I went to bed lay awake for hours listening. A horror was upon me then which has not left me since for a moment, which may never leave me. I shivered with cold that night, the cold born of sheer physical terror. I knew that I was shut up in the house with a soul bent on unreasoning vengeance, the soul of the animal which I had killed prisoned in the body of the woman I had married. I was sick with fear then. I am sick with fear now.

tonight I am so tired. My eyes are heavy and my head aches. No wonder. I have not slept for three nights. I have not dared to sleep.

This strange revolution in my wife's conduct, this passionless change—for I felt instinctively that warm humanity had nothing to do with the transformation—took place three nights ago. These three last days Margot has been playing a part. With what object?

When I sat down to this gray record of two souls—at once dreary and fantastic as it would seem, perhaps, to many—I desired to reassure myself, to write myself into sweet reason, into peace.

I have tried to accomplish the impossible. I feel that the wildest theory may be the truest, after all—that on the border-land of what seems madness, actuality paces.

Every remembrance of my mind confirms the truth first suggested to me by Professor Black.

I know Margot's object now.

The soul of the creature that I tortured, that I killed, has passed into the body of the woman whom I love; and that soul, which once slept in its new cage, is awake now, watching, plotting perhaps. Unconsciously to itself, it recognises me. It stares out upon me with eyes in which the dull terror deepens to hate; but it does not understand why it fears—why, in its fear, it hates. Intuition has taken the place of memory. The change of environment has killed recollection, and has left instinct in its place.

Why did I ever sit down to write? The recalling of facts has set the seal upon my despair.

Instinct only woke in Margot when I brought her to the place the soul had known in the years when it looked out upon the world from the body of an animal.

That first day on the terrace instinct stirred in its sleep, opened its eyes, gazed forth upon me wonderingly, inquiringly.

Margot's faint remembrance of the terrace walk, of the flower-pots, of the grass borders where the cat had often stretched itself in the sun, her eagerness to see the chamber of death, her stealthy visits to that chamber, her growing uneasiness, deepening to acute apprehension, and finally to a deadly malignity—all lead me irresistibly to one conclusion.

The animal's soul within her no longer merely shrinks away in fear of me. It has grown sinister. It lies in ambush, full of a cold, a stealthy intention.

That curious, abrupt change in Margot's demeanour from avoidance to invitation marked the subtle, inward development of feeling, the silent passage from sensation only towards action.

Formerly she feared me. Now I must fear her.

The soul, crouching in its cage, shows its teeth. It is compassing my destruction.

The woman's body twitches with desire to avenge the death of the animal's.

I feel that it is only waiting the moment to spring; and the inherent love of life breeds in me a physical fear of it as of a subtle enemy. For even if the soul is brave, the body dreads to die, and seems at moments to possess a second soul, purely physical, that cries out childishly against pain, against death.

Then, too, there is a cowardice of the imagination that can shake the strongest heart, and this resurrection from the dead, from the murdered, appals my imagination. That what I thought I had long since slain should have companioned me so closely when I knew it not!

I am sick with fear, physical and mental.

Two days ago, when I unlocked my bedroom door in the morning, and saw the autumn sunlight streaming in through the leaded panes of the hall windows, and heard the river dancing merrily down the gully among the trees that will soon be quite bare and naked, I said to myself: "You have been mad. Your mind has been filled with horrible dreams, that have transformed you into a coward and your wife into a demon. Put them away from you."

I looked across the gully. A clear, cold, thin light shone upon the distant mountains. The cloud stacks lay piled above the Scawfell range. The sky was a sheet of faded turquoise. I opened the window for a moment. The air was dry and keen. How sweet it was to feel it on my face!

I went down to the breakfast-room. Margot was moving about it softly, awaiting me. In her white hands were letters. They dropped upon the table as she stole up to greet me. Her lips were set tightly together, but she lifted them to kiss me.

How close I came to my enemy as our mouths touched! Her lips were colder than the wind.

Now that I was with her, my momentary sensation of acute relief deserted me. The horror that oppressed me returned.

I could not eat—I could only make a pretence of doing so; and my hand trembled so excessively that I could scarcely raise my cup from the table.

She noticed this, and gently asked me if I was ill.

I shook my head.

When breakfast was over, she said in a low, level voice:

"Ronald, have you thought over what I said last night?"

"Last night?" I answered, with an effort.

"Yes, about the coldness between us. I think I have been unwell, unhappy, out of sorts. You know that—that women are more subject to moods than men, moods they cannot always account for even to themselves. I have hurt you lately, I know. I am sorry. I want you to forgive me, to—to"—she paused a moment, and I heard her draw in her breath sharply—"to take me back into your heart again."

Every word, as she said it, sounded to me like a sinister threat, and the last sentence made my blood litterally go cold in my veins.

I met her eyes. She did not withdraw hers; they looked into mine. They were the blue eyes of the cat which I had held upon my knees years ago. I had gazed into them as a boy, and watched the horror and the fear dawn in them with a malignant triumph.

"I have nothing to forgive," I said in a broken, husky voice.

"You have much," she answered firmly. "But do not—pray do not bear malice."

"There is no malice in my heart—now," I said; and the words seemed like a cowardly plea for mercy to the victim of the past.

She lifted one of her soft white hands to my breast.

"Then it shall all be as it was before? And tonight you will come back to me?"

I hesitated, looking down. But how could I refuse? What excuse could I make for denying the request? Then I repeated mechanically:

"tonight I will come back to you."

A terrible, slight smile travelled over her face. She turned and left me.

I sat down immediately. I felt too unnerved to remain standing. I was giving way utterly to an imaginative horror that seemed to threaten my reason. In vain I tried to pull myself together. My body was in a cold sweat. All mastery of my nerves seemed gone.

I do not know how long I remained there, but I was aroused by the entrance of the butler. He glanced towards me in some obvious surprise, and this astonishment of a servant acted upon me almost like a scourge. I sprang up hastily.

"Tell the groom to saddle the mare," I said. "I am going for a ride immediately."

Air, action, were what I needed to drive this stupor away. I must get away from this house of tears. I must be alone. I must wrestle with myself, regain my courage, kill the coward in me.

I threw myself upon the mare, and rode out at a gallop towards the moors of Eskdale along the lonely country roads.

All day I rode, and all day I thought of that dark house, of that white creature awaiting my return, peering from the windows, perhaps, listening for my horse's hoofs on the gravel, keeping still the long vigil of vengeance.

My imagination sickened, fainted, as my wearied horse stumbled along the shadowy roads. My terror was too great now to be physical. It was a terror purely of the spirit, and indescribable.

To sleep with that white thing that waited me! To lie in the dark by it! To know that it was there, close to me!

If it killed me, what matter? It was to live and to be near it, with it, that appalled me.

The lights of the house gleamed out through the trees. I heard the sound of the river.

I got off my horse and walked furtively into the hall, looking round me.

Margot glided up to me immediately, and took my whip and hat from me with her soft, velvety white hands. I shivered at her touch.

At dinner her blue eyes watched me.

I could not eat, but I drank more wine than usual.

When I turned to go down to the smoking-room, she said: "Don't be very long, Ronald."

I muttered I scarcely know what words in reply. It was close on midnight before I went to bed. When I entered her room, shielding the light of the candle with my hand, she was still awake.

Nestling against the pillows, she stretched herself curiously and smiled up at me.

"I thought you were never coming, dear," she said.

I knew that I was very pale, but she did not remark it. I got into bed, but left the candle still burning.

Presently she said:

"Why don't you put the candle out?"

I looked at her furtively. Her face seemed to me carved in stone, it was so rigid, so expressionless. She lay away from me at the extreme edge of the bed, sideways, with her hands toward me.

"Why don't you?" she repeated, with her blue eyes on me.

"I don't feel sleepy," I answered slowly.

"You never will while there is a light in the room," she said.

"You wish me to put it out?"

"Yes. How odd you are tonight, Ronald! Is anything the matter?"

"No," I answered; and I blew the light out.

How ghastly the darkness was!

I believed she meant to smother me in my sleep. I knew it. I determined to keep awake.

It was horrible to think that, as we lay there, she could see me all the time as if it were daylight.

The night wore on. She was quite silent and motionless. I lay listening.

It must have been towards morning when I closed my eyes, not because I was sleepy, but because I was so tired of gazing at blackness.

Soon after I had done this there was a stealthy movement in the bed.

"Margot, are you awake?" I instantly cried out sharply.

The movement immediately ceased. There was no reply.

When the light of dawn stole in at the window she seemed to be sleeping.

· · · · · ·

Last night I did not close my eyes once. She did not move.

She means to tire me out, and she has the strength to do it. tonight I feel so intensely heavy. Soon I must sleep, and then——

Shall I seek any longer to defend myself? Everything seems so inevitable, so beyond my power, like the working of an inexorable justice bent on visiting the sin of the father upon the child. For was not the cruel boy the father of the man?

And yet, is this tragedy inevitable? It cannot be. I will be a man. I will rise up and combat it. I will take Margot away from this house that her soul remembers, in which its body so long ago was tortured and slain, and she will—she must forget.

Instinct will sleep once more. It shall be so. I will have it so. I will strew poppies over her soul. I will take her far away from here, far away, to places where she will be once more as she has been.

To-morrow we will go. To-morrow——

.   .   .   .   .   .

Ah, that cry! Was it my own? I am suffocating! What was that? The horror of it! The pen has fallen from my hand. I must have slept; and I have dreamed. In my dream she stole upon me, that white thing! Her velvety hands were on my throat. The soul stared out from her eyes, the soul of the cat! Even her body, her woman's body, seemed to change at the moment of vengeance. She slowly strangled me, and as the breath died from me, and my failing eyes gazed at her, she was no longer woman at all, but something lithe and white and soft. Fur enveloped my throat. Those hands were claws. That breath on my face was the breath of an animal. The body had come back to companion the soul in its vengeance, the body of——

Ah, it was too horrible!

Can vengeance for the dead bring with it resurrection of the dead?

.   .   .   .   .   .

Hark! There is a voice calling to me from upstairs.

"Ronald, are you never coming? I am tired of waiting for you. Ronald!"

"Yes."

"Come to me!"
And I must go.

. . . . . .

Just at the glimmer of dawn the first pale shaft of the sun struck across a bed upon which lay the huddled and distorted corpse of a man. His head was sunk down in the pillows. His eyes, that could not see, stared towards the rising light. And from the open window of the chamber of death a woman in a white wrapper leaned out, watching eagerly with wide blue eyes the birds as they darted to and fro, rested on the climbing creepers, or circled above the gorge through which the river ran. Her set lips smiled. She looked like one calm, easy, and at peace. Presently an unwary sparrow perched on the trellis beneath the window just within her reach. Her white hand darted down softly, closed on the bird. She vanished from the window.

. . . . . .

Can the dead hear? Did he catch the sound of her faint, continuous purring as she crouched with her prey upon the floor?

Of a Promise Broken

Lafcadio Hearn

I

"I am not afraid to die," said the dying wife;—"there is only one thing that troubles me now. I wish that I could know who will take my place in this house."

"My dear one," answered the sorrowing husband, "nobody shall ever take your place in my home. I will never, never marry again."

At the time that he said this he was speaking out of his heart; for he loved the woman whom he was about to lose.

"On the faith of a samurai?" she questioned, with a feeble smile.

"On the faith of a samurai," he responded—stroking the pale thin face.

"Then, my dear one," she said, "you will let me be buried in the garden—will you not?—near those plum-trees that we planted at the farther end? I wanted long ago to ask this; but I thought, that if you were to marry again, you would not like to have my grave so near you. Now you have promised that no other woman shall take my place;—so I need not hesitate to speak of my wish. . . . I want so much to be buried in the garden! I think that in the garden I should sometimes hear your voice, and that I should still be able to see the flowers in the spring."

"It shall be as you wish," he answered. "But do not now speak of burial: you are not so ill that we have lost all hope."

"*I* have," she returned;—"I shall die this morning. . . . But you will bury me in the garden?"

"Yes," he said—"under the shade of the plum-trees that we planted;—and you shall have a beautiful tomb there."

"And will you give me a little bell?"

"Bell—?"

"Yes: I want you to put a little bell in the coffin—such a little bell as the Buddhist pilgrims carry. Shall I have it?"

"You shall have the little bell—and anything else that you wish."

"I do not wish for anything else," she said. . . . "My dear one, you have been very good to me always. Now I can die happy."

Then she closed her eyes and died—as easily as a tired child falls asleep. She looked beautiful when she was dead; and there was a smile upon her face.

She was buried in the garden, under the shade of the trees that she loved; and a small bell was buried with her. Above the grave was erected a handsome monument, decorated with the family crest, and bearing the kaimyō:

Great Elder Sister, Luminous-Shadow-of-the-Plum-Flower-Chamber, dwelling in the Mansion of the Great Sea of Compassion.

·   ·   ·   ·   ·   ·

But, within a twelve-month after the death of his wife, the relatives and friends of the samurai began to insist that he should marry again. "You are still a young man," they said, "and an only son; and you have no children. It is the duty of a samurai to marry. If you die childless, who will there be to make the offerings and to remember the ancestors?"

By many such representations he was at last persuaded to marry again. The bride was only seventeen years old; and he found that he could love her dearly, notwithstanding the dumb reproach of the tomb in the garden.

II

Nothing took place to disturb the happiness of the young wife until the seventh day after the wedding—when her husband was ordered to undertake certain duties requiring his presence at the castle by night. On the first evening that he was obliged to leave her alone, she felt uneasy in a way that she could not explain—vaguely afraid without knowing why. When she went to bed she could not sleep. There was a strange oppression in the air—an indefinable heaviness like that which sometimes precedes the coming of a storm.

About the Hour of the Ox she heard, outside in the night, the clanging of a bell—a Buddhist pilgrim's bell;—and she wondered what pilgrim could be passing through the samurai quarter at such a time. Presently, after a pause, the bell sounded much nearer. Evidently the pilgrim was approaching the house;—but why approaching from the rear, where no road was? . . . Suddenly the dogs began to whine and howl in an unusual and horrible way;—and a fear came upon her like the fear of dreams. . . . That ringing was certainly in the garden. . . . She tried to get up to waken a servant. But she found that she could not rise—could not move—could not call. . . . And nearer, and still more near, came the clang of the bell;—and oh! how the dogs howled! . . . Then, lightly as a shadow steals, there glided into the room a Woman—though every door stood fast, and every screen unmoved—a Woman robed in a grave-robe, and carrying a pilgrim's bell. Eyeless she came—because she had long been dead;—and her loosened hair streamed down about her face;—and she looked without eyes through the tangle of it, and spoke without a tongue:

> Not in this house—not in this house shall you stay! Here I am mistress still. You shall go; and you shall tell to none the reason of your going. If you tell HIM, I will tear you into pieces!

So speaking, the haunter vanished. The bride became senseless with fear. Until the dawn she so remained.

Nevertheless, in the cheery light of day, she doubted the reality of what she had seen and heard. The memory of the warning still weighed upon her so heavily that she did not dare to speak of the vision, either to her husband or to any one else; but she was almost able to persuade herself that she had only dreamed an ugly dream, which had made her ill.

On the following night, however, she could not doubt. Again, at the Hour of the Ox, the dogs began to howl and whine;—again the bell resounded—approaching slowly from the garden;—again the listener vainly strove to rise and call;—again the dead came into the room, and hissed:

> You shall go; and you shall tell to no one why you must go!
> If you even whisper it to HIM, I will tear you in pieces! . . .

This time the haunter came close to the couch—and bent and muttered and mowed above it. . . .

Next morning, when the samurai returned from the castle, his young wife prostrated herself before him in supplication:

"I beseech you," she said, "to pardon my ingratitude and my great rudeness in thus addressing you: but I want to go home;—I want to go away at once."

"Are you not happy here?" he asked, in sincere surprise. "Has any one dared to be unkind to you during my absence?"

"It is not that—" she answered, sobbing. "Everybody here has been only too good to me. . . . But I cannot continue to be your wife;—I must go away. . . ."

"My dear," he exclaimed, in great astonishment, "it is very painful to know that you have had any cause for unhappiness in this house. But I cannot even imagine why you should want to go away—unless somebody has been very unkind to you. . . . Surely you do not mean that you wish for a divorce?"

She responded, trembling and weeping:

"If you do not give me a divorce, I shall die!"

He remained for a little while silent—vainly trying to think of some cause for this amazing declaration. Then, without betraying any emotion, he made answer:

"To send you back now to your people, without any fault on your part, would seem a shameful act. If you will tell me a good reason for your wish—any reason that will enable me to explain matters honorably—I can write you a divorce. But unless you give me a reason, a good reason, I will not divorce you—for the honor of our house must be kept above reproach."

And then she felt obliged to speak; and she told him everything—adding, in an agony of terror:

"Now that I have let you know, she will kill me!—she will kill me! . . ."

Although a brave man, and little inclined to believe in phantoms, the samurai was more than startled for the moment. But a simple and natural explanation of the matter soon presented itself to his mind.

"My dear," he said, "you are now very nervous; and I fear that some one has been telling you foolish stories. I cannot give you a divorce merely because you have had a bad dream in this house. But I am very sorry indeed that you should have been suffering in such a way during my absence. tonight, also, I must be at the castle; but you shall not be alone. I will order two of the retainers to keep watch in your room; and you will be able to sleep in peace. They are good men; and they will take all possible care of you."

Then he spoke to her so considerately and so affectionately that she became almost ashamed of her terrors, and resolved to remain in the house.

III

The two retainers left in charge of the young wife were big, brave, simple-hearted men—experienced guardians of women and children. They told the bride pleasant stories to keep her cheerful. She talked with them a long time, laughed at their good-humoured fun, and almost forgot her fears. When at last she lay down to sleep, the men-at-arms took their places in a corner of the room, behind a screen, and began a game of go[1]— speaking only in whispers, that she might not be disturbed. She slept like an infant.

But again at the Hour of the Ox she awoke with a moan of terror—for she heard the bell! . . . It was already near, and was coming nearer. She started up; she screamed;—but in the room there was no stir—only a silence as of death—a silence growing—a silence thickening. She rushed to the men-at-arms:

---

[1] A game resembling draughts, but much more complicated.

they sat before their checker-table—motionless—each staring
at the other with fixed eyes. She shrieked to them: she shook
them: they remained as if frozen. . . .

Afterwards they said that they had heard the bell—heard also
the cry of the bride—even felt her try to shake them into wake-
fulness;—and that, nevertheless, they had not been able to
move or speak. From the same moment they had ceased to hear
or to see: a black sleep had seized upon them.

· · · · · ·

Entering his bridal-chamber at dawn, the samurai beheld, by
the light of a dying lamp, the headless body of his young wife,
lying in a pool of blood. Still squatting before their unfinished
game, the two retainers slept. At their master's cry they sprang
up, and stupidly stared at the horror on the floor. . . .
The head was nowhere to be seen;—and the hideous
wound showed that it had not been cut off, but *torn off*. A trail
of blood led from the chamber to an angle of the outer gallery,
where the storm-doors appeared to have been riven apart.
The three men followed that trail into the garden—over
reaches of grass—over spaces of sand—along the bank of an
iris-bordered pond—under heavy shadowings of cedar and
bamboo. And suddenly, at a turn, they found themselves face
to face with a nightmare-thing that chippered like a bat: the
figure of the long-buried woman, erect before her tomb—in
one hand clutching a bell, in the other the dripping head. . . .
For a moment the three stood numbed. Then one of the men-
at-arms, uttering a Buddhist invocation, drew, and struck at
the shape. Instantly it crumbled down upon the soil—an
empty scattering of grave-rags, bones, and hair;—and the
bell rolled clanking out of the ruin. But the fleshless right
hand, though parted from the wrist, still writhed;—and its
fingers still gripped at the bleeding head—and tore, and man-
gled—as the claws of the yellow crab cling fast to a fallen
fruit. . . .

"That is a wicked story," I said to the friend who had related it. "The vengeance of the dead—if taken at all—should have been taken upon the man."

"Men think so," he made answer. "But that is not the way that a woman feels. . . ."

He was right.

The Promise

Walter de la Mare

A doctor hears many strange stories, which must for ever remain a secret confidence between himself and his patients. But the story that my old friend, whom we will call Purcell, told me cannot, I think, be so considered. We were sitting one evening in his long garden, just after the fall of dusk, smoking together. His wife had been dangerously (but quite triumphantly) ill; and this was the first evening afterwards. "You know, of course," he said, half-apologetically, "that she has always been very nervous and high-strung; at least——" He broke off and puffed softly on, narrowing his eyes, his hands resting one over the other on his knee. A robin was chattering in the lilac bushes. "I don't think I ever told you how we actually met. There's no harm in telling. . . . Is there?"

"Well, that's best answered when I've heard," I replied. And we laughed.

"Well, you remember—oh, years ago—when I used to live with my mother at Witchelham? It was an absurdly long journey from town. But she liked the country; my father was buried there; and so, nearly two hours every day of my life, except Saturdays and Sundays, were spent in rumbling up and down on that antediluvian branch line. I believe they bought their carriages second-hand. We had an amazing collection of antiques. The stations, too, were that kind of stranded Noah's ark in a garden, which make it rather jolly to look out of the window in the summer, with their banks of flowers, and martins in the eaves. A kind of romance hung over the very engines. You felt in some of the carriages like a savant confronted with a papyrus he can't read. It was all very vague, of course. But there it was.

"One evening, A Tuesday in December, I left my office rather later than usual. There had been a lofty fog most of the day; all the lights flared yellow and amber, and the traffic was muffled to a woolly roar. The station was nearly empty. An early train, the 5.3, coming in late, had carried off most of the usual passengers, and only just we few long-distance ones were left. I walked slowly along the platform, past the silent, illuminated carriages, and got into No. 3399—a second. The number, of course, I noticed afterwards. It was cushioned in deep crimson, lit unusually clear with oil; half a window-strap was gone, and the strings of the luggage bracket hung down in one corner. It was haunted, too, by the very faintest of fragrances, as if it had stood all the summer with windows open in a rose garden. I sat down in the right-hand corner facing the engine, and began to read. Footsteps passed now and again; fog signals detonated out of space; a whistle sounded, and then, rather like an indolent and timid centipede, we crept out of the station. I read on until I presently found that I hadn't for quite some little while been following the sense of what I was reading. Back I went a page or two, and failed again.

"Then I put the book down, and found myself in this rather clearly lit old crimson carriage alone—quite curiously alone. You know what I mean; just as when one is alone in a ball-room when the guests have said good-bye after a dance; just as one's alone after a funeral. It pressed on me. I was rather tired, and perhaps a little run down, so that I quite keenly welcomed all such vague psychological nuances. The carriage was vacant then—richly, delicately, absorbingly vacant. Who had gone out? I know this sounds like utter nonsense. I assure you, though, it was just as it affected me then. There was first this very faint suggestion of flowers in this almost amber lamplight; that was nothing in itself. But there was also an undefined presence of someone, a personality of someone here, too, as obviously reminiscent of a reality as the perfume was reminiscent of once-real flowers.

"The 5.29 did not stop near town—loitered straight on to Thornwood, missed Upland Bois, and launched itself into Witchelham. All that interminable journey (for the fog had fallen low with nightfall) I sat and brooded on this curious impression, on all such impressions, however faint and illusory. So deep did I fall into reverie that when I again came to myself and looked up, I was first conscious that the train was at a standstill, and next that I was no longer alone. In the further and opposite corner of the carriage a lady was sitting. The air between us was the least bit dimmed with fog. But I saw her, none the less, quite clearly—a lady in deep black. Her right hand was gloveless and lay in her lap. On her left hand her chin was resting, so that the face was turned away from me towards the black glass of the window. Whether it was her deep mourning, her utter stillness, something in her attitude, I cannot say. I only know that I had never seen such tragic and complete dejection in any human creature before. And yet something was wanting, something was absent. How can I describe it? I can only say it was as if I was dreaming her there. She was absolutely real to my mind, to myself; and yet I knew, by some extraordinary inward instinct, that if I did but turn my head, withdraw my eyes, she would be gone. I watched her without stirring, simply watched her, overwhelmed with interest and pity, and a kind of faint anxiety or fear. And suddenly, I cannot more exactly express it, I became conscious that my eyes were out of focus, that they were fixed with extreme attention on—nothing at all. I cannot say I was alarmed, nor even astonished. It was rather vexation, disappointment. But as I looked I suddenly became conscious of a small, oblong, brown-paper package, lying parthid under the arm-rest of the seat only just now so mysteriously occupied, and as mysteriously vacated. Directly I became aware of it, it seemed, of course, extraordinarily conspicuous. Could I by the faintest chance in the world have overlooked it on first entering the carriage? Of course, I see now that it must have been so. But at the time I was convinced it was impossible.

"I took up the package, felt it, shook it, and then, without the least excuse or compunction in the world, untied the string and opened the plain wooden case within. It contained a small six-chambered revolver. I scrutinized it for a moment almost in confusion, then I flung down the carriage window, just in time to see the face of the station-master momentarily illuminated in the fog as we crept out of Thornwood. I hastily shut the box and packed it, paper and all, into my pocket. It was entirely intuitive, simply the irresistible caprice of the moment, but I felt I could not surrender it; I felt certain that I should sooner or later meet with its owner. I would surrender it then.

"The next day seemed interminable. Fog still hung over the city. I longed to get back to my haunted carriage. I felt vaguely expectant, as if some very distant, scarcely audible voice were calling to me, questioningly, appealingly. I was convinced that my ghost was really a ghost, a phantasm, an apparition—not an hallucination. Surely an event so rare and inexplicable must have a sequel.

"Out into the misty street (which in the mist, indeed, seemed thronged with phantoms) I turned once more that evening with an excitement I cannot describe—such an excitement as one feels when one is about to meet again a long absent, a very close and intimate friend.

"Again the 5.3 had befriended me. The platform was nearly empty when the 5.27 backed slowly into the station. I had expected no obstacle, had encountered none. Here was my 3399, its lamp, perhaps, not quite so lustrous, its crimson a little dimmed. I entered and sat down in my corner, like a spider in its newly-spun web. What prompted such certainty, such conviction, I can't conceive. The few minutes passed, passengers walked deliberately by. Some glanced in; one old lady, with a reticule and gold spectacles, peered hesitatingly, peered again, all but entered and, as if suddenly alarmed, hastily withdrew. We were already late. And then, just at the last moment, as the doors were beginning to slam, I heard with extraordinary distinctness what it seemed I had for long been waiting for—a light and hurried footfall. It paused, came nearer, paused again, and then (although I simply could not turn my head to look) I knew that there, looking in on me, searchingly, anxiously, stood framed in the misty doorway—my ghost.

"Still she hesitated. But it was too late to retreat. She entered, for I heard the rustling of her gown. And then, at once, the train began to move. At last, when we were really rumbling on, I managed to turn my head. There she sat, completely in black, her left hand in her lap, her chin lightly resting on the other, her eyes gazing gravely and reflectively, yet with a curious fixity, out of the window. She did not stir. So slim, so unreal, she looked in her dead black, it seemed almost that this might be illusion, too—this, too, an apparition. *Almost,* but how surely, how convincingly, not quite. It sounds absurd, but so absorbed again I grew in watching her, so lost in thought, I think I sighed. Whether or no, she suddenly turned her head and looked at me with startled eyes and parted lips. And I think, the faintest red rose in her cheeks.

"I leaned forward. 'You won't please misunderstand me—my speaking, I mean. I think, perhaps, if I might explain . . . you would forgive me . . .' I blundered on. She raised her eyebrows, faintly and distantly smiling. But I felt vaguely certain that somehow she had dimly foreseen my being there. 'I don't quite see why one should *have* to explain,' she said indifferently. 'You could not ask me to forgive anything that would need forgiveness. But tonight, you must please excuse me. I am so very tired I don't really think I could listen. I know I couldn't answer.'

"'It's only this, just this,' I replied in confusion. 'Something has happened: I can't explain now; only if I should seem inexcusably inquisitive—horribly so, perhaps—you will understand when I do explain. . . . You need but answer yes or no to three brief questions—I cannot tell you how deeply interested I am in their answers. May I?' She frowned a little, and turned again to the window. 'What is the first question?' she asked coldly.

"'The first is—please don't suppose that I do not already know the answer, instinctively, as it were, *en rapport*—have you ever travelled in this carriage before, No. 3399?' Could you imagine a more inane way of putting it? I knew that she had, with absolute certainty. But, none the less, she feigned to be unsure. Her eyes scrutinized every corner, but indifferently, and finally settled on the broken netting. 'Yes,' she said simply. 'But as for the number—I don't think I knew railway carriages *were* numbered.' She turned her eyes again directly on mine.

"'Were you alone?' I said, and held my breath.

"She frowned. 'I don't see——' she began. 'But, yes,' she broke off obstinately. 'It was the night before last. I was alone.'

"I turned for a moment to the window. 'The last question,' I went on slowly, 'could only possibly be forgiven to one who was a very real, or hoped to be, a very real, faithful friend.' We looked gently and calmly, and just in that curious instantaneous way, immortally as it were, into each other's eyes.

"'Well?' she said.

"'You were in extreme trouble?'

"She did not at once reply. Her beautiful face grew not paler, more shadowy. She leaned one narrow hand on the crimson seat, and still looked with utterly frank, terribly miserable, desolate eyes into mine.

"'I think—I had got beyond,' she said.

"What sane thing could I offer for a confidence so generous and so childlike? 'Well,' I said, 'it's the same world for all.' She shook her head, and smiled. 'I remember one quite, quite different. But still,' she continued gravely, as if speaking to herself, and still leaning on her hand, 'it is nearly over now. And I can take an interest, a real interest, in what you might tell me; I mean, as to how you came to know, and why you ask.' I told her simply of my dream, the hallucination, psychic experience, or whatever you may care to call it. 'Yes,' she said, 'I *did* sit here. It is very, very strange. It . . .' and then she stopped as if waiting, as if fearing to go on.

"I said nothing for a moment, knowing not what to say. At last I took out the little wooden case just as it was. 'I cannot ask forgiveness *now*,' I said, 'but this—is it yours?'

"She nodded with a slight shudder. Every trace of colour left her face.

"'You left it in the train on Monday?'

"She nodded.

"'And today'—it was a wild, improbable guess—'today you came to town to look for it, to inquire about it?'

"She did not answer, merely sat transfixed, with hard, unmoving eyes and trembling lip.

"'I can't help what you may think, how you may resent my asking. I can't shirk responsibility. I know this is not an accident. I cannot believe it was an accident which sent me here last night.

I cannot believe God ever meant any trouble, any grief to have *this* for an end. If I give it you, will you promise me something?'

"She did not answer.

"'You must promise me,' I said.

"'*What* am I to promise you?' she said, her eyes burning in her still, white, furious face.

"'Need I say?'

"She leaned her elbows on her knees, did not look at me again, merely talked, talked on, as if to her reflection, in that dim crimson, fronting her eyes. 'It is just as it happens, I suppose,' she said. 'It's just this miserable thing we call life, all the world over. You hadn't the ghost of a right to open it—not the faintest right in the world. It is all sheer inference, that is all. As for believing—there's not the faintest proof—not the faintest. Who *can* care *now?* But, no; somehow you got to know, without the least mercy or compunction. Who would believe you? It is simply a blind, pitiless ruse, I suppose. . . . And so . . . you have compelled me, forced me to confess, to explain what no one on earth dreams of, or suspects—you, a complete stranger. Isn't my life my own, then? Oh, yes, I know all that. I know all that. . . . I refuse. You will understand, please, I will *not* promise. Who,' she cried bitterly, flinging scoffingly back her head, 'who gave *you* my life? Who gave *you* the right to question, to persecute me?' And then, suddenly, she hid her face in her hands. 'What am I saying, what am I saying?' she almost whispered. 'I don't know what I am saying.'

"'Please, please,' I said, 'don't think of me. It doesn't in the least matter what you think, or say, of me. Listen, only listen; you must, you *must* promise.'

"'I can't, I can't!' she cried, rising to her feet and facing me once more. The train was slowing down. Here, then, was her station. Was I, after all, to be too late? I, too, stood up.

"'Think what you will of me,' I said; 'I am only, only your friend, now and always. I do believe that I was sent here. I don't understand why, or how: but I cannot, cannot, I mustn't leave you, until you promise.'

"Something seemed to stoop, to look out of her eyes into

mine. How can I possibly put the thought into words?—a fear, a haunting, terrible sorrow and despair, simply, I suppose, her soul's, her spirit's last glance of utter weariness, utter hopelessness; a challenge, a defiance. I know not what I prayed, or to whom, but pray I did, gazing blindly into her face. And then it faded, fainted, died away, that awful presence in those dark, beautiful eyes. She put out her hand with a sob, like a tired-out, beaten child. 'I promise,' she said. . . ."

My friend stopped speaking. Night had fallen deep around us. The garden lay silent, tree and flower obscure and still, beneath the feebly shining stars. We turned towards the house. A white blind in an upper window glimmered faintly in the darkness. And we heard a tiny, impatient, angry, inarticulate voice, crying, crying. "Well," I said, taking his arm, and waving my hand, with my best professional smile, towards the window, "she has kept her promise, hasn't she?"

II. The Terror of Haunted Places

The Ghosts of Austerlitz

A Christmas Story

William Waldorf Astor

On the 25th day of December, in the year of grace 1890, Captain Blythe, formerly of the 10th Rifles, sat in his cosy bachelor rooms in Piccadilly, luxuriously idling away the afternoon, partly in reverie of things past, partly in the perusal of that volume of Thiers' fascinating history of the campaigns of the great Napoleon which bears the suggestive title "Austerlitz." He had pictured the armies confronting one another, the sunrise over the misty snow-fields, the storming of the heights of Pratzen, diluting the martial story, once or twice, with milder reminiscences of his own campaignings in the Crimea and in Zululand, and had finally checked the French pursuit of the Allies for a comfortable anticipation of the turkey and champagne to come by-and-by. And thinking of the Christmas dinners that would that day be eaten in London, he asked himself who should speak so eloquently of the things that grace the season and link themselves with the memory of bygone Christmas days—the bright lights and happy voices, the full stockings and trinket-laden trees, the sleek congregations, the smoking joints and rare old fruity vintages—as that starving poet whom, after twenty years, he had met at the church door, and whom he had bidden to dine that evening. Fine material that, he mused, with a glance at the holly wreath hanging in the window, to kindle a poet's fancy with cheerful suggestions of this frosty season placed midway between the decline of autumn and that flowery spring with whose promise one seeks to wreathe the future. And settling himself at ease before the fire, he thought of his schoolmates trooping, fifty years ago, across the

hayfields, of the honours he took at sixteen, of that ill-fated
courtship at twenty—oh, shame upon thee, faithless Arabella!—
of his poverty-stricken battle with the world, of journeyings and
camp scenes in far countries, of that assegai thrust at Ulundi,
and of the murderous look on the face of that Zulu as he fell shot
through the head. The Captain was a sentimental man, despite
all the hard knocks of life, and was wont to comfort himself with
the reflection that every momentous experience adds a string to
the lute, from the high note of success to the bass of sorrow, so
that the accords of our nature should grow fuller and richer, if
softer, with time. It was pleasanter to remember Arabella, years
ago, as the slip of a girl she was, the night of that midsummer
moonlight walk, than as the stately matron she had grown, surrounded by her rich and obedient husband, and her half-dozen
more or less unruly offspring.

The clock struck four, and lights were brought. In the next house
a German *Fräulein* was lustily singing "Der Erlkönig," and Captain
Blythe could faintly distinguish the weird, sweet ballad of the
knightly and romantic Rhine, of the haunted ride amid storm and
darkness, of the irresistibly persuasive goblin and his fairy daughters,—yet as the words "Erlkönig hat mir ein Leid gethan!" rippled
away, he stirred the fire and pooh-poohed the song, and growled
that none but a German could have dreamt such nonsense as this
of a boy, lured to death in the land of spirits, through his own imagination, while bodily clasped in his father's arms. He walked to the
window and peered through the wintry twilight upon the noiseless
passers. The contrast which a bleak evening and flickering gas
lamps and such indistinct forms presented to his blazing fireside
usually offered a comforting suggestion, but on this particular day
the figures flitted hither and thither with more serious meaning.
Some were, perhaps, returning to cheerless homes; a few to carry
the burden of a secret sorrow into the midst of the care-free; this or
that one to watch this Christmas night beside a bed of illness. Bah!
little concern it was of his whither they went, or what their errands.
He resumed his book and finished the tragic story of the carnage
and rout of the Russian and Austrian troops, until, in the quiet of
that long afternoon, his eyes closed for the forty winks an elderly
gentleman may allow himself before dinner.

He had been asleep but a moment when, in the first impression of what rapidly became a vivid dream, a cold hand closed roughly upon his wrist, and to his bewilderment he found himself in the grasp of a Cossack soldier, one of the very horsemen about whom he had been reading. And it seemed to him that they walked by night across the snow-fields of Austerlitz, passing between great frosted poplars, with glimmering camp-fires in the distance and the stars shining in transcendent splendour overhead.

"Where are you taking me?" he gasped, in such scanty Russian as he had picked up at Sebastopol.

"To the Czar," was the curt answer: "he has need of you."

"To the Czar!—in dressing-gown and slippers!"

"His Majesty is too busy to notice."

"But I shall freeze to death!"

To this objection the Russian vouchsafed only a muttered word that resembled the snarl of a dog not to be trifled with. And looking more closely at his companion, Captain Blythe was startled to discover that it was Arabella's husband disguised as a Cossack, but with an eyeglass in the right eye, and one hand chinking the sovereigns in his trousers pocket, as in life. They walked, as it seemed, for an hour, coming frequently upon vedettes and other tokens of the presence of a vast army. Once they nearly stumbled over the body of a dead Russian soldier, with a bullet through his brain, just where the Captain had shot the Zulu, and bearing, in the darkness, an astonishing resemblance to the black and distorted features of that ill-favoured savage. Farther on they passed a village church which would be fired and stormed on the following morning, and whose graveyard would be strewn with Austrian dead. But now, in the silent and luminous starlight, and beneath the solemn, snow-flecked trees, the headstones and crosses stood out like the sails of a fleet of phantom galleys frozen to a motionless repose.

A distant noise behind them caught the ear, and he and his guide instinctively turned to listen. It was the tumultuous shouting of many voices, a mile away, and with the faint sound, as it moved from one side of the French camp to the other, went a sparkle of torches. Captain Blythe knew that it was the frenzied acclamation of the French soldiers to their Emperor as he made his famous visit to their bivouacs on the night before his greatest victory—an acclamation that, to this day, rings in the ear of whoever reads the story of Austerlitz. The thrilling vibration smote the air like the defiance of a nation, and seemed as prophetic of victory as the jubilant clamour of Gideon. It sounded human, yet savouring of the roar of some ferocious animal. And amid the cheers of an army glorying in its strength could be heard that exultant greeting, *"Vive l'Empereur! Vive l'Empereur!"*

The clock on the mantel struck six, and the sound reached the sleeper indistinctly, like distant land-bells heard at sea; and instantly their reverberation wove itself into his dream in a rhythmical cadence of the bells of the chapel they had left behind. Softly from afar it came, with poesy of incantation—that ringing melody whose voice awakes our happiest and our saddest memories. Its pealing was filled with harmonies of surpassing intensity, like the whisper of breaking waves. All the gladness of youth, all the ecstasy of love rang in the old man's soul through the music of those faint, far-sounding bells, until, with the mystery of an unutterable meaning, their ringing faltered, and was heard no more.

Captain Blythe and the Cossack resumed their walk; and dawn appeared as they sighted the Allied headquarters.

Already the Austrian and Russian camps were astir with drumbeat and bugle-blast, and these reveillés, sounding in a confused medley, impressed the Captain with their droll resemblance to dogs barking at daybreak to one another.

A moment later he stood in the presence of the Czar Alexander and of the Emperor Francis of Austria.

Both were seated at a camp-table, one side of which was covered with a map, whereon the Czar's eyes frequently rested, while upon the other had been spread a frugal breakfast of coffee, biscuit, and ham and eggs, to which the Austrian was applying himself. From a crackling fire of green logs without rose a cloud of aromatic smoke; and before it bent two liveried moujiks, trying to coax forth a brighter blaze. The Czar was a man of fine presence, with florid face, clear gray eyes, thin sandy hair, and salient cheek-bones, which gave an appearance of force to his countenance. He wore a tight green dress-coat with *aiguilettes,* white buckskin breeches, and long polished boots with silver spurs. Upon his shoulders was a mantle, and his cocked hat lay on a chair near by. The Austrian Emperor looked equally splendid in a white dress-coat with gold collar and tight breeches and boots; and he also, while sipping his coffee, held a cloak about him. His intellectual feebleness was apparent, as he asked in guttural German—

"Have my officers their queues properly powdered this morning?"

But before Blythe could declare his ignorance upon this particular, the Czar addressed him in excellent French, with quick, incisive utterance.

"I have sent for you, Monsieur le Capitaine, because you know this field of battle. You have read Thiers' "Histoire du Consulat et de l'Empire," which is more than I have been able to do. You have studied the course the action took eighty-five years ago, and should be able to guard us against a repetition of our blunders. It is not paying you an extravagant compliment to say that you are worth more to me than any of my generals, and that I hold you responsible for Austerlitz."

"*Ach, heilige Maria!*" murmured Kaiser Franz, raising his hand to his thick lips, "verily these eggs are hot."

At the words "responsible for Austerlitz" Captain Blythe realised the weird nature of his position. He understood, as never before, that, in principle, the sleeping intelligence is responsible; for who shall say that the mind which consents to wilful wrong, albeit in the fiction of a dream, sustains no moral blemish? He perceived that the dreamland to which he had passed was a reality, and felt himself under the control of a ghostly influence he could neither shake off nor resist. He was conscious that the scene before him was no more an hallucination than any of the seeming realities of life which vanish at a touch or fade like melting dreams. And for the moment he was appalled at the thought of what might befall him in a trance where the actual pressed so closely upon the visionary, and where the sleeper was answerable to forces and figures apparently as real as himself. He would fain have declined the weighty honour thrust upon him; but the watchful Cossack whispered:—

"Tush, fool! Think you to bandy reasons with a Czar?"

Thus tersely admonished, Captain Blythe made desperate efforts to recall the details of the narrative he had so lately read— to fix the blunders of the fateful battle, the confusion of conflicting orders, the loss of the heights of Pratzen, the catastrophe on the frozen lakes. In the midst of this mental struggle, the Czar buckled on his sword and rode away to where his generals waited; and poor Blythe was left to the maunderings of the Austrian Emperor about his pretty battalions, with their immaculate coats rendered yellow by exposure,—"what would the Viennese say if they could see them now? would they laugh or swear?"

The steady tramp of marching troops was heard, and the blare of drums and trumpets drew near. The Captain beheld a regiment of Austrian *Kaiserlichs* thronging to the front, with great brass-plated conical shakos, and close-fitting coats, and skin-tight trousers that gave them a wasp-like appearance. At their head went a band that filled the air with passionate refrains, stirring the heart with the fire of brave deeds. In his sleep the old man's pulse kindled rapturously, and his face flushed with joy, for the proud air seemed a familiar strain he had sought all his life—to find it at last in the enchantment of a dream. Past him they went—the horns, the cornets, the fifes, the drums, the clashing cymbals—their music filled with martial triumph and touched with the thrilling sweetness of Tyrolean echoes, till, as the march died in the distance, there arose a Babel of commands: Austrian officers speaking German to Hungarian troops; cavalry shouting in Polish to Croat infantry; Italians, Bohemians, Gallicians, Illyrians, side by side, each using their native dialect, to which Russian officers, galloping about, added the bewilderment of a language intelligible to few but themselves.

Before him extended a marvellous panorama. Immediately in front rose the heights of Pratzen, covered with cannon and infantry; to the right and left stretched long lines of troops, the green Russian uniforms contrasting with the Austrian white.

Farther away were Hungarian hussars, in dolmans and colbacks and braided breeches, suggestive of fancy dress; and behind them followed the ubiquitous Cossacks with their shaggy horses and long lances. In the wintry stillness of the Moravian fields, between the assembled armies, rose straight lines of poplars, standing like sentinels between the gathering hosts; and above them came the flush of day and the radiant splendour of the sun of Austerlitz. The smoke of an expiring camp-fire floated lazily across the torquoise-tinted sky, and the snow-crested hill-tops glistened as though touched by an aureole. All sounds were hushed now, and a marvellous quiet prevailed, that, to the dreamer, was intensified by the thought of the storm about to burst. The instant seemed to him one of unspeakable repose, as though the calm of Nature, like a perfect benediction, had over-spread and silenced the passions of Man. The sunrise was one of more than earthly beauty, with such effulgence of transcendent beams, such opalescent hues across the heavens, that the Captain in his bewilderment, with thoughts of Christmas still fresh in his mind, fancied something of the mystical light of Bethlehem must lie behind that brilliant Orient, to touch the earth with such incomparable glory.

The Czar was gesticulating excitedly to his generals, and the Austrian Emperor had finished his ham and eggs, when from the mist in the ravine beneath Pratzen emerged the French infantry and artillery, with glittering squadrons on the flanks. As the fusillade commenced, the Czar motioned Captain Blythe to him. "You perceive," he said, "the solemnity of this hour. Every form you behold is a spectre—the semblance of its former self. The Fates granted that when the last of those who fought at Austerlitz had died, the field should be fought over by their ghosts. The last of them, a Russian drummer, aged fifteen in December 1805, joined us this morning. All now are here: the men, the vivandières, the horses—even the dogs with their little waggons that draw the big drums in the Austrian bands. For sixty-five years I have watched them gather; and you who live on earth, and have the anguish to see your loved ones taken from you, know not the joy that spirits feel as, in our place of waiting, our comrades reappear and greet us as of old."

And, as he spoke, Blythe noticed hundreds of great birds, crows and vultures they seemed, flying at a distance, and wondered if these, too, were spectres. Then the Czar touched him on the shoulder and added, "Remember your duty: follow near, and keep me from the faults and failures of the flesh!"

The battle had commenced, and the first mistake of 1805 had already repeated itself with a strange fatality: through a misunderstanding of orders, a division of Russian cavalry had taken position on the heights of Pratzen, thus causing a delay in the advance of the second infantry line. It seemed as though the force of destiny could make itself felt even in the land of dreams. The Czar turned upon Blythe with a reproachful look: "Could not you," he cried, "have saved us the repetition of that folly?"

The French advanced rapidly, and at sight of his battalions recoiling before their impetuous onset the Czar's face darkened under a sinister presentiment. Nevertheless Miloradovitch, who commanded the Allied centre, exposed himself with daring courage at the front of the division bearing his name, while approaching from behind could be seen the Russian guard, which, by a further repetition of error, had been stationed too far to the rear to be immediately available. At its head rode the Cuirassier Life Guards, the *élite* of the Muscovite army, resplendent in steel and brass, with floating plumes and long straight swords. This corps instantly fell upon one of Vandamme's regiments, which it crushed before the very eyes of Napoleon, capturing its faded and tattered tricolour flag, the emblem of the conquering revolution. This its captor carried back to the two Emperors, with personal triumph undiminished by a bayonet gash through his face, from which the blood trickled slowly down upon the sparking decoration at his breast. Captain Blythe looked on with breathless interest, for never had he beheld so splendid an onset; and, moreover, he vaguely remembered reading, years ago it seemed, in Thiers' pages, of this charge and capture of a flag. The Czar smiled and spoke to the wounded soldier; and the Austrian Emperor, with a sour grimace, remarked, like the philosopher he was, "What shabby standards these Frenchmen bear!"

The battle had become engaged as far as the eye could reach, and as the fire grew hotter and the cannon-balls whizzed through the air or ploughed the ground, Blythe wondered that none of their group of brilliant staff-officers had been struck. But now—simultaneously with a sharp crackling of the fire in his room—a violent explosion rent the air, and an Austrian general near by fell from his horse face downwards. The Czar beckoned Captain Blythe to his side. "You are mismanaging this!" he exclaimed: "these occurrences are merely a renewal of what happened, and if you do not have a care, the result will be no better. Already I see you have allowed Buxhoevden, on the left yonder, to mire his troops on ground Thiers must have told you proved untraversable. Look for yourself, and see that his artillery is imbedded to the axles."

The Englishman saw, indeed, not only that the Allied left was upon dangerous ground, but that a portion of the French centre, wheeling to the right, was marching to strike it in flank. Swiftly he beheld the dire catastrophe that followed,—the Russian infantry, shattered and driven upon the frozen lakes, the storm of cannonballs that rent the ice, the struggling and drowning soldiers, the abandonment of artillery, the flight of the survivors. And now the Allied centre, violently assailed by Soult, gave way. The Austrian soldiers, casting aside their heavy muskets and brass-plated shakos, fled bare-headed and weaponless. Whole batteries of curiously fashioned cannon that had been drawn from Moscow, a thousand miles, were deserted; half a dozen of the gaudy flags of both armies, emblazoned with ravenous, open-mouthed eagles, lay on the ground, in apt token of the woeful fall of those imperial birds, while about them were dead or wounded soldiers, the Austrians in their white, blood-stained coats presenting a ghastly appearance.

Captain Blythe was recalled from the fugitives by a menacing gesture. It was the Czar, his broad face flushed with anger, his lips trembling as though with muttered imprecations. He motioned to some of his infantry who lingered, and pointed fiercely at the Englishman, and in that gesture was a sentence of death. Half a dozen men formed in line, and the Cossack, whose features were those of Arabella's husband, charged now with

Satanic malignity, gave the word of command. Captain Blythe
felt that he was not dreaming; he had drifted from dreamland
into the realm of spirits—about to become, for him, the realm
of death. The scene before him and the events that he had witnessed were not visionary. There was the sun in the sky, and
yonder the leafless December branches. He stamped on the
snow, and the crisp crystal grains flew from under his foot. The
inanimate objects, as well as the men before him, were as real
as himself. He watched the motions of the soldiers with the res-
ignation of a brave man. Every detail of their equipment was
distinct—their dingy uniforms frayed after two months' cam-
paigning, their leather shakos with long *ponpons,* their clumsy
flintlocks and iron bayonets of a previous reign. He heard the
brief order, saw the men tear the paper cartridges with their
teeth and ram them home. Then followed the click of the ram-
rods striking upon the bullets that were to tear his body. In that
supreme instant he had neither heroic thoughts nor useless
regrets; it merely seemed infinitely sad to fancy this beautiful
earth without him—this earth where in the focus of his own
small sphere he seemed to have filled so important a place, yet
whence his removal would not even be noticed.

His heart throbbed violently. Ready! Aim! The flintlocks glittered in the sun; there was a loud report; his heart quivered and
stood still; and Captain Blythe lay dying in his armchair before
his Christmas fireside.

The door had been opened by a valet, who came to remind
him of the hour—dinner would be served at seven, and it was
time to dress. The words faltered on his lips as he perceived that
his master was unconscious. In a few moments a physician had
been summoned, and soon after arrived the poet who had been
bidden to his friend's Christmas dinner, and who seated himself
at the side of what was to prove Captain Blythe's deathbed. For
an hour the sufferer remained speechless, and when at last his
lips moved, his words were so strange that those about him listened in silent wonder to the reiteration:—

"Responsible for Austerlitz! And shot to death!"

Nor could he be wholly recalled from the phantom land to

which he believed that he had wandered, and where he declared he had met his fate. With slow and difficult utterance, that at times sank to a whisper, he told the story of his ghostly adventure.

"But, my dear fellow," said the poet, soothingly, observing that the extraordinary recital agitated him, "you are safe in your own room, which you have not left for an instant."

"Not left in body," replied the dying man; "but in spirit I have been far from here, and those I met have done me a mortal hurt. Believe me, the song of the 'Erlkönig' is founded upon a truth, and the boy's life was charmed from him as he listened."

The doctor applied restoratives, and watched attentively. "It is an aneurism of the heart," he mused within himself.

Then the ill man turned, as if, with faculties supernaturally keen, he had divined the thought:—

"No," he ejaculated: "it is the Russian bullets."

And nothing could dispel this weird hallucination. He believed that at the cost of life he had touched one of the secrets of occult science, and, until final unconsciousness, his mind was persistently running upon the ghostly bourne into which he had strayed, and wither his spirit was about to return. But his vision gradually assumed a softer aspect, and from the words he muttered it appeared that the scene before him had changed to one of matchless beauty, where stretched a winding river with sunlit castles and vineyards, rich with the radiance of a transfigured morning. And beside him the Elf King whispered words of irresistible persuasion, sweet as the song of birds at break of day,— and the Elf King's phantom daughters beckoned from the night of earth towards the shining river. And when his last breath had passed, the poet, bending at the bedside, was so possessed by the mystery of his fate, that he thought of the friend whose cold hand he still clasped as of one who had fallen a victim to the spectres upon whose domain he had unwittingly trespassed.

The Coach

Violet Hunt

It was a lonely part of the country, far away in the north, where the summer nights are pale and scant of shade. There was no moon and yet it was not dark. For hours the flat, deprecating earth had lain prone under a storm of wind and rain. Its patient surface was drenched, blanched, smitten into blindness. The tumbled waters of the Firth splashed on the edges of the plain, their mild commotion dwarfed by the noise of the wind-driven showers, whose gloomy drops tapped the waters into sullen acquiescence. Half a mile inland the great main Roman road was laid. Clear and straight it ran, with never a house or home-stead to break it, viscous with clay here, shining with quartz there, uncompromising, exact, a pallid ribbon stretched from South to North. Its sides were bare, scantily garnished with grass—this was nearly a hedgeless country—but in places the undeviating line of it passed through a little nut coppice or clump of gnarled, ill-conditioned trees. They seemed to lean forward vindictively on either side, snapping their horny fingers at each other, waving their cantankerous branches as the gusts took them, broke them, and whirled the fragments of their ruin far away and out of ken, like a flapping unruly kite which a child has allowed to pass beyond his control. The broad white surface of the road beneath was not suffered to be blotted for a single moment. Nothing could rest for the play of the intriguing air currents, surging backwards and forwards, blind, stupid, unpaci-fied. They had got completely out of hand and defied the archers of the middle sky. Staggering hither and thither like ineffectual giants, they buffeted all impartially; they instigated the hapless boughs at their mercy to savage lashings of each other, to useless accesses of self-destruction. Bending slavishly under the heady gusts, each shabby blade of grass by the road-side rose again and was on the *qui-vive* after the rustling tyrant had passed.

It was then, in the succeeding moments of comparative peace, when the directors of the passionate aerial revolt had managed to call their panting rabble off for the time, that great perpendicular sheets of rain, like stage films, descended, and began moving continuously sideways, like a wall of plate-glass, across the level track, as if slung evenly from heavenly tent-poles. A sheet of whole water, blotting out the stubbly borders of herbage that grew sparsely round the heaps of stones with which the margin was set at intervals, placed there ready for breaking! When the slab of rain had moved on again, the broad road, shining out sturdily with its embedded quartz and milky, kneaded clay, lay clear once more. Calm, ordered and tranquil in the midst of tumult and discord it pursued its appointed course, from its evenly bevelled sides, edging off the noisy moorland streams, that had come jostling each other in their haste to reach it, only to be relegated, noisily plaining, to the swollen unrecognisable gutter.

At a certain point on the line of way, a tall, spare, respectable-looking man in a well-fitting gray frock coat stood waiting. The rain ran down the back of his coat collar, and dripped off the rim of his tall hat. His attitude was that of some weary foredone clerk waiting at the corner of the city street for the omnibus that was to carry him home to slippered comfort and sober pipe of peace. He wore no muffler, but then it was summer—St. John's Eve. He leaned on an iron-headed ebony stick of which he seemed fond, and peered, not very eagerly, along the road, which now, during a lull, lay in dazzling rain-washed clarity, under the struggling moon. He had no luggage, no umbrella, yet his coat looked neat, and his hat shiny.

Far in the distance, southwards, a black clumsy object appeared, labouring along. A coach, of heavy and antique pat-tern. As soon as he had sighted it, the passenger's interest dimin-ished. With a slightly bored air of fulfilment, he took his eyes off, and looked down at the clayey mud at his feet disapprovingly,

although, indeed, the sticky substance did not appear to have
marred the exquisite polish of his shoes. His palm settled com-
posedly on the ivory knob of his trusty stick, as though it were
the hand of an old friend.

With all the signs of difficult going, but no noises of straining
or grinding, the coach at last drew up in front of the expectant
passenger. He looked up quietly, and recognised it as the vehicle wherein it was appointed that he should travel, in this unsuit-
able weather, a stage or two, maybe. All was correct, the coachman, grave, businesslike, headless as of usage, the horses long-
tailed, black, conventional . . .

The door opened noiselessly, and the footboard was let down.
He shook his head as he delicately stepped into it, and observed,
for the benefit, doubtless, of the person or persons inside:

"I see old Diggory on the box in his official trim! Rather
unnecessary, all this ceremony, I venture to think! A few yokels
and old women to impress, if indeed any one not positively
obliged is abroad on a night like this! For form's sake, I suppose."

He took the seat next the window. There were four occupants
of the coach beside himself. They all nodded stiffly, but not
unkindly. He returned their salutations with old-fashioned courtesy, though unacquainted seemingly with any of them.

Sitting next to him was a woman evidently of fashion. Her
dark, rich, valuable furs were negligently cast on one side, to
show a plastron covered with jewels. She wore at least two
enamelled and encrusted watches pinned to her bosom as a
mark for thieves to covet. So at least thought the man in the
frock coat. Her yellow wig was much awry. Her eyes were weak,
strained and fearful, and she aided their vision with a diamond
beset *pince-nez*. Now and again, she glanced over her left shoulder as if in some alarm and at such times she always grasped her
gold net reticule feverishly. She was obviously a rich woman in
the world, a first-class, *train-de-luxe* passenger.

The woman opposite her belonged as unmistakably to the
people. She was hard-featured, worn with a life of sordid toil
and calculation, but withal stout and motherly, a figure to
inspire the fullest confidence. She wore a black bonnet with
strings and black silk gloves heavily darned. Round her sunken

collar, a golden gleam of watch-chain was now and then discernible.

At the other end of the coach, squeezed up into the corner where the vacillating light of the lamp hanging from the roof least penetrated, a neat, sharp-featured man nestled and hid. His forehead retreated, and his bowler hat was set unnecessarily far back, lending him an air of folly and congenital weakness which his long, cold, clever nose could not dissipate. He was white as enamel.

But the man whom the man in the frock coat most affected among his casual fellow travellers was the one sitting directly opposite him, a rough, hearty creature, who alone of all the taciturn coachful seemed disposed to enter into a casual conversation, which might go some way to enliven the dreariness entailed by this somewhat old-fashioned mode of travelling. Speech might help to drown the dashing of the rain against the windows and the ugly roar of the waters of the Firth lying close on the right hand of the section of road they were even now traversing. This—by comparison—cheerful fellow was dressed like a working man, in a shabby suit of corduroys, he wore no collar, but a twisted red cotton handkerchief wound tightly round his thick, squat neck. His little mean eyes, swinish, but twinkling good-humouredly, stared rather enviously at the neat gentleman's stiff collar and the delicate gray tones of his suiting. Crossing and uncrossing his creasy legs, in the unusual effort of an attempt at conviviality, the man in corduroys addressed the man in the frock coat at last, awkwardly enough, but still civilly.

"Well, mate! They've chosen a rare rough night to shift us on! Orders from headquarters, I suppose? I've been here nigh on a year and never set eyes on my boss!"

"We used to call him God the Father," said the elder man slowly. . . . "But whoever it is that orders our ways here, there is no unearthly sense in questioning his arrangements, one can only fall in with them. As you admit, you are fairly new, and perhaps you do not as yet conceive fully of the silent impelling force that sways us here. It is the same in the world we have left, only that there we were only concerned with the titles and standing of our 'boss,' as you call him, and obeyed His laws not a whit. Still, personally, I *must* say I consider this particular system of soul transference very unsettling and productive of restlessness among us. It's a mere survival of a tiresome superstition. It has a single merit; one sees something of the under-world, travelling about as we do, and meeting chance, perhaps kindred, spirits on the road. One realises, too, that Hades is not quite as gray, shall I say, as it is painted? But perhaps"—he added, with a slight touch of class hauteur, "you do not quite follow me?"

"Oh yes, master, I do," eagerly replied the fellow traveller to whom he chose to address his monologue. "Since I've been dead, I have learned the meaning of many things. I turn up my nose at nothing these days. I always neglected my schooling, but now I tell you I try to make up for lost time. From a rough sort of fellow that I was, with not an idea in my head beyond my beer and my prog, I have come to take my part in the whole of knowledge. It was all mine before, so to speak, but I didn't trouble to put my hand out for it. Didn't care, didn't listen to Miss that taught me, or to parson, either. He had some good ideas, too, as I've come to know, though vice isn't vice exactly with us here, now, in a manner of speaking. If God Almighty made us, why did He make us, even in parts, bad, that's what I want to know, and I'll know that when I've been dead a bit longer? Why did He give me rotten teeth so that I couldn't chew properly and didn't care for my food and liked drink better? It's digestion makes drinking, I say."

The smart woman interrupted him, with a kind of languid eagerness, exclaiming:

"I must say I agree with you. Since the pestle fell on my shoulder in that lonely villa at Monte, I have realised what the dreadful gambling fever may lead to. It had made those two inhuman. They were wild beasts. I entered their cage. I should never have accepted their treacherous invitation to luncheon, never tempted them with my outrageous display of jewels! And ah me! I was tarred with the same stick, I gambled, too"—she rummaged in her reticule and fished out a ticket for the rooms at Monte Carlo. "I always call that the ticket for my execution. Though, indeed, my executioners were a little brutal. They will attain unto this place easier than I did. The hand of the law is gentle, compared with the methods of Sir V——"

The man in the gray frock coat raised his finger warningly. "No names, I beg! One of our conventions! . . ."

"Have a drop?" said the calm motherly woman to the excited fine lady. "Your wound is recent, isn't it? Yours was a very severe case! A bloody murder, I call it, if ever there was one, and clumsy at that! And you only passive, which is always so much harder, they say! I can't tell, I was what you may call an active party. *They* don't seem to mind mixing, they that look after us here, they lump us all together, travelling, at any rate! Though when I think of what I was actually turned off for—well, the way I look at it, what I did was a positive benefit to society, and some sections of society knew it, too, and would have liked to preserve me. I have been told that there are people, clever people in the world, who are not ashamed to say so, and who gnashed their teeth with vexation when the verdict went against me. Now Mr. H. B.——"

"No names, again," the man in the frock coat again interposed suavely. "But what, madam, if I may ask, was your little difficulty?"

"It is called, I believe, baby-farming," she replied offhand-edly, receiving her flask back from the smart woman and stow-ing it away in a capacious pocket. As she spoke a shudder, like a transitory ripple on a rain-swept stream, passed over her hear-ers, with the exception of the thin man in the far corner, who preserved his serenity, but raising his sunken chin, observed the last speaker with some slight show of interest.

The man in the gray frock coat apologised.

"Excuse us, madam. A remnant of old-world squeamishness, uncontrollable by us for the moment. Though, perhaps, if you would, you might somewhat dissipate our preconceived notions of your profession, by explaining your point of view a little."

"Delighted, I'm sure," she answered. "Funny, though, how seriously you all take it, even here! The feeling against my pro-fession is so very strong. I was hooted as I left the court, I rec-ollect. It annoyed me then considerably. I thought that those that hooted had more need to be grateful to me if all was known and paid for. I saved their pockets for them and their lovely credit. They knew they owed that to me. For the rest they did

not mind. They went on, carelessly raising up seed for me to
mow down as soon as its head came above ground, and welcome! Sly dogs, no thanks from them! But those shivering
shrinking women that came to me, some of them hardly out of
their teens—some of them so delicate they had no right to have
a baby at all! Ah, if only I hadn't let myself take their money it
would have been a work of pure philanthropy. But I had to live,
then. Now that that tax has been taken off, one has time to think
it out all round. But Lord!—Society, to cry shame on me for
doing its dirty work for it! They might as well hang any other
useful public servant, like dustmen, rat-catchers, and such like
ridders of pests. Good old Herod, that I used to hear about at
school, knew what he was doing when he cleared off all those
useless innocents! He was the first baby-farmer, I take it."

"You take large ground, madam," said the man in the frock
coat, a trifle huffily.

"And I have the right," said she, her large determined chin
emerging boldly from its rolls of fat, in her eagerness. "You men
ought to know it, and you do. I was only the 'scapegoat, and took
on me the little sins of the race. It's an easy job enough, what I
did, but there's few have the stomach for it even then. . . . You
couldn't call it dirty work neither. You just stand by and leave
'em alone—to girn and bloat and die——"

"No blood, eh?" the man in the corner said suddenly. "I like
blood!"

"What a fine night it has turned!" said the man in the gray
frock coat, raising the sash and putting his head out of the window. "Something rather uncanny, eh, about that man?" he
remarked under his breath, half to himself, half to the man in
brown corduroys.

"Take your head in," said the latter almost affectionately, "or
you'll be catching cold, and you've got a nasty scar on your neck
that I could see as you leaned forward, and that you oughtn't to
go getting the cold into."

"Oh, that!" said the other complacently, sitting down again, but
averting his gaze carefully from the man in the corner, for whom
he seemed to feel a repulsion as marked as was his preference
for his cheerful *vis-à-vis*. "That! That's actually the scar of the
blow that killed me. A fearful gash! He was a powerful man that

dealt it me. He got me, of course, from behind, I never even saw him. I was drafted off here at once, his hand had been so sure." He felt nervously in his pockets. "I have a foulard somewhere, but I am apt to mislay it."

"You should do like me, have a good strong handkerchief and knot it round your neck firm. I've got a mark of sorts on my neck, too, but it isn't an open wound—never was. It is sheer vanity with me, but I don't care to have it seen. It goes well all round—mine—done by a rope!" He paused and nodding slyly—"For killing a toff. Nice old gentleman he seemed, too, but I hadn't much time to look at him. Had to get to work——"

He was interrupted by the baby-farmer.

"Lord!" she said. "Do I see another conveyance coming on this lonely road? I'm one for seeing plenty of people. I always liked a crowd and this sort of thing was beginning to get fairly on my nerves."

They all jerked themselves round and peered through the glass pane behind each one of them. The taciturn man reserved his attention. Sure enough, a dark object, plainly outlined in the moonlight which now lit up the heavens, where clouds had obscured the earlier part of their journey, was distinctly visible. It blotted the ribbon of white that lay in front of them. . . . It was a high-hung dog-cart, of the most modern pattern, drawn by a smart little pony, and driven by one of two young girls—the one that wore noticeably white dog-skin gloves that looked immense in the pallid moonshine.

"What an excitement? I've never met any one on the road before!" exclaimed the stout woman.

"I hope—for I'm not a bloodthirsty man—that we're not a-going to give them a shock and send that pony all over the road?" the man in corduroys muttered anxiously. "We mostly do, you know, when we meet them plump like this! 'Orses can't abide the sight of Us, mostly, no more than they could motors at first. And we're worse than motors—they seem to smell us out at once for what we are!"

"If you think that pony likely to swerve," said the man in gray anxiously, "would it be of any use asking old Diggory to drive more slowly?"

"Couldn't go no slower than we are!" the man in corduroys

replied. "Besides, it's not the pace that kills! I'll bet you that pony's all of a sweat already?"

The trap approached. The faces of the two young women were discernible. They were white—with fear—or was it merely an effect of the moonlight? They were disturbed evidently, and the one who was driving, fully realised the necessity of controlling the horse, whose nostrils were quivering. . . .

"It won't pass us!" said the man in the corner, speaking suddenly. "There will be blood!"

"Do stop gloating like that!" said the stout woman. "It turns my stomach to hear you. Wherever have you come from, I wonder? . . . I say, can't we hail them?" she inquired of the man in gray. "All give one big shout?"

"They wouldn't hear us," he replied, shaking his head sadly. "You must remember we're ghosts. We're not really there!"

"And that's what the beasteses know!" cried the man in corduroys. "That 'oss won't be able to stand it! She'll not be able to hold it in!"

"They're on us!" screamed the smart woman. "Oh, my God, do we have to sit still and see it?"

"Yes, missis, and what's more, run away after, like any motor-car that's killed his man. Old Diggory's got his orders . . ."

The frantic snorting of the horse was now audible, the lather of foam dropping from its jaws distinctly visible, and the agonised tension of one girl's hands, and the scared white faces of both, visible by the light of the carriage lamp. . . .

Then the lamp flew downwards and was extinguished, there was a crash, and the road to the north lay clear again. The Coach of Death rolled on remorselessly, past a black heap that filled the ditch by the side, lying quite still, after one heave. . . .

The smart woman fainted, or appeared to do so.

"It's iniquitous!" exclaimed the man in gray. "To leave them behind like that when it's our conveyance has done the mischief!" He groaned.

"We aren't to blame, sir," said the man in corduroys, consoling him. "As you said before—*We ain't really here!*"

"Small consolation!" The old man shook his head, and devoted himself to the smart woman, who revived under his ministrations.

"I shouldn't be surprised if those two girls joined us at the next stage," she observed cheerily, "and then we'll make them tell us all they felt, when they saw the coachful of ghosts coming down upon them. They were both in the ditch, I'm sure, with the cart on top of them. And now, I'm just thinking—suppose, to while away the time, we all told each other the story of how we came to be here? A lively tale might cheer us all up, after the accident."

"Agreed, madam, heartily," said the man in gray. "My own story is by no means a gruesome one, and I regarded the accident that ended me as particularly toward. But—ladies first! Will not you begin?"

"My story, perhaps," she replied modestly, "might not be very new to you. It was in the papers so very recently."

"That will not affect me," he answered. "For if, as I conjecture, it was a murder case, I never read them!"

"I read yours, missis, I expect," said the man in corduroys. "I generally get the missis to read the spicy things out to me."

"It filled the papers for nearly a week," she said eagerly. "And yet the people that did it are not hanged yet. If, indeed, poor souls, they ever are hanged? The French, you know, are lenient, and quite mild and kind in *cold* blood. I am quite anxious to see how it goes. If the pair really are sent here, I suppose I shall be running up against them some night or other, on one of these transference parties. It will be very interesting. But——" she leaned across to the baby-farmer, "could we not persuade you to give us some of your—nursery experiences, madam?"

"There's not much story about the drowning of a litter of squalling puppies or whining kittens," said that lady shortly, "we want something livelier—more personal, if I may say so. From a remark that gentleman in the corner let drop a while ago, I fancy his reminiscences would be quite worth hearing, as good as a shilling shocker."

"My story," the individual thus pointedly addressed replied in a low voice, "is impossible, frankly impossible."

"Indecent, do you mean?" The smart woman's eyes shone. "Oh, let us have it. You can veil it, can't you?"

"Have you ever heard of mental degenerates?" he asked her

compassionately. "I was one. I was called mad—a simple way of expressing it. I was a chemist—a dissector—a bit of a butcher. They did right to exterminate me."

His head dropped. He seemed disinclined to say more. Still the smart woman persisted.

"But the details——?"

"Are purely medical, madam! Not without a psychologico-morbid interest! The——" (he named a daily paper much in vogue) "made a good deal of the implied sense of contrast—the artistic warp, as I might say, of the executant." His head sank again on his chest.

"I do believe," said the baby-farmer, nudging the smart woman, "he's the man who killed his sweetheart, and then tied her poor inside all into true-lovers' knots with sky-blue ribbon. Very common colours—blue and red!"

"Disgusting!" The delicate-minded lady turned away and joined in the petition of the other ghosts to the breezy man in corduroys to relate his experiences.

"Oh, I'll tell you how I came to join you and welcome!" he said, rolling his huge neck about in its setting of red cotton. "Well, to be begin with, I was drunk. Equally, of course, I was hard up. My missus—she's married again, by the way, blast her!—was always nagging me to do something for her and the children. I did. Nation's taking care of them now, along of what I did. Work, she meant, but that was only by the way. I did take on a job, though, on a rich man's estate, building some kind of Folly, lots of glass and that, working away day and night by naphtha flares, you know. He was one of those men, you know the sort, that has more money than a man can properly spend, and feels quite sick about it, and says so, in interviews and so on in the papers a working man reads. That's the mischief. He was always giving away chunks of money to charities, libraries, and that sort of useless lumber, but none of it ever seemed to come the way of those that were in real need of it. They said the money had got on his nerves, and would not let him sleep o' nights, and that he was afraid by day and went about with a loaded stick and I don't know what all. And he was looked after by detectives, at one time, so the papers said—putting things in

people's heads, as it's their way. So one blessed evening I was
very low—funds and all—and my missis and the kids hollering
and complaining as they always do when luck's bad. Lord bless
them, they never thought as they were 'citing their man to murder. Women never do think. And going out with their snivelling
in my ears I passed the station where he landed every evening
after his day in town, and I happened to see him come out of the
train and send away his motor that was awaiting for him all regular, and start out to walk 'ome alone by a short cut across a little
plantation there was, very thick and dark, just the place for a murder. Well—I told you I was half drunk—I raced home and got
something to do it with—a meat chopper, to be particular——"

The old man opposite put his hand up nervously to the back
of his neck.

"Ay, mister, it takes you just there, does it? You look a regular
bundle of nerves, you do. Well, as I was saying, I went round by
a short cut that I happened to know of, and got in front of him
and hid in the hedge. Ten mortal minutes I waited for my man
to come by. Lord, how my hand did tremble! I'd have knocked
off for twopence. I was as nervous as a cat, but all the same, it
didn't prevent me from striking out for wife and children with a
will when my chance came. I caught him behind with my chopper and he fell like a log. Never lifted a hand to defend himself—hadn't got any grit. Ladies, I don't suppose I hurt him
much, for he never even cried out when I struck, or groaned
when it was done. Then I looked him over, turned out his pockets and collared his watch and season ticket and seals and
money. Money—ha!—I had been fairly done over that! Would
you believe it of a rich fellow like that, he hadn't got more than
the change of a sovereign on him?"

"Shame!" ejaculated the taciturn man in the corner.

"I admit it was hard on you," the man in the gray frock coat
observed kindly. "Very hard, for as I read, the retribution came
all to quickly. You foolishly left your chopper about to identify
you, and were apprehended at once, by our excellent rural
police. Yet the law is so dilatory that you lay in gaol a whole year
before you were free to join your victim here?"

"Right you are, mate. Yes, I swung for it, sure enough. Short and sweet it was, when once I stood on the drop, but it still makes my poor old throat ache to think of it." He wriggled and twisted his neck in its cincture. . . . "Now, governor, I'm done, and if you've no objection we'd all like to hear how you came by that ugly gash of yours? It wasn't no rope did that. Common or garden murder, I'll be bound?"

"Certainly, my man, it was a murder—a murder most *à propos*. I suppose you will hardly believe that, but the circumstances were peculiar. I have often longed to get the ear of the jury who tried the man for relieving me of my light purse and my intolerably heavy life, and tell them—the whole labouring twelve of them, trying their best to bring in an honest verdict and avenge my wrongs—my own proper feelings, surely no negligible factor in the case! They could not guess—these ignorant living men, whose eyes had not yet been opened by death to a due sense of the proportions of things—that I bore the poor creature no malice, but was actually grateful for his skilful surgery, that had severed the cord of the life that bored me so neatly and completely."

"It isn't every one would take it like that!" remarked the smart woman. "Yet that is, more or less, how I feel about these things myself. Only in my case it is impossible to speak of skilful surgery! I was disgracefully cut up. I couldn't possibly have worn a low dress again!"

"Have you ever heard," said the man in the gray frock coat thoughtfully, "of the Gold of Rhampsinitos and the inviolable cellar he built to store it in? There it stayed unchanged at least. According to the modern system, in the place where my gold was hoarded fat assets and sordid securities bred and bred all day long. The laws that govern money are hard. You must give it, devise it, you must not allow it to be taken. But for my part I would have welcomed the two sons of the master-builder who broke into the King's Treasure-house. In the strong-room of my brain it was lodged. With one careless calculation, one stroke of a pen, I could make money breed money there to madden me. I was lonely, too. I had no wife to divide my responsibilities. She might have enjoyed them. But I dared approach no woman in the way of love—I would not be loved for my cheque-signing powers. I was not loved at all. I was hated. Unrighteous things were done in my name, by the greedy husbanders of my load of money. I was told that I went in danger of my life, and I condescended to take care of that, for a time—only for a time! One dark winter evening—I forget what had happened during the day, what fresh instance of turpitude or greed had come before me—I was so revolted that I kicked away all the puling safeguards by which my agents guarded their best asset of all, and gave the rein to my instinct. I violently disregarded precautions of every sort—with the exception of my faithful stick, and the carrying of that had come to be a mere matter of habit with me—and I walked home from the station, alone and unattended, up to my big house and good dinner which I hoped— nay, I almost knew—that I should not be alive to eat. And indeed as luck would have it, on that night of all nights the trap was set for me. The appointed death-dealer was waiting—he took me on at once. I got my desire—kind, speedy, merciful, violent death. I never even saw the face of my deliverer."

"By George!" softly swore the man in corduroys. "This beats all. Are you sure you aren't kidding us?"

"No, indeed, that is exactly how I felt about it, and if I had known of knowledge, as I knew of instinct, what was going to happen, I would have managed to realise some of my wealth before setting out to walk through that wood, and made it more worth the honest fellow's while. But as you are aware, a millionaire does not carry portable gold about with him, and my cheque-book, which was on me, would, of course, be of no use to him. Alas, all the poor devil got for his pains was exactly nineteen shillings and elevenpence. I had changed a sovereign at the bookstall to buy a paper, and out of habit, had waited for the change."

The man in corduroys was by this time in a considerable state of excitement. He had pulled the red handkerchief fiercely from his neck and now made as if to tear it across his knee. . . .

"Why, governor!" he exclaimed passionately, "do you mean to say it was through you that I got this here"—he put both hands behind his head and interlocked them—"in return for giving you that there nasty cut at the back of your neck? Yes, sure! Well how things do come about!"

"Gently, gently! my man," the elder soothed him. "Don't be so melodramatic about a very ordinary coincidence. See, the ladies are quite upset! It doesn't do to allow oneself to get excited here—it's not in the rules. If I had made the little discovery you have done, I don't think—no, I really don't think I would have made it public. This undue exhibition of emotion of yours strikes me as belonging to the vulgar world we have all left. But since you have allowed it to come out, and every one is now aware of the peculiar relation in which we stand to each other, you must let me tender you my best thanks, as to a most skilful and firm operator, and believe me to be truly grateful to you for your services in the past."

"Quite the old school!" said the smart woman.

"I must say, sir, I consider you a real gentleman," said the baby-farmer.

"I am a gentleman."

"And a fairly accommodating one!" said the rough man, wiping his brow where, however, no sweat was. "It isn't every man as would give thanks for being scragged!"

"Every man isn't a millionaire," said his victim calmly.

The smart woman, leaning forward, tapped the old gentleman amiably with her jewelled *pince-nez*.

"But we belong to the same world, I perceive," she said, "and so I am quite able to understand your refined feeling. It is as I said in my own case. Indeed, if those two good people, who shall be nameless, had only dealt with me a little more gently, I don't know that I would not forgive them absolutely. I shall at any rate be perfectly civil when I do meet them—only perhaps a *leetle* distant. But that Monte Carlo existence I was leading when they interrupted it, was really becoming intolerable. No one who hasn't done it thoroughly and from the rich inside can realise what it is. Glare, noise, glitter, fever—that heartless, blue, laughing sea——"

The baby-farmer, left behind in this elegant discussion, obviously took no pleasure in it, but, staring straight before her, muttered sulkily:

"Côte d'Azur and Pentonville! There's some little difference, isn't there, between that life and mine? Yet I enjoyed my life, I

did, and as for gratitude, I can't say as I see all those blessed
infants a-coming up to me, and slobbering me for what I did for
'em! It isn't in human nature. Their mothers' thanks was all I got
and they thanked me beforehand, some of them, for what I was
going to do. Lord, what's a rickety baby more or less? I say, we're
slowing up! Going to stop perhaps, and a good thing, too!"

"Yes," said the man in the gray frock coat, speaking very
clearly without observing whether he had listeners or not, "I
cordially thank the man who rid me with one clean scientific
blow of my wretched life and all its tedious accessories. A skilled
workman is worthy of his hire! . . ."

"Mercy!" muttered the baby-farmer. "Is he never going to
stop? If it was for nothing else, he ought to have got scragged for
being a bore!"

But the man in the gray frock coat continued, being fully
wound up, though in the excitement of arrival at the depôt no
one was attending. "Suicide I had thought of, but abhorred,
though on my soul I had nearly come to that, and then it was
merely a question of courage. I had not the courage—you spoke
truly, sir. Mine was a thin, pusillanimous nature, as you said. You
came by, a kind Samaritan, and sacrificed your own good life
freely to rid me of my wretched one. I think I told you that when
you were being tried, I followed urgently all the details of the
trial, and made interest with the authorities here to allow me to
appear to the judge in his sleep, say, and instil into his mind
some inkling of the true state of my feelings towards you. I do
not know, however, if you would have thanked me, for life may
have been no sweeter to you than it was to me—you spoke of an
uncongenial helpmate, I think? Still, one never knows. I might
have been the means of procuring you some good years yet, in
the full exercise of your undeniable vigour and remarkable decision of character. But it was apparently not to be. You followed
me here, after a tedious interval of waiting, and now we have
met, face to face. The introduction on that dark night was worth
nothing. I like your face. We shall probably never meet again—
their ways are dark and devious here—I am the more glad of
this gracious opportunity of opening my mind to you, on a delicate subject, perhaps, but one that has always been very near my

heart. By the way"—he lifted his stick, with its shining ivory crown, into view—"did you notice this? You read the papers, you said, and they told you it was heavily weighted and that I carried it always as a precaution? Well, on that eventful night for both of us, perhaps you were too hurried to notice, but I never used it. Accept it, now, will you not, as a memento? . . . I think from sundry truly unearthly bumpings that we seem to have come at last to our journey's end. . . . I am right, the coachman has got down from his perch and taken his head under his arm. . . . We part. Mesdames, I salute you. Again, sir"—he addressed himself more particularly to the shamefaced man in corduroys—"farewell. Very pleased to have met you!"

One by one, the passengers faded away. For a moment, the polite old man paused; a pale, proud woman's face, tilted up by the coach step, had touched him. She was quite alone. She wore white dog-skin gloves, but no hat. Ah, but on looking closer, he saw that it hung disregarded over her shoulder by an elastic, and was much battered. He decided to speak to her.

"You are the lady we killed, I think?" he asked her gently.

She acknowledged, in a formal, off-hand manner, that it was so.

"We could none of us do anything," said he, "or I hope you will believe——"

"Certainly, sir, it was no fault of yours, I am sure. The accident was quite inevitable," she told him, smiling faintly. There *was* blood on the hair, he was able to assure himself. "Rory, my pony, never can pass things, at the best of times, and the look of your conveyance was certainly rather unusual. But at that time of night, we rarely meet anything on the Great North Road. We chose that time on purpose—my sister and I—we had been away a week, and we were going home. When we saw you coming, she said, half in jest—she is younger than me—suppose that lumbering thing in front were the Coach of Death the foolish country people here talk about. They say it travels in this way once a year, with its cargo of poor souls who have died by violence, on St. John's Eve. And this is St. John's Eve! I asked her not to be superstitious, but I confess I thought the vehicle looked odd, myself, and wondered how Rory would stand it?

When it came nearer, I saw distinctly that the coachman was headless, and I told my sister so. She bade me not disturb her, for dead coach or live coach, she meant to do her best to get Rory past it! She failed——"

The man in gray looked round. He was alone with her. The headless coachman was preparing to ascend to the box-seat again. . . . "Where *is* your sister?" he asked.

"She lies at the bottom of the ditch. Rory has galloped home. She fell on her head, but she is alive still. When they find her in the morning she will be dead, I know that. She will join me. Now I know all. I am at peace—you must have no care for me. . . ."

"Let me at least put you into the coach!" he begged. "Will you not prefer the corner? I see you are going to have all the accommodation to yourself for this stage. I am sorry I cannot offer to accompany you, but I have my marching orders! . . ."

He raised his hat and disappeared, as the coach moved on and was lost in the mist. . . . The summer dawn was breaking.

The Night School

James Hopper

Having laid my last hope beneath heavy flowers, I had drifted back to the village of my youth. The little village was now a large city, a clamorous city, and on the first day I met Dorman. It was on a stone sidewalk, beneath a pale, faint sun. How he recognized me, God only knows; we both had grown very old, and at first I could see nothing in him of the boy with whom I had gone to school.

He stopped and fixed me silently, then from the folds of his cloak his arm stretched out and gripped me as with a claw.

"You are Halton," he said—"Jack Halton, whose desk was next to mine at school."

"I am," I said. "I am Jack Halton."

He stood there, looking at me with eyes gray and round beneath the bristle of his heavy brows.

"I am Dorman," he said—"Nat Dorman, who sat next to you at school."

Of late age has been enwrapping me with its frigid haze, and I have taken to the resource of the old. I stare persistently at the golden days that are gone. And so I remembered.

"I remember," I said.

His hand was still on my arm, his eyes were on my eyes.

"You have a wife, children?" he asked.

"I have had a wife; I have no wife," I answered. "I have had children; I have no children."

"I have never had either wife or children," he said. We stood there on the stone sidewalk, beneath the cheerless sun. "Wife nor children," he nodded; "wife nor children." But it was on my answer he pondered, for finally he said, "Come with me to my house for tonight."

A vast indifference held me. I said:

"Very well, I will go with you to your house for tonight."

He raised his stick, and a carriage which had been wheeling slowly back and forth rushed in sudden animation to the curb. We sank upon the dark cushions within; the door shut upon us. As we rolled along the streets I had known, now unknown to me, I noticed that his hands, folded beneath his chin on the top of his cane, trembled incessantly.

"How old he is!" I thought.

It was a palace, his house, of stone, thick-walled, the interior full of fine, somber things, and muffled with elastic carpets. We dined in a high-ceiled oaken hall, before a blazing grate. We held up our glasses to the flame, and looked at the golden sun of our youth, the ruby blood of our youth. We drank the sun, we drank the blood, but our veins remained cold.

We went up-stairs to his room. Two beds, heavily curtained, were in it, against opposite walls.

"There are two beds," he said. "You will sleep here with me in my room."

I did not care; I answered:

"Yes, I will sleep here in your room with you."

I slept badly. The bed was heaped with blankets, but they were as heavy as a lid, and between the sheets I was as cold as in the tomb. I dreamed.

A bell was ringing somewhere in some one's hand; it had a brazen, persistent sound. When it had ceased with a last rattle of clapper, a drum began to beat. Feet marched to the beat, many of them, light feet, marching a little shufflingly. I could hear their passing from crunched gravel to a resonance of hollow wood; they united in a rhythmic murmur, above which, like gulls eddying over the sea, sharp cries of command hovered, female cries, of women. A door slammed to with a clack as of a whip, the drum died abruptly, there was a silence, then a chorus of fresh young voices rose in song—a song which my bearded, critical self judged harshly, but which was soft to the heart of my youth. Though I thought that I must be asleep, thought that my eyes must be closed, I was aware of my host, in white, standing at one of the three southern windows. He too seemed to listen to the song. I heard him sigh a long, dolorous sigh. Then he must have returned to his bed. The song trailed away in a last, long, gentle note, and now I slept undisturbed, a tenderness tugging at my soul.

When I awoke after the long night, the room was still dark; but when to my gesture a curtain whirred open with a noise as of wings, the day came in warm with sun. I stood at the window and looked out.

I was looking deep into a large, bare yard. Children were playing there, many children, brown-headed and yellow-haired, boys and girls. Above them the layers of air, striated with sun, seemed liquid; they were like goldfish in an aquarium. They zigzagged like butterflies in their bright garments; their cries, muffled to me, came as the little cries of birds.

The front of the yard, to my right, was a big brick building pierced with many windows.

"Do you recognize the place?" Dorman asked.

I turned, and saw him standing at the casement next to mine. He seemed speaking to the glass, not to me.

"It is a school, is it not?" I fenced.

"It is our school," he said.

I looked back far into my memory, and saw that it indeed must be the school to which we had gone when young. But it had changed. The yard had been much wider then, without bonds to the south, where now rose a forest of chimneys and roofs. Then it had stretched away to the south in a grassy meadow that sloped away gently to a brook. And the school-house had not been the big brick pile it now stood. I shut my eyes, and saw again the school-house that had been. I saw clearly the little wooden house, its overlapping boards, softly gray, its peaked roof, as green as moss, the red veins of the carpeting vine, and the long outside stairway, slanting upward to the gallery, along which we marched up to our classroom under the twittering eaves.

"They have changed it, our school!" I exclaimed, absurdly resentful.

"When I returned to this city," he said, "I built here next to the school. I don't know why I built here next to the school."

A bell began to ring in the yard beneath me. The children's

crisscrossing play halted abruptly and petrified in long, decorous lines. A drum began to beat, and the little ones marched into school. The many little feet stamped the ground together; the lines flowed forward. They coiled, straightened, rose, and slid like ribbons into the yawning portals. The drum beat; the little feet tramped, tramped, tramped, along halls, up flights of stairs; the whole building trembled to the tremendous unison of their light, firm tread; and above this basic rumor the commands of the women teachers eddied like the gull's nostalgic cry.

The drum stopped, the outer doors clanged shut, a silence followed, then fresh young voices rose in choral song.

"Why, it must be what I heard last night!" I cried.

But Dorman said:

"It was not they. You heard the others."

I did not understand him.

I stayed again at Dorman's house, for he insisted, and I did not care. My sleep was troubled again that night. The covers lay upon me like a stone, and I was tomb-cold. A bell began to ring. It rang persistently. Its clangs winged off in brazen waves, struck, and rebounded, to mingle with new clangs till my brain pained.

I rose at length to its continued attack, and, groping through the velvet darkness, reached one of the windows. I parted the ponderous curtains, looked, and saw nothing. I was looking into the night, and saw only night. Little by little, though, to the fixity of my stare the blackness seemed to recede, and at last I saw in a brown obscurity. I saw a yard and a school-house. It was a small school-house, of wood. The roof was peaked. Vines veined one wall. Stairs along another wall slanted upward to a gallery beneath the eaves.

Below me, the indistinct floor of the yard was dimly striated with lines. These were animated with a fluid pulsation. After a time I understood them. Children were lined there, grave little children, many of them, with books under their arms or swinging at the end of straps.

I tried to count the children, but they were too many. I tried to count the lines, but they fluctuated like tide-water. There were many. They ran east and west from the little school-house to the fence at the back, then turned flexibly and streamed off to the south, where in my youth the land lay open. I could not see them end over there. My eyes followed them till they merged in the darkness; but even there, and beyond, the void held an undulation of fluid multitudes. Multitudes of children waited in line over there in the vague region beyond the reading of my sight.

The bell came to a stop with a last wicked rattle, and a drum began to beat. A shiver passed along the lines like a breeze; all the small forms bent slightly forward; the lines began to flow; and the night became filled with a measured, soft, and tender tramping sound which was as the muffled heart-beat of the night. The lines passed by; they came glidingly from the void in the south, swung into the yard with a lithe torsion of a fish that turns, crushed across the gravel, stamped up the planking of the stairs, flowed into the yawn of the doors. They passed, the children, by hundreds, by thousands. The stairs shook, the frail building trembled, the night was rhythmic with the soft beat of their feet. The drum beat, they passed, and still the vastness to the south palpitated obscurely with unnumbered reserves. Above the basic rumor the cries of the women were sharp.

"It is our class coming now—our own class," said a voice within the room.

I turned toward it. Dorman was at the window next to mine. Seated in his rich, red armchair, he was looking as I looked, his brow against the pane.

"How our class? How our class?" I said peevishly.

"It is our class; you see if it is not our class."

And then it was truly our class that passed, the little companions of our childhood. They came in line from the dim reservoir to the south, turned into the yard, crunched upon its gravel, and rose along the stairway to the small room beneath the eaves. Their familiar little feet hissed gently against the wooden steps, and we stood there, the two old men, each at his window, watching with cold brows upon the panes.

Dorman, as they passed, told them off to me one by one, their names and their fate. I saw Jack Bennett, the butcher's son, and I remembered that I still owed him a marble; I saw red-headed

Jack Stearns, with his pale, up-tilted nose, and the glass eye which had been our marvel and our pride; and Roscoe Miller, who had become a banker; and Starr, who had ended in the gutter; and Perry, who had wrecked himself against the things that will not move. Up the other stairs, which we could not see, I guessed that the girls were passing, and I knew that among them was a frail, blue-eyed girl—ah, how well I remembered her!

"But," I said, "all those you tell me of have died."

From his window Dorman said:

"I have noticed that. All those that pass here have died." He added after a moment: "And all those with whom we went to school pass here. The class is almost complete."

And still they passed, and still Dorman told them off. Some had been poor, some had been rich; some had been comic, and some tragic; but all had died.

Ralph Dorn passed by. He had been my best chum at school. "Ralph! Ralph!" went my lips, but made no noise, and he did not hear. But I knew now that all my life I had missed him—him and the frail, blue-eyed girl. I knew now what had been ailing my life.

"Here is Keating," said Dorman. "Watch him; he is always funny."

To the stairs came a hunchback boy. He toiled up with much labor, but did not know that he toiled, for his eyes were ahead, far, amid vapory visions; beneath his cap his hair was like a wreath of gold.

"He wrote verse, and he starved," said Dorman. "I have his book in the library; it is funny."

The poet boy toiled up uncertainly. He zigzagged a bit from side to side; the cries of the women teachers eddied over him; he slowed up the line and disordered the march; his eyes were far.

The boy behind him mischievously wiped his feet upon his stockings, but he was unaware of it. The same boy reached within his pocket and took his pencil and his knife, but still he did not notice. He let a book slip from beneath his elbow, and the boy behind trampled upon it. Finally the boy behind gave hm a push. The poet boy fell; his cap jerked off his head, his books scattered down the steps. A woman teacher picked him up and shook him ragefully, while the boy behind looked grave and reproachful.

"If I were there, I would protect him," I thought. "If I were there, I would understand him."

"Who is the boy behind?" I asked of Dorman.

"It is 'Spike' Martin," he answered. "He has been the most successful of us all. His sons are multimillionaires."

I noticed now that this was the end of all the marching. This was the last line. A length of it was still on the stairs, but the yard behind was already empty.

"It is the end," I said.

"Yes," he answered. "They have all passed now; our class is always the last."

"But wait," I said, "here comes another boy, I think."

"Are you sure?" said Dorman. "I have not missed any one."

"Yes, yes, I am sure."

From the vague somberness to the south a dim form was flitting toward us. It neared. It was a boy, running very fast, his books under his arm, his cap in hand.

"But who is that boy? Who is that boy?" Dorman murmured.

The boy was still in the twilight, not quite distinct, but he was nearing very fast. He seemed to pant for his school. Despite his fast running, his hair was orderly and a little damp with late combing, as though to the ring of the bell he had broken away from a mother's lingering touch.

"Who is that boy? Who is that boy?" mumbled Dorman.

The boy was near, and something about his square shoulders, his sturdy legs, the way he swayed slightly from right to left as he ran, gave my memory unrest.

"Who is that boy? Who is that boy?" Dorman cried.

"It seems to me I know. It seems to me I know," I said, my memory more and more restless.

"Who is that boy, Halton? Who is that boy?"

And suddenly I knew.

"It is you, Dorman, it is you!" I cried.

"No, no, Halton, don't say that. Who is that boy?"

"It is you, it is you!" I cried.

The boy came swiftly across the yard, leaped up the steps. He came to the poet boy, drew him aside eagerly, took his place, then with incredible quickness he pulled aside boy after boy till he was first and at the door.

He vanished within; the boys behind, one after the other, vanished within; the poet boy, last of the line, vanished within; the door slapped shut.

The drum stopped beating; there was a silence. I left my window and, going up to Dorman, placed a friendly hand upon his shoulder. And he was dead—dead there in his rich, red armchair, his brow still upon the cold pane.

I think I shall stay here always, and stand at the window at night, till out of the vague region to the south I see a boy come running—a last late boy come running to join his dear comrades.

III. The Terror of Weird Creatures

The Mummy's Foot

Théophile Gautier

I had entered, in an idle mood, the shop of one of those curiosity venders who are called *marchands de bric-à-brac* in that Parisian *argot* which is so perfectly unintelligible elsewhere in France.

You have doubtless glanced occasionally through the windows of some of these shops, which have become so numerous now that it is fashionable to buy antiquated furniture, and that every petty stockbroker thinks he must have his *chambre au moyen âge.*

There is one thing there which clings alike to the shop of the dealer in old iron, the ware-room of the tapestry maker, the laboratory of the chemist, and the studio of the painter: in all those gloomy dens where a furtive daylight filters in through the window-shutters the most manifestly ancient thing is dust. The cobwebs are more authentic than the guimp laces, and the old pear-tree furniture on exhibition is actually younger than the mahogany which arrived but yesterday from America.

The warehouse of my bric-à-brac dealer was a veritable Capharnaum. All ages and all nations seemed to have made their rendezvous there. An Etruscan lamp of red clay stood upon a Boule cabinet, with ebony panels, brightly striped by lines of inlaid brass; a duchess of the court of Louis XV nonchalantly extended her fawn-like feet under a massive table of the time of Louis XIII, with heavy spiral supports of oak, and carven designs of chimeras and foliage intermingled.

Upon the denticulated shelves of several sideboards glittered immense Japanese dishes with red and blue designs relieved by gilded hatching, side by side with enamelled works by Bernard Palissy, representing serpents, frogs, and lizards in relief.

From disembowelled cabinets escaped cascades of silver-lustrous Chinese silks and waves of tinsel, which an oblique sunbeam shot through with luminous beads, while portraits of every era, in frames more or less tarnished, smiled through their yellow varnish.

The striped breastplate of a damascened suit of Milanese armor glittered in one corner; loves and nymphs of porcelain, Chinese grotesques, vases of *céladon* and crackleware, Saxon and old Sèvres cups encumbered the shelves and nooks of the apartment.

The dealer followed me closely through the tortuous way contrived between the piles of furniture, warding off with his hand the hazardous sweep of my coat-skirts, watching my elbows with the uneasy attention of an antiquarian and a usurer.

It was a singular face, that of the merchant; an immense skull, polished like a knee, and surrounded by a thin aureole of white hair, which brought out the clear salmon tint of his complexion all the more strikingly, lent him a false aspect of patriarchal *bonhomie,* counteracted, however, by the scintillation of two little yellow eyes which trembled in their orbits like two louis-d'or upon quicksilver. The curve of his nose presented an aquiline silhouette, which suggested the Oriental or Jewish type. His hands—thin, slender, full of nerves which projected like strings upon the finger-board of a violin, and armed with claws like those on the terminations of bats' wings—shook with senile trembling; but those convulsively agitated hands became firmer than steel pincers or lobsters' claws when they lifted any precious article—an onyx cup, a Venetian glass, or a dish of Bohemian crystal. This strange old man had an aspect so thoroughly rabbinical and cabalistic that he would have been burnt on the mere testimony of his face three centuries ago.

"Will you not buy something from me today, sir? Here is a Malay kreese with a blade undulating like flame. Look at those grooves contrived for the blood to run along, those teeth set backward so as to tear out the entrails in withdrawing the weapon. It is a fine character of ferocious arm, and will look well in your collection. This two-handed sword is very beautiful. It is the work of Josepe de la Hera; and this *coliche-marde,* with its fenestrated guard—what a superb specimen of handicraft!"

"No; I have quite enough weapons and instruments of carnage. I want a small figure, something which will suit me as a paper-weight, for I cannot endure those trumpery bronzes which the stationers sell, and which may be found on everybody's desk."

The old gnome foraged among his ancient wares, and finally arranged before me some antique bronzes, so-called at least; fragments of malachite, little Hindoo or Chinese idols, a kind of poussah-toys in jade-stone, representing the incarnations of Brahma or Vishnoo, and wonderfully appropriate to the very undivine office of holding papers and letters in place.

I was hesitating between a porcelain dragon, all constellated with warts, its mouth formidable with bristling tusks and ranges of teeth, and an abominable little Mexican fetich, representing the god Vitziliputzili *au naturel,* when I caught sight of a charming foot, which I at first took for a fragment of some antique Venus.

It had those beautiful ruddy and tawny tints that lend to Florentine bronze that warm living look so much preferable to the gray-green aspect of common bronzes, which might easily be mistaken for statues in a state of putrefaction. Satiny gleams played over its rounded forms, doubtless polished by the amorous kisses of twenty centuries, for it seemed a Corinthian bronze, a work of the best era of art, perhaps moulded by Lysippus himself.

"That foot will be my choice," I said to the merchant, who regarded me with an ironical and saturnine air, and held out the object desired that I might examine it more fully.

I was surprised at its lightness. It was not a foot of metal, but in sooth a foot of flesh, an embalmed foot, a mummy's foot. On examining it still more closely the very grain of the skin, and the almost imperceptible lines impressed upon it by the texture of the bandages, became perceptible. The toes were slender and delicate, and terminated by perfectly formed nails, pure and transparent as agates. The great toe, slightly separated from the rest, afforded a happy contrast, in the antique style, to the position of the other toes, and lent it an aërial lightness—the grace of a bird's foot. The sole, scarcely streaked by a few almost imperceptible cross lines, afforded evidence that it had never touched the bare ground, and had only come in contact with the finest matting of Nile rushes and the softest carpets of panther skin.

"Ha, ha, you want the foot of the Princess Hermonthis!" exclaimed the merchant, with a strange giggle, fixing his owlish eyes upon me. "Ha, ha, ha! For a paperweight! An original idea!—artistic idea! Old Pharaoh would certainly have been surprised had some one told him that the foot of his adored daughter would be used for a paper-weight after he had had a mountain of granite hollowed out as a receptacle for the triple coffin, painted and gilded, covered with hieroglyphics and beautiful paintings of the Judgment of Souls," continued the queer little merchant, half audibly, as though talking to himself.

"How much will you charge me for this mummy fragment?"

"Ah, the highest price I can get, for it is a superb piece. If I had the match of it you could not have it for less than five hundred francs. The daughter of a Pharaoh! Nothing is more rare."

"Assuredly that is not a common article, but still, how much do you want? In the first place let me warn you that all my wealth consists of just five louis. I can buy anything that costs five louis, but nothing dearer. You might search my vest pockets and most secret drawers without even finding one poor five-franc piece more."

"Five louis for the foot of the Princess Hermonthis! That is very little, very little indeed. 'Tis an authentic foot," muttered the merchant, shaking his head, and imparting a peculiar rotary motion to his eyes. "Well, take it, and I will give you the bandages into the bargain," he added, wrapping the foot in an ancient damask rag. "Very fine! Real damask—Indian damask which has never been redyed. It is strong, and yet it is soft," he mumbled, stroking the frayed tissue with his fingers, through the trade-acquired habit which moved him to praise even an object of such little value that he himself deemed it only worth the giving away.

He poured the gold coins into a sort of mediæval alms-purse hanging at his belt, repeating:

"The foot of the Princess Hermonthis to be used for a paperweight!"

Then turning his phosphorescent eyes upon me, he exclaimed in a voice strident as the crying of a cat which has swallowed a fish-bone:

"Old Pharaoh will not be well pleased. He loved his daughter, the dear man!"

"You speak as if you were a contemporary of his. You are old enough, goodness knows! but you do not date back to the Pyramids of Egypt," I answered, laughingly, from the threshold.

I went home, delighted with my acquisition.

With the idea of putting it to profitable use as soon as possible, I placed the foot of the divine Princess Hermonthis upon a heap of papers scribbled over with verses, in themselves an undecipherable mosaic work of erasures; articles freshly begun; letters forgotten, and posted in the table drawer instead of the letter-box, an error to which absent-minded people are peculiarly liable. The effect was charming, *bizarre,* and romantic.

Well satisfied with this embellishment, I went out with the gravity and pride becoming one who feels that he has the ineffable advantage over all the passers-by whom he elbows, of possessing a piece of the Princess Hermonthis, daughter of Pharaoh.

I looked upon all who did not possess, like myself, a paper-weight so authentically Egyptian as very ridiculous people, and it seemed to me that the proper occupation of every sensible man should consist in the mere fact of having a mummy's foot upon his desk.

Happily I met some friends, whose presence distracted me in my infatuation with this new acquisition. I went to dinner with them, for I could not very well have dined with myself.

When I came back that evening, with my brain slightly confused by a few glasses of wine, a vague whiff of Oriental perfume delicately titillated my olfactory nerves. The heat of the room had warmed the natron, bitumen, and myrrh in which the *paraschistes,* who cut open the bodies of the dead, had bathed the corpse of the princess. It was a perfume at once sweet and penetrating, a perfume that four thousand years had not been able to dissipate.

The Dream of Egypt was Eternity. Her odors have the solidity of granite and endure as long.

I soon drank deeply from the black cup of sleep. For a few hours all remained opaque to me. Oblivion and nothingness inundated me with their sombre waves.

Yet light gradually dawned upon the darkness of my mind. Dreams commenced to touch me softly in their silent flight.

The eyes of my soul were opened, and I beheld my chamber as it actually was. I might have believed myself awake but for a vague consciousness which assured me that I slept, and that something fantastic was about to take place.

The odor of the myrrh had augmented in intensity, and I felt a slight headache, which I very naturally attributed to several glasses of champagne that we had drunk to the unknown gods and our future fortunes.

I peered through my room with a feeling of expectation which I saw nothing to justify. Every article of furniture was in its proper place. The lamp, softly shaded by its globe of ground crystal, burned upon its bracket; the water-color sketches shone under their Bohemian glass; the curtains hung down languidly; everything wore an aspect of tranquil slumber.

After a few moments, however, all this calm interior appeared to become disturbed. The woodwork cracked stealthily, the ash-covered log suddenly emitted a jet of blue flame, and the disks of the pateras seemed like great metallic eyes, watching, like myself, for the things which were about to happen.

My eyes accidentally fell upon the desk where I had placed the foot of the Princess Hermonthis.

Instead of remaining quiet, as behooved a foot which had been embalmed for four thousand years, it commenced to act in a nervous manner, contracted itself, and leaped over the papers like a startled frog. One would have imagined that it had suddenly been brought into contact with a galvanic battery. I could distinctly hear the dry sound made by its little heel, hard as the hoof of a gazelle.

I became rather discontented with my acquisition, inasmuch as I wished my paperweights to be of a sedentary disposition, and thought it very unnatural that feet should walk about without legs, and I commenced to experience a feeling closely akin to fear.

Suddenly I saw the folds of my bed-curtain stir, and heard a bumping sound, like that caused by some person hopping on one foot across the floor. I must confess I became alternately hot and cold, that I felt a strange wind chill my back, and that my suddenly rising hair caused my night-cap to execute a leap of several yards.

The bed-curtains opened and I beheld the strangest figure imaginable before me.

It was a young girl of a very deep coffee-brown complexion, like the bayadere Amani, and possessing the purest Egyptian type of perfect beauty. Her eyes were almond-shaped and oblique, with eyebrows so black that they seemed blue; her nose was exquisitely chiselled, almost Greek in its delicacy of outline; and she might indeed have been taken for a Corinthian statue of bronze but for the prominence of her cheek-bones and the slightly African fullness of her lips, which compelled one to recognize her as belonging beyond all doubt to the hieroglyphic race which dwelt upon the banks of the Nile.

Her arms, slender and spindle-shaped like those of very young girls, were encircled by a peculiar kind of metal bands and bracelets of glass beads; her hair was all twisted into little cords, and she wore upon her bosom a little idol-figure of green paste, bearing a whip with seven lashes, which proved it to be an image of Isis; her brow was adorned with a shining plate of gold, and a few traces of paint relieved the coppery tint of her cheeks.

As for her costume, it was very odd indeed.

Fancy a *pagne*, or skirt, all formed of little strips of material bedizened with red and black hieroglyphics, stiffened with bitumen, and apparently belonging to a freshly unbandaged mummy.

In one of those sudden flights of thought so common in dreams I heard the hoarse falsetto of the bric-à-brac dealer, repeating like a monotonous refrain the phrase he had uttered in his shop with so enigmatical an intonation:

"Old Pharaoh will not be well pleased. He loved his daughter, the dear man!"

One strange circumstance, which was not at all calculated to restore my equanimity, was that the apparition had but one foot; the other was broken off at the ankle!

She approached the table where the foot was starting and fidgetting about more than ever, and there supported herself upon the edge of the desk. I saw her eyes fill with pearly gleaming tears.

Although she had not as yet spoken, I fully comprehended the thoughts which agitated her. She looked at her foot—for it was indeed her own—with an exquisitely graceful expression of coquettish sadness, but the foot leaped and ran hither and thither, as though impelled on steel springs.

Twice or thrice she extended her hand to seize it, but could not succeed.

Then commenced between the Princess Hermonthis and her foot—which appeared to be endowed with a special life of its own—a very fantastic dialogue in a most ancient Coptic tongue, such as might have been spoken thirty centuries ago in the syrinxes of the land of Ser. Luckily I understood Coptic perfectly well that night.

The Princess Hermonthis cried, in a voice sweet and vibrant as the tones of a crystal bell:

"Well, my dear little foot, you always flee from me, yet I always took good care of you. I bathed you with perfumed water in a bowl of alabaster; I smoothed your heel with pumice-stone mixed with palm oil; your nails were cut with golden scissors and polished with a hippopotamus tooth; I was careful to select *tat-bebs* for you, painted and embroidered and turned up at the toes, which were the envy of all the young girls in Egypt. You wore on your great toe rings bearing the device of the sacred Scarabæus, and you supported one of the lightest bodies that a lazy foot could sustain."

The foot replied in a pouting and chagrined tone:

"You know well that I do not belong to myself any longer. I have been bought and paid for. The old merchant knew what he was about. He bore you a grudge for having refused to espouse him. This is an ill turn which he has done you. The Arab who violated your royal coffin in the subterranean pits of the necropolis of Thebes was sent thither by him. He desired to prevent you from being present at the reunion of the shadowy nations in the cities below. Have you five pieces of gold for my ransom?"

"Alas, no! My jewels, my rings, my purses of gold and silver were all stolen from me," answered the Princess Hermonthis, with a sob.

"Princess," I then exclaimed, "I never retained anybody's foot unjustly. Even though you have not got the five louis which it cost me, I present it to you gladly. I should feel unutterably wretched to think that I were the cause of so amiable a person as the Princess Hermonthis being lame."

I delivered this discourse in a royally gallant, troubadour tone which must have astonished the beautiful Egyptian girl.

She turned a look of deepest gratitude upon me, and her eyes shone with bluish gleams of light.

She took her foot, which surrendered itself willingly this time, like a woman about to put on her little shoe, and adjusted it to her leg with much skill.

This operation over, she took a few steps about the room, as though to assure herself that she was really no longer lame.

"Ah, how pleased my father will be! He who was so unhappy because of my mutilation, and who from the moment of my birth set a whole nation at work to hollow me out a tomb so deep that he might preserve me intact until that last day, when souls must be weighed in the balance of Amenthi! Come with me to my father. He will receive you kindly, for you have given me back my foot."

I thought this proposition natural enough. I arrayed myself in a dressing-gown of large-flowered pattern, which lent me a very Pharaonic aspect, hurriedly put on a pair of Turkish slippers, and informed the Princess Hermonthis that I was ready to follow her.

Before starting, Hermonthis took from her neck the little idol of green paste, and laid it on the scattered sheets of paper which covered the table.

"It is only fair," she observed, smilingly, "that I should replace your paper-weight."

She gave me her hand, which felt soft and cold, like the skin of a serpent, and we departed.

We passed for some time with the velocity of an arrow through a fluid and grayish expanse, in which half-formed silhouettes flitted swiftly by us, to right and left.

For an instant we saw only sky and sea.

A few moments later obelisks commenced to tower in the distance; pylons and vast flights of steps guarded by sphinxes became clearly outlined against the horizon.

We had reached our destination.

The princess conducted me to a mountain of rose-colored granite, in the face of which appeared an opening so narrow and low that it would have been difficult to distinguish it from the fissures in the rock, had not its location been marked by two stelæ wrought with sculptures.

Hermonthis kindled a torch and led the way before me.

We traversed corridors hewn through the living rock. Their walls, covered with hieroglyphics and paintings of allegorical processions, might well have occupied thousands of arms for thousands of years in their formation. These corridors of interminable length opened into square chambers, in the midst of which pits had been contrived, through which we descended by cramp-irons or spiral stairways. These pits again conducted us into other chambers, opening into other corridors, likewise decorated with painted sparrow-hawks, serpents coiled in circles, the symbols of the *tau* and *pedum*—prodigious works of art which no living eye can ever examine—interminable legends of granite which only the dead have time to read through all eternity.

At last we found ourselves in a hall so vast, so enormous, so immeasurable, that the eye could not reach its limits. Files of monstrous columns stretched far out of sight on every side, between which twinkled livid stars of yellowish flame; points of light which revealed further depths incalculable in the darkness beyond.

The Princess Hermonthis still held my hand, and graciously saluted the mummies of her acquaintance.

My eyes became accustomed to the dim twilight, and objects became discernible.

I beheld the kings of the subterranean races seated upon

thrones—grand old men, though dry, withered, wrinkled like parchment, and blackened with naphtha and bitumen—all wearing *pshents* of gold, and breastplates and gorgets glittering with precious stones, their eyes immovably fixed like the eyes of sphinxes, and their long beards whitened by the snow of centuries. Behind them stood their peoples, in the stiff and constrained posture enjoined by Egyptian art, all eternally preserving the attitude prescribed by the hieratic code. Behind these nations, the cats, ibixes, and crocodiles contemporary with them—rendered monstrous of aspect by their swathing bands—mewed, flapped their wings, or extended their jaws in a saurian giggle.

All the Pharaohs were there—Cheops, Chephrenes, Psammetichus, Sesostris, Amenotaph—all the dark rulers of the pyramids and syrinxes. On yet higher thrones sat Chronos and Xixouthros, who was contemporary with the deluge, and Tubal Cain, who reigned before it.

The beard of King Xixouthros had grown seven times around the granite table, upon which he leaned, lost in deep reverie, and buried in dreams.

Farther back, through a dusty cloud, I beheld dimly the seventy-two preadamite kings, with their seventy-two peoples, forever passed away.

After permitting me to gaze upon this bewildering spectacle a few moments, the Princess Hermonthis presented me to her father Pharaoh, who favored me with a most gracious nod.

"I have found my foot again! I have found my foot!" cried the princess, clapping her little hands together with every sign of frantic joy. "It was this gentleman who restored it to me."

The races of Kemi, the races of Nahasi—all the black, bronzed, and copper-colored nations repeated in chorus:

"The Princess Hermonthis has found her foot again!"

Even Xixouthros himself was visibly affected.

He raised his heavy eyelids, stroked his mustache with his fingers, and turned upon me a glance weighty with centuries.

"By Oms, the dog of Hell, and Tmei, daughter of the Sun and of Truth, this is a brave and worthy lad!" exclaimed Pharaoh, pointing to me with his sceptre, which was terminated with a lotus-flower.

"What recompense do you desire?"

Filled with that daring inspired by dreams in which nothing seems impossible, I asked him for the hand of the Princess Hermonthis. The hand seemed to me a very proper antithetic recompense for the foot.

Pharaoh opened wide his great eyes of glass in astonishment at my witty request.

"What country do you come from, and what is your age?"

"I am a Frenchman, and I am twenty-seven years old, venerable Pharaoh."

"Twenty-seven years old, and he wishes to espouse the Princess Hermonthis who is thirty centuries old!" cried out at once all the Thrones and all the Circles of Nations.

Only Hermonthis herself did not seem to think my request unreasonable.

"If you were even only two thousand years old," replied the ancient king, "I would willingly give you the princess, but the disproportion is too great; and, besides, we must give our daughters husbands who will last well. You do not know how to preserve yourselves any longer. Even those who died only fifteen centuries ago are already no more than a handful of dust. Behold, my flesh is solid as basalt, my bones are bars of steel!

"I will be present on the last day of the world with the same body and the same features which I had during my lifetime. My daughter Hermonthis will last longer than a statue of bronze.

"Then the last particles of your dust will have been scattered abroad by the winds, and even Isis herself, who was able to find the atoms of Osiris, would scarce be able to recompose your being.

"See how vigorous I yet remain, and how mighty is my grasp," he added, shaking my hand in the English fashion with a strength that buried my rings in the flesh of my fingers.

He squeezed me so hard that I awoke, and found my friend Alfred shaking me by the arm to make me get up.

"Oh, you everlasting sleeper! Must I have you carried out into the middle of the street, and fireworks exploded in your ears? It is afternoon. Don't you recollect your promise to take me with you to see M. Aguado's Spanish pictures?"

"God! I forgot all, all about it," I answered, dressing myself hurriedly. "We will go there at once. I have the permit lying there on my desk."

I started to find it, but fancy my astonishment when I beheld, instead of the mummy's foot I had purchased the evening before, the little green paste idol left in its place by the Princess Hermonthis!

The Discomfited Demon

Ambrose Bierce

I never clearly knew why I visited the old cemetery that night. Perhaps it was to see how the work of removing the bodies was getting on, for they were all being taken up and carted away to a more comfortable place where land was less valuable. It was well enough; nobody had buried himself there for years, and the skeletons that were now exposed were old mouldy affairs for which it was difficult to feel any respect. However, I put a few bones in my pocket as souvenirs. The night was one of those black, gusty ones in March, with great inky clouds driving rapidly across the sky, spilling down sudden showers of rain which as suddenly would cease. I could barely see my way between the empty graves, and in blundering about among the coffins I tripped and fell headlong. A peculiar laugh at my side caused me to turn my head, and I saw a singular old gentleman whom I had often noticed hanging about the Coroner's office, sitting cross-legged upon a prostrate tombstone.

"How are you, sir?" said I, rising awkwardly to my feet; "nice night."

"Get off my tail," answered the elderly party, without moving a muscle.

"My eccentric friend," rejoined I, mockingly, "may I be permitted to inquire your street and number?"

"Certainly," he replied, "No. 1, Marle Place, Asphalt Avenue, Hades."

"The devil!" sneered I.

"Exactly," said he; "oblige me by getting off my tail."

I was a little staggered, and by way of rallying my somewhat dazed faculties, offered a cigar: "Smoke?"

"Thank you," said the singular old gentleman, putting it under his coat; "after dinner. Drink?"

I was not exactly prepared for this, but did not know if it would be safe to decline, and so putting the proferred flask to my lips pretended to swig elaborately, keeping my mouth tightly closed the while. "Good article," said I, returning it. He simply remarked, "You're a fool," and emptied the bottle at a gulp.

"And now," resumed he, "you will confer a favour I shall highly appreciate by removing your feet from my tail."

There was a slight shock of earthquake, and all the skeletons in sight arose to their feet, stretched themselves and yawned audibly. Without moving from his seat, the old gentleman rapped the nearest one across the skull with his gold-headed cane, and they all curled away to sleep again.

"Sire," I resumed, "indulge me in the impertinence of inquiring your business here at this hour."

"My business is none of yours," retorted he, calmly; "what are you up to yourself?"

"I have been picking up some bones," I replied, carelessly.

"Then you are——"

"I am——"

"A Ghoul!"

'My good friend, you do me injustice. You have doubtless read very frequently in the newspapers of the Fiend in Human Shape whose actions and way of life are so generally denounced. Sire, you see before you that maligned party!"

There was a quick jerk under the soles of my feet, which pitched me prone upon the ground. Scrambling up, I saw the old gentleman vanishing behind an adjacent sandhill as if the devil were after him.

The Tortoise

W. F. Harvey

O ne word as to the documentary part of my story.
The letter was written by Tollerton, the butler, five weeks before his death. Sandys, to whom he addressed it, was, I believe, his brother; in any case the man was not known at Revelstoke Mansions, and the letter came back to Baldby Manor unopened.

I read it twice before it dawned upon me that the man was writing of himself. I then remembered the diary which, with the rest of his belongings, had never been claimed. Each partly explains the other. Nothing to my mind will ever explain the tortoise.

Here is the letter—

"BALDBY MANOR.

"MY DEAR TOM.—You asked in your last for particulars. I suppose, as the originator of the story, I am the only person able to supply them, but the task is rather hard. First as to the safety of the hero. You need not be alarmed about that; my stories have always ended happily.

"You wonder how it all came about so successfully. Let me give you the general hang of the plot. To begin with, the man was old, a miser, and consequently eccentric. The villain of the piece (the same in this case as the hero, you know) wanted money badly, and moreover knew where the money was kept.

"Do you remember Oppenheim's *Forensic Medicine,* and how we used to laugh over the way they always bungled these jobs? There was no bungling here, and consequently no use for the luck that attended the hero. (I still think of him as hero, you see; each man is a hero to himself.)

"The victim occasionally saw the doctor, and the doctor knew that the old fellow was suffering from a disease which might end suddenly. The hero knew that the graver symptoms of the disease were, and with diabolical cunning told the doctor's coachman how his master had begun to complain, but refused to see any medical man. Three days later that 'intelligent old butler— I rather think he must have come down in the world, poor fellow'—is stopped in the village street by Æsculapius.

"'How is your master, John?' 'Very bad, sir.' Then follows an accurate account of signs and symptoms, carefully cribbed up from old Banks's *Handbook*. Æsculapius is alarmed at the gravity of the case, but delighted at the accuracy of the observations. The butler suggests that an unofficial visit should be paid on the morrow; he complains of the responsibility. Æsculapius replies that he was about to suggest the very same thing himself. 'I fear I can do little,' he adds as he drives away.

"The old man sleeps soundly at night. The butler goes his usual round at twelve, and enters his master's room to make up the fire, and then—well, after all the rest can be imagined. De Quincey himself would have approved of the tooling, cotton-wool wrapped in a silk handkerchief. There was no subsequent bleeding, no fracture of the hyoid or thyroid, and this because the operator remembered that aphorism in Oppenheim, that murderers use unnecessary violence. Only gold is taken, and only a relatively small quantity. I have invented another aphorism: The temperate man is never caught.

"Next day the butler enters the bedroom with his master's breakfast. The tray drops to the floor with a crash, he tugs frantically at the bell-rope, and the servants rush into the room. The groom is sent off post haste for help. The doctor comes, shakes his head, and says, 'I told you so; I always feared the end would be this!'

"Even if there had been an inquest, nothing would have been discovered. The only thing at all suspicious was a slight hæmorrhage into the right conjunctiva, and that would be at best a very doubtful sign.

"The butler stays on; he is re-engaged by the new occupier, a half-pay captain, who has the sincerity not to bemoan his cousin's death.

"And here comes a little touch of tragedy. When the will is read, a sum of two hundred pounds is left to John the butler, as 'some slight reward for faithful service rendered.' Question for debate: 'Would a knowledge of the will have induced a different course of action?' It is difficult to decide. The man was seventy-seven and almost in his dotage, and, as you say, the option of taking up those copper shares is not a thing to be lightly laid aside.

"It's not a bad story, is it? But I am surprised at your wanting to hear more than I told you at first. One of the captain's friends—I have forgotten his name—met you last winter in Nice; he described you as 'respectability embalmed.' We hear all these things in the servants' hall. That I got from the parlourmaid, who was uncertain of the meaning of the phrase. Well, so long. I shall probably chuck this job at the end of the year.

"*P.S.*—Invest anything that is over in Arbutos Rubbers. They are somewhere about 67 at present, but from a straight tip I overheard in the smoke-room, they are bound to rise."

That is the letter. What follows are extracts from Tollerton's diary.

"Kingsett came in this morning with a large tortoise they had found in the kitchen-garden. I suppose it is one of the half-dozen Sir James let loose a few years ago. The gardeners are always turning them out, like the ploughshares did the skulls in that rotten poem we used to learn at school about the battle of Blenheim. This one I haven't seen before. He's much bigger than the others, a magnificent specimen of Chelonia what's-its-name.

"They brought it into the conservatory and gave it some milk, but the beast was not thirsty. It crawled to the back of the hot-water pipes, and there it will remain until the children come back from their aunt's. They are rather jolly little specimens, and like me are fond of animals.

•   •   •   •   •   •

"The warmth must have aroused the tortoise from its lethargy, for this morning I found it waddling across the floor of the hall. I took it with me into my pantry; it can sleep very well with the cockroaches in the bottom cupboard. I rather think tortoises are vegetable feeders, but I must look the matter up.

•   •   •   •   •   •

"There is something fascinating in a tortoise. This one reminds one of a cat in a kennel. Its neck muscles are wonderfully active, especially the ones that withdraw the head. There is something quite feline in the eyes—wise eyes, unlike a dog's in never for a moment betraying the purpose of the brain behind them.

•   •   •   •   •   •

"The temperature of the pantry is exactly suited to the tortoise. He keeps awake and entertains me vastly, but has apparently no wish to try the draughty passages again. A cat in a kennel is a bad simile; he is more like a god in a shrine. The shrine is old, roofed with a great ivory dome. Only occasionally do the faithful see the dweller in the shrine, and then nothing but two eyes, all-seeing and all-knowing. The tortoise should have been worshipped by the Egyptians.

•   •   •   •   •   •

"I still hear nothing from Tom; he ought to have replied by now. But he is one of those rare men whom one can trust implicitly. I often think of the events of the past two months, not at night, for I let nothing interfere with that excellent habit of sleeping within ten minutes from the time my head has touched the pillow, but in the daytime when my hands are busy over their work.

"I do not regret what I have done, though the two hundred

would weigh on my mind if I allowed it to do so. I am thankful
to say I bore my late master no ill-will. I never annoyed him; he
always treated me civilly. If there had been spite or malice on
my side I should never have acted as I did, for death would only
have removed him beyond my reach. I have found out by bitter
experience that by fostering malice one forfeits that peaceable
equanimity which to my mind is the crown of life, besides
dwarfing one's nature. As it is, I can look back with content to
the years we have spent together, and if in some future existence
we should meet again, I, for my part, shall bear no grudge.

"Tortoises do not eat cockroaches. Mine has been shut up in
a box for the last half-hour with three of the largest I can find.
They are still undevoured.

·   ·   ·   ·   ·   ·

"Some day I shall write an essay upon tortoises, or has the
thing been already botched by some one else? I should lead off
with that excellent anecdote of Sydney Smith's. A child, if I
remember, was found by that true-hearted divine stroking the
back of a tortoise. 'My dear,' he said, 'you might as well stroke
the dome of St. Paul's in order to propitiate the Dean and
Chapter.' Tortoises are not animals to be fondled. They have too
much dignity, they are far too aloof to be turned aside from their
purpose by any of our passing whims.

·   ·   ·   ·   ·   ·

"The pantry has grown too warm, and the tortoise has taken
to perambulating the passages, returning always at night to the
cupboard. He seems to have been tacitly adopted as an indoor
fixture, and what is more, he has been named. I named him.
The subject cropped up at lunch time. The captain suggested
'Percy' because he was so 'Shelley,' a poor sort of joke with
which to honour the illustrious dead, but one which of course
found favour with a table full of limerick makers. There followed a host of inappropriate suggestions. I am the last person
to deny the right of an animal to a name, but there is invariably

one name, and one name only, that is suitable. The guests seemed to think as I did, for all agreed that there was some one of whom the beast was the very image, not the vicar, not Dr. Baddely, not even Mrs. Gilchrist of the Crown. As they talked, I happened to notice an enlargement of an old portrait of Sir James, which had just come back from being framed. It showed him seated in his bath-chair, the hood of which was drawn down. He was wrapped up in his great sealskin cape; his seal-skin cap was on his head, with the flaps drawn close over his ears. His long, scraggy neck, covered with shrivelled skin, was bent forward, and his eyes shone dark and penetrating. He had not a vestige of eyebrow to shade their brilliance. The captain laughingly turned to me to end their dispute. The old man's name was on my lips. As it was, I stuttered out 'Jim,' and so Jim he is in the dining-room. He will never be anything else than Sir James in the butler's pantry.

"Tortoises do not drink milk; or, to avoid arguing from the particular to the general, Sir James does not drink milk, or indeed anything at all. If it were not so irreverent I should dearly like to try him with some of our old port.

· · · · · ·

"The children have come back. The house is full of their laughter. Sir James, of course, was a favourite at once. They take him with them everywhere, in spite of his appalling weight. If I would let them they would be only too glad to keep him upstairs in the dolls'-house: as it is, the tortoise is in the nursery half the day, unless he is being induced to beat his own record from the night-nursery door to the end of the passage.

"I still have no news of Tom. I have made up my mind to give notice next month; I well deserve a holiday.

"Oh, I must not forget. Sir James does, as I thought, take port. One of the gentlemen drank too deep last night; I think it must have been the Admiral. Anyhow there was quite a pool of dark liquid on the floor that exactly suited my purpose. I brought Sir James in. He lapped it up in a manner that seemed to me uncanny. It is the first time I ever used that word, which, till

now, has never conveyed any meaning to my mind. I must try
him some day with hot rum and water.

. . . . . .

"I was almost forgetting the fable of the hare and the tortoise.
That must certainly figure in my essay; for the steady plod plod
of Sir James as he follows one (I have taught him to do that)
would be almost pathetic if one did not remember that perseverance can never be pathetic, since perseverance means ultimate success. He reminds me of those old lines, I forget whose
they are, but I think they must be Elizabethan—

> 'Some think to lose him
> By having him confined;
> And some do suppose him,
> Poor heart, to be blind;
> But if ne'er so close ye wall him,
> Do the best that ye may,
> Blind love, if so ye call him,
> He will find out his way.
>
> 'There is no striving
> To cross his intent;
> There is no contriving
> His plots to prevent;
> But if once the message greet him
> That his True Love doth stay,
> If Death should come and meet him
> Love will find out the way.'

"I have given notice. The captain was exceedingly kind.
Kindness and considerate treatment to servants seem to belong
to the family. He said that he was more than sorry to lose me,
but quite understood my wish to settle down. He asked me if
there was any favour he could do me. I told him yes, I should
like to take 'Jim' with me. He seemed amused, but raised no
objection, but I can imagine the stormy scenes in the nursery.

"Mem. important.—There is a broken rail in the balustrade
on the top landing overlooking the hall. The captain has twice
asked me to see to it, as he is afraid one of the children might

slip through. Only the bottom part of the rail is broken, and there should be no fear of any accidents. I cannot think how with a good memory like mine I have forgotten to see to this."

These are the only extracts from Tollerton's diary that have a bearing upon what followed. They are sufficient to show his extraordinary character, his strong imagination, and his stronger self-control.

I, the negligible half-pay captain of his story, little dreamed what sort of a man had served me so well as butler; but strange as his life had been, his death was stranger.

The hall at Baldby Manor is exceedingly lofty, extending the full height of the three-storied house. It is surrounded by three landings; from the uppermost a passage leads to the nursery. The day after the last entry in the diary I was crossing the hall on my way to the study, when I noticed the gap in the banisters. I could hear distinctly the children's voices as they played in the corridor. Doubly annoyed at Tollerton's carelessness (he was usually the promptest and most methodical of servants), I rang the bell. I could see at once that he was vexed at his own for-getfulness. "I made a note of it only last night," he said. Then as we looked upward a curious smile stole across his lips. "Do you see that?" he said, and pointed to the gap above. His sight was keener than mine, but I saw at last the thing that attracted his gaze—the two black eyes of the tortoise, the withered head, the long, protruded neck stretched out from the gap in the rail. "You'll excuse a liberty, sir, I hope, from an old servant, but don't you see the extraordinary resemblance between the tortoise and the old master? He's the very image of Sir James. Look at the portrait behind you." Half instinctively I turned. I must have passed the picture scores of times in the course of a day, I must have seen it in sunlight and lamplight, from every point of view; it was a clever picture, well painted, if the subject was not exactly a pleasing one, but that was all.

Yes, I knew at once what the butler meant. It was the eyes— no, the neck—that caused the resemblance, or was it both? together with the half-open mouth with its absence of teeth.

I had been used to think of the smile as having something

akin to benevolence about it; time had seemed to be sweetening a nature once sour. Now I saw my mistake—the expression was wholly cynical. The eyes held me by their discerning power, the lips with their subtle mockery.

Suddenly the silence was broken by a cry of terror, followed by an awful crash.

I turned round in amazement.

The body of Tollerton lay stretched on the floor, strangely limp; in falling he had struck the corner of a heavy oak table.

His head lay in a little pool of blood, which the tortoise—I shudder as I think of it—was lapping greedily.

IV. The Terror of the Superhuman

Borrhomeo the Astrologer
A Monkish Tale

J. Sheridan LeFanu

A t the period of the famous plague of Milan in 1630, a frenzy
of superstition seized upon the population high and low.
Old prophecies of a diabolical visitation reserved for their city,
in that particular year of grace, prepared the way for this wild
panic of the imagination. When the plague broke out terror
seems to have acted to a degree scarcely paralleled upon the
fancy or the credulity of the people. Excitement in very many
cases produced absolutely the hallucinations of madness.
Persons deposed, in the most solemn and consistent terms, to
having themselves witnessed diabolical processions, spoken
with an awful impersonation of Satan, and been solicited amidst
scenes and personages altogether supernatural, to lend their
human agency to the nefarious designs of the fiend, by consent-
ing to disseminate by certain prescribed means, the virus of the
pestilence.

Some of the stories related of persons possessed by these
awful fancies are in print; and by no means destitute of a certain
original and romantic horror. That which I am about to tell,
however, has I believe, never been printed. At all events I saw it
only in MSS., sewed up in vellum, with a psaltery and half-a-
dozen lives of saints, in the library of the old Dominican
monastery which stands about two leagues to the north-east of
the city. With your permission I am about to give you the best
translation I was able to make of this short but odd story, of the
truth of which, judging from the company in which I found it,
the honest monks entertained no sort of doubt. You are to
remember that all sorts of tales of wonder were at that time

flying about and believed in Milan, and that many of these were authenticated in such a way as to leave no doubt as to the *bona fides* of those who believed themselves to have been eye-witnesses of what they told. Monks and country padres of course believed; but so did men who stood highest in the church, and who, unless fame belied them, believed little else.

In the year of our Lord, 1630, when Satan, by divine permission, appearing among us in person, afflicted our beautiful city of Milan with a pestilence unheard of in its severity, there lived in the *Strada Piana,* which has lately been pulled down, an astrologer calling himself Borrhomeo. Some say he came from Perrugia, others from Venice; I know not. He it was who first predicted, in the year of our Lord, 1628, by means of his art, that the pale comet which then appeared would speedily be followed, not by war or by famine, but by pestilence; which accordingly came to pass. Beside his skill in astrology, which was wonderful, he was profoundly versed in alchymy. He was a man great in stature, and strong, though old in years, and with a most reverent beard. But though seemingly austere in his life, it is said that he was given up, in secret, to enormous wickedness.

Having shut himself up in his house for more than a month, with his furnace and crucibles (truly he had made repeated and near approaches to the grand arcanum) he had arrived, as he supposed, at the moment of projection.

He collects the powder and tries it on molten lead; it was a failure. He was too wise to be angry; the long pursuit of his art had taught him patience. But while he is pondering in a profound and gloomy reverie, a retort, which he had forgotten in the furnace, explodes.

He sees in the smoke a pale young man, dressed in mourning, with black hair, and viewing him with a sad and reproachful countenance.

Borrhomeo who lived among chimæras, is not utterly overcome, as another man might be, and confronts him, amazed, indeed, but not terrified.

The stranger shook his head like a holy young confessor, who hears an evil shrift; and says he, rather sternly—"Borrhomeo! Beware of covetousness which is idolatry. On this sordid pursuit which you call a science, have you wasted your days on earth and your peace hereafter."

"Young man," says the alchymist, too much struck by the manner and reproof of the stranger to ask himself how he came there—"Wealth is power to do good as well as evil. To seek it is, therefore, an ambition as honourable as any other."

"We both know why you seek it, and how you would employ it," answers the young man gravely.

The old man's face flushed with anger at this rebuke, and he looked down frowningly to the table whereon lay the book of his spells. But he bethought him this must be a good spirit, and he was abashed. Nevertheless, he roused his courage, and shook his white mane back, and was on the point of answering sternly, when the young man said with a melancholy smile—

"Besides, you will never discover the grand arcanum—the elixir vitæ, or the philosopher's stone."

His words, which were as soft as snow flakes, fell like an iron mace upon the heart of the seer.

"Perhaps not," said the astrologer frigidly.

"Not perhaps," said the stranger.

"At all events, young man—for as such you appear—and I know what spirits seek who take that shape, the science has its charms for me; and when the pleasures of the young are as harmless as the amusements of the aged I'll hear you question mine."

"You know not what spirit you are of. As for me, I am contrite and humble—well I may," says the stranger faintly with a sigh. "Besides, what you have pursued in vain, and will never by your own researches find, I have discovered."

"What! the"——

"Yes, the tincture that can prolong life to virtual immortality, and the dust that can change that lead into gold; but I care for neither."

"Why, young man, if this be true," says Borrhomeo in a rapture of wonder, "you stand before me an angel of wisdom, in power and immortality like a god!"

"No," says the stranger, "a long-lived fellow, with a long purse—that's all."

"All?—every thing?" cries the old man. "Will you—*will you*"——

"Yes, sir, you shall see," says the young man in black. "Give me that crucible. It is all a matter of proportions. Water, clay, and air are the material of all the vegetable world—the flowers and forests, the wines and the fruits—the seed is both the laboratory and the chemist, and knows how, with the sun's help, to apportion and combine."

While he said this with the abstracted manner of one whose mind is mazed in a double reverie, while his hands work out some familiar problem, he tumbled over the alchymist's papers, and unstopped and stopped his bottles of crystals, precipitates, and elixirs—taking a little from this and a little from that, and throwing all into a small gold cup that stood on the table; but like a juggler, he moved those bottles so deftly, that the quick eyes and retentive soul of the old man vainly sought to catch or keep the order of the process. When he had done there was hardly a thimblefull.

"Is that it?" whispered the old man, twinkling with greedy eyes.

"No," said the stranger, with a sly smile, "there is one very simple ingredient which you have forgotten."

He took a large, flat, oval gold box, with some hair set under a crystal in the lid of it, and looking at it for a moment, he seemed to sigh. He tapped it like a snuff-box—there was within it a powder like vermilion, and on the inside of the lid, in the centre, was the small enamel portrait of a beautiful but sinister female face. The features were so very beautiful, and the expression so strangely blended with horror, that it fixed the gaze of the old man for a moment; and—was it illusion?—he thought he saw the face steadily dilating as if it would gradually fill the lid of the box, and even expand to human dimensions.

"Yes," said the stranger, as having taken some of the red powder, he shut the cover down again with a snap, "she was beautiful, and her lineaments are still clear and bright—nothing like darkness to keep them from fading, and so the poor little miniature is again in prison"; and he dropped the black box into his pocket.

Then he took two iron ladles, and heating in the one his powder to a white heat, and bidding the alchymist melt a pellet of lead in the other, and pour it into the ladle which held the powder, there arose a beautiful purple fire in the bottom of it, with an intense fringe of green and yellow; and when it subsided there was a little nut of gold there of the bigness of the leaden pellet.

The fiery eyes of the alchymist almost leaped from their sockets into the iron cup, and he could have clasped his marvellous visitor round the knees and worshipped him.

"And now," says the stranger very gently and earnestly, "in return for satisfying your curiosity, I ask only your solemn promise to prosecute this dread science no more. Ha! you'll not give it. Take, then, my warning, and remember the wages of this knowledge is sorrow."

"But won't you tell me how to commute—and—and—you have not produced the elixir," the old man cried.

"'Tis folly—and, as I've told you, worse—a snare," answered the young man, sighing heavily. "I came not to satisfy but to rebuke your dangerous though fruitless frenzy. Besides, I hear my friend still pacing the street. Hark! he taps at the window."

Then came a sharp rattle as of a cane tapping angrily on the window.

The young man bowed, smiling sadly, and somehow got himself away, though without hurry, yet so quickly that the old man could not reach the door till after it had closed and he was gone.

"Oaf that I am!" cried the astrologer, losing patience and stamping on the ground, "how have I let him go? He hesitated—he would have yielded—his scruples, benevolent perhaps, I could have quieted—and yet in the very crisis I was tongue-tied and motionless, and let him go!"

He pushed open the little window, from which he observed the street, and thought he saw the stranger walking round the corner, conversing with a little hunchback in a red cloak, and followed by an ugly dog.

At sight of the great white head and beard, and the fierce features of the alchymist, bleared and tanned in the smoke of his furnace, people stopped and looked. So he withdrew, and in haste got him ready for the street, waiting for no refreshment, though he had fasted long; for he had the strength as well as the stature of a giant, and forth he went.

By this time the twilight had passed into night. He had his mantle about him, and his rapier and dagger—for the streets were dangerous, and a feather in his cap, and his white beard hidden behind the fold of his cloak. So he might have passed for a tall soldier of the guard.

The pestilence kept people much within doors, and the streets more solitary than was customary. He had walked through the town two hours and more, before he met with any thing to speak of. Then—lo!—on a sudden, near the Fountain of the Lion—it being then moonlight—he discovers, in a solitude, the figure of his visitor, standing with the hunchback and the dog, which he knew by its ungainly bones, and its carrying its huge head so near the ground.

So he shouts along the silent street, "Stay a moment, signor," and he mends his pace.

But they were parting company there, it seemed, and away went the deformed, with his unsightly beast at his heels, and this way came the youth in black.

So standing full in his way, and doffing his cap, and throwing back his cloak, that his snowy beard and head might appear, and the stranger recognize him when he drew nigh. He cried—

"Borrhomeo implores thee to take pity on his ignorance."

"What! still mad?" said the young man. "This man will waste the small remnant of his years in godless search after gold and immortality; better he should know all, and feel their vanity."

"Better a thousand times!" cried the old man, in ecstacy.

"There is in this city, signor, at this time, in great secrecy, the master who taught me," says the youth, "the master of all alchymists. Many centuries since he found out the elixir vitæ. From him I've learned the few secrets that I know, and without his leave I dare not impart them. If you desire it, I will bring you before him; but, once in his presence, you cannot recede, and his conditions you must accept."

"All, all, with my whole heart. But some reasonable pleasures"——

"With your pleasures he will not interfere; he cannot change

your heart," said the young man, with one of his heavy sighs;
"but you know what gold is, and what the elixir is, and power
and immortality are not to be had for nothing."

"Lead on, signor, I'm ready," cries the old man, whose face
flushed, and his eyes burned with the fires of an evil rapture.

"Take my hand," said the young man, more stern and pale
than he had yet appeared. So he did, and his conductor seized it
with a cold gripe, and they walked swiftly on.

Now he led him through several streets, and on their way
Borrhomeo passes his notary, and, lingering a moment, asks him
whether he has a bond, signed by a certain merchant, with
whom he had contracted for a loan. The notary, who was talking
to another, says, suddenly, to that other—

"Per Baccho! I've just called to mind a matter that must be
looked after for Signor Borrhomeo"; and he called him a nick-
name, which incensed the astrologer, who struck him a lusty box
upon the ear.

"There's a humming in my ear tonight," said the notary, going
into his house; "I hope it is no sign of the plague."

So on they walked, side by side, till they reached the shop of
a vintner of no good repute. It was well known to Borrhomeo—
a house of evil resort, where the philosopher sometimes stole,
disguised, by night, to be no longer a necromancer, but a man,
and, so, from a man to become a beast.

They passed through the shop. The host, with a fat pale face,
and a villainous smile, was drawing wine, which a handsome
damsel was waiting to take away with her. He kissed her as she
paid, and she gave him a cuff on his fat white chops, and laughed.

"What's become of Signor Borrhomeo," said the girl, "that he
never comes here now."

'Why, here he is!" cried Borrhomeo, with a saturnine smile,
and he slaps his broad palm on her shoulder.

But the girl only shrugged, with a little shiver, and said, "What
a chill down my back—they're walking over my grave now."

[The Italian phrase here is very nearly equivalent.]

"Why they neither hear nor see me!" said the astrologer,
amazed.

They went into the inner room, where guests used to sit and

drink. But the plague had stopped all that, and the room was empty.

"He's in there," said the young man; "you'll see him presently."

Borrhomeo was filled with an awful curiosity. He knew the room, he thought, well; and there never had been, he thought, a door where the young man had pointed; but there was now a drapery there like what covers a doorway, and it swelled and swayed slowly in the wind.

"Some centuries?" said the astrologer, looking on the dark drapery. Geber, perhaps, or Alfarabi"——

"It matters not a pin's point what his name; you'll call him 'my lord,' simply; and—observe—wealchymists are a potent order, and it behoves you to keep your word with us."

"I will be true," said Borrhomeo.

"And use the powers you gain, beneficently," repeated his guide.

"I'm but a sinner. I will strive, with only an exception, in favour of such things as make wealth and life worth having," answered the philosopher.

"See, take this, and do as I bid you," said the youth, giving him a thin round film of human skin.

[How the honest monk who wrote the tale, or even Borrhomeo himself, knew this and many other matters he describes, 'tis for him to say.]

"Breathe on it," said he.

And when he did so he made him stretch it to the size of a sheet of paper, which he did quite easily.

"Now cover your face with it as with a napkin."

So he did.

"'Twill do; give it to me. It is but a picture. See."

And it slowly shrunk until its disc was just the same as that of the lady's miniature in the lid of the box, over which he fixed it.

Borrhomeo beheld his own picture.

"Every adept has his portrait here," said the young man. "So good a likeness is always pleasant; but these have a power beside, and establish a sympathy between their originals and their possessor which secures discipline and silence."

"How does it work?" asked Borrhomeo.

"Have I not been your good angel?" said the young man, sitting before him. He extends his legs—pushing out his feet, and letting his chin sink on his chest—he fixes his eyes upon him with a horrible and sarcastic glare, and one of his feet contracts and divides into a goatish stump.

Borrhomeo would have burst into a yell, but he could not.

"It is a nightmare, is it not?" said the stranger, who seemed delighted to hold him, minute after minute, in that spell. At last the shoe and hose that seemed to have shrunk apart like burning parchment, closed over the goatish shin and hoof; and rising, he shook him by the shoulder. With a gasp, the astrologer started to his feet.

"There, I told you it was a nightmare, or—or what you please. I could not have done it but through the picture. You see how fast we have you. You must for once resemble a Christian, Borrhomeo, and with us deal truly and honestly."

"You've promised me the elixir vitæ," the old man said, fearful lest the secret should escape him.

"And you shall have it. Go, bring a cup of wine. He'll not see you, nor the wine, nor the cup."

So he brought a cup of Falernian, which he loved the best.

"There's fifty years of life for every drop," said the youth.

"Let me live a thousand years, to begin with," cries Borrhomeo.

"Beware. You'll tire of it"——

"Nay. Give me the twenty drops."

So he took the cup, and measured the drops; and as they fell, the wine was agitated with a gentle simmer all over, and threw out ring after ring of purple, green, and gold. And Borrhomeo drank it, and sucked in the last drop in ecstacy, and cried out, blaspheming, with joy and sensual delight—

"And I'm to have this secret, too."

"This and all others, when you claim them," said the young man.

"See, 'tis time," he added.

And Borrhomeo saw that the great misshapen dog he had seen in the street, was sniffing by the stranger's feet.

When they went into the inner room there was a large table,

and many men at either side; and at the head a gigantic man, with a face like the face of a beast, but the flesh was as of a man. Borrhomeo quaked in his presence.

"I am aware of what hath passed, Borrhomeo," he said. "The condition is this:—You take this vial, and with the fluid it contains and the sponge trace the letter S on every door of every church and religious house within the walls of Milan. The dog will go with you."

It was a fiend in dog's shape, says the monkish writer; and had he failed in his task would have torn him in pieces.

So Borrhomeo, that old arch-villain, undertook this office cheerfully, well knowing what its purpose was. For it was a thing notorious, that Satan was himself in a bodily, though phantasmal, shape seen before in Milan, and that he had tempted others to a like fascinorous action; but, happily for their souls, in vain. The Stygian satellites of the fiend had power to smear the door of every unconsecrated house in Milan with that pestilential virus, as, indeed, the citizens with their own eyes, when first the plague broke out, beheld upon their own doors. But they could not defile the church gates, nor the doors of the monasteries; and according to the conditions under which their infernal malice is bound, they could in nowise effect it save by the hand of one who was baptized, which, to the baleful abuse of that holy sacrament, the wretch, Borrhomeo, had been.

He did his accursed and murderous office well and fearlessly. His reward mammon and indefinite long life. The hell-dog by his side compelling him, and the belief in his invisibility making him confident withal. But therein was shown forth to all the world the craft of the fiend, and the just judgment of heaven; for he was plainly seen in the very act by the Sexton of the Church of Saint Mary of the Passion, and by the Pastor of the convent of Saint Justina of Padua, and the same officer of the Olivetans of Saint Victor. So, finding in the morning the only too plain and fatal traces of what he had been doing, with a mob at their heels, who would have had his life but for the guard, they arrested him in his house next morning, and the mob breaking in, smashed all the instruments of his infernal art, and would have burnt the house had they been allowed.

He being duly arraigned was, according to law, put to the torture, and forthwith confessed all the particulars I have related. So he was cast into a dungeon to await execution, which secretly he dreaded not, being confident in the efficacy of the elixir he had swallowed.

He was not to be put to death by decapitation. It was justly thought too honourable for so sordid a miscreant. He was sentenced to be hanged, and after hanging a day and a night he was to be laid in an open grave outside the gate on the Roman road, and there impaled, and after three days' exposure to be covered in, and so committed to the keeping of the earth, no more to groan under his living enormities.

The night before his execution, thinking deeply on the virtue of the elixir, and having assured himself, by many notable instances, which he easily brought to remembrance, that they could not deprive him, even by this severity, of his life, he lifted up his eyes and beheld the young man, in mourning suit, whose visit had been his ruin, standing near him in the cell.

This slave of Satan affected a sad countenance at first; and said he, "We are cast down, Borrhomeo, by reason of thy sentence."

"But we've cheated them," answers he, pretending, maybe, more confidence than he had; "they can't kill me."

"That's certain," rejoins the fiend.

"I shall live for a thousand years," says he.

"Ay, you must continue to live for full one thousand years; 'tis a fair term—is it not?"

"A great deal may be done in that time," says the old man, while beads of perspiration covered his puckered forehead, and he thought that, perhaps, he might cheat *him* too, and make his peace with heaven.

"They can't hang me," says Borrhomeo.

"Oh! yes, they will certainly hang you; but, then, you'll live through it."

"Ay, the elixir," cried the prisoner.

"Thus stands the case: when an ordinary man is hanged he dies outright; but you can't die."

"No—ha, ha!—I can't die!"

"Therefore, when you are hanged, you feel, think, hear, and soforth during the process."

"St. Anthony! But then 'tis only an hour—one hour of agony—and it ends."

"You are to hang for a whole day and night," continued the fiend; "but that don't signify. Then when they take you down, you continue to feel, hear, think, and, if they leave your eyes open, to see, just as usual."

"Why, yes, certainly, I'm alive," cries Borrhomeo.

"Yes, alive, quite alive, although you appear to be dead," says the dæmon with a smile.

"Ay; but what's the best moment to make my escape?" says Borrhomeo.

"Escape! why, you *have* escaped. They can't kill you. No one can kill you, until your time is out. Then you know they lay you in an open grave and impale you."

"What! ah, ha!" roared the old sinner, "you are jesting."

"Hush! depend upon it they will go through with it."

The old man shook in every joint.

"Then, after three days and nights, they bury you," said his visitor.

"I'll lose my life, or I'll break from them!" shouts the gigantic astrologer.

"But you can't lose your life, and you can't break from them," says the fiend, softly.

"Why not? Oh! blessed saints! I'm stronger than you think."

"Ay, muscles, bones—you are an old giant!"

"Surely," cries the old man, "and the terror of a dead man rising; ha! don't you see? They fly before me, and so I escape."

"But you can't rise."

"Say—say in heaven's name what you mean," thundered old Borrhomeo.

"Do you remember, signor, that nightmare, as we jocularly called it, at the sign of the 'Red Hat'?"

"Yes."

"Well, a man who having swallowed the elixir vitæ, suffers that sort of shock which in other mortals is a violent death, is afflicted during the remainder of his period of life, whether he be decapitated, or dismembered, or is laid unmutilated in the grave, with that sort of catalepsy, which you experienced for a minute—a catalepsy that does not relax or intermit. For that reason you ought to have carefully avoided this predicament."

"'Tis a lie," roared the old man, and he ground his teeth, "*that's* not living."

"You'll find, upon my honour, that it *is* living," answered the fiend, with a gentle smile, and withdrawing from the cell.

Borrhomeo told all this to a priest, not under seal of confession, but to induce him to plead for his life. But the good man seeing he had already made himself the liegeman and accomplice of Satan, refused. Nor would his intercession have prevailed in any wise.

So Borrhomeo was hanged, impaled, and buried, according to his sentence; and it came to pass that fourteen years afterwards, that grave was opened in making a great drain from the group of houses thereby, and Borrhomeo was found just as he was laid therein, in no wise decayed, but fresh and sound, which, indeed, showed that there did remain in him that sort of life which was supposed to ward off the common consequences of death.

So he was thrown into a great pit, and with many curses, covered in with stones and earth, where his stupendous punishment proceeds.

Get thee hence, Satan.

The Diary of a God

Barry Pain

During the week there had been several thunderstorms. It was after the last of these, on a cool Saturday evening, that he was found at the top of the hill by a shepherd. His speech was incoherent and disconnected; he gave his name correctly, but could or would add no account of himself. He was wet through, and sat there pulling a sprig of heather to pieces. The shepherd afterwards said that he had great difficulty in persuading him to come down, and that he talked much nonsense. In the path at the foot of the hill he was recognized by some people from the farmhouse where he was lodging, and was taken back there. They had, indeed, gone out to look for him. He was subsequently removed to an asylum, and died insane a few months later.

• • • • • •

Two years afterwards, when the furniture of the farmhouse came to be sold by auction, there was found in a little cupboard in the bedroom which he had occupied an ordinary penny exercise-book. This was partly filled, in a beautiful and very regular handwriting, with what seems to have been something in the nature of a diary, and the following are extracts from it:

June 1st.—It is absolutely essential to be quiet. I am beginning life again, and in quite a different way, and on quite a different scale, and I cannot make the break suddenly. I must have a pause of a few weeks in between the two different lives. I saw the advertisement of the lodgings in this farmhouse in an

170

evening paper that somebody had left at the restaurant. That
was when I was trying to make the change abruptly, and I may
as well make a note of what happened.

After attending the funeral (which seemed to me an act of
hypocrisy, as I hardly knew the man, but it was expected of me)
I came back to my Charlotte Street rooms and had tea. I slept
well that night. Then next morning I went to the office at the
usual hour, in my best clothes, and with a deep band still on my
hat. I went to Mr. Toller's room and knocked. He said, "Come
in," and after I had entered: "Can I do anything for you? What
do you want?"

Then I explained to him that I wished to leave at once. He
said:

"This seems sudden, after thirty years' service."

"Yes," I replied. "I have served you faithfully for thirty years,
but things have changed, and I have now three hundred a year
of my own. I will pay something in lieu of notice, if you like, but
I cannot go on being a clerk any more. I hope, Mr. Toller, you
will not think that I speak with any impertinence to yourself,
or any immodesty, but I am really in the position of a private
gentleman."

He looked at me curiously, and as he did not say anything I
repeated:

"I think I am in the position of a private gentleman."

In the end he let me go, and said very politely he was sorry to
lose me. I said good-bye to the other clerks, even to those who
had sometimes laughed at what they imagined to be my pecu-
liarities. I gave the better of the two office-boys a small present
in money.

I went back to the Charlotte Street rooms, but there was
nothing to do there. There were figures going on in my head,
and my fingers seemed to be running up and down columns. I
had a stupid idea that I should be in trouble if Mr. Toller were
to come in and catch me like that. I went out and had a capital
lunch, and then I went to the theatre. I took a stall right in the
front row, and sat there all by myself. Then I had a cab to the
restaurant. It was too soon for dinner, so I ordered a whisky-
and-soda, and smoked a few cigarettes. The man at the table

next me left the evening paper in which I saw the advertisement
of these farmhouse lodgings. I read the whole of the paper, but
I have forgotten it all except that advertisement, and I could say
it by heart now—all about bracing air and perfect quiet and the
rest of it. For dinner I had a bottle of champagne. The waiter
handed me a list, and asked which I would prefer. I waved the
list away and said:

"Give me the best."

He smiled. He kept on smiling all through dinner until the
end; then he looked serious. He kept getting more serious. Then
he brought two other men to look at me. They spoke to me, but
I did not want to talk. I think I fell asleep. I found myself in my
rooms in Charlotte Street next morning, and my landlady gave
me notice because, she said, I had come home beastly drunk.
Then that advertisement flashed into my mind about the bracing air. I said:

"I should have given you notice in any case; this is not a suitable place for a gentleman."

June 3rd.—I am rather sorry that I wrote down the above. It
seems so degrading. However, it was merely an act of ignorance
and carelessness on my part, and, besides, I am writing solely for
myself. To myself I may own freely that I made a mistake, that
I was not used to the wine, and that I had not fully gauged what
the effects would be. The incident is disgusting, but I simply put
it behind me, and think no more about it. I pay here two pounds
ten shillings a week for my two rooms and board. I take my
meals, of course, by myself in the sitting-room. It would be
rather cheaper if I took them with the family, but I do not care
about that. After all, what is two pounds ten shillings a week?
Roughly speaking, a hundred and thirty pounds a year.

June 17th.—I have made no entry in my diary for some days.
For a certain period I have had no heart for that or for anything
else. I had told the people here that I was a private gentleman
(which is strictly true), and that I was engaged in literary pursuits. By that latter I meant to imply no more than that I am
fond of reading, and that it is my intention to jot down from time
to time my sensations and experiences in the new life which has
burst upon me. At the same time I have been greatly depressed.

Why, I can hardly explain. I have been furious with myself. Sitting in my own sitting-room, with a gold-tipped cigarette between my fingers, I have been possessed (even though I recognized it as an absurdity) by a feeling that if Mr. Toller were to come in suddenly I should get up and apologize. But the thing which depressed me most was the open country. I have read, of course, those penny stories about the poor little ragged boys who never see the green leaf in their lives, and I always thought them exaggerated. So they are exaggerated: there are the Embankment Gardens with the Press Band playing; there are parks; there are Sunday-school treats. All these little ragged boys see the green leaf, and to say they do not is an exaggeration—I am afraid a wilful exaggeration. But to see the open country is quite a different thing. Yesterday was a fine day, and I was out all day in a place called Wensley Dale. On one spot where I stood I could see for miles all round. There was not a single house, or tree, or human being in sight. There was just myself on the top of a moor; the bigness of it gave me a regular scare. I suppose I had got used to walls: I had got used to feeling that if I went straight ahead without stopping I should knock against something. That somehow made me feel safe. Out on that great moor—just as if I were the last man left alive in the world—I do not feel safe. I find the track and get home again, and I tremble like a half-drowned kitten until I see a wall again, or somebody with a surly face who does not answer civilly when I speak to him. All these feelings will wear off, no doubt, and I shall be able to enter upon the new phase of my existence without any discomfort. But I was quite right to take a few months quiet retirement. One must get used to things gradually. It was the same with the champagne—to which, by the way, I had not meant to allude any further.

June 20th.—It is remarkable what a fascination these very large moors have for me. It is not exactly fear any more—indeed, it must be the reverse. I do not care to be anywhere else. Instead of making this a mere pause between two different existences, I shall continue it. To that I have quite made up my mind. When I am out there in a place where I cannot see any trees, or houses, or living things, I am the last person left alive

in the world. I am a kind of a god. There is nobody to think anything at all about me, and it does not matter if my clothes are
not right, or if I drop an "h"—which I rarely do except when
speaking very quickly. I never knew what real independence was
before. There have been too many houses around, and too many
people looking on. It seems to me now such a common and
despicable thing to live among people, and to have one's character and one's ways altered by what they are going to think. I
know now that when I ordered that bottle of champagne I did it
far more to please the waiter and to make him think well of me
than to please myself. I pity the kind of creature that I was then,
but I had not known the open country at that time. It is a grand
education. If Toller were to come in now I should say, "Go away.
Go back to your bricks and mortar, and account-books, and
swell friends, and white waistcoats, and rubbish of that kind.
You cannot possibly understand me, and your presence irritates
me. If you do not go at once I will have the dog let loose upon
you." By the way, that was a curious thing which happened the
other day. I feed the dog, a mastiff, regularly, and it goes out
with me. We had walked some way, and had reached that spot
where a man becomes the last man alive in the world. Suddenly
the dog began to howl, and ran off home with its tail between its
legs, as if it were frightened of something. What was it that the
dog had seen and I had not seen? A ghost? In broad daylight?
Well, if the dead come back they might walk here without con-
tamination. A few sheep, a sweep of heather, a gray sky, but
nothing that a living man planted or built. They could be alone
here. If it were not that it would seem a kind of blasphemy, I
would buy a piece of land in the very middle of the loneliest
moor and build myself a cottage there.

June 23rd.—I received a letter today from Julia. Of course
she does not understand the change which has taken place in
me. She writes as she always used to write, and I find it very
hard to remember and realize that I liked it once, and was glad
when I got a letter from her. That was before I got into the habit
of going into the empty places alone. The old clerking, account-
book life has become too small to care about. The swell life of
the private gentleman, to which I looked forward, is also not

worth considering. As for Julia, I was to have married her; I used to kiss her. She wrote to say that she thought a great deal of me; she still writes. I don't want her. I don't want anything. I have become the last man alive in the world. I shall leave this farmhouse very soon. The people are all right, but they are *people,* and therefore insufferable. I can no longer live or breathe in a place where I see people, or trees which people have planted, or houses which people have built. It is an ugly word—people.

July 7th.—I was wrong in saying that I was the last man alive in the world. I believe I am dead. I know now why the mastiff howled and ran away. The whole moor is full of them; one sees them after a time when one has got used to the open country— or perhaps it is because one is dead. Now I see them by moonlight and sunlight, and I am not frightened at all. I think I must be dead, because there seems to be a line ruled straight through my life, and the things which happened on the further side of the line are not real. I look over this diary, and see some references to a Mr. Toller, and to some champagne, and coming into money. I cannot for the life of me think what it is all about. I suppose the incidents described really happened, unless I was mad when I wrote about them. I suppose that I am not dead, since I can write in a book, and eat food, and walk, and sleep and wake again. But since I see them now—these people that fill up the lonely places—I must be quite different to ordinary human beings. If I am not dead, then what am I? today I came across an old letter signed "Julia Jarvis"; the envelope was addressed to me. I wonder who on earth she was?

July 9th.—A man in a frock coat came to see me, and talked about my best interest. He wanted me, so far as I could gather, to come away with him somewhere. He said I was all right, or, at any rate, would become all right, with a little care. He would not go away until I said that I would kill him. Then the woman at the farmhouse came up with a white face, and I said I would kill her too. I positively cannot endure people. I am not alive, and I am not dead. I cannot imagine what I am.

July 16th.—I have settled the whole thing to my complete satisfaction. I can without doubt believe the evidence of my own senses. I have seen, and I have heard. I know now that I am a

god. I had almost thought before that this might be. What was
the matter was that I was too diffident: I had no self-confidence;
I had never heard before of any man, even a clerk in an old-
established firm, who had become a god. I therefore supposed
it was impossible until it was distinctly proved to be.

I had often made up my mind to go to that range of hills that
lies to the north. They are purple when one sees them far off. At
nearer view they are gray, then they become green, then one
sees a silver network over the green. The silver network is made
by streams descending in the sunlight. I climbed the hill slowly;
the air was still, and the heat was terrible. Even the water which
I drank from the running stream seemed flat and warm. As I
climbed, the storm broke. I took but little notice of it, for the
dead that I had met below on the moor had told me that lightning could not touch me. At the top of the hill I turned, and saw
the storm raging beneath my feet. It is the greatest of mercies
that I went there, for that is where the other gods gather, at such
times as the lightning plays between them and the earth, and
the black thunder-clouds, hanging low, shut them out from the
sight of men.

Some of the gods were rather like the big pictures that I have
seen on the hoardings advertising plays at the theatre, or some
food which is supposed to give great strength and muscular
development. They were handsome in face, and without any
expression. They never seemed to be angry or pleased, or hurt.
They sat there in great long rows, resting, with the storm raging
in between them and the earth. One of them was a woman. I
spoke to her, and she told me that she was older than this earth;
yet she had the face of a young girl, and her eyes were like eyes
that I have seen before somewhere. I cannot think where I saw
the eyes like those of the goddess, but perhaps it was in that part
of my life which is forgotten and ruled off with a line. It gave
one the greatest and most majestic feelings to stand there with
the gods, and to know that one was a god one's self, and that
lightning did not hurt one, and that one would live for ever.

July 18th.—This afternoon the storm returned, and I hurried
to the meeting-place, but it is far away to the hills, and though I

climbed as quickly as I could the storm was almost passed, and
they had gone.

August 1st.—I was told in my sleep that to-morrow I was to
go back to the hill again, and that once more the gods would be
there, and that the storm would gather round us, and would shut
us from profane sight, and the steely lightnings would blind any
eye that tried to look upon us. For this reason I have refused
now to eat or drink anything; I am a god and have no need of
such things. It is strange that now when I see all real things so
clearly and easily—the ghosts of the dead that walk across the
moors in the sunlight and the concourse of the gods on the hill-
top above the storm—men and women with whom I once
moved before I became a god are no more to me than so many
black shadows. I scarcely know one from the other, only that the
presence of a black shadow anywhere near me makes me angry,
and I desire to kill it. That will pass away; it is probably some
faint relic of the thing that I once was in the other side of my life
on the other side of the line which has been ruled across it.
Seeing that I am a god it is not natural that I can feel anger or
joy any more. Already all feeling of joy has gone from me, for to-
morrow, so I was told in my sleep, I am to be betrothed to the
beautiful goddess that is older than the world, and yet looks like
a young girl, and she is to give me a sprig of heather as a token
and——

·   ·   ·   ·   ·   ·

It was on the evening of August 1 he was found.

The Three Drugs

E. Nesbit

I

Roger Wroxham looked round his studio before he blew out the candle, and wondered whether, perhaps, he looked for the last time. It was large and empty, yet his trouble had filled it, and, pressing against him in the prison of those four walls, forced him out into the world, where lights and voices and the presence of other men should give him room to draw back, to set a space between it and him, to decide whether he would ever face it again—he and it alone together. The nature of his trouble is not germane to this story. There was a woman in it, of course, and money, and a friend, and regrets and embarrassments—and all of these reached out tendrils that wove and interwove till they made a puzzle-problem of which heart and brain were now weary. It was as though his life depended on his deciphering the straggling characters traced by some spider who, having fallen into the ink-well, had dragged clogged legs in a black zig-zag across his map of the world.

He blew out the candle and went quietly downstairs. It was nine at night, a soft night of May in Paris. Where should he go? He thought of the Seine, and took—an omnibus. The chestnut trees of the Boulevards brushed against the sides of the one that he boarded blindly in the first light street. He did not know where the omnibus was going. It did not matter. When at last it stopped he got off, and so strange was the place to him that for an instant it almost seemed as though the trouble itself had been left behind. He did not feel it in the length of three or four streets that he traversed slowly. But in the open space, very light and lively, where he recognised the Taverne de Paris and knew himself in Montmartre, the trouble set its teeth in his heart

178

again, and he broke away from the lamps and the talk to struggle with it in the dark quiet streets beyond.

A man braced for such a fight has little thought to spare for the details of his surroundings. The next thing that Wroxham knew of the outside world was the fact that he had known for some time that he was not alone in the street. There was someone on the other side of the road keeping pace with him—yes, certainly keeping pace, for, as he slackened his own, the feet on the other pavement also went more slowly. And now they were four feet, not two. Where had the other man sprung from? He had not been there a moment ago. And now, from an archway a little ahead of him, a third man came.

Wroxham stopped. Then three men converged upon him, and, like a sudden magic-lantern picture on a sheet prepared, there came to him all that he had heard and read of Montmartre—dark archways, knives, Apaches, and men who went away from homes where they were beloved and never again returned. He, too—well, if he never returned again, it would be quicker than the Seine, and, in the event of ultramundane possibilities, safer.

He stood still and laughed in the face of the man who first reached him.

"Well, my friend?" said he, and at that the other two drew close.

"Monsieur walks late," said the first, a little confused, as it seemed, by that laugh.

"And will walk still later, if it pleases him," said Roger. "Goodnight, my friends."

"Ah!" said the second, "friends do not say adieu so quickly. Monsieur will tell us the hour."

"I have not a watch," said Roger, quite truthfully.

"I will assist you to search for it," said the third man, and laid a hand on his arm.

Roger threw it off. That was instinctive. One may be resigned to a man's knife between one's ribs, but not to his hands pawing one's shoulders. The man with the hand staggered back.

"The knife searches more surely," said the second.

"No, no," said the third quickly, "he is too heavy. I for one will not carry him afterwards."

They closed round him, hustling him between them. Their
pale, degenerate faces spun and swung round him in the struggle.
For there was a struggle. He had not meant that there should be
a struggle. Someone would hear—someone would come.

But if any heard, none came. The street retained its empty
silence, the houses, masked in close shutters, kept their reserve.
The four were wrestling, all pressed close together in a writhing
bunch, drawing breath hardly through set teeth, their feet slipping, and not slipping, on the rounded cobble-stones.

The contact with these creatures, the smell of them, the
warm, greasy texture of their flesh as, in the conflict, his face or
neck met neck or face of theirs—Roger felt a cold rage possess
him. He wrung two clammy hands apart and threw something
off—something that staggered back clattering, fell in the gutter,
and lay there.

It was then that Roger felt the knife. Its pointed glanced off
the cigarette-case in his breast pocket and bit sharply at his inner
arm. And at the sting of it Roger knew that he did not desire to
die. He feigned a reeling weakness, relaxed his grip, swayed sideways, and then suddenly caught the other two in a new grip,
crushed their faces together, flung them off, and ran. It was but
for an instant that his feet were the only ones that echoed in the
street. Then he knew that the others too were running.

It was like one of those nightmares wherein one runs for ever,
leaden-footed, through a city of the dead. Roger turned sharply
to the right. The sound of the other footsteps told that the pur-
suers also had turned that corner. Here was another street—a
steep ascent. He ran more swiftly—he was running now for his
life—the life that he held so cheap three minutes before. And
all the streets were empty—empty like dream-streets, with all
their windows dark and unhelpful, their doors fast closed against
his need.

Far away down the street and across steep roofs lay Paris,
poured out like a pool of light in the mist of the valley. But
Roger was running with his head down—he saw nothing but the
round heads of the cobble stones. Only now and again he
glanced to right or left, if perchance some window might show
light to justify a cry for help, some door advance the welcome of
an open inch.

There was at last such a door. He did not see it till it was almost behind him. Then there was the drag of the sudden stop—the eternal instant of indecision. Was there time? There must be. He dashed his fingers through the inch-crack, grazing the backs of them, leapt within, drew the door after him, felt madly for a lock or bolt, found a key, and, hanging his whole weight on it, strove to get the door home. The key turned. His left hand, by which he braced himself against the door-jamb, found a hook and pulled on it. Door and door-post met—the latch clicked—with a spring as it seemed. He turned the key, leaning against the door, which shook to the deep sobbing breaths that shook him, and to the panting bodies that pressed a moment without. Then someone cursed breathlessly outside; there was the sound of feet that went away.

Roger was alone in the strange darkness of an arched carriage-way, through the far end of which showed the fainter darkness of a courtyard, with black shapes of little formal tubbed orange trees. There was no sound at all there but the sound of his own desperate breathing; and, as he stood, the slow, warm blood crept down his wrist, to make a little pool in the hollow of his hanging, half-clenched hand. Suddenly he felt sick.

This house, of which he knew nothing, held for him no terrors. To him at that moment there were but three murderers in all the world, and where they were not, there safety was. But the spacious silence that soothed at first, presently clawed at the set, vibrating nerves already overstrained. He found himself listening, listening, and there was nothing to hear but the silence, and once, before he thought to twist his handkerchief round it, the drip of blood from his hand.

By and by, he knew that he was not alone in this house, for from far away there came the faint sound of a footstep, and, quite near, the faint answering echo of it. And at a window, high up on the other side of the courtyard, a light showed. Light and sound and echo intensified, the light passing window after window, till at last it moved across the courtyard, and the little trees threw back shifting shadows as it came towards him—a lamp in the hand of a man.

It was a short, bald man, with pointed beard and bright, friendly eyes. He held the lamp high as he came, and when he saw Roger, he drew his breath in an inspiration that spoke of surprise, sympathy, and pity.

"Hold! hold!" he said, in a singularly pleasant voice, "there has been a misfortune? You are wounded, monsieur?"

"Apaches," said Roger, and was surprised at the weakness of his own voice.

"Your hand?"

"My arm," said Roger.

"Fortunately," said the other, "I am a surgeon. Allow me."

He set the lamp on the step of a closed door, took off Roger's coat, and quickly tied his own handkerchief round the wounded arm.

"Now," he said, "courage! I am alone in the house. No one comes here but me. If you can walk up to my rooms, you will save us both much trouble. If you cannot, sit here and I will fetch you a cordial. But I advise you to try and walk. That *porte cochère* is, unfortunately, not very strong, and the lock is a common spring lock, and your friends may return with *their* friends; whereas the door across the courtyard is heavy and the bolts are new."

Roger moved towards the heavy door whose bolts were new. The stairs seemed to go on for ever. The doctor lent his arm, but the carved bannisters and their lively shadows whirled before Roger's eyes. Also, he seemed to be shod with lead, and to have in his legs bones that were red-hot. Then the stairs ceased, and there was light, and a cessation of the dragging of those leaden feet. He was on a couch, and his eyes might close. There was no need to move any more, nor to look, nor to listen.

When next he saw and heard, he was lying at ease, the close intimacy of a bandage clasping his arm, and in his mouth the vivid taste of some cordial.

The doctor was sitting in an armchair near a table, looking benevolent through gold-rimmed pince-nez.

"Better?" he said. "No, lie still, you'll be a new man soon."

"I am desolated," said Roger, "to have occasioned you all this trouble."

"Not at all," said the doctor. "We live to heal, and it is a nasty cut, that in your arm. If you are wise, you will rest at present. I shall be honoured if you will be my guest for the night."

Roger again murmured something about trouble.

"In a big house like this," said the doctor, as it seemed a little sadly, "there are many empty rooms, and some rooms which are not empty. There is a bed altogether at your service, monsieur, and I counsel you not to delay in seeking it. You can walk?"

Wroxham stood up. "Why, yes," he said, stretching himself. "I feel, as you say, a new man."

A narrow bed and rush-bottomed chair showed like doll's-house furniture in the large, high, gaunt room to which the doctor led him.

"You are too tired to undress yourself," said the doctor, "rest—only rest," and covered him with a rug, roundly tucked him up, and left him.

"I leave the door open," he said, "in case you have any fever. Good night. Do not torment yourself. All goes well."

Then he took away the lamp, and Wroxham lay on his back and saw the shadows of the window-frames cast on the wall by the moon now risen. His eyes, growing accustomed to the darkness, perceived the carving of the white panelled walls and mantelpiece. There was a door in the room, another door from the one which the doctor had left open. Roger did not like open doors. The other door, however, was closed. He wondered where it led, and whether it were locked. Presently he got up to see. It was locked. He lay down again.

His arm gave him no pain, and the night's adventure did not seem to have overset his nerves. He felt, on the contrary, calm, confident, extraordinarily at ease, and master of himself. The trouble—how could that ever have seemed important? This calmness—it felt like the calmness that precedes sleep. Yet sleep was far from him. What was it that kept sleep away? The bed was comfortable—the pillows soft. What was it? It came to him presently that it was the scent which distracted him, worrying him with a memory that he could not define. A faint scent of—what was it? Perfumery? Yes—and camphor—and something else—something vaguely disquieting. He had not noticed it before he had risen and tried the handle of that other door. But now—— He covered his face with the sheet, but through the sheet he smelt it still. He rose and threw back one of the

long French windows. It opened with a click and a jar, and he
looked across the dark well of the courtyard. He leaned out,
breathing the chill, pure air of the May night, but when he withdrew his head, the scent was there again. Camphor—perfume—and something else. What was it that it reminded him
of? He had his knee on the bed-edge when the answer came to
that question. It was the scent that had struck at him from a
darkened room when, a child, clutching at a grown-up hand, he
had been led to the bed where, amid flowers, something white
lay under a sheet—his mother they had told him. It was the
scent of death, disguised with drugs and perfumes.

He stood up and went, with carefully controlled swiftness,
towards the open door. He wanted light and a human voice. The
doctor was in the room upstairs; he——

The doctor was face to face with him on the landing, not a
yard away, moving towards him quietly in shoeless feet.

"I can't sleep," said Wroxham, a little wildly, "it's too dark——"

"Come upstairs," said the doctor, and Wroxham went.

There was comfort in the large, lighted room, with its shelves
and shelves full of well-bound books, its tables heaped with
papers and pamphlets—its air of natural everyday work. There
was a warmth of red curtain at the windows. On the window ledge
a plant in a pot, its leaves like red misshapen hearts. A green-
shaded lamp stood on the table. A peaceful, pleasant interior.

"What's behind that door," said Wroxham, abruptly—"that
door downstairs?"

"Specimens," the doctor answered, "preserved specimens.
My line is physiological research. You understand?"

So that was it.

"I feel quite well, you know," said Wroxham, laboriously
explaining—"fit as any man—only I can't sleep."

"I see," said the doctor.

"It's the scent from your specimens, I think," Wroxham went
on; "there's something about that scent——"

"Yes," said the doctor.

"It's very odd." Wroxham was leaning his elbow on his knee
and his chin on his hand. "I feel so frightfully well—and yet—
there's a strange feeling——"

"Yes," said the doctor. "Yes, tell me exactly what you feel."

"I feel," said Wroxham, slowly, "like a man on the crest of a wave."

The doctor stood up.

"You feel well, happy, full of life and energy—as though you could walk to the world's end, and yet——"

"And yet," said Roger, "as though my next step might be my last—as though I might step into my grave."

He shuddered.

"Do you," asked the doctor, anxiously—"do you feel thrills of pleasure—something like the first waves of chloroform—thrills running from your hair to your feet?"

"I felt all that," said Roger, slowly, "downstairs before I opened the window."

The doctor looked at his watch, frowned and got up quickly. "There is very little time," he said.

Suddenly Roger felt an unexplained opposition stiffen his mind.

The doctor went to a long laboratory bench with bottle-filled shelves above it, and on it crucibles and retorts, test tubes, beakers—all a chemist's apparatus—reached a bottle from a shelf, and measured out certain drops into a graduated glass, added water, and stirred it with a glass rod.

"Drink that," he said.

"No," said Roger, and as he spoke a thrill like the first thrill of the first chloroform wave swept through him, and it was a thrill, not of pleasure, but of pain. "No," he said, and "Ah!" for the pain was sharp.

"If you don't drink," said the doctor, carefully, "you are a dead man."

"You may be giving me poison," Roger gasped, his hands at his heart.

"I may," said the doctor. "What do you suppose poison makes you feel like? What do you feel like now?"

"I feel," said Roger, "like death."

Every nerve, every muscle thrilled to a pain not too intense to be underlined by a shuddering nausea.

"Then drink," cried the doctor, in tones of such cordial entreaty, such evident anxiety, that Wroxham half held his hand out for the glass. "Drink! Believe me, it is your only chance."

Again the pain swept through him like an electric current. The beads of sweat sprang out on his forehead.

"That wound," the doctor pleaded, standing over him with the glass held out. "For God's sake, drink! Don't you understand, man? You *are* poisoned. Your wound——"

"The knife?" Wroxham murmured, and as he spoke, his eyes seemed to swell in his head, and his head itself to grow enormous. "Do you know the poison—and its antidote?"

"I know all." The doctor soothed him. "Drink, then, my friend."

As the pain caught him again in a clasp more close than any lover's he clutched at the glass and drank. The drug met the pain and mastered it. Roger, in the ecstasy of pain's cessation, saw the world fade and go out in a haze of vivid violet.

II

Faint films of lassitude, shot with contentment, wrapped him round. He lay passive, as a man lies in the convalescence that follows a long fight with Death. Fold on fold of white peace lay all about him.

"I'm better now," he said, in a voice that was a whisper—tried to raise his hand from where it lay helpless in his sight, failed, and lay looking at it in confident repose—"much better."

"Yes," said the doctor, and his pleasant, soft voice had grown softer, pleasanter. "You are now in the second stage. An interval is necessary before you can pass to the third. I will enliven the interval by conversation. Is there anything you would like to know?"

"Nothing," said Roger; "I am quite contented."

"This is very interesting," said the doctor. "Tell me exactly how you feel."

Roger faintly and slowly told him.

"Ah!" the doctor said, "I have not before heard this. You are the only one of them all who ever passed the first stage. The others——"

"The others? said Roger, but he did not care much about the others.

"The others," said the doctor frowning, "were unsound. Decadent students, degenerate, Apaches. You are highly trained—in fine physical condition. And your brain! God be good to the Apaches, who so delicately excited it to just the degree of activity needed for my purpose."

"The others?" Wroxham insisted.

"The others? They are in the room whose door was locked. Look—you should be able to see them. The second drug should lay your consciousness before me, like a sheet of white paper on which I can write what I choose. If I choose that you should see my specimens—*Allons donc.* I have no secrets from you now. Look—look—strain your eyes. In theory, I know all that you can do and feel and see in this second stage. But practically— enlighten me—look—shut your eyes and look!"

Roger closed his eyes and looked. He saw the gaunt, uncarpeted staircase, the open doors of the big rooms, passed to the locked door, and it opened at his touch. The room inside was like the others, spacious and panelled. A lighted lamp with a blue shade hung from the ceiling, and below it an effect of spread whiteness. Roger looked. There *were* things to be seen.

With a shudder he opened his eyes on the doctor's delightful room, the doctor's intent face.

"What did you see?" the doctor asked. "Tell me!"

"Did you kill them all?" Roger asked back.

"They died—of their own inherent weakness," the doctor said. "And you saw them?"

"I saw," said Roger, "the quiet people lying all along the floor in their death clothes—the people who have come in at that door of yours that is a trap—for robbery, or curiosity, or shelter, and never gone out any more."

"Right," said the doctor. "Right. My theory is proved at every point. You can see what I choose you to see. Yes, decadents all. It was in embalming that I was a specialist before I began these other investigations."

"What," Roger whispered—"what is it all for?"

"To make the superman," said the doctor. "I will tell you."

He told. It was a long story—the story of a man's life, a man's work, a man's dreams, hopes, ambitions.

"The secret of life," the doctor ended. "That is what all the alchemists sought. They sought it where Fate pleased. I sought it where I have found it—in death."

Roger thought of the room behind the locked door.

"And the secret is?" he asked.

"I have told you," said the doctor impatiently; "it is in the third drug that life—splendid, superhuman life—is found. I have tried it on animals. Always they became perfect, all that an animal should be. And more, too—much more.They were too perfect, too near humanity. They looked at me with human eyes. I could not let them live. Such animals it is not necessary to embalm. I had a laboratory in those days—and assistants. They called me the Prince of Vivisectors."

The man on the sofa shuddered.

"I am naturally," the doctor went on, "a tender-hearted man. You see it in my face; my voice proclaims it. Think what I have suffered in the sufferings of these poor beasts who never injured me. My God! Bear witness that I have not buried my talent. I have been faithful. I have laid down all—love, and joy, and pity, and the little beautiful things of life—all, all, on the altar of science, and seen them consume away. I deserve my heaven, if ever man did. And now by all the saints in heaven I am near it!"

"What is the third drug?" Roger asked, lying limp and flat on his couch.

"It is the Elixir of Life," said the doctor. "I am not its discoverer; the old alchemists knew it well, but they failed because they sought to apply the elixir to a normal—that is, a diseased and faulty—body. I knew better. One must have first a body abnormally healthy, abnormally strong. Then, not the elixir, but the two drugs that prepare. The first excites prematurely the natural conflict between the principles of life and death, and then, just at the point where Death is about to win his victory, the second drug intensifies life so that it conquers—intensifies, and yet chastens. Then the whole life of the subject, risen to an ecstasy, falls prone in an almost voluntary submission to the coming super-life. Submission—submission! The garrison must surrender before the splendid conqueror can enter and make the citadel his own. Do you understand? Do you submit?"

"I submit," said Roger, for, indeed, he did. "But—soon—quite soon—I will not submit."

He was too weak to be wise, or those words had remained unspoken.

The doctor sprang to his feet.

"It works too quickly!" he cried. "Everything works too quickly with you. Your condition is too perfect. So now I bind you."

From a drawer beneath the bench where the bottles gleamed, the doctor drew rolls of bandages—violet, like the haze that had drowned, at the urgence of the second drug, the consciousness of Roger. He moved, faintly resistant, on his couch. The doctor's hands, most gently, most irresistibly, controlled his movement.

"Lie still," said the gentle, charming voice. "Lie still; all is well." The clever, soft hands were unrolling the bandages—passing them round arms and throat—under and over the soft narrow couch. "I cannot risk your life, my poor boy. The least movement of yours might ruin everything. The third drug, like the first, must be offered directly to the blood which absorbs it. I bound the first drug as an unguent upon your knife-wound."

The swift hands, the soft bandages, passed back and forth, over and under—flashes of violet passed to and fro in the air, like the shuttle of a weaver through his warp. As the bandages clasped his knees, Roger moved.

"For God's sake, no!" the doctor cried; "the time is so near. If you cease to submit it is death."

With an incredible, accelerated swiftness he swept the bandages round and round knees and ankles, drew a deep breath—stood upright.

"I must make an incision," he said—"in the head this time. It will not hurt. See! I spray it with the Constantia Nepenthe; that also I discovered. My boy, in a moment you know all things—you are as God. For God's sake, be patient. Preserve your submission."

And Roger, with life and will resurgent hammering at his heart, preserved it.

He did not feel the knife that made the cross-cut on his temple, but he felt the hot spurt of blood that followed the cut; he felt the cool flap of a plaster, spread with some sweet, clean-smelling unguent that met the blood and stanched it. There was a moment—or was it hours?—of nothingness. Then from that cut on his forehead there seemed to radiate threads of infinite length, and of a strength that one could trust to—threads that linked one to all knowledge past and present. He felt that he controlled all wisdom, as a driver controls his four-in-hand. Knowledge, he perceived, belonged to him, as the air belongs to the eagle. He swam in it, as a great fish in a limitless ocean.

He opened his eyes and met those of the doctor, who sighed as one to whom breath has grown difficult.

"Ah, all goes well. Oh, my boy, was it not worth it? What do you feel?"

"I. Know. Everything," said Roger, with full stops between the words.

"Everything? The future?"

"No. I know all that man has ever known."

"Look back—into the past. See someone. See Pharaoh. You see him—on his throne?"

"Not on his throne. He is whispering in a corner of his great gardens to a girl, who is the daughter of a water-carrier."

"Bah! Any poet of my dozen decadents, who lie so still could have told me that. Tell me secrets—the *Masque de Fer.*"

The other told a tale, wild and incredible, but it satisfied the teller.

"That too—it might be imagination. Tell me the name of the woman I loved and——"

The echo of the name of the anæsthetic came to Roger; "Constantia," said he, in an even voice.

"Ah," the doctor cried, "now I see you know all things. It was not murder. I hoped to dower her with all the splendours of the superlife."

"Her bones lie under the lilacs, where you used to kiss her in the spring," said Roger, quite without knowing what it was that he was going to say.

"It is enough," the doctor cried. He sprang up, ranged certain bottles and glasses on a table convenient to his chair. "You know all things. It is not a dream, this, the dream of my life. It is true. It is a fact accomplished. Now I, too, will know all things. I will be as the gods."

He sought among leather cases on a far table, and came back swiftly into the circle of light that lay below the green-shaded lamp.

Roger, floating contentedly on the new sea of knowledge that seemed to support him, turned eyes on the trouble that had driven him out of that large, empty studio so long ago, so far away. His new-found wisdom laughed at that problem, laughed and solved it. "To end that trouble I must do so-and-so, say such-and-such," Roger told himself again and again.

And now the doctor, standing by the table, laid on it his pale, plump hand outspread. He drew a knife from a case—a long, shiny knife—and scored his hand across and across its back, as a cook scores pork for cooking. The slow blood followed the cuts in beads and lines.

Into the cuts he dropped a green liquid from a little bottle, replaced its stopper, bound up his hand and sat down.

"The beginning of the first stage," he said; "almost at once I shall begin to be a new man. It will work quickly. My body, like yours, is sane and healthy."

There was a long silence.

"Oh, but this is good," the doctor broke it to say. "I feel the hand of Life sweeping my nerves like harp-strings."

Roger had been thinking, the old common sense that guides an ordinary man breaking through this consciousness of illimitable wisdom. "You had better," he said, "unbind me; when the hand of Death sweeps your nerves, you may need help."

"No," the doctor said, "and no, and no, and no many times. I am afraid of you. You know all things, and even in your body you are stronger than I. When I, too, am a god, and filled with the wine of knowledge, I will loose you, and together we will drink of the fourth drug—the mordant that shall fix the others and set us eternally on a level with the immortals."

"Just as you like, of course," said Roger, with a conscious effort after commonplace. Then suddenly, not commonplace any more—

"Loose me!" he cried; "loose me, I tell you! I am wiser than you."

"You are also stronger," said the doctor, and then suddenly and irresistibly the pain caught him. Roger saw his face contorted with agony, his hands clench on the arm of his chair; and it seemed that, either this man was less able to bear pain than he, or that the pain was much more violent than had been his own. Between the grippings of the anguish the doctor dragged on his watch-chain; the watch leapt from his pocket, and rattled as his trembling hand laid it on the table.

"Not yet," he said, when he had looked at its face, "not yet, not yet, not yet." It seemed to Roger, lying there bound, that the other man repeated those words for long days and weeks. And the plump, pale hand, writhing and distorted by anguish, again and again drew near to take the glass that stood ready on the table, and with convulsive self-restraint again and again drew back without it.

The short May night was waning—the shiver of dawn rustled the leaves of the plant whose leaves were like red misshaped hearts.

"Now!" The doctor screamed the word, grasped the glass, drained it and sank back in his chair. His hand struck the table beside him. Looking at his limp body and head thrown back, one could almost see the cessation of pain, the coming of kind oblivion.

III

The dawn had grown to daylight, a poor, gray, rain-stained daylight, not strong enough to pierce the curtains and persiennes, and yet not so weak but that it could mock the lamp, now burnt low and smelling vilely.

Roger lay very still on his couch, a man wounded, anxious, and extravagantly tired. In those hours of long, slow dawning, face to face with the unconscious figure in the chair, he had felt, slowly and little by little, the recession of that sea of knowledge on which he had felt himself float in such content. The sea had withdrawn itself, leaving him high and dry on the shore of the normal. The only relic that he had clung to and that he still grasped was the answer to the problem of the trouble—the only wisdom that he had put into words. These words remained to him, and he knew that they held wisdom—very simple wisdom, too.

"To end the trouble, I must do so-and-so and say such-and-such."

But of all that had seemed to set him on a pinnacle, had evened him with the immortals, nothing else was left. He was just Roger Wroxham—wounded, and bound, in a locked house, one of whose rooms was full of very quiet people, and in another room himself and a dead man. For now it was so long since the doctor had moved that it seemed he must be dead. He had got to know every line of that room, every fold of drapery, every flower on the wall-paper, the number of the books, the shapes and sizes of things. Now he could no longer look at these. He looked at the other man.

Slowly a dampness spread itself over Wroxham's forehead and tingled among the roots of his hair. He writhed in his bonds. They held fast. He could not move hand or foot. Only his head could turn a little, so that he could at will see the doctor or not see him. A shaft of desolate light pierced the persienne at its hinge and rested on the table, where an overturned glass lay.

Wroxham thrilled from head to foot. The body in the chair stirred—hardly stirred—shivered rather—and a very faint, far-away voice said:—

"Now the third—give me the third."

"What?" said Roger, stupidly; and he had to clear his throat twice before he could say even that.

"The moment is now," said the doctor. "I remember all. I made you a god. Give me the third drug."

"Where is it?" Roger asked.

"It is at my elbow," the doctor murmured. "I submit—I submit. Give me the third drug, and let me be as you are."

"As *I* am?" said Roger. "You forget. *I* am bound."

"Break your bonds," the doctor urged, in a quick, small voice. "I trust you now. You are stronger than all men, as you are wiser. Stretch your muscles, and the bandages will fall asunder like snow-wreaths."

"It is too late," Wroxham said, and laughed; "all that is over. I am not wise any more, and I have only the strength of a man. I am tired and wounded. I cannot break your bonds—I cannot help you!"

"But if you cannot help me—it is death," said the doctor.

'It is death," said Roger. "Do you feel it coming on you?"

"I feel life returning," said the doctor; "it is now the moment—the one possible moment. And I cannot reach it. Oh, give it me—give it me!"

Then Roger cried out suddenly, in a loud voice: "Now, by God in heaven, you damned decadent, I am *glad* that I cannot give it. Yes, if it costs me my life, it's worth it, you madman, so that your life ends too. Now be silent, and die like a man, if you have it in you."

Only one word seemed to reach the man in the chair.

"A decadent!" he repeated. "I? But no, I am like you—I see what I will. I close my eyes, and I see—no—not that—ah!—not that!" He writhed faintly in his chair, and to Roger it seemed that for that writhing figure there would be no return of power and life and will.

"Not that," he moaned. "Not that," and writhed in a gasping anguish that bore no more words.

Roger lay and watched him, and presently he writhed from the chair to the floor, tearing feebly at it with his fingers, moaned, shuddered, and lay very still.

Of all that befell Roger in that house, the worst was now. For now he knew that he was alone with the dead, and between him and death stretched certain hours and days. For the *porte cochère* was locked; the doors of the house itself were locked—heavy doors and the locks new.

"I am alone in the house," the doctor had said. "No one comes here but me."

No one would come. He would die there—he, Roger Wroxham—"poor old Roger Wroxham, who was no one's enemy but his own." Tears pricked his eyes. He shook his head impatiently and they fell from his lashes.

"You fool," he said, "can't *you* die like a man either?"

Then he set his teeth and made himself lie still. It seemed to him that now Despair laid her hand on his heart. But, to speak truth, it was Hope whose hand lay there. This was so much more than a man should be called on to bear—it could not be true. It was an evil dream. He would wake presently. Or if it were, indeed, real—then someone would come, someone must come. God could not let nobody come to save him.

And late at night, when heart and brain had been stretched to the point where both break and let in the sea of madness, someone came.

The interminable day had worn itself out. Roger had screamed, yelled, shouted till his throat was dried up, his lips baked and cracked. No one heard. How should they? The twilight had thickened and thickened, till at last it made a shroud for the dead man on the floor by the chair. And there were other dead men in that house; and as Roger ceased to see the one he saw the others—the quiet, awful faces, the lean hands, the straight, stiff limbs laid out one beyond another in the room of death. They at least were not bound. If they should rise in their white wrappings and, crossing that empty sleeping chamber very softly, come slowly up the stairs—

A stair creaked.

His ears, strained with hours of listening, thought themselves befooled. But his cowering heart knew better.

Again a stair creaked. There was a hand on the door.

"Then it is all over," said Roger in the darkness, "and I *am* mad."

The door opened very slowly, very cautiously. There was no light. Only the sound of soft feet and draperies that rustled.

Then suddenly a match spurted—light struck at his eyes; a flicker of lit candle-wick steadying to flame. And the things that had come were not those quiet people creeping up to match their death with his death in life, but human creatures, alive, breathing, with eyes that moved and glittered, lips that breathed and spoke.

"He must be here," one said. "Lisette watched all day; he never came out. He must be here—there is nowhere else."

Then they set up the candle-end on the table, and he saw their faces. They were the Apaches who had set on him in that lonely street, and who had sought him here—to set on him again.

He sucked his dry tongue, licked his dry lips, and cried aloud:—

"Here I am! Oh, kill me! For the love of God, brothers, kill me *now!*"

And even before they spoke, they had seen him, and seen what lay on the floor.

"He died this morning. I am bound. Kill me, brothers; I cannot die slowly here alone. Oh, kill me, for Christ's sake!"

But already the three were pressing on each other at the doorway suddenly grown too narrow. They could kill a living man, but they could not face death, quiet, enthroned.

"For the love of Christ," Roger screamed, "have pity! Kill me outright! Come back—come back!"

And then, since even Apaches are human, one of them did come back. It was the one he had flung into the gutter. The feet of the others sounded on the stairs as he caught up the candle and bent over Roger, knife in hand.

"Make sure," said Roger, through set teeth.

"*Nom d'un nom,*" said the Apache, with worse words, and cut the bandages here, and here, and here again, and there, and lower, to the very feet.

Then this good Samaritan helped Roger to rise, and when he could not stand, the Samaritan half pulled, half carried him down those many steps, till they came upon the others putting on their boots at the stair-foot.

Then between them the three men who could walk carried the other out and slammed the outer door, and presently set him against a gate-post in another street, and went their wicked ways.

And after a time, a girl with furtive eyes brought brandy and hoarse, muttered kindnesses, and slid away in the shadows.

Against that gate-post the police came upon him. They took him to the address they found on him. When they came to question him he said, "Apaches," and his late variations on that theme were deemed sufficient, though not one of them touched truth or spoke of the third drug.

There has never been anything in the papers about that house. I think it is still closed, and inside it still lie in the locked room the very quiet people; and above, there is the room with the narrow couch and the scattered, cut, violet bandages, and the thing on the floor by the chair, under the lamp that burned itself out in that May dawning.

The Window of Horrors

H. L. Mencken

The little shops nestle elegantly along the bright avenue. The tall buildings preen themselves in the sunlight. Their windows glisten and are like ranks upon ranks of little golden and silver butterflies. The people who stroll in the avenue are also quite elegant. They look idly at the luxurious automobiles which glide back and forth down the street. They seem very happy, as if nothing were wrong with the world, as if a carefully manicured and pomaded God were in his boudoir heaven.

They look at the little shop windows, these strollers; at the windows in which such pretty pictures are for sale, in which bizarre knick-knacks lure the eye.

Sometimes they pause in little polite clusters to gaze upon jewels which lie on black velveted surfaces or to admire the Japanese oddities—those fantastically colored and shaped bird cages and Mandarin gowns, potteries and silks—which make you dream for the moment. But always before the window of the *Maison des Robes* they gather most thickly, they pause most delightedly.

For the window of the *Maison des Robes* is entirely the despair of all the other shop keepers in the avenue. It is a Paradise of windows. It is a window of enchantments. It is a fairyland of chiffons and satins, tulles and cloths which I cannot name. The women who stroll in the Avenue sigh when they pause before it. Here are other windows which exhibit clothes. But they are not like the window of the *Maison des Robes*.

Here there is something strange, something which fascinates. It has an air, just as a Princess has an air. Even men stop to look into it. They behold Romance and Mystery and a loveliness which pales the effulgence of the sun.

Women behold their dreams herein. Before them float gowns which are to their souls as beautiful thoughts are to the souls of the poets. These gowns are worn by strange inanimate figures which stand remarkably silent, in attitudes so startling, so perfect that men often feel their hearts beat faster when they look at them and women always smile with envy.

It is not as if these things were real within the window of the *Maison des Robes*. They are beyond reality. They belong in the region of masterpieces, of things which surpass nature and gladden the eyes of the world with visions of the ideal.

The shopkeepers often come to look upon this window and to study it. They search the world for and sometimes find such gowns as Mr. Hugo Blute manages to discover and place in his window. They buy of the best figures and employ the most artistic drapers and window trimmers. But even as Reynolds sought to learn the secrets of Titian by scraping the colors from the Venetian's canvas, even as Wilde sought to untangle the tints of Huysmans, they fail.

You see in their windows only clothes, merely a conventional beauty which makes you think of money and of corsets. But in the window of the *Maison des Robes* there are things you do not see and you search in your mind for fantasies, you dream of ball rooms and grottos, and the boulevard seems to you for the moment like some elegant and exquisite street in an Arabian Night.

II

On the morning of a certain day early in June the *Maison des Robes* was unusually crowded. Usually but a woman or two was to be seen therein beside the very polite and pretty clerks. But this day witnessed twenty-seven women, all of them young, all of them possessed of various beauty. They entered one at a time, surveyed for a moment the gray walls, the costly modulated furnishings, and were approached by a matron with white hair and a regal step.

Thus one by one they were ushered through the sumptuous salesroom past the two great black framed mirrors and into an office which was at the rear. The pretty clerks seemed undisturbed by their advent. They stood in their places like figures in a stage set for Maeterlinck. At one side a willowy black-haired young woman walked slowly back and forth before the gaze of two customers who had alighted from an electric. The elder customer surveyed the willowy one through a lorgnette. A girl with her watched with intent interest the influx of the twenty-seven.

In the office the twenty-seven found chairs to sit upon and two long benches. Only a few were obliged to remain standing.

They had come in answer to a tiny advertisement which had appeared in the columns of the morning newspapers.

The advertisement read:

Wanted—Six of the most beautiful young women in Chicago to work as manikins. No references required. Foreign girls preferred. Apply in person to Mr. Hugo Blute,—East Michigan avenue, at 5 p.m., sharp.

The young women who now waited for Mr. Blute to arrive preserved a dignified silence and gazed at each other speculatively. Some were obviously of the *demi monde*—bold and artificial Venuses. Some were less elaborately dressed, but fresher looking and possessed of a reposeful prettiness. A few were remarkable-looking, remarkably featured, with eyes which glowed with violet fires.

They had been waiting less than ten minutes when Mr. Blute entered. There was a hurried shuffling of feet and a stir of great portent.

Mr. Blute was a Paganini of shopkeepers—a dwarf-like Paganini. He was a short man with a large head on which lay a mop of black hair, that gave him an appearance of incongruous ferocity. For otherwise he was an elegantly dressed little man, in an afternoon coat, carefully tapering and pressed trousers, pointed black patent leather shoes and linen quite resplendent.

Yet above this almost doll-like costume arose Mr. Blute's massive head and hair. It was apparent that Mr. Blute gave this part of his person a great deal of attention. His face was carefully massaged, his hair was violently combed. His eyebrows, alas, were slightly stenciled and the swarthiness of his skin was relieved by a faint pink flush of some careful cosmetic.

But despite these things Mr. Blute's nose remained obtrusively large, his lips obtrusively heavy, his eyes glistening and in an inexplicable manner, malignant. His hair remained likewise moplike. There was something pathetic, in fact, about Mr. Blute when he powdered his nose as he did at frequent intervals, to remove the oily glisten which lay upon his skin.

He entered his office with the dapper step of a man who has small feet. He held a silk hat in his hand and a pair of yellow gloves in the other, together with a black lacquer cane.

The twenty-seven who awaited him eyed him with a kindred emotion. They were somewhat startled. It was always this way with people who gazed upon Mr. Blute for the first time. There was always something vaguely startling and dwarfish about the man until one became inured to him. People who encountered him suddenly would often feel an impulse to gasp.

"Good evening, ladies," said Mr. Blute, in a thin, sweet voice, and depositing his hat, gloves and cane on top of a large mahogany desk he sat down in the swivel chair and surveyed the twenty-seven beauties his advertisement had brought together.

After his polite salutation he seemed to become all business at once.

He eyed his visitors with a general keenness, as one eyes an ensemble.

He announced:

"You will first fill out these blanks which I give you and then return them to me. Come forward one at a time, please."

With an exaggerated restraint the twenty-seven obeyed. As they approached to receive their blanks a queer light kindled in Mr. Blute's little black eyes.

The printed matter on the blanks requested each to state her age, her name, her address, her birthplace, and to give what relatives she had in the city, if any. There was a great scribbling among the twenty-seven, who had removed their gloves and revealed an assortment of beautiful and jeweled hands.

Mr. Blute appeared to wax mysteriously excited. He so far forgot himself as to open a drawer of his desk, extract a small

powder puff and powder his heavy nose. He also rubbed his
palms together and clucked genially with his tongue. One by
one the twenty-seven returned the blanks amid a silence. In this
silence Mr. Blute then studied the blanks for fully twenty minutes with an expression of intense absorption on his face. Each
one he read carefully and placed in one of three divisions.

Finally he called the names of eight of the young women in
the office and added:

"Those whose names I have called may go home."

The eight beautiful women whose names had been pronounced arose frowning and walked with great dignity out of the
office.

When they had left Mr. Blute clucked his tongue again and
said:

"We can now proceed with more despatch. Will Miss
Margaret Swinburne step forward, please?"

A tall blonde detached herself and approached.

Mr. Blute eyed her closely.

"You have no father or mother," he said, waving one of the
blanks before him. "You are an orphan, yes?"

Miss Swinburne said, "Yes."

"Good," Mr. Blute chuckled.

He looked at her and bade her turn around.

He studied her features intently and after the pause
announced, somewhat inanely, as may be seen:

"Excellent. I am devoted to orphans. I favor them in my shop.
I employ them. I will employ you. Your duties, you know, will be
only to wear beautiful clothes. Silks and laces. You understand
what a manikin is?"

Miss Swinburne nodded graciously.

"To show my fashionable customers how beautiful are my
clothes," said Mr. Blute, as if Miss Swinburne hadn't understood.

An excitement again appeared to possess him and as if to contain himself he added abruptly:

"You are accepted, Miss Swinburne. Will you sit over there?"

In this same peculiar and abrupt manner Mr. Blute selected
the five others from the group. There were several whom Mr.

Blute dismissed reluctantly, gazing with glowing eyes upon their lovely faces and turning them around and around before him.

"Ah—ah—" he murmured each time. "You are what I want—what I desire—but—unsuited. Too bad."

He shook his massive head sorrowfully, clucked dismally with his tongue and waved his hand toward the door. But on the whole the six whom he had chosen were among the most remarkable of the beautiful young women.

When the others had departed Mr. Blute sprang from his chair and announced sweetly.

"So. It is settled. You shall all wear beautiful clothes and receive twenty-five dollars each a week. Hugo Blute is not cheap. No. He is—ha!"

He indulged in a vague trilling little laugh and, paused thus in his praise, he assumed a droll position, his short arms folded across his bulky chest, his large head thrown back.

"But there must be a contract, ladies," he went on. "You must agree to place yourselves in my hands for two days. I will take you to the St. John Hotel and send you my most beautiful dresses to become acquainted with. I wish you to try them on and become used to their lines and able to wear them—magnificently."

Here Mr. Blute indulged in his little trilling laugh again and the six beautiful young women regarded his mysterious amusement with six beautiful smiles.

"You will wear them a long time," he said. "I employ orphans and am kind to them. I employ them as long as they remain beautiful. Your only duties while I employ you will be to show off my exquisite dresses to the fashionable ladies. Do I speak plainly? Am I understood?"

A chorus of "Yesses" answered him.

Mr. Blute became suddenly animate. His short legs seemed to prance. He passed among the six manikins to be and shook hands with each of them, patting them tenderly on their arms and clucking up at them.

"Follow me, young ladies," he added. "My automobile will take you to the hotel. Is there anyone of you will have to notify someone of her absence?"

There was a pause. During this pause Mr. Blute became dark and his face glistened.

He eyed each of the six beautiful young women with an ominous, somewhat aggrieved frown, and waited.

After a brief silence a pretty black-haired girl raised her voice. "I must tell my uncle," she said.

"What's your name?" Mr. Blute asked curtly.

"Miss Marlow."

"Miss Marlow," said Mr. Blute, "you may go home to your uncle. Now, is there anyone else?"

The dismissed one hesitated. Mr. Blute ignored her. The remaining five then watched Miss Marlow leave the office and appeared slightly puzzled. But when she had gone, Mr. Blute diverted their attention with a violent laugh.

"Very well," he cried. "Follow me."

He led his smiling and elated troupe through the luxurious salesroom to a large green limousine which waited at the curb.

It had grown dark. The avenue glowed in the dusk. Vivid patches of light gleamed over the pavements. Clusters of lamps shone gayly down the line of the curbing. People were still strolling leisurely, elegantly by. But now over the avenue was an air of quest, a spirit of masquerade. The hurrying cabs and motors perforated the gloom with their long shafts of light.

"Step in," said Mr. Blute to his troupe. "The chauffeur will be here directly. All arrangements have been made."

One by one the five disappeared into the tonneau. He waited and closed the door upon them. He exuded a joyous politeness, laughing aimlessly, bowing elaborately to the laden tonneau, returning briskly to his establishment. Inside Mr. Blute spoke briefly to two of his pretty clerks who were covering the stock and fixtures preparatory to leaving.

"Run along," he ordered, "and play. Run along, children. Don't waste time. Time is valuable, very valuable to the young. Ah, make the most of life."

He patted the two clerks upon the arm in a happy, paternal fashion and approached the white-haired and regal stepping matron—his bookkeeper.

"Run along, run along, Miss Jones," he said to her.

He waited until his staff had clothed itself and bidden him good evening, and, as the last one passed through the door, he hurried into his office.

Five minutes later a man in a great black coat wearing goggles and a pointed cap mounted the driver's seat of Mr. Blute's machine. This person clucked with his tongue in a way highly reminiscent of his employer, Mr. Blute, and in fact seemed possessed of another of his habits. For, as he adjusted himself in the seat, he extracted a little powder puff from one of his large pockets and dabbed whimsically at his nose. This tell-tale ritual accomplished, the mysterious chauffeur swung his car into the mass of traffic and spun away in the direction of the St. John Hotel.

III

Mr. Blute, looking tired and slightly disheveled, entered the *Maison des Robes* the following morning. He glanced keenly at his pretty clerks who were standing in a solemn little group near the center of the room and bending over an opened newspaper. Mr. Blute paused, he came near them.

"Too bad, ladies," he said. "It is a terrible thing."

"Oh, we are so sorry," one of them answered, and Mr. Blute, shaking his head, sadly passed on into his office.

He closed the door and drew from his pocket a newspaper and sitting down at his desk read the account of the tragedy which had overtaken five young women and an intoxicated chauffeur.

The newspaper stated the young women had been selected by Mr. Blute as the most beautiful in Chicago and were being escorted to the St. John Hotel in the automobile belonging to the proprietor of the *Maison des Robes*. The chauffeur as he guided the machine had appeared to be intoxicated to at least several crossing policemen who remembered his passing. He had, this diabolical chauffeur, finally ended by crashing through the slight guard at the river's edge and into the river, at Adams street. The bridge at this point had been open at the time. Repairs which were being made on the structure had necessitated the closing of the street and thus it was that the accident had been witnessed by no one. An officer named Maloney was the first to arrive on the scene. He peered into the black water and saw great ripples dancing under the red lights of the bridge. It was eight o'clock according to Policeman Maloney.

Mr. Blute studied the story closely as he read, rereading several paragraphs.

Pressing a button, he summoned one of his pretty clerks and ordered her to secure him copies of the afternoon papers as soon as they appeared.

As he waited their arrival, two policemen desecrated the interior of the establishment with their heavy feet and loud voices, and ended by being ushered into the proprietor's presence. They informed him that his limousine had been fished out of the river, little the worse for wear, but that the police had been unable to recover the bodies of the five young women.

Mr. Blute listened gravely. He answered their questions freely, telling them of the chauffeur whom he had only hired two days before and whose first name was Harold.

"It is awful," said Mr. Blute, covering his face with his hands. "I had prepared rooms at the St. John Hotel and given the man instructions to go there at once. The tragedy has unnerved me, gentlemen."

"We are draggin' fer the ladies and the chauffeur," said one of the policemen, "and will let you know, Mr. Blute, as soon as we find anything."

To the newspaper reporters who arrived at the *Maison des Robes* as the police were leaving, Mr. Blute announced that he would bestow a sum of $100 upon each of the families of the deceased five young women. He revealed their names, as he had done to the police, described their beauties, dwelt bitterly upon the drunkenness of the miserable chauffeur, wrung his hands and clucked solemnly with his tongue.

For eight days the police continued to drag the river for the bodies of the six victims. During this time, apparently overcome by the disaster, Mr. Blute relapsed into a morose condition. His pretty clerks saw him but little. He called upon the police captain in charge of the search for the bodies daily.

At the end of the eighth day the body of a young woman was found near the mouth of the river. The body was taken to the morgue and there identified by a young man as the remains of Mary Collins, his sister. Miss Collins, it developed at once, was one of the five beautiful women who had been chosen by the discriminating Mr. Blute.

The brother identified the body by means of the clothes the young woman wore and a signet ring which she had borrowed from him only a week before. The features were discolored beyond recognition by the water, seeming also to have sustained certain bruises.

In quick succession during that night four other bodies were recovered from the mouth of the river. Like the first, their faces were disfigured by discolorations and bruises. The coroner and police explained this fact by the theory that the bruises had been sustained in the accident itself, the plunge into the river, and the discolorations had been brought on by the abrasions.

Three of the bodies were identified by landladies. One was a Miss Helen Lowrey. The second, Miss Dorothy Janes. The third, Miss Anna Hyde. The landladies wept and declared the victims had roomed with them when alive. The identifications were made by means of the clothing, of rings, ornaments, shoes and hosiery. Mr. Blute himself established the identity of the fourth, remembering in particular the black and white checked suit in which the body was attired—and the long gray gloves.

An inquest was held and the bodies buried. The search for the drunken chauffeur was discontinued. Mr. Blute reimbursed the brother of one of the victims with his check for $100, and thus two weeks after the evening of the tragedy the matter was forgotten, and business at the *Maison des Robes* was resumed.

Even Mr. Blute appeared to have recovered some of his joyous and paternal air which the incident had for the time taken from him. The elegant people who walked in the avenue passed the window of the famous establishment and soon forgot, as they gazed at the exquisite interior, the story of the five beautiful women, the drunken chauffeur and the open bridge.

The night after the inquest, Mr. Blute walked briskly towards

his home. His automobile was still suffering repair. He had rid-
den to a point within four blocks of where he lived in the street
car. It was warm and the promise of a storm was in the sultry air.

Mr. Blute's home was a large red brick house located in a
peculiarly dismal part of the city which had once been the center of wealth and society. The mansions which had once lent an
air of solid and tasteful affluence to the street now stood with
their windows broken, their porches sunken, their stairs over-
grown. Large "For Sale" signs painted white, shone out of the
darkness. Here and there were some still inhabited.

A stagnation had apparently overtaken the district. To the
south furious building activities had converted the almost
prairies of twenty years ago into populous resident sections. To
the north the avenue had changed the scene into one of glitter
and prosperity.

But in this space, where stood the home of Mr. Blute a decay
had fallen. The night lay somberly upon it, the sagging outlines
of the tumble-down mansions appeared faintly out of the unrelieved gloom.

Before one of the more preserved of these mansions Mr.
Blute stopped. A single light burned in an upper window.

Mr. Blute, peering into the darkness about him, suddenly
mounted the steps and let himself into the house with a key.

He locked the door carefully behind him.

For a moment he stood still and listened and then he walked
to a front window in the large barren room to the right of the
hall and dropped to his knees in front of a cracked pane.

He remained thus on his knees for ten minutes, peering cautiously into the street, only his mop of hair and gleaming eyes
visible above the ledge.

After gazing into the vacant street in this odd manner, Mr.
Blute arose, rubbed his palms together and, smiling, tiptoed
gently up the stairs.

The old mansion became full of creakings and groanings as
Mr. Blute progressed. But at the top of the flight he paused and
the noises ceased.

He paused and peered intently at a door behind which a light burned. Into his eyes came, it seemed, an answering light, a faintly ecstatic gleam.

Mr. Blute inserted a key in the door lock and turned it. The door opened slowly.

The room in front of Mr. Blute was illuminated by a lighted gas jet. Across the walls fell long trembling shadows. He walked directly to the jet and turned on the light fuller. Two cabinets, in which a variety of odd surgical instruments and bottles of colored liquids reposed, came into view. Also ranged across one end of the room there appeared to be five long tables on which lay the bodies of the five young women, who had entered Mr. Blute's automobile one evening two weeks ago.

IV

Mr. Blute, as if remembering something, dashed back to the door and locked it with the key. He then returned to the other end of the room and surveyed the contents of the five tables. Each of them was partially covered with a black cloth.

"Ah, my beauties," said Mr. Blute softly. "Everything is settled. You have been decently buried. And one of you has cost me an extra $100."

He frowned at the middle figure and wagged a reproving forefinger at it.

"Why didn't you mention that brother of yours, eh? Pah! Women are never to be trusted," he growled.

But recovering his good spirits Mr. Blute clucked genially with his tongue, walked to one of the cabinets and proceeded to remove an array of apparatus, instruments and bottles.

As he made these preparations his eyes strayed continually to the bodies on the tables. He kept mumbling to himself:

"Orphans, excellent. Ah, beauties. I have made no mistakes . . . no mistakes."

The proprietor of the *Maison des Robes* then spread out his strange paraphernalia on a sixth and smaller table. His mop of hair became awry, his eyes gleamed and an unlovely oil gradually overspread his face.

But his hands were busy, dexterously busy. They mixed the
liquids of the bottles, they lighted little gas burners and cooked
little pots. There was an elaborate methodicality about Mr.
Blute during these operations. He counted things, he insisted
upon laying everything straight and keeping everything clean.

Towards the end of his labors he grew excited, gazing into the
bubbling pots, clucking with his tongue and finally prancing up
and down and rubbing his palms vigorously together.

It was obvious that Mr. Blute was preparing a solution, a delicate, difficult solution from the intensity of his maneuverings.
Having prepared this in at least five different ways—there were
five little pots, Mr. Blute filled a long hollow needle-like instrument with the bubbling liquid from one of the pots.

"It is perfect," he mumbled, "perfect. The perfect fluid. Ah,
what would the Ptolomies have given for it?"

He then folded his short arms across his bosom and surveyed
with dignity the five bodies which lay stiff and beautiful upon
the five tables.

"One more injection," he mumbled, "and it is complete. But
first another bath—one more bath."

Opening a drawer beneath one of the cabinets, Mr. Blute
extracted a large bottle containing a violet liquid.

With this in his hand he approached first the body of
Margaret Swinburne, looking as she had looked when he had
asked her her name in his office two weeks ago. With the violet
liquid he proceeded to bathe her face.

An odd spicy smell crept into the room.

The inanimate face underwent simultaneously a remarkable
change.

The skin appeared to revive, the flesh seemed to bloom, a
glowing tint of life suffused the throat.

"Four baths," mumbled Mr. Blute, "I must remember. Only
four. And I must not forget the hair."

Darting to the cabinet he returned with a bottle of dark liquid
and this he applied expertly to the head. The blonde hair, which
he loosened, shimmered under the application. Slowly its color
changed, Mr. Blute drenching it delicately with the contents of

the bottle. It became a smouldering auburn. This accomplished, Mr. Blute returned to his long needle instrument.

"Now," he addressed the figure upon which he had been working: "We shall see. This way."

With quick little movements he inserted the point of the needle into the tips of the slender fingers, each time loosing some of the liquid by means of the silver plunger which formed the upper part of the instrument. The eleventh injection Mr. Blute made into the heart.

As soon as they were finished he seized the body in a frenzy and staggering under its weight carried it to a bench which stood near the cabinets.

"Now," he cried, "the pose, the pose. This way. No. Turn the head. The foot out. You will sit. A morning costume. So. The right foot in. The arm out. The fingers. My God, are you stupid! The fingers, so; open one. Close the other. The knee less bent. Ah! Excellent. Leaning forward a bit. Ah, what grace. As if you listened. So. As if you had something to say, ha, ha."

As he spoke or rather ejaculated, Mr. Blute's hands manipulated the body before him. It resembled, the operation did, some weird sculpturing. But the pose he finally achieved seemed to delight him. He hovered around it. Now and then he added a finishing touch, a final angle. But soon the limbs ceased to obey his sensitive movements. He strained the wrist in an effort to undo a curve. He might as well have sought to undo the curve of some marble wrist. A gleam of triumph came into his eyes.

"You harden quickly," he gasped. "Quicker than ever. An hour quicker! I have barely time to adjust! Eh! And this time you will last longer; yes. Two years, my beauty. And then perhaps—who knows—the fluid which is forever. I think now, that you will do."

The remainder of the night Mr. Blute spent in similar ministrations upon the other four bodies. Each he bathed in the peculiarly smelling liquid. Each revived under his touch, losing its still ghastly stiffness, growing mysteriously alive, acquiring a delicate blooming transparency of skin as of death made beautiful. The hair of each Mr. Blute dyed a different color!

At dawn Mr. Blute had finished. The five were posed. They

lay now upon the tables in impossible posturings, ludicrously sinister, lovely and vicious, like a family of houris caught by some sudden enchantment which had perpetuated them in their casual graces. Each had suffered the careful and elaborate adjusting of Mr. Blute.

Tired and disheveled, he stood in the center of the room and panted. The air was full of an almost suffocating odor. But a prodigious strength seemed to be his.

With a great sigh he lifted the body of Miss Swinburne upon his shoulder and carried her into an adjacent room.

On the floor of this room were laid six oblong boxes. Their lids had been opened and each of the boxes contained a naked wax model to which was affixed a wire standard.

It was Mr. Blute's purpose to sever the wire standards from the wax models and attach them to the bodies of his five young women. This he did carefully, placing each of the bodies, when he had finished, into each box occupied by the wax dummies.

V

An hour later Mr. Blute sat and waited for the arrival of the wagon from the *Maison des Robes.* He had washed his face and hands, changed his clothes, powdered his nose and violently brushed his hair.

The wagon came and Mr. Blute supervised the loading of the oblong boxes, which had been recrated and carefully relabeled by their owner. Seated then on one of them, the erratic Mr. Blute was driven into the avenue and around to a point in the rear of the *Maison des Robes.*

He emerged into his establishment and ordered his clerks to bring out the five costumes which had been selected. Then standing with the fluffy silken mass in his arms, he announced: "I do not wish to be disturbed until I ring," and retired into his office where the five oblong boxes had been taken.

He uncrated them one at a time, attiring them in lingerie petticoats, shoes and the costumes.

To the first he pinned a bit of paper on the hem of the petticoat. On the paper were the initials M. C. which, in Mr. Blute's mind, were obviously the initials of Mary Collins.

He placed the carefully dressed body in a corner and proceeded with the second. His actions were tender, wistful and expert.

It was well along in the afternoon when Mr. Blute issued from his office and summoned his pretty clerks.

"We will not place the figures in the window. We will take the figures which are in there out and put them in the boxes. Handle everything carefully, ladies."

The clerks stepped at the door of Mr. Blute's private office and gasped.

Confronting them were five beautiful young women attired in the height of exquisite fashion. One of them was standing smiling with a simple and yet startling grace to her outlines. A second was seated and gazing nonchalantly at her dainty boot. She seemed to be meditating upon the filmiest of secrets. A third was standing with her head turned and her mouth slightly opened in a look of pleasant surprise. A fourth was seated, leaning forward as if in conversation. Words trembled on her lips and there was about her the air of a woman who is struggling to reveal something of piquant importance. The fifth stood straight and tall, her eyes lowered, her arms listless, as if she were dreaming for the instant of some memories far distant. They were all radiant and appeared to the astounded clerks to be alive.

"Beauties, eh?" clucked Mr. Blute, rubbing his palms together.

The clerks admired his handiwork without a word.

Then amid the delighted exclamations of his employees and three fashionable customers, the five models were carried one by one into the spacious and wonderfully draped window of the *Maison des Robes*.

From the sidewalk Mr. Blute surveyed the effect and pranced excitedly up and down. His face moved with queer grimaces and he appeared obsessed by a deep and silent joy. He raised his eyes to the sky and blinked in a solemn sort of thanksgiving or prayer.

Within the shop his clerks talked among themselves.

"Those are certainly the most beautiful figures Blute has had yet," said the first one. "They are remarkable. I never saw anything like them."

The second one came out of the window shaking her head solemnly.

"Yes," she agreed. "They are far superior to the last three figures we had, although I can't see why Mr. Blute is throwing those last three out. They were better than anything on the avenue and hadn't begun to melt. *These* must have cost a fortune."

Miss Jones, the white-haired and regal-stepping one interrupted in a superior manner.

"A man like Mr. Blute," she said, "does not balk at expense in pursuing his art. I have been here for eight years and during that time he has had four shipments from France, each one better than the other. This is the fifth."

The conversation ceased as Mr. Blute re-entered his establishment. After gracefully receiving the congratulations of the occupants he retired to his office.

He closed the door behind him.

Then after a pause he opened the steel door of a wall safe and extracted from its interior a large ledger. This he carried to his desk.

Opening it to a blank page he wrote in it as follows:

Fifth Importation
For bodies from the Merville, Holmes, Wilmot and City Hospitals.

$10 each	$ 50
For poison gun and limousine attachment	25
For embalming, mummifying chemicals..............	200
For rash statement to the press....................	100
For expressage of hospital bodies to mouth of the river ...	30
For wax models from France, destroyed..............	400

"I guess that's all," murmured Mr. Blute, and with a sigh he totalled the column.

A light of mystic satisfaction shone from him. He powdered his nose with the puff and rubbing his hands together added to himself:

"Eight hundred and five dollars! Twice as much as last time, ha! Hobbies cost money. Ah, well, art for art's sake."

Mr. Blute then returned the ledger in the wall safe, locked the steel door and with a light brisk step re-entered his display room.

On the sidewalk a crowd of men and women had gathered. The men stared intensely into the window, their eyes smiling, their hearts beating fast. The women gazed enviously fascinated as always by this Paradise of windows, this fairyland of silks and laces and tulles, and graces. Exclamations of delight and wonder came from all sides, exclamations of astonishment and joy.

Mr. Blute stood in the plate glass door of his establishment, his large head thrown back, his hands clasped behind him and regarded the admiring throng with an expansive, though modest, smile.

The Man Who Lost His Head

Thomas Burke

The accident that befell Peter Smothe was no such accident as is met by compensation from our popular daily papers. Their catholic and imaginative lists stop short of that kind of accident.

It is said of many of us when, in times demanding the packed thought of an hour, we are unable to attain even a moment's reflection—that we have lost our heads. The term is one of those passionately tropical images which fall so glibly from the lips of accountants, stockbrokers, cricket-umpires and other repressed poets. But with Peter Smothe the thing happened. He did actually lose his head, and lived to know that he had lost it.

It began in that restiveness which comes to many a man at fifty. He came to see his life as flat and unprofitable. He looked about him and saw—or thought he saw—other men leading vivid-coloured lives; lives as full of zest and effulgence as a fire-opal; while his own had been safe, warm—and dull. He was fifty, and he had had none of that highly-charged life of which he read in the newspapers. He forgot, of course, that they were they, and he was he; and that a man cannot choose his way of life. He can be only what his chemistry and his karma allow him to be. He can be only himself. To seek to be something else is to throw the whole mechanism of his being out of gear.

But Peter Smothe was sick of being himself, and at fifty he decided to be something else; anything else. He felt it a sorry thing that a man's life should run on one set of rails. That a man should spend his little span in being but one kind of man—a soldier, an actor, a geologist, a scholar, a lawyer, a painter. Why couldn't he have a little of each? He realized that at fifty it was

too late to try for a little of each, but at least he would have
something different. He had had enough of his rails, and since
most of his life was gone, this was the time, if ever, while he was
yet able and healthy, to try something new; something utterly
alien to his previous experience.

So, upon a fine morning, he packed a small bag, and left his
Kensington flat without any word of his intention; and was never
again seen in it.

He had no clear plan, other than escape into a new world. A
passing delivery van gave him his first pointer. He saw the words
"Pentonville Road," and he hailed a taxi, and said, "Pentonville
Road." He stopped the taxi half-way up the long ascent of that
road, and went down a side turning. There he took the first
turning on the right. He walked down this littered street, studying its decrepit houses. One of them, not so decrepit as the rest,
had a card in its window—"Lodgings for a Respectable Single
Man." He knocked at its door, and when it was opened he
crossed the threshold of that house and of his former life.

• • • • • •

In that street he remained for four months. He was within a
three-penny bus-ride of his own home, yet, after a week or two,
as far from it as if he were in Iceland. He became one more of
the annual hundreds of Mysterious Disappearances.

And he became a new man. He ate in squalid little eating-
houses. He hung about the Islington streets and talked to all
sorts and conditions. He consorted in bars with the less favoured
specimens. He learned to use their talk, and do their things, and
soon to accept their thought. He told himself that he was having
a high old time. He looked back on his staid bourgeois life with
impatience and contempt. To think of the years he had wasted
on it. He wondered how he had endured it so long. He wondered why he had looked with shivers on the kind of life he was
now leading. He gave his old self a grimy laugh.

He felt that he was now leading the real Bohemian life; not
the well-to-do imitation of it; and realized that it was the life he
had always, secretly, wanted to lead. His friends, he thought,

would call it *going to pieces*. He himself called it *branching out*.
He thought of the anecdotage with which he could surprise
them when the mood took him to return. He thought of the wisdom by which he could shock the innocence of two of them,
who claimed to know things because they dabbled in social service. He did not know that he was not going back.

There came a night when he met, in an obscure tavern near
King's Cross, a man from whom he would have shrunk a few
months ago, but whom now he saw as an Interesting Man. The
creature was dark-haired and untidy; his face and hands were so
unclean that they gave dreadful hints about the rest of his body.
He wore a tattered overcoat with the collar turned up. The collar was buttoned and the rest of the coat hung from him in a
fork. He used the unclean hands to stress the key-word of every
sentence in a way that suggested the Near East. He, too, was
about fifty, but he had led a more tumbled life than Peter
Smothe, and his face was lined and drawn. But the eyes were
brighter and more alert than Peter Smothe's. They had been
called to look upon strange and unexpected things in their fifty
years, while Peter Smothe, until four months ago, had seen little
that was strange and unexpected. He still had, in moments of
repose, the calm eye of the club-man.

The stranger, having selected Peter Smothe for his audience,
began to talk of things he had seen. He revealed not only alert
eyes but a brain. It was not the kind of brain Peter Smothe knew
in Kensington and in his clubs; but he would have been disap-
pointed if it were. The man talked of really strange things, and
talked of them as casually as men talk of a visit to the theatre.
He talked of The Power. He talked of the *Petit Albert* as others
talk of the latest novel. He talked of the sword and the cup, and
of things he had seen done in Greece.

"Mind you, I don't talk in this way to these people here. It
would be a waste. But you, sir, I perceived at once, are an educated man. You think. These people"—he waved the soiled
hand and the funereal fingernails—"these people—cattle—
dross for cemeteries. Impossible to talk to. But you, I see, think
things out. You are not bemused by such childish nonsense as

laws, and such artificially-created things as crime. Dope—
don't you agree? All dope. When I see the way that tenth-rate
little humbugs in power bemuse the mass of the people with
their stale old tricks, I could——" He finished on a crescendo
of profanity.

Peter Smothe hugged himself. "Most interesting man," he
thought. "Lovely Type. Quite like one of these master-criminals."
Aloud he said, "Won't you have a drink with me?"

"Don't mind. Make it a whiskey and peppermint." When the
drinks came he said, "Suppose we sit down. Could you pull that
other chair over to this table?" Smothe went over and fetched
the chair. The soiled hand shot into the pocket of the soiled
overcoat. The soiled hands carried the glasses to the table. The
hand that held the glass of Peter Smothe went back to the overcoat pocket. "Now we can talk. . . . My views perhaps may seem
extreme to you, but often to reach the desirable middle it is necessary to exert ourselves towards the extreme. There was a man
I knew in Greece. An extraordinary man. You'd have liked him.
Satan we called him. I learned a lot from him. Oh, a lot. Not all
I wanted to learn, or I wouldn't be in this place talking to you.
But enough to be useful from time to time. *His* views I used to
consider extreme, but I found he was only aiming further than
he wished to reach. Which is what I always do. I remember once
in Marseilles, when I was in some little trouble——"

Peter Smothe repeated to himself that This was Lovely. He
was in touch with the real underworld of which he had read in
novels. This man, talking a farrago of street profanity and sham
education, good phrases and illiterate phrases, was a Find. He
decided that he must cultivate him.

After a return of drinks they parted on Peter Smothe's suggestion that they meet the next evening. The stranger thought it
likely that they would. He could not be sure; affairs might detain
him; but he hoped to be there. If not, some other night. As they
went out Smothe trod on a tiny empty capsule which lay by the
stranger's feet. He did not notice that he had trod on anything.

He walked to his dingy room in a queer state of elation and
fatigue. The man's appearance and talk had elated him, but
something else about the man had exhausted him. It was as

though he had sucked all vitality from the air about them, and left Smothe only the nitrogen. His head was light and his legs were heavy. It was a clear, dry night, and still early—just the night for one of those prowls in dim quarters which had become a habit with him. But he found that he wanted only to be in bed. The ten-minute climb from King's Cross to that bed called for an effort. It seemed unattainably distant. Every hundred yards seemed a mile. But after some hours of plodding he made it, and was surprised to see that his clock showed that he had left King's Cross twelve minutes ago.

•   •   •   •   •   •

His first awareness of himself next morning was that he was a living Thirst. He could not realize arms or legs, or life itself. His whole being was Thirst, and his only sense-perception came through the throat. He got up to seek water, and drained three glasses. Within a few minutes his mind and body resumed the normal coursing of life, and he felt able to wash and dress.

Having washed and half-dressed, he prepared to shave, and it was here that the normal coursing of life was again arrested, and his being became one extreme sickness. He had just taken up the shaving-stick, and had tilted the mirror, when he dropped the shaving-stick and almost knocked the little mirror to the floor.

The face that looked back at him from the mirror wasn't his.

He had tilted the mirror in the casual faith that it would show him what it had shown him throughout every day of all his years—a chubby pink face, a little blond moustache, blue eyes and thin blond hair. What it did show him was black, lank hair, a lined and drawn face, dark, restless eyes, a black forecast of beard, and a general air of grubbiness.

Wondering whether it were nightmare, or if he were still suffering from last night, he rubbed his hand heavily across his face, and looked again. There was no doubt of it. He was awake; from the street came the cries of the morning; from below came the familiar sounds of that dingy house; from the window he saw the bedraggled figures he saw every morning. And in the mirror he saw a face that was not his.

Before he understood the full implication of what had happened, and the frightful dilemma in which it placed him, he was aware only of that sickness which comes to all men in presence of the unaccountable. Something had happened which *didn't* happen; something out of nature; something against the sun. We live by a peaceable faith in the course of nature; a faith which takes so much for granted that if the morning sun were to shine upon us from the west, and the stars appear in daylight, we should stand still in dismay. For the moment Peter Smothe stood still in dismay. Four times he went to the mirror, and four times he sat down and stared at the carpet. The impossible thing *had* happened. He had a new face. The rest of his body was the body he had known for fifty years. His hands and legs, which he examined slowly and in fear, were his. The face was not.

At the fourth examination of it, he felt that, strange and repellent as it was, he had seen it before. He spent some minutes in trying to remember where he had seen it, and only after searching about all the queer faces he had seen in the last few months did he recall last night. The Interesting Man in the bar. And then he recalled the unusual effect of two glasses of light beer. The face he saw in the mirror was the face of the Interesting Man.

When, in the course of an hour, he came to consider his position in relation to everyday affairs, he realized that he could not face the woman of the house. He would be a stranger. He would be a stranger everywhere. One thought came to him; the thought that comes to every man in every kind of disaster. Flight.

At eleven o'clock when, as he knew by custom, the woman was out, he fled. He took his bag and fled, and boarded the first bus that came along. He sat in the bus with the desolate feeling of being Nobody. His light pretence in leaving home and sinking his identity under an assumed name was now changed to dismal fact. He was not Peter Smothe, and he was not really the Interesting Man in the bar. He had achieved completely what he had thought he wanted: he had got away from himself.

He left the bus at the Strand, and took the bus behind it, which was labelled for Waterloo. He did not know why he should go to Waterloo, but he decided that he might as well go there as anywhere else. It was distant from Islington and from Kensington, and it was a quarter which, outside the platforms of its station, was known to nobody of his own sort.

In a dim street off Lower Marsh he found a room to let, and into it he took his misery. He hunched himself on the narrow bed, and tried to realize what had happened, and to follow out its implications. But the thing would not resolve itself into thought; he could only look at it and wonder. A wild hope came to him that as this mad thing had happened, so it might un-happen. It might last only for a while. Whatever madness was at work upon him might exhaust itself, and he would find himself again Peter Smothe. He thought of his Kensington flat, and prayed that the thing might pass, and that he might be again Peter Smothe, and abandon his foolish antics of the last few months. Every fifteen minutes he went to the mirror, but the mirror had nothing for him.

Towards late afternoon his feeling of sickness increased, and he realized that he had eaten nothing. With an effort he dragged himself out to seek some secluded eating-house. But he went no farther in his search than some twenty paces.

He had scarcely left the house when two men confronted him. They confronted him very solidly, one on either side of him. The stouter of the two said, "Just a moment. We are police-officers. What's your name?"

"Er—what—er—Peter—er—Arthur Exford."

The man studied him. "You answer to the description of a man wanted by the Southampton police. Known as Boris Gudlatch."

"That's not my name. And I've never in my life been in Southampton."

"I see." The officer looked at the poor street and the shabby creature, and seemed trying to reconcile the street and the shabbiness with the delicate voice. He made his decision on the street and the shabbiness, and took Peter Smothe by the arm. "You better come along to the station. If there's a mistake we can soon settle it." He turned to his companion and nodded towards the house. His companion went to the house, and Peter Smothe was taken to the station.

At first he was bewildered and incoherent, as all respectable men are when their arms are taken by policemen. He could not clearly grasp what was happening, or why, or what he should do. He could only utter feeble protests. At the station he was told that he must expect to wait awhile, as officers were coming from Southampton with witnesses. If a mistake had been made, he would no doubt understand that the interests of justice must be served even at inconvenience to innocent people. He continued to protest. "I don't know what it's all about. I've never been in Southampton in my life, and my name isn't the name you mentioned. I'll admit that it isn't the name I gave." Under this new trouble he forgot the trouble that had come upon him in the morning. There was no mirror in the station, and he talked to them as himself. "No. It isn't the name I gave. I had a private reason for giving that. Nothing to do with anything that would interest you. I've just been going about London seeing life. Actually, my name is Peter Smothe. My address is Helsingfors Mansions, Kensington. You'll find me in the telephone book. And you can ring up and ask my man to come along."

"You were there yesterday?"

"Er—no. No, I wasn't there yesterday. I haven't been there for a month or so. I told you I've been wandering about London. But I left my man enough to go on with, and he'll probably be there."

"Well, we'll ring him up."

They rang up, and they told Peter Smothe that his man was coming along by taxi, and had expressed some anxiety concerning the disappearance of his employer. The officer, not certain whether he had an amiable eccentric, or a bluffing criminal, gave the benefit to courtesy, and assured him that if he were the man he claimed to be, everything would be all right, save for the inconvenience, which couldn't be avoided.

Within half an hour his man arrived, and he got up from his hard chair with a gasp of relief. "Hendrick!" Hendrick took no notice. He turned to the officer, "Where's Mr. Smothe?" The officer said, "There." Hendrick looked round the room. "No. That's not him." Peter Smothe became indignant. "What's the matter with you, Hendrick? I *am* here." Hendrick look again at him. "Don't know what you're talking about. You're not *my* Mr. Smothe."

"But I *am*. Hendrick—my parrot—Mulvaney. You know the parrot, Mulvaney. And my collection of enamels. And the cabinet in the corner with the Bohemian glass. Hendrick!"

The officer looked at both of them. Hendrick looked at the officer and indicated Peter Smothe with a nod. "Seems to know a lot about Mr. Smothe's habits and his flat. But that ain't Mr. Smothe. I been with Mr. Smothe eleven years. I ought to know him. He went off sudden-like some months ago, and I haven't seen him since. But that ain't him. My Mr. Smothe was yellow-haired and pink. Chubby face, sort of. Blue eyes. Always very neat and what you might call spruce. *That's* no more him than I am."

"But, Hendrick——"

Hendrick was thanked for coming, and Peter Smothe was left alone. He was left alone for half an hour, which gave him time to realize his folly in sending for Hendrick. The impossibility of explaining to Hendrick that though he had lost his head he was still Peter Smothe. The impossibility of explaining to police-officers that a man could lose his head, and go about with a head that didn't belong to him. The impossibility of explaining anything.

And then his loneliness was broken. Four other men came into the room. They were ushered in by an officer and they sat down on chairs, gingerly and self-consciously. An odd lot. A man who looked like a clerk; a man who smelt of fish; a man who looked wicked enough to double-cross Satan; and a man who couldn't look anything because his eyes were everywhere and his face was constantly changing. The only point they had in common was shabby appearance.

They had had only the time to look round the room and grin or grimace at each other when a big man came in and presented a young girl to the company. She stood in the doorway and looked them over one by one. The big man said, "Well?" Without hesitation she pointed to Peter Smothe. "That one." "Sure?" "Absolutely. Wearing different clothes, but the face is unmistakable. I saw it quite clearly when he stood in the light before he started running." "Thank you." He called through the door: "Take Miss Jones to the next room. Don't let her see the young man. Then send the young man."

A young man came in. He, too, studied the company. The officer lifted his head in enquiry. The young man nodded. "Yes—over there by the window. That one." He pointed to Peter Smothe.

"Sure? He says he's never been in Southampton at any time."

"I'm certain that's the man I saw. Different clothes, but the face—I saw it quite clearly for some seconds. Don't see faces like that every day. Not in Southampton, anyway."

The young man was waved out, and when he was gone the four other men in the room were waved out. The officer turned to Smothe.

"Two witnesses have identified you as a man wanted by the Southampton police. I hold a warrant for the arrest of that man, known, among other names, as Boris Gudlatch, on a charge of murder."

"Mur——"

"It is my duty to detain you and take you to Southampton to answer a charge of robbery at a jeweller's shop in Humstrum Street, at five o'clock yesterday afternoon, and of murdering John Smith. It is my du——"

"But I tell you again I've never in my life been in Southampton. It's ridiculous. It's rubbish. These people are making a mistake. I——"

"You are at liberty to make a statement, or not; as you please. If you wish to make a statement, it is my duty to warn you that anything you may say may be used in——"

"I've not been out of London at all the last four months. I was in London all day yesterday. I was wandering about all the afternoon, and I can call witnesses who saw me at nine o'clock near King's Cross, and——"

The officer had held up his hand, but it wasn't the warning hand that made him break off. It was the realization that he had spoken to nobody through the whole afternoon, and had stopped nowhere; and the realization that a man could have been in Southampton at five o'clock, and yet have reached a King's Cross bar by nine o'clock.

"If you don't wish to make a statement," the officer said, "it would be better to say nothing for the present."

So Peter Smothe said nothing. He saw the utter futility of making a statement. He saw the impossibility of an alibi, and the idiocy of telling this man, or any man, that somebody took his head away last night and gave him his present head in exchange. He closed his mouth and dropped his hands, and suffered himself to be taken to Southampton and confronted with three more eye-witnesses.

Six weeks later he learnt his lesson. He learnt in exaggerated form what every man learns in some degree who commits his kind of folly. He learnt that when a man wilfully flies from his life; when he willfully loses his true self—or his head—he has lost it for ever.

V. The Terror of Fantasy

The Queen of the Bees

Erckmann-Chatrian

"As you go from Motiers-Navers to Boudry, on your way
to Neufchatel," said the young professor of botany, "you
follow a road between two walls of rocks of immense height;
they reach a perpendicular elevation of five or six hundred feet,
and are hung with wild plants, the mountain basil (thymus alpi-
nus), ferus (polypodium), the whortleberry (vitis idœa), ground
ivy, and other climbing plants producing a wonderful effect.

"The road winds along this defile; it rises, falls, turns, sometimes tolerably level, sometimes broken and abrupt, according
to the thousand irregularities of the ground. Gray rocks almost
meet in an arch overhead, others stand wide apart, leaving the
distant blue visible, and discovering sombre and melancholy-
looking depths, and rows of firs as far as the eye could reach.

"The Reuss flows along the bottom, sometimes leaping along
in waterfalls, then creeping through thickets, or steaming, foam-
ing, and thundering over precipices, while the echoes prolong
the tumult and roar of its torrents in one immense endless hum.
Since I left Tubingen the weather had continued fine; but when
I reached the summit of this gigantic staircase, about two
leagues distant from the little hamlet of Novisaigne, I suddenly
noticed great gray clouds begin passing overhead, which soon
filled up the defile entirely; this vapour was so dense that it soon
penetrated my clothes as a heavy dew would have done.

"Although it was only two in the afternoon, the sky became
clouded over as if darkness was coming on; and I foresaw a
heavy storm was about to break over my head.

"I consequently began looking about for shelter, and I
saw through one of those wide openings which afford you a

perspective view of the Alps, about two or three hundred yards distant on the slope leading down to the lake, an ancient-looking gray châlet, moss-covered, with its small round windows and sloping roof loaded with large stones, its stairs outside the house, with a carved rail, and its basket-shaped balcony, on which the Swiss maidens generally hang their snowy linen and scarlet petticoats to dry.

"Precisely as I was looking down, a tall woman in a black cap was folding and collecting the linen which was blowing about in the wind.

"To the left of this building a very large apiary supported on beams, arranged like a balcony, formed a projection above the valley.

"You may easily believe that without the loss of a moment I set off bounding through the heather to seek for shelter from the coming storm, and well it was I lost no time, for I had hardly laid my hand on the handle of the door before the hurricane burst furiously overhead; every gust of wind seemed about to carry the cottage bodily away; but its foundations were strong, and the security of the good people within, by the warmth of their reception, completely reassured me about the probability of any accident.

"The cottage was inhabited by Walter Young, his wife Catherine, and little Rœsel, their only daughter.

"I remained three days with them; for the wind, which went down about midnight, had so filled the valley of Neufchatel with mist, that the mountain where I had taken refuge was completely enveloped in it; it was impossible to walk twenty yards from the door without experiencing great difficulty in finding it again.

"Every morning these good people would say, when they saw me buckle on my knapsack—

"'What are you about, Mr. Hennetius? You cannot mean to go yet; you will never arrive anywhere. In the name of Heaven stay here a little longer!'

"And Young would open the door and exclaim—

"'Look there, sir; you must be tired of your life to risk it among these rocks. Why, the dove itself would be troubled to find the ark again in such a mist as this.'

"One glance at the mountain side was enough for me to make up my mind to put my stick back again in the corner.

"Walter Young was a man of the old times. He was nearly sixty; his grand head wore a calm and benevolent expression—a real Apostle's head. His wife, who always wore a black silk cap, pale and thoughtful, resembled him much in disposition. Their two profiles, as I looked at them defined sharply against the little panes of glass in the châlet's windows, recalled to my mind those drawings of Albert Durer the sight of which carried me back to the age of faith and the patriarchal manners of the fifteenth century. The long brown rafters of the ceiling, the deal table, the ashen chairs with the carved backs, the tin drinking-cups, the sideboard with its old-fashioned painted plates and dishes, the crucifix with the Saviour carved in box on an ebony cross, and the wormeaten clock-case with its many weights and its porcelain dial, completed the illusion.

"But the face of their little daughter Rœsel was still more touching. I think I can see her now, with her flat horsehair cap and watered black silk ribbons, her trim bodice and broad blue sash down to her knees, her little white hands crossed in the attitude of a dreamer, her long fair curls—all that was graceful, slender, and ethereal in nature. Yes, I can see Rœsel now, sitting in a large leathern armchair, close to the blue curtain of the recess at the end of the room, smiling as she listened and meditated.

"Her sweet face had charmed me from the first moment I saw her and I was continually on the point of inquiring why she wore such an habitually melancholy air, why did she hold her pale face down so invariably, and why did she never raise her eyes when spoken to?"

"Alas! the poor child had been blind from her birth.

"She had never seen the lake's vast expanse, nor its blue sheet blending so harmoniously with the sky, the fishermen's boats which ploughed its surface, the wooded heights which crowned it and cast their quivering reflection on its waters, the rocks covered with moss, the green Alpine plants in their vivid and brilliant colouring; nor had she ever watched the sun set behind the glaciers, nor the long shades of evening draw across the valleys, nor the golden broom, nor the endless heather—nothing. None of these things had she ever seen; nothing of what we saw every day from the windows of the châlet.

"'What an ironical commentary on the gifts of Fortune!' thought I, as I sat looking out of the window at the mist, in expectation of the sun's appearing once more, 'to be blind in this place! here in presence of Nature in its sublimest form, of such limitless grandeur! To be blind! Oh, Almighty God, who shall dare to dispute Thy impenetrable decrees, or who shall venture to murmur at the severity of Thy justice, even when its weight falls on an innocent child? But to be thus blind in the presence of Thy grandest creations, of creations which ceaselessly renew our enthusiasm, our love, and our adoration for Thy genius, Thy power, and Thy goodness; of what crime can this poor child have been guilty thus to deserve Thy chastisement?'

"And my reflections continually reverted to this topic.

"I asked myself, too, what compensation Divine pity could make its creature for the deprival of its greatest blessing, and, finding none, I began to doubt its power.

"'Man, in his presumption,' said the royal poet, "dares to glorify himself in his knowledge, and judge the Eternal. But his wisdom is but folly, and his light darkness.'

"On that day one of Nature's great mysteries was revealed to me, doubtless with the purpose of humbling my vanity, and of teaching me that nothing is impossible to God, and that it is in His power only to multiply our senses, and by so doing gratify those who please Him."

Here the young professor took a pinch from his tortoiseshell snuff-box, raised his eyes to the ceiling with a contemplative air, and then, after a short pause, continued in these terms:—

"Does it not often happen to you, ladies, when you are in the country in fine weather in summer, especially after a brief storm, when the air is warm, and the exhalations from the ground filling it with the perfume of thousands of plants, and their sweet scent penetrates and warms you; when the foliage from the trees in the solitary avenues, as well as from the bushes, seems to lean over you as if it sought to take you in its arms and embrace you; when the minutest flowers, the humble daisy, the blue forget-me-not, the convolvulus in the hedgerows raise their heads and follow you with a longing look—does it not happen to you to experience an inexpressible sensation of languor, to sigh for no apparent reason, and even to feel inclined to shed tears, and to ask yourselves, 'Why does this feeling of love oppress me? why do my knees bend under me? whence these tears?'

"Whence indeed, ladies? Why from life, and the thousands of living things which surround you, lean to you, and call to you to stay with them, while they gently murmur, 'We love you; love us, and do not leave us.'

"You can easily imagine, then, the deep enthusiastic feeling and the religious sentiment of a person always in a similar state of ecstasy. Even if blind, abandoned by his friends, do you think there is nothing to envy in his lot? or that his destiny is not infinitely happier than our own? For my own part I have not the slightest doubt of it.

"But you will, doubtless, say such a condition is impossible—the mind of man would break down under such a load of happiness. And, moreover, whence could such happiness be derived? What organs could transmit, and where could it find, such a sensation of universal life?

"This, ladies, is a question to which I can give you no answer; but I ask you to listen and then judge.

"The very day I arrived at the châlet I had made a singular remark—the blind girl was especially uneasy about the bees.

"While the wind was roaring without Rœsel sat with her head on her hands listening attentively.

"'Father,' said she, 'I think at the end of the apiary the third hive on the right is still open. Go and see. The wind blows from the north; all the bees are home; you can shut the hive.'

"And her father having gone out by a side door, when he returned he said—

"'It is all right, my child; I have closed the hive.'

"Half an hour afterwards the girl, rousing herself once more from her reverie, murmured—

"'There are no more bees about, but under the roof of the apiary there are some waiting; they are in the sixth hive near the door; please go and let them in, father.'

"The old man left the house at once. He was away more than

a quarter of an hour; then he came back and told his daughter that everything was as she wished it—the bees had just gone into their hive.

"The child nodded, and replied—

"'Thank you, father.'

"Then she seemed to doze again.

"I was standing by the stove, lost in a labyrinth of reflections; how could that poor blind girl know that from such or such a hive there were still some bees absent, or that such a hive had been left open? This seemed inexplicable to me; but having been in the house hardly one hour, I did not feel justified in asking my hosts any questions with regard to their daughter, for it is sometimes painful to talk to people on subjects which interest them very nearly. I concluded that Young gave way to his daughter's fancies in order to induce her to believe she was of some service in the family, and that her forethought protected the bees from several accidents. That seemed the simplest explanation I could imagine, and I thought no more about it.

"About seven we supped on milk and cheese, and when it was time to retire Young led me into a good-sized room on the first floor, with a bed and a few chairs in it, panelled in fir, as is generally the case in the greater number of Swiss châlets. You are only separated from your neighbours by a deal partition, and you can hear every footstep and nearly every word.

"That night I was lulled to sleep by the whistling of the wind and the sound of the rain beating against the window-panes. The next day the wind had gone down and we were enveloped in mist. When I awoke I found my windows quite white, quite padded with mist. When I opened my window the valley looked like an immense stove; the tops of a few fir-trees alone showed their outlines against the sky; below, the clouds were in regular layers down to the surface of the lake; everything was calm, motionless, and silent.

"When I went down to the sitting-room I found my hosts seated at table, about to begin breakfast.

"'We have been waiting for you,' cried Young gaily.

"'You must excuse us,' said the mother; 'this is our regular breakfast hour.'

"'Of course, of course; I am obliged to you for not noticing my laziness.'

"Rœsel was much more lively than the preceding evening; she had a fresh colour in her cheeks.

"'The wind has gone down,' said she; 'the storm has passed away without doing any harm.'

"'Shall I open the apiary?' asked Young.

"'No, not yet; the bees would lose themselves in this mist. Besides, everything is drenched with rain; the brambles and mosses are full of water; the least puff of wind would drown many of them. We must wait a little while. I know what is the matter: they feel dull, they want to work; they are tormented at the idea of devouring their honey instead of making it. But I cannot afford to lose them. Many of the hives are weak—they would starve in winter. We will see what the weather is like to-morrow.'

"The two old people sat and listened without making any observations.

"About nine the blind girl proposed to go and visit her bees; Young and Catherine followed her, and I did the same, from a very natural feeling of curiosity.

"We passed through the kitchen by a door which opened on to a terrace. Above us was the roof of the apiary; it was of thatch, and from its ledge honeysuckle and wild grapes hung in magnificent festoons. The hives were arranged on three shelves.

"Rœsel went from one to the other, patting them, and murmuring—

"'Have a little patience; there is too much mist this morning. Ah! the greedy ones, how they grumble!'

"And we could hear a vague humming inside the hive, which increased in intensity until she had passed.

"That awoke all my curiosity once more. I felt there was some strange mystery which I could not fathom, but what was my surprise, when, as I went into the sitting-room, I heard the blind girl say in a melancholy tone of voice—

"'No, father, I would rather not see at all today than lose my eyes. I will sing, I will do something or other to pass the time, never mind what; but I will not let the bees out.'

"While she was speaking in this strange manner I looked at Walter Young, who glanced out of the window and then quietly replied—

"'You are right, child; I think you are right. Besides, there is nothing to see; the valley is quite white. It is not worth looking at.'

"And while I sat astounded at what I heard, the child continued—

"'What lovely weather we had the day before yesterday! Who would have thought that a storm on the lake would have caused all this mist? Now one must fold up its wings and crawl about like a wretched caterpillar.'

"Then again, after a few moments' silence—

"'How I enjoyed myself under the lofty pines on the Grinderwald! How the honey-dew dropped from the sky! It fell from every branch. What a harvest we made, and how sweet the air was on the shores of the lake, and in the rich Tannemath pastures—the green moss, and the sweet-smelling herbs! I sang, I laughed, and we filled our cells with wax and honey. How delightful to be everywhere, see everything, to fly humming about the woods, the mountains, and the valleys!'

"There was a fresh silence, while I sat, with mouth and eyes open, listening with the greatest attention, not knowing what to think or what to say.

"'And when the shower came,' she went on, 'how frightened we were! A great humble-bee, sheltered under the same fern as myself, shut his eyes at every flash; a grasshopper had sheltered itself under its great green branches, and some poor little crickets had scrambled up a poppy to save themselves from drowning. But what was most frightful was a nest of warblers quite close to us in a bush. The mother hovered round about us, and the little ones opened their beaks, yellow as far as their windpipes. How frightened we were! Good Lord, we were frightened indeed! Thanks be to Heaven, a puff of wind carried us off to the mountain side; and now the vintage is over we must not expect to get out again so soon.'

"On hearing these descriptions of Nature so true, at this worship of day and light, I could no longer entertain the least doubt on the subject.

"'The blind girl sees,' said I to myself; 'she sees through thousands of eyes; the apiary is her life, her soul. Every bee carries a part of her away into space, and then returns drawn to her by thousands of invisible threads. The blind girl penetrates the flowers and the mosses; she revels in their perfume; when the sun shines she is everywhere; in the mountain side, in the valleys, in the forests, as far as her sphere of attraction extends.'

"I sat confounded at this strange magnetic influence, and felt tempted to exclaim—

"'Honour, glory, honour to the power, the wisdom, and the infinite goodness of the Eternal God! For Him nothing is impossible. Every day, every instant of our lives reveals to us His magnificence.'

"While I was lost in these enthusiastic reflections, Rœsel addressed me with a quiet smile.

"'Sir,' said she.

"'What, my child?'

"'You are very much surprised at me, and you are not the first person who has been so. The rector Hegel, of Neufchatel, and other travellers have been here on purpose to see me: they thought I was blind. You thought so too, did you not?'

"'I did indeed, my dear child, and I thank the Lord that I was mistaken.'

"'Yes,' said she, 'I know you are a good man—I can tell it by your voice. When the sun shines I shall open my eyes to look at you, and when you leave here I will accompany you to the foot of the mountain.'

"Then she began to laugh most artlessly.

"'Yes,' said she, 'you shall have music in your ears, and I will seat myself on your cheek; but you must take care—take care. You must not touch me, or I should sting you. You must promise not to be angry.'

"'I promise you, Rœsel, I promise you I will not,' I said with tears in my eyes, 'and, moreover, I promise you never to kill a bee or any other insect except those which do harm.'

"'They are the eyes of the Lord,' she murmured. 'I can only see by my own poor bees, but He has every hive, every ant's nest, every leaf, every blade of grass. He lives, He feels, He loves, He suffers, He does good by means of all these. Oh, Monsieur Hennetius, you are right not to pain the Lord, who loves us so much!"

"Never in my life had I been so moved and affected, and it was a full minute before I could ask her—

"'So, my dear child, you see by your bees; will you explain to me how that is?'

"'I cannot tell, Monsieur Hennetius; it may be because I am so fond of them. When I was quite a little child they adopted me, and they have never once hurt me. At first I liked to sit for hours in the apiary all alone and listen to their humming for hours together. I could see nothing then, everything was dark to me; but insensibly light came upon me. At first I could see the sun a little, when it was very hot, then a little more, with the wild vine and the honeysuckle like a shade over me, then the full light of day. I began to emerge from myself; my spirit went forth with the bees. I could see the mountains, the rocks, the lake, the flowers and mosses, and in the evening, when quite alone, I reflected on these things. I thought how beautiful they were, and when people talked of this and that, of whortleberries, and mulberries, and heaths, I said to myself, "I know what all these things are like— they are black, or brown, or green." I could see them in my mind, and every day I became better acquainted with them, thanks to my dear bees; and therefore I love them dearly, Monsieur Hennetius. If you knew how it grieves me when the time comes for robbing them of their wax and their honey!'

"'I believe you, my child—I believe it does.'

"My delight at this wonderful discovery was boundless.

"Two days longer Rœsel entertained me with a description of her impressions. She was acquainted with every flower, every Alpine plant, and gave me an account of a great number which have as yet received no botanical names, and which are probably only to be found in inaccessible situations.

"The poor girl was often much affected when she spoke of her dear friends, some little flowers.

"'Often and often,' said she, 'I have talked for hours with the golden broom or the tender blue-eyed forget-me-not, and shared in their troubles. They all wished to quit the earth and fly about; they all complained of their being condemned to dry up in the ground, and of being exposed to wait for days and weeks ere a drop of dew came to refresh them.'

"And so Rœsel used to repeat to me endless conversations of this sort. It was marvellous! If you only heard her you would be capable of falling in love with a dogrose, or of feeling a lively sympathy and a profound sentiment of compassion for a violet, its misfortunes and its silent sufferings.

"What more can I tell you, ladies? It is painful to leave a subject where the soul has so many mysterious emanations; there is such a field for conjecture; but as everything in this world must have an end, so must even the pleasantest dreams.

"Early in the morning of the third day of my stay a gentle breeze began to roll away the mist from off the lake. I could see its folds become larger every second as the wind drove them along, leaving one blue corner in the sky, and then another; then the tower of a village church, some green pinnacles on the tops of the mountains, then a row of firs, a valley, all the time the immense mass of vapour slowly floated past us; by ten it had left us behind it, and the great cloud on the dry peaks of the Chasseron still wore a threatening aspect; but a last effort of the wind gave it a different direction, and it disappeared at last in the gorges of Saint-Croix.

"Then the mighty nature of the Alps seemed to me to have born young again; the heather, the tall pines, the old chestnut-trees dripping with dew, shone with vigorous health; there was something in the view of them joyous, smiling, and serious all at once. One felt the hand of God was in it all—His eternity.

"I went downstairs lost in thought; Rœsel was already in the apiary. Young opened the door and pointed her out to me sitting in the shade of the wild vine, with her forehead resting on her hands, as if in a doze.

"'Be careful,' said he to me, 'not to awake her; her mind is elsewhere; she sleeps; she is wandering about; she is happy.'

"The bees were swarming about by thousands, like a flood of gold over a precipice.

"I looked on at this wonderful sight for some seconds, praying the Lord would continue His love for the poor child.

"Then turning round—

"'Master Young,' said I, 'it is time to go.'

"He buckled my knapsack on for me himself, and put my stick into my hand.

"Mistress Catherine looked on kindly, and they both accompanied me to the threshold of the châlet.

"'Farewell!' said Walter, grasping my hand; 'a pleasant journey; and think of us sometimes!'

"'I can never forget you,' I replied, quite melancholy; 'may your bees flourish, and may Heaven grant you are as happy as you deserve to be!'

"'So be it, M. Hennetius,' said good Dame Catherine; 'amen; a happy journey, and good health to you.'

"I moved off.

"They remained on the terrace until I reached the road.

"Thrice I turned round and waved my cap, and they responded by waving their hands.

"Good people; why cannot we meet with such every day?"

"Little Rœsel accompanied me to the foot of the mountain, as she had promised. For a long time her musical hum lightened the fatigue of my journey; I seemed to recognise her in every bee which came buzzing about my ears, and I fancied I could hear her say in a small shrill tone of voice—

"'Courage, M. Hennetius, courage; it is very hot, is it not? Come, let me give you a kiss; don't be afraid; you know we are very good friends.'

"It was only at the end of the valley that she took leave of me, when the sound of the lake drowned her gentle voice; but her idea followed me all through my journey, nor do I think it will ever leave me."

The Caves of Death

Gertrude Atherton

I cannot tell whether I had been asleep hours or moments, but I awoke suddenly as if shaken from my unconsciousness by some unseen hand. And immediately I was aware that a change had come over the night. The moon still shone clearly down into the little amphitheatre of hills wherein I lay, the redwoods still loomed unswayingly on the mountain beyond, the stars still glittered undisturbed in the heavens above, but yet there was a change. And the change, I realized, sprang from other than earthly conditions. The air was full of unheard sighs, the night of unseen shapes. How I knew this I cannot tell, for I saw nothing, and no voice spoke; reason and analysis had no part in my knowledge, but a heretofore unknown consciousness seemed suddenly awake and abnormally acute. In a moment I knew that something had happened on the hill behind me, and I turned with a sense of expectancy which was almost foreknowledge, and looked up. Something had appeared over the brow of the hill and was slowly descending. What was it? A chariot, a carriage, a vehicle, ancient or modern? I could not tell. Its outlines and substance were too dim, too shadowy, too unsubstantial, too elusive, but perhaps it bore more resemblance to a hearse than to any other human object. But whatever it may have been, it was followed by another, then another, and another, in a funereal procession of a kind never seen on earth. The long, ghostly train wound slowly down the hill, and traversing the space at its foot, disappeared in a cave which yawned opposite. Would it never end? Hundreds and hundreds of these hearses, half seen, imponderable as a mountain mist, vanished through the mouth of the cave, but hundreds still wound over the brow of the hill

241

until I knew that the number had swelled to thousands, and that time had passed. I knew, also, what it meant. That newly awakened, or newly born Consciousness supplied the place of externally derived knowledge. It was the funeral train of the souls of the dead, coming from the graves of their bodies, under earth and sea, where they had gone for one hour to weep, and on their way to their yearly rendezvous in the Christmas House of Death.

How long it was before the last of those pale chariots floated down the hill, I cannot tell, but after a time I found myself following the procession into the cave below. And as the light and the familiar objects of the outer world were left behind, my consciousness of this midnight phenomenon became still more acute, and sight and hearing developed themselves into more than mortal sensitiveness. In the long line of hearses winding before me through the depths of the hills, I caught, again and again, a glimpse of what was now a point of luminous white light, now expanded into the semblance of a human form, then contracting into shapelessness, or vanishing into nothingness. The air was torn with cries and groans, and more than once a shriek, frail and shadowy as the thing that gave it vent, came to my ears. But this was not all. I had learned in the great world above that no sound, once born and given to the waves of the air, can die until time and space shall be alike annihilated. In that wonderful expanse above, where the atmosphere vibrated with the sounds of men, or the million audible manifestations of Nature, and where human Consciousness was happily limited, that endless continuity of sound was dumb to human ears. But in this long, dark, silent passage in the heart of a mountain no sounds penetrated either of nature or of man, and the ocular sensitiveness of which I found myself in possession, gave me a new and terrible power. The wails and groans, the pale, wan shrieks, the occasional awful bursts of laughter, hollow as a dead man's skull, the feeble, colorless cry of the infant, the distant, dream-like sobs of pulsating wraiths, which once had lived in woman's form, the curses and cries of those who had sinned and died unrepentant, the smiling whispers of those few at perfect rest, echoed on and on and on in the vaulted roof above until sense was strained to the utmost limit of human endurance.

Fainter and fainter they grew until it seemed as if sound, human or ghostly, could survive no longer. But the end never came. Softer, softer, remoter, hollower, more unearthly, more difficult of perception grew those terrible echoes of ghostly woe, and sharper grew the strain to follow. Nor would they blend. The ear followed the bitter cry of the murderer, the groping wail of the solitary babe, the sob of the woman for the lover she had left, down to their infinitesimal vibrations and in all their individual separateness. If it had lasted much longer, my soul would have joined that pale army before me in one terrific human shriek, which would have echoed through all Eternity, overriding those thunder bubbles of air which called it forth.

But presently I saw that my journey was over, and that things were about to occur which would consign sound to temporary oblivion. The last hearse had disappeared, I could not tell where, and I stood at the entrance of a vast succession of caves, wide and white, and illuminated with a soft, dull radiance, which came from no visible lamp. Far down in their dim perspective that soft, cold light still shone, and I knew that endless caverns stretched beyond, and that mountain upon mountain must lie upon their heads. The floors, the walls, the mighty vaulted roof were of purest white, and softly polished, but of what they were composed no man could tell. That which lay about and looked down from above was finer than cobweb and denser than marble; it looked as if a sigh would blow it away, and as if the instruments of man would glance back, impotent, at its contact. It was so beautiful, so typical of stern and awful purity, so unearthly in its fairness that I took for a moment no note of anything beyond. The souls of sinners and saints, I knew, were summoned alike to these caves of loveliness and calm, that the latter might find more infinite peace and the former know greater anguish in the emblem afforded them of a bliss to be theirs, only after a punishment and probation extending over millions of years. Only from midnight until dawn of Christmas day were the gates to this wonderful realm thrown open, and in it all sounds, whether of joy or of pain, were inaudible save one. Far away, down in that dim perspective, I could see a white-robed choir, and the strains they gave forth, sad as the wail of a harp, and unearthly as the

Gertrude Atherton

forms of the choristers, floated through all that vast expanse and filled the air with a sweetness and an infinite harmony which the imagination of no mortal who has not heard it can conceive.

After a time I lowered my eyes and looked about me. The great hall formed by the ever multiplying caves was crowded with luminous, shadowy, transparent forms, visible at last under this all-searching light, in dim but distinct outline. I passed into a cave at my right and saw the faint negatives of faces I had known in my youth. In a moment I paused before a familiar form. It was that of a man who had posed for a cynic in the existence above, and for a blasé man of the world in the small community he had never left, and in which he had found the Alpha and Omega of his experience of life. French novels had convinced him that in common with the world he had no morality, and French dinners had sent him to rejoice the spirit world prematurely. And in the spirit world he was not comfortable. He had been wont to argue to admiring friends that there was no God, no future, no soul; therefore, when he found himself in the future and at the disposal of a God who insisted upon recognition, he felt somewhat vague and upset. But he had another and yet more trying grievance. Having disbelieved in the existence of a soul it was discomfiting to find himself a soul, pure and simple, merely that and nothing more. He did not know from what point of view to regard himself; that he must admire himself went without saying; but it was hard to be obliged to learn the lesson all over again. He was very much worried and he longed for the old existence artificial, where no one had ever accused him of being an entity.

My attention was quickly diverted from him to a group just beyond. On the floor crouched a man young in years but with the egotism of age speaking in every line. On a bench on a platform above him sat a thin, wiry, sardonic little man, his face "stamped deep with grins that had no merriment," his intelligent brow contracted in a savage frown, his coarse mouth set in a pitiless line. In his heart was a knife, and, as I gazed, he drew it slowly out and bent over the man at his feet. The motion was as deliberate as that of a snake curving itself to strike, and the other watched him with the fascinated gaze of the bird under the charm of the serpent. Then, with a swift motion, the arm of the man on the bench darted down and plunged the knife into the heart of the other, who rolled upon the floor, uttering voiceless cries of agony. Then I saw that the knife was not even as palpable in the form as the hand which had sent it home, but the wound it inflicted was sharp as the sting of Conscience. The man who had dealt the blow then raised himself upright on his bench and beckoned to a figure behind me. The figure approached and conferred with him, and I saw that he had been a man of much physical perfection, and I knew that the intelligence, which was all that was left of his earthly attributes had once been of great service to the little man on the bench. At his back was a large and interesting army of retainers, one and all of whom bore the outlines of woman's form. Of all shapes and sizes, of all color and style, of all conditions, mental, moral and social, they formed a beautiful illustration of the variety which may exist in one man's mind. They all wore a mocking smile, and its meaning was obvious. Upon earth he had had the privilege of beaming upon one at a time, but here he had the whole collection, with all their various and conflicting characteristics perpetually evident to eye and ear. He turned, after a moment, and I saw his face. He did not look happy.

I wandered into the next cave, but found few faces there that I knew. Before I left it, however, I paused a moment before a group which no observer could pass without noticing. Leaning with what in flesh would have been a heavy attitude against the wall of the cave was a man. He had the brutish face of the criminal cast, haggard and lined with cowardice and shameful punishment, and in his hand was a knife from which ghastly colorless drops dripped, dripped, with eternal persistence. Before him stood a girl, young, beautiful, with a hideous, gaping wound in her throat. She was saying nothing to the man who had murdered her, even in silent spirit-thought; she uttered no reproaches or words of forgiveness. She merely *looked*—looked at him with great, wide, transparent, horror-stricken eyes; eyes fixed forever in the look he had seen flash into them as he dealt the blow which cut short her brief life on earth, and which were destined to follow him throughout all eternity.

I entered the next cave and paused before a strange picture. In the middle of the room, the light shining full on his villainous, unintelligent face and ignoble head, stood a man who, during the trial which scandalized Europe and America, had been the most talked of and best hated man in the Great Republic. But the man he had murdered knelt at his feet and kissed his hands. "I have power here," he murmured in that voiceless interchange of thought, which was all that was allowed in these halls of silence. "Command me as you will in return for the immortality you conferred upon me." "Yes," said the other grimly, "if it had not been for me, you would have had favors of another sort today. You had already made as many mistakes as man ever contrives to crowd into so short a space of time, and you were just about to mount your steed and go down hill at a gallop when I stepped in and saved you. Now you wear a martyr's crown, and half the children in the nation are named after you. Moreover, you have been remembered for more than four years; you can never repay me for that." "Never!" murmured the other. "You can command me to any extent you please," and he settled the martyr's crown more firmly on his brow. Another man came by at the moment and joined the group. He had been a man of splendid make, and he bore himself with the air of a personage who yet had not sprung from the alleys and gutters. He looked enviously at the kneeling man. "You are fortunate," he said. "I died in bed, and had only a paragraph and one headline, while you monopolized the entire sheet and all the pictorials. I did my duty for the allotted time, incurred but little reproach, and killed myself by the exertion, yet I am forgotten, and you are a saint. Such is human destiny." And he passed on.

I glanced from the group which had claimed my attention for several moments, towards a figure calculated to attract the notice of the passer-by. Not that he was particularly striking in appearance, for he had a heavy, rather fishy face, but his occupation was a somewhat curious one, and not to be defined at first glance. His fingers were wandering with great precision in the empty air, now as if pulling, now adjusting, now changing and substituting objects invisible to even my quickened sense. It seemed, however, as if a delicate vibrating sound should have followed those manipulations. Finally he confined himself to one movement only, and pulled and pulled and pulled with a methodical persistency which commanded my admiration, but with no change of expression on his stolid face, varying as the results must have been. The kneeling man rose and approached him. "The ruling passion strong in death," he conveyed. "Yes," replied the other with a frown and a sigh. "It is a great pity I couldn't have stayed longer. I wouldn't have needed a bullet." "No," replied the other, "you would have hanged yourself with red tape." I smiled at this interchange of ghostly amenities, and went my way. Presently I met a woman whose face had been familiar to me in the brilliant societies of the world. She still bore vague, shadowy marks of beauty, and still held herself with the professional air. Her face assumed an aggrieved expression as she saw me. "I am not happy," she murmured. "No one admires me here." "That is unfortunate," I said. "Will nothing else satisfy you?" She opened wide the pale eyes which once had been so beautiful in their dark brilliancy. "What else is there?" she demanded. "You might recite," I suggested lamely. Her lip curled scornfully. "They do not appreciate my collection here," she replied. "I gave up trying to please them long ago. And they care nothing for my beauty, and toilettes I have none. My fame is gone! My fame is gone!" "Your notoriety," I amended mildly. "What is the difference!" she demanded. "All the newspapers babbled of me. And there is not a newspaper in spirit-land— woe is me!" "Would that I could dwell permanently in spirit-land," I sighed, and bade her farewell.

Suddenly I became aware that hours had passed, although no bell had tolled their flight; and I knew that the dawn of earth approached, for one and all of the ghostly multitude about me had turned their faces toward the choir, and were pressing down the long perspective of the caves. Just behind that choir, I knew, was an inner chamber, a holy of holies, which all who were forgiven were allowed to enter before departure, and experience one moment of a happiness which even that wonderful new Consciousness which had been granted me would not allow me to dimly picture. I followed the throng, however, and, looking through them, I saw the small band of the elect walking ahead

and apart. When they reached the outer portals of the Chamber
of Perfect Blessedness, the choir paused a moment, raising their
eyes and their hands; then, when the fortunate few had passed
within and the doors swung behind them, they burst into such a
wonderful peal of song that I thought the wretched beings without must be compensated for what was denied them. But it was
otherwise. They cast themselves face downward upon the
ground and burst into a voiceless wail of anguish which I felt but
could not bear, which thrilled all my being with its terrible
dumbness, but which must find no outlet to disturb the immortal sweetness of sound alone tolerated in these caves of beauty
and death.

Almost immediately the great doors behind the choir opened
again and the few who had passed through them reappeared.
And, although they had known but one moment of perfect bliss,
their faces were transfigured with the radiance of what would
preclude the possibility of further suffering in all spirit time to
come. In re-embodiment they would again experience the trials
of humanity, but in a modified degree, and until then they were
exempt. They passed the prostrate millions, retraversed the long
line of the caves, and disappeared through the entrance into the
darkness beyond. Then the others rose and with bowed heads
followed, the music going with them in strains of sadness and
compassion, and passed in turn into the gloom of the way by
which they had come. Then voice came to them once more, and
the beauty and melody and harmony of the past hours vanished
for the moment from my memory. Shrieks and groans, wails and
cries, curses and sobs once more rent the air. The turmoil of
their coming faded into insignificance beside that of their going;
the air seemed literally creaking and groaning beneath the burden cast upon it and of which it would never be freed. Again my
ear strained itself to follow those dying waves of sound, until I
longed for the peace of the outer world with a longing equaling
in intensity that of the sinners before me for the one moment of
happiness which awaited them in the twilight of coming centuries. But it was not in my power to pass that funeral train, and
it was only after what, in my torment, seemed interminable
hours that I stood at length under the stars without and watched

the last filmy chariot of the dead pass up the hill and disappear over its brow. I followed, but when I reached the hill's summit no trace of that ghostly cortege could be seen. Nothing met my gaze but nature slumbering peacefully under her coverlid of dew. Then I glanced toward the east and saw a line of rosy light. The dawn had come. It was Christmas morning.

The Soldiers' Rest

Arthur Machen

The soldier with the ugly wound in the head opened his eyes at last, and looked about him with an air of pleasant satisfaction.

He still felt drowsy and dazed with some fierce experience through which he had passed, but so far he could not recollect much about it. But an agreeable glow began to steal about his heart—such a glow as comes to people who have been in a tight place and have come through it better than they had expected. In its mildest form this set of emotions may be observed in passengers who have crossed the Channel on a windy day without being sick. They triumph a little internally, and are suffused with vague, kindly feelings.

The wounded soldier was somewhat of this disposition as he opened his eyes, pulled himself together, and looked about him. He felt a sense of delicious ease and repose in bones that had been racked and weary, and deep in the heart that had so lately been tormented there was an assurance of comfort—of the battle won. The thundering, roaring waves were passed; he had entered into the haven of calm waters. After fatigues and terrors that as yet he could not recollect he seemed now to be resting in the easiest of all easy chairs in a dim, low room.

In the hearth there was a glint of fire and a blue, sweet-scented puff of wood smoke; a great black oak beam roughly hewn crossed the ceiling. Through the leaded panes of the windows he saw a rich glow of sunlight, green lawns, and against the deepest and most radiant of all blue skies the wonderful far-lifted towers of a vast Gothic cathedral—mystic, rich with imagery.

"Good Lord!" he murmured to himself. "I didn't know they had such places in France. It's just like Wells. And it might be the other day when I was going past the Swan, just as it might be past that window, and asked the ostler what time it was, and he says, 'What time? Why, summer-time'; and there outside it looks like summer that would last for ever. If this was an inn they ought to call it 'The Soldiers' Rest.'"

He dozed off again, and when he opened his eyes once more a kindly looking man in some sort of black robe was standing by him.

"It's all right now, isn't it?" he said, speaking in good English.

"Yes, thank you, sir, as right as can be. I hope to be back again soon."

"Well, well; but how did you come here? Where did you get that?" He pointed to the wound on the soldier's forehead.

The soldier put his hand up to his brow and looked dazed and puzzled.

"Well, sir," he said at last, "it was like this, to begin at the beginning. You know how we came over in August, and there we were in the thick of it, as you might say, in a day or two. An awful time it was, and I don't know how I got through it alive. My best friend was killed dead beside me as we lay in the trenches. By Cambrai, I think it was.

"Then things got a little quieter for a bit, and I was quartered in a village for the best part of a week. She was a very nice lady where I was, and she treated me proper with the best of everything. Her husband he was fighting; but she had the nicest little boy I ever knew, a little fellow of five, or six it might be, and we got on splendid. The amount of their lingo that kid taught me— 'We, we' and 'Bong swor' and 'Commong voo porty voo,' and all—and I taught him English. You should have heard that nipper say '"Arf a mo', old un'! It was a treat.

"Then one day we got surprised. There was about a dozen of us in the village, and two or three hundred Germans came down on us early one morning. They got us; no help for it. Before we could shoot.

.   .   .   .   .   .

"Well, there we were. They tied our hands behind our backs, and smacked our faces and kicked us a bit, and we were lined up opposite the house where I'd been staying.

"And then that poor little chap broke away from his mother, and he run out and saw one of the Boshes, as we call them, fetch me one over the jaw with his clenched fist. Oh dear! oh dear! he might have done it a dozen times if only that little child hadn't seen him.

"He had a poor bit of a toy I'd bought him at the village shop; a toy gun it was. And out he came running, as I say, crying out something in French like 'Bad man! bad man! don't hurt my Anglish or I shoot you'; and he pointed that gun at the German soldier. The German, he took his bayonet, and he drove it right through the poor little chap's throat."

The soldier's face worked and twitched and twisted itself into a sort of grin, and he sat grinding his teeth and staring at the man in the black robe. He was silent for a little. And then he found his voice, and the oaths rolled terrible, thundering from him, as he cursed that murderous wretch, and bade him go down and burn for ever in hell. And the tears were raining down his face, and they choked him at last.

"I beg your pardon, sir, I'm sure," he said, "especially you being a minister of some kind, I suppose; but I can't help it. He was such a dear little man."

The man in black murmured something to himself: *"Pretiosa in conspectu Domini mors innocentium ejus"*—Dear in the sight of the Lord is the death of His innocents. Then he put a kind hand very gently on the soldier's shoulder.

"Never mind," said he; "I've seen some service in my time, myself. But what about that wound?"

"Oh, that; that's nothing. But I'll tell you how I got it. It was just like this. The Germans had us fair, as I tell you, and they shut us up in a barn in the village; just flung us on the ground and left us to starve seemingly. They barred up the big door of the barn, and put a sentry there, and thought we were all right.

"There were sort of slits like very narrow windows in one of the walls, and on the second day it was, I was looking out of these slits down the street, and I could see those German devils were up to mischief. They were planting their machine guns everywhere handy where an ordinary man coming up the street would never see them, but I see them, and I see the infantry lining up behind the garden walls. Then I had a sort of a notion of what was coming; and presently, sure enough, I could hear some of our chaps singing 'Hullo, hullo, hullo!' in the distance; and I says to myself, 'Not this time.'

"So I looked about me, and I found a hole under the wall; a kind of a drain I should think it was, and I found I could just squeeze through. And I got out and crept round, and away I goes running down the street, yelling for all I was worth, just as our chaps were getting round the corner at the bottom. 'Bang, bang!' went the guns, behind me and in front of me, and on each side of me, and then—bash! something hit me on the head and over I went; and I don't remember anything more till I woke up here just now."

The soldier lay back in his chair and closed his eyes for a moment. When he opened them he saw that there were other people in the room besides the minister in the black robes. One was a man in a big black cloak. He had a grim old face and a great beaky nose. He shook the soldier by the hand.

"By God! sir," he said, "you're a credit to the British Army; you're a damned fine soldier and a good man, and, by God! I'm proud to shake hands with you."

And then someone came out of the shadow, someone in queer clothes such as the soldier had seen worn by the heralds when he had been on duty at the opening of Parliament by the King.

"Now, by Corpus Domini," this man said, "of all knights ye be noblest and gentlest, and ye be of fairest report, and now ye be a brother of the noblest brotherhood that ever was since this world's beginning, since ye have yielded dear life for your friends' sake."

The soldier did not understand what the man was saying to him. There were others, too, in strange dresses, who came and spoke to him. Some spoke in what sounded like French. He could not make it out; but he knew that they all spoke kindly and praised him.

"What does it all mean?" he said to the minister. "What are they talking about? They don't think I'd let down my pals?"

"Drink this," said the minister, and he handed the soldier a great silver cup, brimming with wine.

The soldier took a deep draught, and in that moment all his sorrows passed from him.

"What is it?" he asked.

"Vin nouveau du Royaume," said the minister. "New Wine of the Kingdom, you call it." And then he bent down and murmured in the soldier's ear.

"What," said the wounded man, "the place they used to tell us about in Sunday School? With such drink and such joy——"

His voice was hushed. For as he looked at the minister the fashion of his vesture was changed. The black robe seemed to melt away from him. He was all in armour, if armour be made of starlight, of the rose of dawn, and of sunset fires; and he lifted up a great sword of flame.

> *Full in the midst, his Cross of Red*
> *Triumphant Michael brandished,*
> *And trampled the Apostate's pride.*

VI. The Terror of the Cosmic

Romance

Lord Dunsany

At a certain hour of the night, when the house is quiet and one candle is burning alone in some old large room, burning and flickering from unknown draughts, the diaphanous figure of Romance comes softly in.

He comes over the cold fields by way of Camelot, past Avalon and Arcady and Fairyland, from painting the faces of the ancient years that lie in the tombs of Time. Full of glamour then becomes all that he touches; he reveals hidden meanings and histories never chronicled. His cloak is woven of shadows, cast by the moon, of spiders' webs in old deserted chambers.

When I saw this robe about Romance I perceived for the first time the fearful wonder in the dark spider's art. He works in his cornices silently like the stars, till his terrible fortress is built and his door is ready for the travellers that only come one way. Never a night ekes out its long dark hours but screams are heard in that fortress by all whose ears are attuned to the grief of the gnat or fly.

Picture yourself pursuing an uncertain way by night in a land shut in by mountains. Suddenly you stumble through a vast door. It closes, and bolts are shot. You are in a great hall full of doors. A grand staircase sweeps up into remote darkness, and you have a fear of that staircase. Some of the doors open and lead nowhere; some are already barred; portcullises are falling all round you and closing possible exits. Bells are ringing continually in a dark tower at the top of the stairs that you dread. They ring worse whenever you move. You try door after door and look askance at the stairs. Chains begin to come creeping down the wall from dungeons up above you invisible in the darkness. Pits are opening in the floor, but still you watch the staircase. Presently the banisters begin to ripple, and far up the staircase, as far as you can see, the worst happens. And a fearful thing is coming softly downstairs, a crab-like tiger with lolling bags of eyes; and you know him by the marks upon his back. And then you scream; and he goes up to a little cupboard and takes out some chains. Then he comes towards you lightly on his toes. It was like that when I dreamed that I was a fly.

When Romance came I guessed the history of the dust that lay in the spider's web. It came on an old east wind from Babylon. He has despoiled Assyria to pave his court. Where are the colours faded from old tapestry?

"I have them," said the spider.

"Hast thou the blue of the eyes of painted queens?" I said.

"It is mine," said the spider.

He has the purple cloaks of moths that have foundered long since in the night through which they used to sail.

He is very still on his feet. He has no song like the gnat, for he would not break the silence. The silence is his goodly ornament that the dead years have left him for a heritage.

I thought I heard the rats go round and round because they would not rest. But it was Romance bringing back dead feet again. Why do you come, dead feet? The years are here. You are seeking for something that you cannot find. The years have taken it. Go back to your place, dead feet, where you are safe from the years.

Still going to and fro! Still walking round and round! You seek for our weeping, ye dead feet. We have forgotten you, and weep no more. The years have made us forget, not our hearts, dead feet.

And then Romance sat down beside me and looked into the fire. And we saw old gardens in it, and people walking in them long ago; and always the smoke went up and up the chimney. And they that walked in those gardens long ago met with one another under the tall sunflowers, and Romance knew to what region of the sky the echoes of their footsteps have gone quivering away. Crunch, crunch on the gravel, and a rustle of dress. Now a sigh and now a word; the echoes are living yet. They go to cheer perhaps the furthest stars, even the lonely ones that feel the chill of Space. How soon they tumble in, those gardens in the fire; and the smoke goes up and up. Very soon it will be up, far up, in the cold night, and the world will leave it behind.

And Romance knows how lonely it is for the smoke in the great spaces to which he arises from the homely hearth. He stands up god-like up above the world, and takes his warmth no more from the hearths of men but from the tremendous sun. As little gray patches appear to him whole cities, whence his brethren leap up to him singing of the sky. He beholds and knows the errands of the stars. He is among the four primeval winds, and there he stands in the heights regretting Earth. As we look into the fire, Romance and I, a great number of people are sitting just behind me. They used to look into this fireplace years and years ago. If I turn my head to see them they will all go away.

Romance has made a wreath for his head out of the shadows of broken toys in silent nurseries where dead echoes are.

There is no reason why I should weep, if I look at the wreath on his head. Nevertheless I do not look at it, for it sits mournfully upon his head, and the great draughts that roam about the room when the house is lonely blow through and through the wreath and make it sigh.

Sometimes Romance rises and goes all round the house, and I go with him into empty, sounding rooms. I said unto Romance, "Show me old ghosts and bring the old songs back." But he has a way of touching quite common things. He touched a billiard ball as he passed by. And then I knew that in its ivory core it cares not much for its little skilful journeys round and round the table, the slave of men at play, but in indolent hours dreams, in the quest house, of terrible journeys through warm African forests, when it was moist with rains and glittered with stars and moon and with the fearful sagacity of two little eyes. It is not a joy to it to hear men laugh at their play; they never laughed near it in the days gone by. And then it turns over in its ivory core horrible old memories of the days of its strength.

As we went round the house, Romance and I, we heard a clock ticking loudly. And a look of anger came over the face of Romance, for he hates and despises Time. There is the blood of old ghosts on the hands of the clock, ghosts that Romance has loved. One by one it has hammered their days away. And those bloody hands Romance could not bear to see. But he turned from me slowly and faded as he turned, and, gathering about him a retinue of dreams, passed through the window over night-haunted fields and so went back to his lair in Nineveh.

And there in the corner stands the tall old clock, swinging his long pendulum to and fro, even as a headsman that has grown old at his trade swings up and down his axe—and not in idleness but to strike the deadlier blow.

The Man Who Found Out

(A Nightmare)

Algernon Blackwood

1

P rofessor Mark Ebor, the scientist, led a double life, and the only persons who knew it were his assistant, Dr. Laidlaw, and his publishers. But a double life need not always be a bad one, and, as Dr. Laidlaw and the gratified publishers well knew, the parallel lives of this particular man were equally good, and indefinitely produced would certainly have ended in a heaven somewhere that can suitably contain such strangely opposite characteristics as his remarkable personality combined.

For Mark Ebor, F.R.S., etc., etc., was that unique combination hardly ever met with in actual life, a man of science and a mystic.

As the first, his name stood in the gallery of the great, and as the second—but there came the mystery! For under the pseudonym of "Pilgrim" (the author of that brilliant series of books that appealed to so many), his identity was as well concealed as that of the anonymous writer of the weather reports in a daily newspaper. Thousands read the sanguine, optimistic, stimulating little books that issued annually from the pen of "Pilgrim," and thousands bore their daily burdens better for having read; while the Press generally agreed that the author, besides being an incorrigible enthusiast and optimist, was also—a woman; but no one ever succeeded in penetrating the veil of anonymity and discovering that "Pilgrim" and the biologist were one and the same person.

Mark Ebor, as Dr. Laidlaw knew him in his laboratory, was one man; but Mark Ebor, as he sometimes saw him after work was over, with rapt eyes and ecstatic face, discussing possibilities of "union with God" and the future of the human race, was quite another.

"I have always held, as you know," he was saying one evening as he sat in the little study beyond the laboratory with his assistant and intimate, "that Vision should play a large part in the life of the awakened man—not to be regarded as infallible, of course, but to be observed and made use of as a guide-post to possibilities——"

"I am aware of your peculiar views, sir," the young doctor put in deferentially, yet with a certain impatience.

"For Visions come from a region of the consciousness where observation and experiment are out of the question," pursued the other with enthusiasm, not noticing the interruption, "and, while they should be checked by reason afterwards, they should not be laughed at or ignored. All inspiration, I hold, is of the nature of interior Vision, and all our best knowledge has come— such is my confirmed belief—as a sudden revelation to the brain prepared to receive it——"

"Prepared by hard work first, by concentration, by the closest possible study of ordinary phenomena," Dr. Laidlaw allowed himself to observe.

"Perhaps," sighed the other; "but by a process, none the less, of spiritual illumination. The best match in the world will not light a candle unless the wick be first suitably prepared."

It was Laidlaw's turn to sigh. He knew so well the impossibility of arguing with his chief when he was in the regions of the mystic, but at the same time the respect he felt for his tremendous attainments was so sincere that he always listened with attention and deference, wondering how far the great man would go and to what end this curious combination of logic and "illumination" would eventually lead him.

"Only last night," continued the elder man, a sort of light coming into his rugged features, "the vision came to me again— the one that has haunted me at intervals ever since my youth, and that will not be denied."

Dr. Laidlaw fidgeted in his chair.

"About the Tablets of the Gods, you mean—and that they lie somewhere hidden in the sands," he said patiently. A sudden

gleam of interest came into his face as he turned to catch the
professor's reply.

"And that I am to be the one to find them, to decipher them,
and to give the great knowledge to the world——"

"Who will not believe," laughed Laidlaw shortly, yet interested in spite of his thinly-veiled contempt.

"Because even the keenest minds, in the right sense of the
word, are hopelessly—unscientific," replied the other gently, his
face positively aglow with the memory of his vision. "Yet what is
more likely," he continued after a moment's pause, peering into
space with rapt eyes that saw things too wonderful for exact language to describe, "than that there should have been given to
man in the first ages of the world some record of the purpose
and problem that had been set him to solve? In a word," he
cried, fixing his shining eyes upon the face of his perplexed
assistant, "that God's messengers in the far-off ages should have
given to His creatures some full statement of the secret of the
world, of the secret of the soul, of the meaning of life and
death—the explanation of our being here, and to what great end
we are destined in the ultimate fullness of things?"

Dr. Laidlaw sat speechless. These outbursts of mystical
enthusiasm he had witnessed before. With any other man he
would not have listened to a single sentence, but to Professor
Ebor, man of knowledge and profound investigator, he listened
with respect, because he regarded this condition as temporary
and pathological, and in some sense a reaction from the intense
strain of the prolonged mental concentration of many days.

He smiled, with something between sympathy and resigna-
tion as he met the other's rapt gaze.

"But you have said, sir, at other times, that you consider the
ultimate secrets to be screened from all possible——"

"The *ultimate* secrets, yes," came the unperturbed reply; "but
that there lies buried somewhere an indestructible record of the
secret meaning of life, originally known to men in the days of
their pristine innocence, I am convinced. And, by this strange
vision so often vouchsafed to me, I am equally sure that one day
it shall be given to me to announce to a weary world this glorious and terrific message."

And he continued at great length and in glowing language to describe the species of vivid dream that had come to him at intervals since earliest childhood, showing in detail how he discovered these very Tablets of the Gods, and proclaimed their splendid contents—whose precise nature was always, however, withheld from him in the vision—to a patient and suffering humanity.

"The *Scrutator,* sir, well described 'Pilgrim' as the Apostle of Hope," said the young doctor gently, when he had finished; "and now, if that reviewer could hear you speak and realize from what strange depths comes your simple faith——"

The professor held up his hand, and the smile of a little child broke over his face like sunshine in the morning.

"Half the good my books do would be instantly destroyed," he said sadly; "they would say that I wrote with my tongue in my cheek. But wait," he added significantly; "wait till I find these Tablets of the Gods! Wait till I hold the solutions of the old world-problems in my hands! Wait till the light of this new revelation breaks upon confused humanity, and it wakes to find its bravest hopes justified! Ah, then, my dear Laidlaw——"

He broke off suddenly; but the doctor, cleverly guessing the thought in his mind, caught him up immediately.

"Perhaps this very summer," he said, trying hard to make the suggestion keep pace with honesty; "in your explorations in Assyria—your digging in the remote civilization of what was once Chaldea, you may find—what you dream of——"

The professor held up his hand, and the smile of a fine old face.

"Perhaps," he murmured softly, "perhaps!"

And the young doctor, thanking the gods of science that his leader's aberrations were of so harmless a character, went home strong in the certitude of his knowledge of externals, proud that he was able to refer his visions to self-suggestion, and wondering complaisantly whether in his old age he might not after all suffer himself from visitations of the very kind that afflicted his respected chief.

And as he got into bed and thought again of his master's rugged face, and finely shaped head, and the deep lines traced by years of work and self-discipline, he turned over on his pillow and fell asleep with a sigh that was half of wonder, half of regret.

2

It was in February, nine months later, when Dr. Laidlaw made his way to Charing Cross to meet his chief after his long absence of travel and exploration. The vision about the so-called Tablets of the Gods had meanwhile passed almost entirely from his memory.

There were few people in the train, for the stream of traffic was now running the other way, and he had no difficulty in finding the man he had come to meet. The shock of white hair beneath the low-crowned felt hat was alone enough to distinguish him by easily.

"Here I am at last!" exclaimed the professor, somewhat wearily, clasping his friend's hand as he listened to the young doctor's warm greetings and questions. "Here I am—a little older, and *much* dirtier than when you last saw me!" He glanced down laughingly at his travel-stained garments.

"And *much* wiser," said Laidlaw, with a smile, as he bustled about the platform for porters and gave his chief the latest scientific news.

At last they came down to practical considerations.

"And your luggage—where is that? You must have tons of it, I suppose?" said Laidlaw.

"Hardly anything," Professor Ebor answered. "Nothing, in fact, but what you see."

"Nothing but this hand-bag?" laughed the other, thinking he was joking.

"And a small portmanteau in the van," was the quiet reply. "I have no other luggage."

"You have no other luggage?" repeated Laidlaw, turning sharply to see if he were in earnest.

"Why should I need more?" the professor added simply.

Something in the man's face, or voice, or manner—the doctor hardly knew which—suddenly struck him as strange. There was a change in him, a change so profound—so little on the surface, that is—that at first he had not become aware of it. For a moment it was as though an utterly alien personality stood before him in that noisy, bustling throng. Here, in all the homely, friendly turmoil of a Charing Cross crowd, a curious feeling of cold passed over his heart, touching his life with icy finger, so that he actually trembled and felt afraid.

He looked up quickly at his friend, his mind working with startled and unwelcome thoughts.

"Only this?" he repeated, indicating the bag. "But where's all the stuff you went away with? And—have you brought nothing home—no treasures?"

"This is all I have," the other said briefly. The pale smile that went with the words caused the doctor a second indescribable sensation of uneasiness. Something was very wrong, something was very queer; he wondered now that he had not noticed it sooner.

"The rest follows, of course, by slow freight," he added tactfully, and as naturally as possible. "But come, sir, you must be tired and in want of food after your long journey. I'll get a taxi at once, and we can see about the other luggage afterwards."

It seemed to him he hardly knew quite what he was saying; the change in his friend had come upon him so suddenly and now grew upon him more and more distressingly. Yet he could not make out exactly in what it consisted. A terrible suspicion began to take shape in his mind, troubling him dreadfully.

"I am neither very tired, nor in need of food, thank you," the professor said quietly. "And this is all I have. There is no luggage to follow. I have brought home nothing—nothing but what you see."

His words conveyed finality. They got into a taxi, tipped the porter, who had been staring in amazement at the venerable figure of the scientist, and were conveyed slowly and noisily to the house in the north of London where the laboratory was, the scene of their labours of years.

And the whole way Professor Ebor uttered no word, nor did Dr. Laidlaw find the courage to ask a single question.

It was only late that night, before he took his departure, as the two men were standing before the fire in the study—that study where they had discussed so many problems of vital and absorbing interest—that Dr. Laidlaw at last found strength to come to the point with direct questions. The professor had been giving him a superficial and desultory account of his travels, of his journeys by camel, of his encampments among the mountains and in the desert, and of his explorations among the buried temples, and, deeper, into the waste of the pre-historic sands, when suddenly the doctor came to the desired point with a kind of nervous rush, almost like a frightened boy.

"And you found——" he began stammering, looking hard at the other's dreadfully altered face, from which every line of hope and cheerfulness seemed to have been obliterated as a sponge wipes markings from a slate—"you found——"

"I found," replied the other, in a solemn voice, and it was the voice of the mystic rather than the man of science—"I found what I went to seek. The vision never once failed me. It led me straight to the place like a star in the heavens. I found—the Tablets of the Gods."

Dr. Laidlaw caught his breath, and steadied himself on the back of a chair. The words fell like particles of ice upon his heart. For the first time the professor had uttered the well-known phrase without the glow of light and wonder in his face that always accompanied it.

"You have—brought them?" he faltered.

"I have brought them home," said the other, in a voice with a ring like iron; "and I have—deciphered them."

Profound despair, the bloom of outer darkness, the dead sound of a hopeless soul freezing in the utter cold of space seemed to fill in the pauses between the brief sentences. A silence followed, during which Dr. Laidlaw saw nothing but the white face before him alternately fade and return. And it was like the face of a dead man.

"They are, alas, indestructible," he heard the voice continue, with its even, metallic ring.

"Indestructible," Laidlaw repeated mechanically, hardly knowing what he was saying.

Again a silence of several minutes passed, during which, with a creeping cold about his heart, he stood and stared into the eyes of the man he had known and loved so long—aye, and worshipped, too; the man who had first opened his own eyes when they were blind, and had led him to the gates of knowledge, and no little distance along the difficult path beyond; the man who, in another direction, had passed on the strength of his faith into the hearts of thousands by his books.

"I may see them?" he asked at last, in a low voice he hardly recognized as his own. "You will let me know—their message?"

Professor Ebor kept his eyes fixedly upon his assistant's face as he answered, with a smile that was more like the grin of death than a living human smile.

"When I am gone," he whispered; "when I have passed away. Then you shall find them and read the translation I have made. And then, too, in your turn, you must try, with the latest resources of science at your disposal to aid you, to compass their utter destruction." He paused a moment, and his face grew pale as the face of a corpse. "Until that time," he added presently, without looking up, "I must ask you not to refer to the subject again— and to keep my confidence meanwhile—*ab—so—lute-ly.*"

3

A year passed slowly by, and at the end of it Dr. Laidlaw had found it necessary to sever his working connexion with his friend and one-time leader. Professor Ebor was no longer the same man. The light had gone out of his life; the laboratory was closed; he no longer put pen to paper or applied his mind to a single problem. In the short space of a few months he had passed from a hale and hearty man of late middle life to the con- dition of old age—a man collapsed and on the edge of dissolu- tion. Death, it was plain, lay waiting for him in the shadows of any day—and he knew it.

To describe faithfully the nature of this profound alteration in his character and temperament is not easy, but Dr. Laidlaw summed it up to himself in three words: *Loss of Hope.* The splendid mental powers remained indeed undimmed, but the incentive to use them—to use them for the help of others—had gone. The character still held to its fine and unselfish habits of years, but the far goal to which they had been the leading strings had faded away. The desire for knowledge—knowledge for its own sake—had died, and the passionate hope which hitherto had animated with tireless energy the heart and brain of this splendidly equipped intellect had suffered total eclipse. The central fires had gone out. Nothing was worth doing, thinking, working for. There *was* nothing to work for any longer!

The professor's first step was to recall as many of his books as possible; his second to close his laboratory and stop all research. He gave no explanation, he invited no questions. His whole personality crumbled away, so to speak, till his daily life became a mere mechanical process of clothing the body, feeding the body, keeping it in good health so as to avoid physical discomfort, and, above all, doing nothing that could interfere with sleep. The professor did everything he could to lengthen the hours of sleep, and therefore of forgetfulness.

It was all clear enough to Dr. Laidlaw. A weaker man, he knew, would have sought to lose himself in one form or another of sensual indulgences—sleeping-draughts, drink, the first pleasures that came to hand. Self-destruction would have been the method of a little bolder type; and deliberate evil-doing, poisoning with his awful knowledge all he could, the means of still another kind of man. Mark Ebor was none of these. He held himself under fine control, facing silently and without complaint the terrible facts he honestly believed himself to have been unfortunate enough to discover. Even to his intimate friend and assistant, Dr. Laidlaw, he vouchsafed no word of true explanation or lament. He went straight forward to the end, knowing well that the end was not very far away.

And death came very quietly one day to him, as he was sitting in the armchair of the study, directly facing the doors of the laboratory—the doors that no longer opened. Dr. Laidlaw, by happy chance, was with him at the time, and just able to reach his side in response to the sudden painful efforts for breath; just in time, too, to catch the murmured words that fell from the pallid lips like a message from the other side of the grave.

"Read them, if you must; and, if you can—destroy. But"—his voice sank so low that Dr. Laidlaw only just caught the dying syllables—"but—never, never—give them to the world."

And like a gray bundle of dust loosely gathered up in an old garment the professor sank back into his chair and expired.

But this was only the death of the body. His spirit had died two years before.

4

The estate of the dead man was small and uncomplicated, and Dr. Laidlaw, as sole executor and residuary legatee, had no difficulty in settling it up. A month after the funeral he was sitting alone in his upstairs library, the last sad duties completed, and his mind full of poignant memories and regrets for the loss of a friend he had revered and loved, and to whom his debt was so incalculably great. The last two years, indeed, had been for him terrible. To watch the swift decay of the greatest combination of heart and brain he had ever known, and to realize he was powerless to help, was a source of profound grief to him that would remain to the end of his days.

At the same time an insatiable curiosity possessed him. The study of dementia was, of course, outside his special province as a specialist, but he knew enough of it to understand how small a matter might be the actual cause of how great an illusion, and he had been devoured from the very beginning by a ceaseless and increasing anxiety to know what the professor had found in the sands of "Chaldea," what these precious Tablets of the Gods might be, and particularly—for this was the real cause that had sapped the man's sanity and hope—what the inscription was that he had believed to have deciphered thereon.

The curious feature of it all to his own mind was, that whereas his friend had dreamed of finding a message of glorious hope and comfort, he had apparently found (so far as he had found anything intelligible at all, and not invented the whole thing in his dementia) that the secret of the world, and the meaning of life and death, was of so terrible a nature that it robbed the heart of courage and the soul of hope. What, then, could be the contents of the little brown parcel the professor had bequeathed to him with his pregnant dying sentences?

Actually his hand was trembling as he turned to the writing-table and began slowly to unfasten a small old-fashioned desk on which the small gilt initials "M.E." stood forth as a melancholy memento. He put the key into the lock and half turned it. Then, suddenly, he stopped and looked about him. Was that a sound at the back of the room? It was just as though someone had laughed and then tried to smother the laugh with a cough. A slight shiver ran over him as he stood listening.

"This is absurd," he said aloud; "too absurd for belief—that I should be so nervous! It's the effect of curiosity unduly prolonged." He smiled a little sadly and his eyes wandered to the blue summer sky and the plane trees swaying in the wind below his window. "It's the reaction," he continued. "The curiosity of two years to be quenched in a single moment! The nervous tension, of course, must be considerable."

He turned back to the brown desk and opened it without further delay. His hand was firm now, and he took out the paper parcel that lay inside without a tremor. It was heavy. A moment later there lay on the table before him a couple of weather-worn plaques of gray stone—they looked like stone, although they felt like metal—on which he saw markings of a curious character that might have been the mere tracings of natural forces through the ages, or, equally well, the half-obliterated hieroglyphics cut upon their surface in past centuries by the more or less untutored hand of a common scribe.

He lifted each stone in turn and examined it carefully. It seemed to him that a faint glow of heat passed from the substance into his skin, and he put them down again suddenly, as with a gesture of uneasiness.

"A very clever, or a very imaginative man," he said to himself, "who could squeeze the secrets of life and death from such broken lines as those!"

Then he turned to a yellow envelope lying beside them in the desk, with the single word on the outside in the writing of the professor—the word *Translation*.

"Now," he thought, taking it up with a sudden violence to conceal his nervousness, "now for the great solution. Now to learn the meaning of the worlds, and why mankind was made, and why discipline is worth while, and sacrifice and pain the true law of advancement."

There was the shadow of a sneer in his voice, and yet something in him shivered at the same time. He held the envelope as though weighing it in his hand, his mind pondering many things. Then curiosity won the day, and he suddenly tore it open with the gesture of an actor who tears open a letter on the stage, knowing there is no real writing inside at all.

A page of finely written script in the late scientist's handwriting lay before him. He read it through from beginning to end, missing no word, uttering each syllable distinctly under his breath as he read.

The pallor of his face grew ghastly as he neared the end. He began to shake all over as with ague. His breath came heavily in gasps. He still gripped the sheet of paper, however, and deliberately, as by an intense effort of will, read it through a second time from beginning to end. And this time, as the last syllable dropped from his lips, the whole face of the man flamed with a sudden and terrible anger. His skin became deep, deep red, and he clenched his teeth. With all the strength of his vigorous soul he was struggling to keep control of himself.

For perhaps five minutes he stood there beside the table without stirring a muscle. He might have been carved out of stone. His eyes were shut, and only the heaving of the chest betrayed the fact that he was a living being. Then, with a strange quietness, he lit a match and applied it to the sheet of paper he held in his hand. The ashes fell slowly about him, piece by piece, and he blew them from the window-sill into the air, his eyes following them as they floated away on the summer wind that breathed so warmly over the world.

He turned back slowly into the room. Although his actions and movements were absolutely steady and controlled, it was clear that he was on the edge of violent action. A hurricane might burst upon the still room any moment. His muscles were tense and rigid. Then, suddenly, he whitened, collapsed, and sank backwards into a chair, like a tumbled bundle of inert matter. He had fainted.

In less than half an hour he recovered consciousness and sat up. As before, he made no sound. Not a syllable passed his lips. He rose quietly and looked about the room.

Then he did a curious thing.

Taking a heavy stick from the rack in the corner he approached the mantelpiece, and with a heavy shattering blow he smashed the clock to pieces. The glass fell in shivering atoms.

"Cease your lying voice for ever," he said, in a curiously still, even tone. "There is no such thing as *time!*"

He took the watch from his pocket, swung it round several times by the long gold chain, smashed it into smithereens against the wall with a single blow, and then walked into his laboratory next door, and hung its broken body on the bones of the skeleton in the corner of the room.

"Let one damned mockery hang upon another," he said smiling oddly. "Delusions, both of you, and cruel as false!"

He slowly moved back to the front room. He stopped opposite the bookcase where stood in a row the "Scriptures of the World," choicely bound and exquisitely printed, the late professor's most treasured possession, and next to them several books signed "Pilgrim."

One by one he took them from the shelf and hurled them through the open window.

"A devil's dreams! A devil's foolish dreams!" he cried, with a vicious laugh.

Presently he stopped from sheer exhaustion. He turned his eyes slowly to the wall opposite, where hung a weird array of Eastern swords and daggers, scimitars and spears, the collections of many journeys. He crossed the room and ran his finger along the edge. His mind seemed to waver.

"No," he muttered presently; "not that way. There are easier and better ways than that."

He took his hat and passed downstairs into the street.

5

It was five o'clock, and the June sun lay hot upon the pavement. He felt the metal door-knob burn the palm of his hand.

"Ah, Laidlaw, this is well met," cried a voice at his elbow; "I was in the act of coming to see you. I've a case that will interest you, and besides, I remembered that you flavoured your tea with orange leaves!—and I admit——"

It was Alexis Stephen, the great hypnotic doctor.

"I've had no tea today," Laidlaw said, in a dazed manner, after staring for a moment as though the other had struck him in the face. A new idea had entered his mind.

"What's the matter?" asked Dr. Stephen quickly. "Something's wrong with you. It's this sudden heat, or overwork. Come, man, let's go inside."

A sudden light broke upon the face of the younger man, the light of a heaven-sent inspiration. He looked into his friend's face, and told a direct lie.

"Odd," he said, "I myself was just coming to see you. I have something of great importance to test your confidence with. But in *your* house, please," as Stephen urged him towards his own door—"in your house. It's only round the corner, and I—I cannot go back there—to my rooms—till I have told you."

"I'm your patient—for the moment," he added stammeringly as soon as they were seated in the privacy of the hypnotist's sanctum, "and I want—er——"

"My dear Laidlaw," interrupted the other, in that soothing voice of command which had suggested to many a suffering soul that the cure for its pain lay in the powers of its own reawakened will, "I am always at your service, as you know. You have only to tell me what I can do for you, and I will do it." He showed every desire to help him out. His manner was indescribably tactful and direct.

Dr. Laidlaw looked up into his face.

"I surrender my will to you," he said, already calmed by the other's healing presence, "and I want you to treat my hypnotically—and at once. I want you to suggest to me"—his voice became very tense—"that I shall forget—forget till I die— everything that has occurred to me during the last two hours; till I die, mind," he added, with solemn emphasis, "till I die."

He floundered and stammered like a frightened boy. Alexis Stephen looked at him fixedly without speaking.

"And further," Laidlaw continued, "I want you to ask me no

questions. I wish to forget for ever something I have recently discovered—something so terrible and yet so obvious that I can hardly understand why it is not patent to every mind in the world—for I have had a moment of absolute *clear vision*—of merciless clairvoyance. But I want no one else in the whole world to know what it is—least of all, old friend, yourself."

He talked in utter confusion, and hardly knew what he was saying. But the pain on his face and the anguish in his voice were an instant passport to the other's heart.

"Nothing is easier," replied Dr. Stephen, after a hesitation so slight that the other probably did not even notice it. "Come into my other room where we shall not be disturbed. I can heal you. Your memory of the last two hours shall be wiped out as though it had never been. You can trust me absolutely."

"I know I can," Laidlaw said simply, as he followed him in.

6

An hour later they passed back into the front room again. The sun was already behind the houses opposite, and the shadows began to gather.

"I went off easily?" Laidlaw asked.

"You were a little obstinate at first. But though you came in like a lion, you went out like a lamb. I let you sleep a bit afterwards.

Dr. Stephen kept his eyes rather steadily upon his friend's face.

"What were you doing by the fire before you came here?" he asked, pausing, in a casual tone, as he lit a cigarette and handed the case to his patient.

"I? Let me see. Oh, I know; I was worrying my way through poor old Ebor's papers and things. I'm his executor, you know. Then I got weary and came out for a whiff of air." He spoke lightly and with perfect naturalness. Obviously he was telling the truth. "I prefer specimens to papers," he laughed cheerily.

"I know, I know," said Dr. Stephen, holding a lighted match for the cigarette. His face wore an expression of content. The experiment had been a complete success. The memory of the last two hours was wiped out utterly. Laidlaw was already chatting gaily and easily about a dozen other things that interested him. Together they went out into the street, and at his door Dr. Stephen left him with a joke and a wry face that made his friend laugh heartily.

"Don't dine on the professor's old papers by mistake," he cried, as he vanished down the street.

Dr. Laidlaw went up to his study at the top of the house. Half way down he met his housekeeper, Mrs. Fewings. She was flustered and excited, and her face was very red and perspiring.

"There've been burglars here," she cried excitedly, "or something funny! All your things is just any'ow, sir. I found everything all about everywhere!" She was very confused. In this orderly and very precise establishment it was unusual to find a thing out of place.

"Oh, my specimens!" cried the doctor, dashing up the rest of the stairs at top speed. "Have they been touched or——"

He flew to the door of the laboratory. Mrs. Fewings panted up heavily behind him.

"The labatry ain't been touched," she explained, breathlessly, "but they smashed the libry clock and they've 'ung your gold watch, sir, on the skelinton's hands. And the books that weren't no value they flung out er the window just like so much rubbish. They must have been wild drunk, Dr. Laidlaw, sir!"

The young scientist made a hurried examination of the rooms. Nothing of value was missing. He began to wonder what kind of burglars they were. He looked up sharply at Mrs. Fewings standing in the doorway. For a moment he seemed to cast about in his mind for something.

"Odd," he said at length. "I only left here an hour ago and everything was all right then."

"Was it, sir? Yes, sir." She glanced sharply at him. Her room looked out upon the courtyard, and she must have seen the books come crashing down, and also have heard her master leave the house a few minutes later.

"And what's this rubbish the brutes have left?" he cried, taking up two slabs of worn gray stone, on the writing-table. "Bath brick, or something, I do declare."

He looked very sharply again at the confused and troubled housekeeper.

"Throw them on the dust heap, Mr. Fewings, and—and let me know if anything is missing in the house, and I will notify the police this evening."

When she left the room he went into the laboratory and took his watch off the skeleton's fingers. His face wore a troubled expression, but after a moment's thought it cleared again. His memory was a complete blank.

"I suppose I left it on the writing-table when I went out to take the air," he said. And there was no one present to contradict him.

He crossed to the window and blew carelessly some ashes of burned paper from the sill, and stood watching them as they floated away lazily over the tops of the trees.

A Negligible Experiment

J. D. Beresford

"I can't get him right, somehow," the young sculptor said, but he looked tenderly at the little figure of the man he was modelling in plasticine, as if, despite its very obvious defects, he found something to admire in his creation.

"Wants stiffening, doesn't he?" I suggested. "Couldn't you put a wire or something up his legs and back?"

"Well, you see," my young friend explained, "I could if I knew beforehand exactly what I was going to do with him. Only I don't. I like to make him up as I go along. I'm no good at it really. I can't think it all out ahead and then sit down and do it right off. I have to experiment and—see how it comes, you know. Do you think his head is too big?"

I thought it was rather big.

The young modeller regarded his creation with a look in which fondness still seemed to preponderate.

"Perhaps if. . . ." he said; then speech died out of him as his hands again began to fashion and improve his little image of humanity.

And as I watched him a vision came to me. I lost consciousness of the boy and his workshop. I wandered away into a dreamland of the imagination, following the lure of a fantasy deeper and more satisfying than the reality of life.

. . . . . .

When I read in my morning's paper of the "Nova" in the constellation of Sagittarius, I thought first of H. G. Wells's story of 'The New Star,' and smiled. Later, I turned with a little shiver of

278

anxiety to that chapter in Professor Lowell's *Evolution of Worlds* in which he describes the possible coming of a 'dark stranger' out of the depths of space. Already there were points of striking resemblance between Lowell's imaginative accounts and the details that were appearing casually, in the intervals between more important news, in the newspapers. This new star differed from those other *novæ* so many of which have been recorded at various times. *They* brought us tidings of a collision that had already occurred, blazing out suddenly into a short-lived splendour and quickly waning again to invisibility. This stranger, astronomers were agreed, shone not by its own light but by the reflected light of the sun. Then it must be, relatively, near. Lowell's calculations gave us something like thirty years to prepare before the invader wrought the destruction of the solar system. But, obviously, that calculation depended on various assumptions that the reality need not verify. This strange visitor might be much smaller than he had assumed—he had taken the enormous mass of the sun as his standard—its albedo might be lower; its speed greater. Also Lowell's stranger was assumed to be coming at right angles to the plane of the ecliptic; this one would, as it were, skim the edge of that swimming saucer. Would any of the outer planets be interposed between us and this dreadful visitor? Neptune, Uranus, Saturn, Jupiter, Mars, might any of them be a buffer to us—provide us, perhaps, with some stupendous display in the heavens, but save us from ultimate disaster?

Everyone treated the thing so lightly. Here and there alarmist paragraphs appeared, but they only displayed the hand of the sensation-monger. No one took the threat seriously. And yet the astronomers must know? They had had more than a week, now, in which to make their calculations.

And then the shadow fell with such suddenness that it was impossible to say how the certainty had come to us. Everyone knew. The astronomers confirmed one another without a dissentient. And there was nothing in the way. With a horrible unanimity the outer plants had left a clear space for the intruder, while the Earth, with that blundering indifference which is surely its chief characteristic, was stolidly marching straight into the path of destruction. Is there any esoteric significance in the fact that the Earth has a greater density than any other member of the solar system?

Everyone knew, but little was changed. We went on with our affairs; with little zest, no doubt—we could never forget the deepening shadow. But what else was there for us to do but go on? We could not instantly alter ourselves or our way of life. Religions blazed into a spasmodic fever as men and women sought refuge from the dreadful reality. Crimes of lust and greed increased for the same reason. But for the most part we continued in the old ways by sheer inertia, though there was a new and smaller moon visible to us in the night sky, a moon that waxed with infinite slowness towards the full, and grew larger night by night. We knew by then that the stranger was as big as Jupiter, and with a density little less than that of the Earth.

The first portents of disaster came when our own moon was approaching the new. The stranger's mass had begun to affect the tides, and we were warned to evacuate all low lands, near the sea, upon the estuaries, and incidentally the river level in London. Four days before the highest tide the Thames flooded Farringdon Street, Westminster, and great districts on the south bank, and the retreating river laid bare the river-bed as far down as Greenwich.

The population of London had fled to the heights North and South before the great floods that devastated all the low lands of Essex, Kent, Surrey, and Middlesex. And with that rush for safety and the rapidly increasing portents of disaster the routine of civilisation was definitely broken. It seemed as if in the mass we were being gradually stripped of all our tediously-acquired virtues and vices, until but one instinct remained, the instinct for self-preservation. That, however, was only the effect produced by the panic movement of the crowd; when one came to individuals. . . .

I can, however, only speak of two, myself and another man. We sat together on a hill in Derbyshire and watched through the last night.

A certain calmness had come to me, then, mingled with the queerest feelings of excitement and expectation. Within sight of death, I could still enjoy this amazing celestial adventure. The new planet that was rushing in upon us had already torn us from our steady path about the sun, and our old familiar moon dwindled to the size of a sixpence, and, diminishing almost visibly, was within a few hours of destruction. For the moon had fled its old allegiance to the Earth and was rushing to the arms of this great stranger like some passionate, unfaithful lover.

But the new planet itself drowned all consciousness of lesser things when it rose magnificently above the eastern horizon. That night it was a full circle of yellow light, and across its great expanse moved one circle of intense blackness, the size of our old moon, a circle that was slowly increasing in size, the shadow of our own Earth. So great a thing appeared this new planet, then, that when its lower rim was at last clear of the horizon, its upper limb towered half-way to the zenith. It had few markings, but from one pole, which was turned markedly towards us, radiated uneven, dark lines—chains of mountains, perhaps—that definitely produced the effect of a solid globe long before its actual convexity was recognisable. All the rest of the planet presented a smooth, unbroken expanse, possibly the vast bed of some long-vanished sea.

For an hour or more my companion and I had sat in silence watching this gigantic spectacle; then he said quietly, 'We are witnessing the failure of a negligible experiment."

I did not answer at once. I had not caught his drift. I was struggling with a foolish preoccupation, the result of an almost lifelong habit. As I watched I was searching for words to describe what I saw. I wanted to write my experience; yes, even there, under the sentence of death pronounced not only upon me, but upon all humanity, I was struggling with this meaningless desire to create a record that none could ever read.

I made an effort and roused myself from this inane preoccupation. "Negligible?" I said, grasping at what seemed to be his most prominent word.

"Proved to be negligible," he asserted. "You are a serious man? You don't cling to straws? You have no doubt that this is the end of the Earth? Very well then, you know that we are to be destroyed? By an accident? Possibly. Or it may be that this arrow that has been discharged at us was shot deliberately; with a definite purpose.

"It isn't as if the same thing had not happened before," he continued after a pause. "We have seen it—seen the effects at least. When some temporary star blazed up in the sky, we inferred some such collision as this. It may very well be that from a planet in some other system men may catch sight of this tiny blaze of ours—and wonder. It will be relatively a very small affair. Some of those we've seen must have been many thousand times greater.

"But the point is that this experiment of making men upon the Earth is now proved to be negligible. In a few hours it will be finished, wiped out. And whether that termination is the result of accident or design makes no difference to the effect. This is an answer to all our philosophies and religions. Either we are the creatures of some chance evolutionary process, or we are an experiment that has failed."

I looked at him, and noted with a curious stir of unplaceable recollection that his head was too large.

"It is certain that we shall go off like an exploded shell?" I asked.

"I don't fancy that many of us will live to see that," he replied. "Most of us will be drowned in the next tide. It will come in a wall of water many thousand feet high. Don't you notice a feeling of lightness in your body? The attraction of this great stranger is beginning to drag at us. On the other side of the Earth men are feeling an intolerable heaviness. And our speed increases. We have been drawn out of our orbit. We are rushing now to greet the stranger with a kiss of fire. Our circling about the sun is done for ever. We and the stranger are leaping together like two bubbles in a cup."

I believe some hours passed before I spoke again. A sense of imminence had grown upon me in the meantime. I was aware of the guards that were fetching me to execution.

"After all," I cried, "there may still be such a thing as an immortal soul. Though every physical expression is smashed at one blow, that does not prove. . . ."

"There is no such thing as proof possible," my companion

interrupted. "But don't you know in your heart that it's no good?"

•   •   •   •   •   •

"No good. It's no good." I woke with a start at the repetition of that statement.

My young modeller was rolling a great ball of plasticine, and before I could stop him he had thrown it with deadly accuracy at his effigy of man.

"He wouldn't come right," he explained, picked up the shapeless mass of clay, and tossed it carelessly into a corner of the workshop.

"Oh, but you shouldn't have done that," I said, with the incurable didacticism of the pedagogue.

The Root-Gatherers

R. H. Barlow

The red sun was nearly lost behind a welter of dark trees, and night thickened about us. It was then I first noticed that my mother had a dim fear of the ancient lost place through which we must go. I did not mind seeing ruined buildings; in truth rumours of the corpse-town had fascinated my young ears. You see, I had accompanied her only a few times to hunt foot-roots, and had never before gone the way lying directly through the city. Tubers grew well in the clay caverns beyond that place of ruins, and in order that no one else might find them, my mother always chose a time when she could go unobserved. This was in the brief period before nightfall, while the tribe was engaged in cooking.

About us spread once cultivated fields where straggling bean and pea-vines persisted after a time past reckoning, but since man did not care for them, or fight the weeds, few plants bore anything edible. A horde of pale blossoms, hued like the summer evening, and bearing five points, overspread leagues of unused soil and crowded onto the rotten highway. This land about us, these ancient, sun-covered fields, we knew had once been great and flourishing; but in a forgotten time, something wrong had happened. We are the children of the old race, but no one cares now about the ancient things and the world of dead memories. Such things they say are of no use, for they cannot help us to obtain food. Only two or three of us take interest in the past. Perhaps it is a fortunate thing, because those who do are half-restive in the life about them.

A last reflection from the sky spread a golden mantle over the fields as we came to the wood of black fir-trees which hinted at

the nearness of the first ruin. Their foliage shut out the ending
glory of the sun, and for a breathless period we hastened
through premature night. I pushed my way among the bushes,
following my mother, and soon the ebbing daylight sparkled
rewardingly again in leaves of summer greenery.

When we were beyond the trees I looked at the small figure
beside me, and felt a pang because of half-recollected stories of
our ancient grandeur, when we had made cities like the dead
ones before us, and did not fear storms and animals. But then a
glimpse of the most outlying ruin changed my thoughts, and
wonder and astonishment hid from me the knowledge that we
were frail and lonely and trivial amid surroundings that thought
of a vanished day.

Forgotten now was our humble errand and the dust of the
road. Before us lay a fallen tower, very nearly complete, girt with
thin pillars like fingers clasped about it. The base of this brick
spire lay near us and the little wood, but what remained of the
highest tier was half buried, very far away. It had been fashioned
strongly, and had fallen like a chimney, intact save where a few
centuried pines (lean and tortured) found root-hold in the
encircling facade.

There was nothing to show the purpose for which it had been
made, and tradition only knew of it that men had drawn the
lightning there in magical ways, and sent out again the glory of
the skies in a throbbing halo. My regret that we have no memories is a pang more difficult than hunger, for hunger can be satisfied, but for the nostalgic beckoning of old centuries there is
no assuagement. I would like so much to fill out the gap of years
which binds us to the past, when men built that old city; and to
know the hues and forms of a life vanished utterly. But there are
only ruins on which to speculate, fragments of a life existing
nowhere, and the people of that place are lonely in the desolate
grave of night. A rain of centuries has obliterated most of the
traditions about them and all that I may ever recapture is as
nothing when it is weighed against the ignorance of our time.
Forest and wooded glen, and tales of ancient huntings are the
joys of my race.

There are two ruins which even yet hold for me the greatest

lure, and I saw them both, that day, now likewise gone into the forgotten abyss of time. The first is that Gargantuan tower of slim embracing pillars, whose foundation—jagged on the sky— seemed to my childish eyes much like a crowd of vultures, and the other, a metal bridge farther on the way, seen only as one nears the city. The bridge is not so great in height as the tower must have been, but it spans a great sluggish river. Men have used it forever when they wished to go into the place of ruins, and wild things scurry over the perilous span in darkness. Sometimes apes and bears are tracked across the old bridge, and slain upon it, though since my youth these are grown scarce.

We came to it later, when the broken tower was out of sight. It was lost overhead in perspective and darkness, and I beheld the corroded girders with a vague fear. The end near us was choked with trees, and beneath it the river flowed green, with spots of diseased yellow. There were five arches upon pillars of old brick, for the river is wide in that part, and had been that way even when the city was built. The weedy stream forms a lagoon where great rushes and lilies grow, and there is only a stirring of the tired water. It is a vivid and chromatic scene that I remember—the dead green surface and the vague glitter of the bridge at dusk—though years have gone since I was there last.

I looked about as we started across the ruinous structure, and saw a few pale stars where a girder had fallen away overhead. They watched like indifferent eyes, through the faint evening, from a timeless vantage point. Vague emotions moved in me, and I felt again the regret that ruins must lie unpeopled and forgotten. It was a brief sensation that the noises of a dying thing might arouse; not pity, for pity is then of no use, but an ineffable emotion as near to sorrow as the mist is to rain. It was not sharp enough to analyze, but I have kept the memory of a child who felt, beyond the netted, broken girders, the regard of those unseeing stars.

There was only in places a floor, so for the most part we walked on iron beams. In the blackness under us the water rustled past some obstruction which I did not see, and on the curving shores was a cluster of stooping trees. The far end of the bridge was in shadow, but I knew from my mother's words that we should come out between the metal ankles of a guarding statue into the vast silent ruins of a city. Tottering in the gloom, the old bridge was like a man whose ribs are sharped by the years. As we traversed it, I looked up in apprehension, and saw that above us tons of insecure metal swayed like a broken spider web. I feared that it would fall, but it had been suspended in that fashion before memory, and yet the cables are intact and the girders whole.

Then we came into the city, passing below the mute colossi whose downward gaze had the frightening indifference of all ancient things. There was an aspect of waiting about the metal statue, whose head touched the darkness and the increasing stars. No one has guessed when it was made and set there as guardian of the bridge. It is of the same material, and built of cunning segments, rather than sculptured. Looking briefly at the high, indistinct face, I turned away from the bridge and the nameless crouching giant to go into the ruinous streets.

Here was Doom. The shards of a city that once knew merchants and toilers and the glittering rich—peopled now with memories and shadows and the whisper of the breeze. Silent now were the streets whose paving had sounded with the trample of multitudes; silent also the tumbled houses. There were no high structures; these had fallen unmarked during the years of neglect. The air was stagnant and weary, and the dark holes in the street and buildings were like the orifices of a nameless skull.

A moon had come up out of the chaos of stars, and swung above the fretted outline of the ruined city, where an immemorial silence reigned. No throb of bird-wing, no rustle of furred feet disturbed the still evening. There were only stars attendant on the moon, and a bluish silence which filled the town like water.

For centuries the vines and roots of jungle things had accumulated about the city, enveloping it and gnawing at outlying districts. For centuries the bubbling hues of sunset had glazed with yellow lacquer those dark streets, and crept along unseen walls. Throughout the multitudinous days of its collapse there had been clouds over it and bright skies and rains: the thunder of the elements had beaten down on it, and sun and storm had battled, each claiming it his fortress. But that night, all was fled save silence.

I saw what once had been a shop—the front was crumbled, and a rotten beam lay half across the opening, but there was a litter of incredible wreckage within—goods that had been fashioned for purchasers dead a thousand years, despised even by the beast. Someone had come there and sorted out the useful, undamaged things, but like the rest, these lay in an unclaimed pile. Perhaps the scavenger was there a day before us—perhaps he had become the prey of some animal eight hundred years ago. There was nothing to tell why he had not borne off his spoil.

I would have liked to go into some of the buildings which ranged spectrally along the road. Now one, and then another took my fancy, but we had no time if we meant to end our mission by a safe hour. There was one pile of white marble standing alone in a little field, as if it had been a temple or a strong man's house. And I saw another; round, with many bordering pillars, like an immense spider; whose purpose I could not understand. I would have explored these had there been no hurry. But I knew that we must get back before there was too much moonlight, and the beasts came out. They are very terrible at such times.

And so we went on, and found many roots in the caverns beyond the city.

Notes on the Authors

WILLIAM WALDORF ASTOR (1848–1919) was born in New York, a son of John Jacob Astor. After serving in the New York state legislature, Astor was appointed U.S. Minister to Italy (1882–85); during this period he absorbed the background to write his historical novels, *Valentino* (1885) and *Sforza: A Story of Milan* (1889). In 1889 he became a naturalized British citizen, and in 1917 he was made first Viscount Astor. His one collection of tales, *Pharaoh's Daughter and Other Stories* (1900), is distinctive in melding the horror story with the historical tale. Astor published additional, uncollected weird tales in the *Pall Mall Magazine* up to 1911. "The Ghosts of Austerlitz" appeared in the *Pall Mall Magazine* (December 1893) and was included in *Pharaoh's Daughter.*

GERTRUDE ATHERTON (1857–1948) traveled the world but remained faithful to her native San Francisco. A prolific author of novels and tales, she established her claim as a leading California writer with the story collections *Before the Gringo Came* (1894; revised in 1902 as *The Splendid Idle Forties*), about the original Spanish settlers of California, and *The Bell in the Fog and Other Stories* (1905), which includes her most famous tale of terror, "The Striding Place." Her novel *Black Oxen* (1923) was a best-seller. The fantasy "The Caves of Death" appeared in the *San Francisco News Letter* (25 December 1886) and has never been reprinted.

ROBERT HAYWARD BARLOW (1918–1951) spent much of his youth in Florida, where, from the age of thirteen onward, he established contacts with the leading American pulp writers of the day, including H. P. Lovecraft and Clark Ashton Smith. Barlow's early writings—some of them revised by Lovecraft—reveal a precocious and vivid imagination; perhaps the best of them are "A Dim-Remembered Story" (1935) and "The Night Ocean" (1936). In 1937 he was appointed Lovecraft's literary executor. In the 1940s he moved to Mexico, where he became a leading anthropologist, devoting much time to the study of native peoples. "The Root-Gatherers" was first published in *Polaris* (March 1940) and has never been reprinted.

British novelist JOHN DAVYS BERESFORD (1873–1947) left school at the age of seventeen to become a draughtsman in an architect's office, but soon took to writing. He gained a position on the *Westminster Gazette* in 1907 and shortly thereafter began writing novels and tales. *The Hampdenshire Wonder* (1911) is a classic of early science fiction in its portrayal of a modern superman. Other works of imaginative fiction include *Goslings* (1913; also published as *A World of Women*), a depiction of an all-female society, and the utopian novel "*What Dreams May Come . . .*" (1941). Beresford's weird tales are scattered through two volumes, *Nineteen Impressions* (1918) and *Signs and Wonders* (1921). The cosmic vignette "A Negligible Experiment" derives from the latter collection.

AMBROSE BIERCE (1842–1914?) served in some of the bloodiest battles of the Civil War before settling in San Francisco, where he became a renowned journalist, writing for such papers as the *Argonaut* (1877–79), the *Wasp* (1881–86), and William Randolph Hearst's *San Francisco Examiner* (1887–1906), and developing a reputation as a fearless exposer of fraud, folly, and hypocrisy. His stories of the Civil War and of psychological terror were collected in *Tales of Soldiers and Civilians* (1891; later titled *In the Midst of Life*), and his tales of supernatural horror were gathered in *Can Such Things Be?* (1893). He supervised his own *Collected Works* (1909–12), published in twelve volumes, but it included only a fraction of his journalism. Also omitted were many items he had written early in his career, among them "The Discomfited Demon," based upon a sketch published in the *San Francisco News Letter* (May 7, 1870) and, in revised form, included in his early volume of miscellany, *The Fiend's Delight* (1873). It is Bierce's first venture into weird fiction.

ALGERNON BLACKWOOD (1869–1951), a towering figure in twentieth-century weird fiction, traveled widely (including voyages to Germany, Canada, and New York), but resided mostly in his native England and in Switzerland. He was the author of numerous collections of weird tales, including *The Empty House* (1906), *The Listener* (1907), *John Silence: Physician Extraordinary* (1908), *The Lost Valley* (1910), *Pan's Garden* (1913), and *Incredible Adventures* (1914), as well as several novels, among them *The Centaur* (1911) and *The Bright Messenger*

(1921). His most characteristic work is mystical, pantheistic, and evocative of awe rather than terror. "The Man Who Found Out," first published in the *Canadian Magazine* (December 1912), was collected in *The Wolves of God and Other Fey Stories* (1921).

THOMAS BURKE (1886–1945) left school at fifteen and published his first story at sixteen. He later worked for several years at a literary agency while continuing to write poetry and fiction. He gained celebrity with *Limehouse Nights* (1916), a gripping series of tales about the Limehouse district of London, largely occupied by Chinese immigrants. *More Limehouse Nights* followed in 1920. Burke went on to write numerous volumes, including several books of essays focusing on his rambles throughout London. *Night-Pieces* (1935) is a collection of weird tales from which "The Man Who Lost His Head" is taken.

WALTER DE LA MARE (1873–1956) began writing as a young man and became a prolific short story writer, novelist, and poet. In his lifetime he perhaps achieved greatest renown as a writer for children, with such volumes as *The Three Mulla-Mulgars* (1910), *Broomsticks and Other Tales* (1925), and *The Lord Fish and Other Tales* (1933). De la Mare's weird work is known for its subtlety, delicacy, and occasional obscurity. His powerful novel of psychic possession, *The Return* (1910; revised 1922; reprinted by Dover, 1997), is his greatest contribution to weird fiction; but he wrote numerous other shorter weird tales, most notably "Seaton's Aunt"; they were included in *The Riddle* (1923), *The Connoisseur* (1926), *On the Edge* (1930), and *The Wind Blows Over* (1936). A few weird specimens were not collected by de la Mare; among them is the elusive tale "The Promise," published in the *English Review* (January 1919).

Anglo-Irish fantasist LORD DUNSANY (1878–1957), born Edward John Moreton Drax Plunkett, joins Algernon Blackwood, H. P. Lovecraft, and Arthur Machen as one of the leading weird writers of his generation. Creating an entire fantastic theogony in his first volume, *The Gods of Pegana* (1905), Dunsany went on to write many volumes of tales—*Time and the Gods* (1906), *The Sword of Welleran* (1908), *A Dreamer's Tales* (1910), *The Book of Wonder* (1912)—several noteworthy novels, including *The King of Elfland's Daughter* (1924), *The Blessing of Pan* (1927), and *The Curse of the Wise Woman* (1933). A distinctive facet of his work is a series of five volumes of stories recounting the tall tales of the clubman Joseph Jorkens. Never before reprinted, Dunsany's early prose poem "Romance" was one of many stories and sketches he contributed to the London *Saturday Review* in his early career. This item appeared in the issue of May 29, 1909.

EMILE ERCKMANN (1822–1899) and ALEXANDER CHATRIAN (1826–1890) met in 1847 and, a decade later, began collaborating on many works of fiction that made them among the most widely read French authors of the nineteenth century. Many of their works are historical novels, including *L'Ami Fritz* (1864; translated as *Friend Fritz*), *Histoire d'un conscrit de 1813* (1864; translated as *The History of a Conscript of 1813*), *Histoire d'un homme du peuple* (1865; translated as *A Man of the People*), and *Le Blocus* (1867; translated as *The Blockade of Phalsburg*). They also wrote many tales, gathered in *Contes fantastiques* (1860), *Contes de la montagne* (1862), and other volumes. "The Queen of the Bees" ("La Reine des abeilles") appeared in French in *Contes du bords du Rhin* (1862) and in English in *The Man-Wolf and Other Tales* (1876), translated by F. A. Malleson.

THÉOPHILE GAUTIER (1811–1872) was a leading French novelist, critic, and journalist of the nineteenth century. His most notable work is *Mademoiselle de Maupin* (1835), in the lengthy preface to which Gautier definitively enunciated the "art for art's sake" attitude that would influence the aesthetic movement later in the century. Throughout his career Gautier wrote several tales of horror and fantasy, including "One of Cleopatra's Nights," "Avatar," and "Clarimonde." Many of these tales (among them "The Mummy's Foot") were gathered in *One of Cleopatra's Nights and Other Fantastic Romances* (1882), translated by Lafcadio Hearn.

Born in Yorkshire, WILLIAM FRYER HARVEY (1885–1937) published a relatively small body of work, including three novels and four story collections; but among this output are two of the most popular weird tales in all literature, "August Heat" (included in *Midnight House*, 1910) and "The Beast with Five Fingers" (included in *The Beast with Five Fingers and Other Tales*, 1928). A later collection, *Moods and Tenses* (1933), also contains some weird work. "The Tortoise" was published in *Midnight House*.

LAFCADIO HEARN (1850–1904) was born in Greece, brought up in Dublin, educated in England, and was a journalist in Cincinnati and New Orleans before moving to Japan and become a Japanese citizen, taking the name Koisumi Yakumo. Among his bountiful work are the weird collections *Some Chinese Ghosts* (1887), *In Ghostly Japan* (1899), and *Kwaidan* (1904; reprinted by Dover, 1968), containing Hearn's skillful retellings of Chinese and Japanese legendry. The posthumously published *Fantastics* (1914) reprints some of Hearn's early journalism devoted to the weird and horrific. Hearn was also a notable translator from the French, and was particularly taken with the work of Théophile Gautier, Gustave Flaubert, and Anatole France. "Of a Promise Broken" is a grim tale from *A Japanese Miscellany* (1901).

ROBERT HICHENS (1864–1950) became one of the most popular British writers of his generation, publishing an enormous quantity of novels and tales. He first gained notoriety with the anonymously published novel *The Green Carnation* (1894), featuring a thinly disguised portrayal of Oscar Wilde. His mystery novel *The Paradine Case* (1933) was filmed by Alfred Hitchcock. His weird novels *Flames: A London Phantasy* (1897) and *The Dweller on the Threshold* (1911) are noteworthy. His tales of terror are scattered through several volumes, including *Bye-Ways* (1897), *Tongues of Conscience* (1900), *The Black Spaniel* (1905), and *Snake-Bite* (1919). "The Return of the Soul" first appeared as "A Re-incarnation" in the *Pall Mall Magazine* (August 1895) and was included in *The Folly of Eustace and Other Stories* (1896).

JAMES HOPPER (1876–1956) was born in Paris but came with his family to the United States at the age of ten. He attended the University of California from 1894 to 1898, becoming a star football player. Among Hopper's works are the story collections *Caybigan* (1906) and *What Happened in the Night* (1913), the novels *The Trimming of Goosie* (1909) and *The Freshman* (1912), and a scathing exposé of prison life, *9009* (1908), cowritten with Fred R. Bechdolt. "The Night School," a haunting ghost story published in the *Century Magazine* for March 1914, is not typical of Hopper's work but displays the delicacy and subtlety of his portrayal of character. It has not been previously reprinted.

VIOLET HUNT (1866–1942) was the daughter of British painter Alfred Hunt and spent many years as the companion of Ford Madox Ford. A prolific novelist, biographer, and journalist, she wrote such novels as *A Hard Woman* (1895) and *The Human Interest* (1899) and several collections of tales. Her weird work is chiefly gathered in two volumes, *Tales of the Uneasy* (1911) and *More Tales of the Uneasy* (1925). "The Coach," first published in the *English Review* (March 1909), was collected in the former volume.

JOSEPH SHERIDAN LEFANU (1814–1873) was Ireland's greatest writer of weird fiction before the emergence of Bram Stoker and Lord Dunsany. He was owner and editor of the *Dublin University Magazine* (1861–69), where many of his novels and tales appeared. His story collections include *Ghost Stories and Tales of Mystery* (1851), *In a Glass Darkly* (1872), and *The Purcell Papers* (1880). Among his novels, *The House by the Churchyard* (1863), *Uncle Silas* (1864; reprinted by Dover, 1966), and *Wylder's Hand* (1864) are the ones that feature the greatest proportion of the weird. His best horror tales can be found in two collections published by Dover, *Best Ghost Stories* (1964) and *Ghost Stories and Mysteries* (1975). In recent years several anonymous tales have been convincingly attributed to LeFanu based upon additional research and internal evidence. One of these is "Borrhomeo the Astrologer," published in the *Dublin University Magazine* (January 1862).

Welsh-born ARTHUR MACHEN (1863–1947) is one of the towering figures in the history of weird fiction. Spending much of his life in London as a journalist, Machen created a sensation with *The Great God Pan and The Inmost Light* (1894), which were condemned as the outpourings of a diseased mind. Other notable works of weird fiction include the episodic novel *The Three Imposters* (1895) and the story collection *The House of Souls* (1906). On the borderline of the weird are the delicate novels *The Hill of Dreams* (1907) and *The Secret Glory* (1922). "The Soldiers' Rest," first published in the London *Evening News* (October 20, 1914), was collected in a volume of wartime fantasies, *The Angels of Mons* (1915), which includes the celebrated tale "The Bowmen," an account of the ghosts of ancient British soldiers coming to the rescue of their modern counterparts in a World War I battle; it was widely accepted as an authentic narrative, in spite of Machen's repeated claims that it was pure fiction.

HENRY LOUIS MENCKEN (1880–1956) became the most celebrated American journalist and literary critic of his day, as a columnist for the *Baltimore Evening Sun* (1906–48), as editor and book reviewer of the *Smart Set* (1914–23), and as founder and editor of the *American Mercury* (1924–33). His six-volume series, *Prejudices* (1919–27), is a landmark in criticism, as his *American Language* (1919) is a landmark in philology. Early in his career, however, Mencken attempted to establish himself as a short story writer. His tales run the gamut from satire to social drama to farce; one of his last stories is the grim non-supernatural horror tale, "The Window of Horrors," published in the *Smart Set* (September 1917) under the pseudonym "William Drayham."

EDITH NESBIT (1858–1924) gained celebrity as a prolific author of fantasies for children, including *The Story of the Treasure-Seekers* (1899), *The Wouldbegoods* (1901), *Five Children and It* (1902), and other volumes. Early in her career, however, she published a small volume of weird tales for adults, *Grim Tales* (1893). Some of the contents of this collection were reprinted in the collection *Fear* (1910), augmented with more recent stories. "The Three Drugs" first appeared in the *Strand Magazine* (February 1908) and was included in *Fear*.

BARRY PAIN (1864–1928) attended Cambridge, where he edited *Granta*, before deciding to seek his fortune as a writer and journalist. He wrote widely for magazines of the period, and was for a time editor of *today*. Best known in his day for his humorous sketches and for *Memoirs of Constantine Dix* (1905), a collection of stories about a female criminal, Pain is today remembered almost entirely for the weird tales scattered through his many volumes of tales. *Stories in the Dark* (1901), from which "The Diary of a God" is taken, is his principal weird collection, but other horror tales can be found in *Stories and Interludes* (1893), *Here and Hereafter* (1911), and *The New Gulliver and Other Stories* (1913). Pain also wrote a weird novel, *An Exchange of Souls* (1911).

SIR ARTHUR QUILLER-COUCH (1863–1944), the first King Edward VII Professor of English Literature at Cambridge, became a leading British literary critic, author of such volumes as *Shakespeare's Workmanship* (1918) and *The Art of Reading* (1920). With J. Dover Wilson, he edited the New Cambridge Edition of Shakespeare's plays. Quiller-Couch was also a prolific novelist and short story writer; many of his tales are set in his native Cornwall. His weird fiction was scattered in various collections, including *Noughts and Crosses* (1891), *Wandering Heath* (1895), and *Old Fires and Profitable Ghosts* (1900). "The Haunted Dragoon" first appeared in *I Saw Three Ships and Other Winter's Tales* (1892).

WILLIAM SHARP (1855–1905) was a Scottish poet, novelist, and critic, whose biographies of Rossetti, Shelley, Heine, and Browning were well received. He achieved greatest celebrity, however, by novels, tales, and poems written under the pseudonym "Fiona Macleod," including *The Sin-Eater and Other Tales* (1895) and *The Dominion of Dreams* (1899). To the end of his life he managed to conceal his authorship of the works published by Fiona Macleod. "The Graven Image" is a story included in *The Gypsy Christ and Other Tales* (1895), a volume published under his own name.

A CATALOG OF SELECTED DOVER
BOOKS IN ALL FIELDS OF INTEREST

CONCERNING THE SPIRITUAL IN ART, Wassily Kandinsky. Pioneering work by father of abstract art. Thoughts on color theory, nature of art. Analysis of earlier masters. 12 illustrations. 80pp. of text. 5⅜ x 8½.   0-486-23411-8

CELTIC ART: The Methods of Construction, George Bain. Simple geometric techniques for making Celtic interlacements, spirals, Kells-type initials, animals, humans, etc. Over 500 illustrations. 160pp. 9 x 12. (Available in U.S. only.)   0-486-22923-8

AN ATLAS OF ANATOMY FOR ARTISTS, Fritz Schider. Most thorough reference work on art anatomy in the world. Hundreds of illustrations, including selections from works by Vesalius, Leonardo, Goya, Ingres, Michelangelo, others. 593 illustrations. 192pp. 7⅛ x 10¼.   0-486-20241-0

CELTIC HAND STROKE-BY-STROKE (Irish Half-Uncial from "The Book of Kells"): An Arthur Baker Calligraphy Manual, Arthur Baker. Complete guide to creating each letter of the alphabet in distinctive Celtic manner. Covers hand position, strokes, pens, inks, paper, more. Illustrated. 48pp. 8¼ x 11.   0-486-24336-2

EASY ORIGAMI, John Montroll. Charming collection of 32 projects (hat, cup, pelican, piano, swan, many more) specially designed for the novice origami hobbyist. Clearly illustrated easy-to-follow instructions insure that even beginning papercrafters will achieve successful results. 48pp. 8¼ x 11.   0-486-27298-2

BLOOMINGDALE'S ILLUSTRATED 1886 CATALOG: Fashions, Dry Goods and Housewares, Bloomingdale Brothers. Famed merchants' extremely rare catalog depicting about 1,700 products: clothing, housewares, firearms, dry goods, jewelry, more. Invaluable for dating, identifying vintage items. Also, copyright-free graphics for artists, designers. Co-published with Henry Ford Museum & Greenfield Village. 160pp. 8¼ x 11.   0-486-25780-0

THE ART OF WORLDLY WISDOM, Baltasar Gracian. "Think with the few and speak with the many," "Friends are a second existence," and "Be able to forget" are among this 1637 volume's 300 pithy maxims. A perfect source of mental and spiritual refreshment, it can be opened at random and appreciated either in brief or at length. 128pp. 5⅜ x 8½.   0-486-44034-6

JOHNSON'S DICTIONARY: A Modern Selection, Samuel Johnson (E. L. McAdam and George Milne, eds.). This modern version reduces the original 1755 edition's 2,300 pages of definitions and literary examples to a more manageable length, retaining the verbal pleasure and historical curiosity of the original. 480pp. 5³⁄₁₆ x 8¼.   0-486-44089-3

ADVENTURES OF HUCKLEBERRY FINN, Mark Twain, Illustrated by E. W. Kemble. A work of eternal richness and complexity, a source of ongoing critical debate, and a literary landmark, Twain's 1885 masterpiece about a barefoot boy's journey of self-discovery has enthralled readers around the world. This handsome clothbound reproduction of the first edition features all 174 of the original black-and-white illustrations. 368pp. 5⅜ x 8½.   0-486-44322-1

A MODERN HERBAL, Margaret Grieve. Much the fullest, most exact, most useful compilation of herbal material. Gigantic alphabetical encyclopedia, from aconite to zedoary, gives botanical information, medical properties, folklore, economic uses, much else. Indispensable to serious reader. 161 illustrations. 888pp. 6½ x 9¼. 2-vol. set. (Available in U.S. only.) Vol. I: 0-486-22798-7 Vol. II: 0-486-22799-5

HIDDEN TREASURE MAZE BOOK, Dave Phillips. Solve 34 challenging mazes accompanied by heroic tales of adventure. Evil dragons, people-eating plants, blood-thirsty giants, many more dangerous adversaries lurk at every twist and turn. 34 mazes, stories, solutions. 48pp. 8¼ x 11. 0-486-24566-7

LETTERS OF W. A. MOZART, Wolfgang A. Mozart. Remarkable letters show bawdy wit, humor, imagination, musical insights, contemporary musical world; includes some letters from Leopold Mozart. 276pp. 5⅜ x 8½. 0-486-22859-2

BASIC PRINCIPLES OF CLASSICAL BALLET, Agrippina Vaganova. Great Russian theoretician, teacher explains methods for teaching classical ballet. 118 illustrations. 175pp. 5⅜ x 8½. 0-486-22036-2

THE JUMPING FROG, Mark Twain. Revenge edition. The original story of The Celebrated Jumping Frog of Calaveras County, a hapless French translation, and Twain's hilarious "retranslation" from the French. 12 illustrations. 66pp. 5⅜ x 8½. 0-486-22686-7

BEST REMEMBERED POEMS, Martin Gardner (ed.). The 126 poems in this superb collection of 19th- and 20th-century British and American verse range from Shelley's "To a Skylark" to the impassioned "Renascence" of Edna St. Vincent Millay and to Edward Lear's whimsical "The Owl and the Pussycat." 224pp. 5⅜ x 8½. 0-486-27165-X

COMPLETE SONNETS, William Shakespeare. Over 150 exquisite poems deal with love, friendship, the tyranny of time, beauty's evanescence, death and other themes in language of remarkable power, precision and beauty. Glossary of archaic terms. 80pp. 5³⁄₁₆ x 8¼. 0-486-26686-9

HISTORIC HOMES OF THE AMERICAN PRESIDENTS, Second, Revised Edition, Irvin Haas. A traveler's guide to American Presidential homes, most open to the public, depicting and describing homes occupied by every American President from George Washington to George Bush. With visiting hours, admission charges, travel routes. 175 photographs. Index. 160pp. 8¼ x 11. 0-486-26751-2

THE WIT AND HUMOR OF OSCAR WILDE, Alvin Redman (ed.). More than 1,000 ripostes, paradoxes, wisecracks: Work is the curse of the drinking classes; I can resist everything except temptation; etc. 258pp. 5⅜ x 8½. 0-486-20602-5

SHAKESPEARE LEXICON AND QUOTATION DICTIONARY, Alexander Schmidt. Full definitions, locations, shades of meaning in every word in plays and poems. More than 50,000 exact quotations. 1,485pp. 6½ x 9¼. 2-vol. set. Vol. 1: 0-486-22726-X Vol. 2: 0-486-22727-8

SELECTED POEMS, Emily Dickinson. Over 100 best-known, best-loved poems by one of America's foremost poets, reprinted from authoritative early editions. No comparable edition at this price. Index of first lines. 64pp. 5³⁄₁₆ x 8¼. 0-486-26466-1

THE INSIDIOUS DR. FU-MANCHU, Sax Rohmer. The first of the popular mystery series introduces a pair of English detectives to their archnemesis, the diabolical Dr. Fu-Manchu. Flavorful atmosphere, fast-paced action, and colorful characters enliven this classic of the genre. 208pp. 5³⁄₁₆ x 8¼. 0-486-29898-1

THE MALLEUS MALEFICARUM OF KRAMER AND SPRENGER, translated by Montague Summers. Full text of most important witchhunter's "bible," used by both Catholics and Protestants. 278pp. 6⅝ x 10. 0-486-22802-9

SPANISH STORIES/CUENTOS ESPAÑOLES: A Dual-Language Book, Angel Flores (ed.). Unique format offers 13 great stories in Spanish by Cervantes, Borges, others. Faithful English translations on facing pages. 352pp. 5⅜ x 8½.
0-486-25399-6

GARDEN CITY, LONG ISLAND, IN EARLY PHOTOGRAPHS, 1869–1919, Mildred H. Smith. Handsome treasury of 118 vintage pictures, accompanied by carefully researched captions, document the Garden City Hotel fire (1899), the Vanderbilt Cup Race (1908), the first airmail flight departing from the Nassau Boulevard Aerodrome (1911), and much more. 96pp. 8⅞ x 11¾. 0-486-40669-5

OLD QUEENS, N.Y., IN EARLY PHOTOGRAPHS, Vincent F. Seyfried and William Asadorian. Over 160 rare photographs of Maspeth, Jamaica, Jackson Heights, and other areas. Vintage views of DeWitt Clinton mansion, 1939 World's Fair and more. Captions. 192pp. 8⅞ x 11. 0-486-26358-4

CAPTURED BY THE INDIANS: 15 Firsthand Accounts, 1750-1870, Frederick Drimmer. Astounding true historical accounts of grisly torture, bloody conflicts, relentless pursuits, miraculous escapes and more, by people who lived to tell the tale. 384pp. 5⅜ x 8½. 0-486-24901-8

THE WORLD'S GREAT SPEECHES (Fourth Enlarged Edition), Lewis Copeland, Lawrence W. Lamm, and Stephen J. McKenna. Nearly 300 speeches provide public speakers with a wealth of updated quotes and inspiration—from Pericles' funeral oration and William Jennings Bryan's "Cross of Gold Speech" to Malcolm X's powerful words on the Black Revolution and Earl of Spenser's tribute to his sister, Diana, Princess of Wales. 944pp. 5⅜ x 8⅜. 0-486-40903-1

THE BOOK OF THE SWORD, Sir Richard F. Burton. Great Victorian scholar/adventurer's eloquent, erudite history of the "queen of weapons"—from prehistory to early Roman Empire. Evolution and development of early swords, variations (sabre, broadsword, cutlass, scimitar, etc.), much more. 336pp. 6⅛ x 9¼.
0-486-25434-8

AUTOBIOGRAPHY: The Story of My Experiments with Truth, Mohandas K. Gandhi. Boyhood, legal studies, purification, the growth of the Satyagraha (nonviolent protest) movement. Critical, inspiring work of the man responsible for the freedom of India. 480pp. 5⅜ x 8½. (Available in U.S. only.) 0-486-24593-4

CELTIC MYTHS AND LEGENDS, T. W. Rolleston. Masterful retelling of Irish and Welsh stories and tales. Cuchulain, King Arthur, Deirdre, the Grail, many more. First paperback edition. 58 full-page illustrations. 512pp. 5⅜ x 8½. 0-486-26507-2

THE PRINCIPLES OF PSYCHOLOGY, William James. Famous long course complete, unabridged. Stream of thought, time perception, memory, experimental methods; great work decades ahead of its time. 94 figures. 1,391pp. 5⅜ x 8½. 2-vol. set.
Vol. I: 0-486-20381-6   Vol. II: 0-486-20382-4

THE WORLD AS WILL AND REPRESENTATION, Arthur Schopenhauer. Definitive English translation of Schopenhauer's life work, correcting more than 1,000 errors, omissions in earlier translations. Translated by E. F. J. Payne. Total of 1,269pp. 5⅜ x 8½. 2-vol. set.   Vol. 1: 0-486-21761-2   Vol. 2: 0-486-21762-0

MAGIC AND MYSTERY IN TIBET, Madame Alexandra David-Neel. Experiences among lamas, magicians, sages, sorcerers, Bonpa wizards. A true psychic discovery. 32 illustrations. 321pp. 5⅜ x 8½. (Available in U.S. only.) 0-486-22682-4

THE EGYPTIAN BOOK OF THE DEAD, E. A. Wallis Budge. Complete reproduction of Ani's papyrus, finest ever found. Full hieroglyphic text, interlinear transliteration, word-for-word translation, smooth translation. 533pp. 6½ x 9¼. 0-486-21866-X

HISTORIC COSTUME IN PICTURES, Braun & Schneider. Over 1,450 costumed figures in clearly detailed engravings–from dawn of civilization to end of 19th century. Captions. Many folk costumes. 256pp. 8⅜ x 11¾. 0-486-23150-X

MATHEMATICS FOR THE NONMATHEMATICIAN, Morris Kline. Detailed, college-level treatment of mathematics in cultural and historical context, with numerous exercises. Recommended Reading Lists. Tables. Numerous figures. 641pp. 5⅜ x 8½. 0-486-24823-2

PROBABILISTIC METHODS IN THE THEORY OF STRUCTURES, Isaac Elishakoff. Well-written introduction covers the elements of the theory of probability from two or more random variables, the reliability of such multivariable structures, the theory of random function, Monte Carlo methods of treating problems incapable of exact solution, and more. Examples. 502pp. 5⅜ x 8½. 0-486-40691-1

THE RIME OF THE ANCIENT MARINER, Gustave Doré, S. T. Coleridge. Doré's finest work; 34 plates capture moods, subtleties of poem. Flawless full-size reproductions printed on facing pages with authoritative text of poem. "Beautiful. Simply beautiful."–*Publisher's Weekly*. 77pp. 9¼ x 12. 0-486-22305-1

SCULPTURE: Principles and Practice, Louis Slobodkin. Step-by-step approach to clay, plaster, metals, stone; classical and modern. 253 drawings, photos. 255pp. 8⅛ x 11. 0-486-22960-2

THE INFLUENCE OF SEA POWER UPON HISTORY, 1660–1783, A. T. Mahan. Influential classic of naval history and tactics still used as text in war colleges. First paperback edition. 4 maps. 24 battle plans. 640pp. 5⅜ x 8½. 0-486-25509-3

THE STORY OF THE TITANIC AS TOLD BY ITS SURVIVORS, Jack Winocour (ed.). What it was really like. Panic, despair, shocking inefficiency, and a little heroism. More thrilling than any fictional account. 26 illustrations. 320pp. 5⅜ x 8½. 0-486-20610-6

ONE TWO THREE . . . INFINITY: Facts and Speculations of Science, George Gamow. Great physicist's fascinating, readable overview of contemporary science: number theory, relativity, fourth dimension, entropy, genes, atomic structure, much more. 128 illustrations. Index. 352pp. 5⅜ x 8½. 0-486-25664-2

DALÍ ON MODERN ART: The Cuckolds of Antiquated Modern Art, Salvador Dalí. Influential painter skewers modern art and its practitioners. Outrageous evaluations of Picasso, Cézanne, Turner, more. 15 renderings of paintings discussed. 44 calligraphic decorations by Dalí. 96pp. 5⅜ x 8½. (Available in U.S. only.) 0-486-29220-7

ANTIQUE PLAYING CARDS: A Pictorial History, Henry René D'Allemagne. Over 900 elaborate, decorative images from rare playing cards (14th–20th centuries): Bacchus, death, dancing dogs, hunting scenes, royal coats of arms, players cheating, much more. 96pp. 9¼ x 12¼. 0-486-29265-7

MAKING FURNITURE MASTERPIECES: 30 Projects with Measured Drawings, Franklin H. Gottshall. Step-by-step instructions, illustrations for constructing handsome, useful pieces, among them a Sheraton desk, Chippendale chair, Spanish desk, Queen Anne table and a William and Mary dressing mirror. 224pp. 8⅛ x 11¼. 0-486-29338-6

NORTH AMERICAN INDIAN DESIGNS FOR ARTISTS AND CRAFTSPEOPLE, Eva Wilson. Over 360 authentic copyright-free designs adapted from Navajo blankets, Hopi pottery, Sioux buffalo hides, more. Geometrics, symbolic figures, plant and animal motifs, etc. 128pp. 8⅜ x 11. (Not for sale in the United Kingdom.) 0-486-25341-4

THE FOSSIL BOOK: A Record of Prehistoric Life, Patricia V. Rich et al. Profusely illustrated definitive guide covers everything from single-celled organisms and dinosaurs to birds and mammals and the interplay between climate and man. Over 1,500 illustrations. 760pp. 7½ x 10⅛. 0-486-29371-8

VICTORIAN ARCHITECTURAL DETAILS: Designs for Over 700 Stairs, Mantels, Doors, Windows, Cornices, Porches, and Other Decorative Elements, A. J. Bicknell & Company. Everything from dormer windows and piazzas to balconies and gable ornaments. Also includes elevations and floor plans for handsome, private residences and commercial structures. 80pp. 9⅜ x 12¼. 0-486-44015-X

WESTERN ISLAMIC ARCHITECTURE: A Concise Introduction, John D. Hoag. Profusely illustrated critical appraisal compares and contrasts Islamic mosques and palaces–from Spain and Egypt to other areas in the Middle East. 139 illustrations. 128pp. 6 x 9. 0-486-43760-4

CHINESE ARCHITECTURE: A Pictorial History, Liang Ssu-ch'eng. More than 240 rare photographs and drawings depict temples, pagodas, tombs, bridges, and imperial palaces comprising much of China's architectural heritage. 152 halftones, 94 diagrams. 232pp. 10¾ x 9⅞. 0-486-43999-2

THE RENAISSANCE: Studies in Art and Poetry, Walter Pater. One of the most talked-about books of the 19th century, *The Renaissance* combines scholarship and philosophy in an innovative work of cultural criticism that examines the achievements of Botticelli, Leonardo, Michelangelo, and other artists. "The holy writ of beauty."–Oscar Wilde. 160pp. 5⅜ x 8½. 0-486-44025-7

A TREATISE ON PAINTING, Leonardo da Vinci. The great Renaissance artist's practical advice on drawing and painting techniques covers anatomy, perspective, composition, light and shadow, and color. A classic of art instruction, it features 48 drawings by Nicholas Poussin and Leon Battista Alberti. 192pp. 5⅜ x 8½. 0-486-44155-5

THE MIND OF LEONARDO DA VINCI, Edward McCurdy. More than just a biography, this classic study by a distinguished historian draws upon Leonardo's extensive writings to offer numerous demonstrations of the Renaissance master's achievements, not only in sculpture and painting, but also in music, engineering, and even experimental aviation. 384pp. 5⅜ x 8½. 0-486-44142-3

WASHINGTON IRVING'S RIP VAN WINKLE, Illustrated by Arthur Rackham. Lovely prints that established artist as a leading illustrator of the time and forever etched into the popular imagination a classic of Catskill lore. 51 full-color plates. 80pp. 8⅜ x 11. 0-486-44242-X

HENSCHE ON PAINTING, John W. Robichaux. Basic painting philosophy and methodology of a great teacher, as expounded in his famous classes and workshops on Cape Cod. 7 illustrations in color on covers. 80pp. 5⅜ x 8½. 0-486-43728-0

LIGHT AND SHADE: A Classic Approach to Three-Dimensional Drawing, Mrs. Mary P. Merrifield. Handy reference clearly demonstrates principles of light and shade by revealing effects of common daylight, sunshine, and candle or artificial light on geometrical solids. 13 plates. 64pp. 5⅜ x 8½. 0-486-44143-1

ASTROLOGY AND ASTRONOMY: A Pictorial Archive of Signs and Symbols, Ernst and Johanna Lehner. Treasure trove of stories, lore, and myth, accompanied by more than 300 rare illustrations of planets, the Milky Way, signs of the zodiac, comets, meteors, and other astronomical phenomena. 192pp. 8⅜ x 11. 0-486-43981-X

JEWELRY MAKING: Techniques for Metal, Tim McCreight. Easy-to-follow instructions and carefully executed illustrations describe tools and techniques, use of gems and enamels, wire inlay, casting, and other topics. 72 line illustrations and diagrams. 176pp. 8¼ x 10⅞. 0-486-44043-5

MAKING BIRDHOUSES: Easy and Advanced Projects, Gladstone Califf. Easy-to-follow instructions include diagrams for everything from a one-room house for bluebirds to a forty-two-room structure for purple martins. 56 plates; 4 figures. 80pp. 8¾ x 6⅜. 0-486-44183-0

LITTLE BOOK OF LOG CABINS: How to Build and Furnish Them, William S. Wicks. Handy how-to manual, with instructions and illustrations for building cabins in the Adirondack style, fireplaces, stairways, furniture, beamed ceilings, and more. 102 line drawings. 96pp. 8¾ x 6⅜. 0-486-44259-4

THE SEASONS OF AMERICA PAST, Eric Sloane. From "sugaring time" and strawberry picking to Indian summer and fall harvest, a whole year's activities described in charming prose and enhanced with 79 of the author's own illustrations. 160pp. 8¼ x 11. 0-486-44220-9

THE METROPOLIS OF TOMORROW, Hugh Ferriss. Generous, prophetic vision of the metropolis of the future, as perceived in 1929. Powerful illustrations of towering structures, wide avenues, and rooftop parks–all features in many of today's modern cities. 59 illustrations. 144pp. 8¼ x 11. 0-486-43727-2

THE PATH TO ROME, Hilaire Belloc. This 1902 memoir abounds in lively vignettes from a vanished time, recounting a pilgrimage on foot across the Alps and Apennines in order to "see all Europe which the Christian Faith has saved." 77 of the author's original line drawings complement his sparkling prose. 272pp. 5⅜ x 8½. 0-486-44001-X

THE HISTORY OF RASSELAS: Prince of Abissinia, Samuel Johnson. Distinguished English writer attacks eighteenth-century optimism and man's unrealistic estimates of what life has to offer. 112pp. 5⅜ x 8½. 0-486-44094-X

A VOYAGE TO ARCTURUS, David Lindsay. A brilliant flight of pure fancy, where wild creatures crowd the fantastic landscape and demented torturers dominate victims with their bizarre mental powers. 272pp. 5⅜ x 8½. 0-486-44198-9

Paperbound unless otherwise indicated. Available at your book dealer, online at **www.doverpublications.com**, or by writing to Dept. GI, Dover Publications, Inc., 31 East 2nd Street, Mineola, NY 11501. For current price information or for free catalogs (please indicate field of interest), write to Dover Publications or log on to **www.doverpublications.com** and see every Dover book in print. Dover publishes more than 500 books each year on science, elementary and advanced mathematics, biology, music, art, literary history, social sciences, and other areas.